THY
BROTHER'S
WIFE

THY
BROTHER'S
WIFE

Andrew M. Greeley

WARNER BOOKS

A Warner Communications Company

A BERNARD GEIS ASSOCIATES
BOOK

To the Memory
of
James F. Andrews

Ubi caritas et amor, ibi Deus est.
"Where there is charity and love, God is always present."
(Hymn sung at the Washing of the Feet on Holy Thursday)

DISCLAIMER

Those readers who insist, contrary to a writer's protests, that they "know" the persons on whom the characters in a novel are based cannot be prevented, I suppose, from playing their guessing games, even when they are told that they are inevitably going to be wrong. Nonetheless they are wrong about the characters in this book, all of whom are the products of my imagination.

In particular, Chicago has never been blessed by an Archbishop as wise as Eamon McCarthy. Moreover, the courage of Sean Cronin, however bizarre his motivations, is far greater than that of any American hierarch of whom I am aware.

—Andrew M. Greeley

PASSOVER: A NOTE

The Passover is a Jewish and Christian Springtime Feast—in most languages Easter and Passover have the same name—of liberation and renewal. Its origins are to be found in three different pagan spring festivals which antedate the Sinai experience of the Hebrew tribes: the Feast of the Unleavened Bread, the Feast of the Pascal Lamb, and the Feast of Fire and Water. In the Christian Passover these three festivals are celebrated on three separate days. Holy Thursday is especially the Feast of the Unleavened Bread, Good Friday the Feast of the Pascal Lamb, and Easter Eve the Feast of the Fire and Water. On Holy Thursday, while eating the unleavened bread of the Seder with his followers, Jesus committed himself to them irrevocably.

The passages from St. John's Gospel quoted in this story are descriptions of the final Seder Jesus ate with his followers.

❧ BOOK I ❧

*I pray for them . . . for those whom thou hast given me
. . . protect them by the power of thy name that they may be
one as we are one . . . I pray thee not to take them out of the
world but to keep them from evil.*

—John 17:9, 12, 15

CHAPTER ONE

1951

After supper on Holy Thursday evening, Father McCabe motioned Sean Cronin away from the black line of seminarians filing in silence out of the house chapel. "Mistah Cronin," he snapped, "go to my office."

Sean walked down the dimly lit corridor and waited at the door of the disciplinarian's office, his heart beating rapidly. What would his father say if he were sent home in disgrace? As far as he could remember, he hadn't violated any rules, but in the atmosphere of suspicion and distrust that permeated Mundelein a sudden and final decision to expel a student could be made arbitrarily on the basis of very little evidence.

When the last of the seminarians finished reporting minor infractions of the rules to Father McCabe—being late for class; not turning out lights at 9:45; violating the "great silence" between lights out and the end of morning mass. McCabe shuffled out of his office, a tall lean shaggy dog of a man, and, almost without looking at Sean, beckoned him inside.

"Your father called earlier this afternoon," he said abruptly. "Your brother has been reported missing in action. He led a night patrol on the Punchbowl. They ran into a Chinese outpost. He didn't come back."

Time stood still for Sean. Abstractedly he noticed the rancid cigar smoke that filled the room, the disarray of papers and books tossed about on desks and chairs. Fighting nausea, he groped des-

perately for control of his voice. "May I phone my father?" Why
had they waited hours to tell him about Paul?

"I see no point in that," said Father McCabe. "Missing isn't
dead."

"On the Punchbowl it probably is." Sean felt as though life
were ebbing out of his body, just as it must have from his
brother's. "May I go to my room?"

"Don't pamper yourself." Father McCabe's voice took on the
machine-gun quality that was a sign of his impatience with a seminarian. "You may go to the chapel for five minutes and then
join your classmates at recreation. Others besides the Cronin family have suffered loss in this world."

"Yes, Father," Sean said meekly, controlling his desire to smash
his fists against the five-o'clock shadow on McCabe's jaw.

In the chapel, Sean was numb. Paul Martin Cronin, the bright,
brash Medal of Honor winner who was supposed to become president of the United States one day, either a prisoner or dead. What
was his father feeling now? And Aunt Jane? The favorite of her
two nephews gone; what light would be left in her life?

And Nora. . . . What happens to a sixteen-year-old when the
man she has always known she would marry vanishes in fog and
the snowdrifts of Korea?

A dry sob burst from Sean's chest. "Oh, my God! Why Paul?"

The five minutes allotted by Father McCabe quickly spent.
Sean blessed himself with holy water and left the chapel. He de-
scended to the first floor of the building and walked out from dark
hallway into the twilight of the half-hour evening smoking period.

The knot of his classmates standing on the porch of the red
brick colonial-style building opened to make room for him. Most
of his classmates liked and even admired Sean—despite his family's wealth, his father's obvious ecclesiastical ambitions for him,
and his own careful observance of the rules. They kidded him
about being a "model seminarian," yet they always seemed
pleased when he joined a group of them.

"What did the Moose want?" Jimmy McGuire, Sean's closest
friend, used the nickname given to McCabe in recognition of his
shambling walk and unkempt appearance.

Sean could not bring himself to share his grief. "He wanted to
make sure that my sister is coming visiting Sunday." Sean tried to
grin suggestively.

Nora was indeed the principal attraction of visiting Sundays. The seminary only grudgingly recognized the existence of family. Seminarians were not permitted to go home at Christmastime, and even on the day of their ordination their families were packed off back to Chicago while the young priests ate dinner with the faculty and the other clergy. It was the way Cardinal Mundelein wanted it; even though Cardinal Mundelein had been dead for more than a decade, it was the way things were still done.

Visiting Sunday, then, was a privilege conceded reluctantly three times each semester. The seminarian and his family—limited to three members—were permitted to visit for two hours in a classroom building with disciplinarians like McCabe watching with beady eyes to see that no contraband food or affection was exchanged.

In such an edgy and resentful environment, Nora was a sturdy spring flower who caused every male and most of the female heads to turn when she entered the large lecture hall. She was just a bit over five feet nine inches tall, with the lithe body of a woman athlete. Her flawless complexion was framed by rich auburn hair that fell halfway to a willowy waist. Nora was dazzling.

Joe Cleary, the class mimic, reenacted the now-famous scene between Sean and Father McCabe that had taken place earlier in the year, with perfect imitation of both their voices:

"Mistah Cronin, who was that *woman* who visited you today?"

"That was my Aunt Jane, Father. She's my father's sister and housekeeper."

"I don't mean her, boy; I mean the younger one. Who was that younger woman, Mistah Cronin?"

"My sister, Nora, Father. She's been here every visiting Sunday."

"That young woman has never been here before, Mistah Cronin."

"Sure she has, Father. She's just—uh, er, I mean she's grown up some since last year."

The cluster on the porch howled at Cleary's imitation of Sean.

"Is she your *blood* sister?"

"No, Father, she's my foster sister, but she's lived with us since she was a little girl."

"Then she may not visit you, Mistah Cronin. Only blood sisters are permitted. No foster sisters."

"Yes, Father. I didn't know that was one of the rules."

"Mistah Cronin, we make up the rules as we go along."

More laughter from the class. The last line, however true to character, had not really been spoken by Father McCabe.

"It's a good thing for all of us, Sean," said Jimmy McGuire, "that your father leaned on the Cardinal. What would visiting Sunday be without Nora?"

Roger Fitzgibbon, a smoothly handsome young man with black hair, pale white skin, and infinite charm, said, "I thought Nora was your adopted sister."

"Not really. My father never did get around to the formalities of adoption." Sean did not add that, as a foster daughter, Nora Riley was far more dependent on Michael James Arthur Cronin than any adopted daughter would ever be. Mike Cronin liked to keep his women dependent, however much he loved them.

At seven thirty the bell rang the end of the smoking period. Jimmy McGuire caught his eye, and Sean lagged behind the others to talk to him.

"Is it Paul?" Jimmy's freckled face was anxious in the fading twilight, the cheery leprechaun changing into the solemn good friend.

Sean nodded.

"Dead?" Jimmy asked incredulously.

Sean shook his head. "No, missing."

"While there's life there's hope, Sean. You know that," Jimmy said.

"Do I? I guess so. I'm too numb right now to know much of anything."

"Women are lucky," Jimmy said. "They can cry and get some of the pain out."

"Nora isn't crying," Sean said as they entered the building. "She's not that kind."

"A real Cronin!" said Jimmy with a soft laugh. He patted Sean on the back, expressing more sympathy with that gesture than any words could possibly have.

"A real Cronin," agreed Sean sadly, thus breaking the rule against talking in the building, a violation he decided he would not report to Father McCabe.

• • •

In his room Sean took off his cassock and hung it carefully in the closet. They did not strictly insist that you wear a cassock in your room, although it was praised as a sign of virtue if you wore it all the time. He closed one of the windows; the late March evening was turning cool. He looked out on the courtyard across the neatly landscaped grass and shrubbery, toward the gymnasium and the dark night sky beyond it. The last thing he wanted to do was turn to his desk and see the picture of Paul.

Finally he forced himself to sit on the hard wooden chair and confront his brother's handsome face, with its devil-may-care grin and mischief-filled eyes: a black Irish warrior with the looks of a movie star. "Goddamn reckless fool," he said. "Paul Martin Cronin, you won one Medal of Honor up at the Reservoir. Why did you have to be a hero a second time?"

He laid his head on his arm and began to sob. It had all come so quickly. Only nine months ago Paul had graduated from Notre Dame with a diploma he had just barely earned and a commission in the Marine Corps that was awarded only because the NROTC commanding officer chose to ignore a couple of drinking episodes. The summer had been devoted not to water skiing and girls at their Oakland Beach home but to advanced officers' training at Quantico. Then, just as Sean returned to the seminary, Paul was fighting toward the Yalu River with the Tenth Corps, commanding a platoon of Marines who were even younger than he was. Five months later he was the recipient of a Congressional Medal of Honor from Douglas MacArthur himself.

Sean raised his head from the desk. Thank God no one had seen him cry. Especially his father. Michael Cronin had set rigid standards for his sons. He had mapped out their futures with a precision rarely seen outside of a war council room. There was no allowance in his plan for any sign of weakness, in his sons or in himself. He was a man of enormous energy and charm, the kind of person people turned to watch as he walked down the street, although he was only five feet nine inches tall and already balding. His body radiated vitality, his green eyes sparkled with rapidly changing emotions. His finely shaped jaw, tilted ever so slightly in the air, promised a fight or an evening of fun, or possibly both. Women, as Sean had learned all too well, found Michael Cronin irresistible, and men delighted in his quick wit and intelligence.

Unfortunately for his children, Michael Cronin firmly believed that you raised two motherless sons by the same kind of quick, intuitive thrusts with which you assaulted an enemy position, courted a woman, or sank hundreds of thousands of dollars into pork belly futures.

Sean wondered what his father would be doing now. Calling the Pentagon for news? Cursing Truman and the Marine Corps? Damning the "Communist conspiracy" that had sent his son on "police action" in Korea?

Would Martha, the latest of his father's chic socialite friends, be around? Probably not. In times of rage and grief, Michael Cronin disdained the company of his always very discreet companions. He would doubtless be furious with the seminary for not letting him talk to Sean on the phone. On the other hand, his position had always been that seminary discipline was a good thing for someone like Sean; it would make a man out of him. So he would not push either Father McCabe or Monsignor Flaherty, the rector, to bend the rules—as he had forced them to bend the rules to permit Nora to come on visiting Sundays.

"Missing isn't dead," Sean told himself. The Moose was right about that at least. If he had any faith at all, he would resign himself to God's will and hope for the best.

Reluctantly he reached for the battered brown spiral notebook in which he was keeping a journal—an idea he had not shared with his spiritual director, who would strongly disapprove, especially since he would guess quite correctly that Sean was doing it in imitation of Thomas Merton's *Seven Storey Mountain,* a book upon which Father Meisterhorst frowned. Sean began to write.

Holy Thursday. The Last Supper. The First Mass. The beginning of the Priesthood. The night Jesus washed the feet of his disciples to show what authority meant. The night he called us not servants but friends. The night that he prayed to the Heavenly Father to protect his friends from evil. Dammit, Lord, you didn't protect Paul from evil. What will I do without him? Sometimes I don't understand him, but I love him and I don't want to lose him. I would give up the priesthood, give up anything, if he were still alive.

Why am I writing these lines? Are you out there listening, out there in the night sky with the half moon coming up over the lake?

He hesitated, his pen poised over the page.

> *Life seems to be nothing but heartbreaks. Mother dead. Aunt Jane the way she is. Now Paul probably gone. This Holy Thursday evening, I don't think I believe in you at all.*

He tossed the pen aside and slammed the notebook closed. He must get back to work. McCabe was right. He ought not to pamper himself. He reached for the green-covered Latin philosophy textbook. He would memorize the pages he needed to know for tomorrow's recitation. He opened the philosophy book and flipped to the appropriate page. It was not required that you understood what Carolus Boyer was saying. It was only necessary that you be able to repeat it verbatim to the professor.

Suddenly he put the philosophy text aside and opened the notebook again. In large, bold print he scrawled three words: *MISSING ISN'T DEAD!*

A week later, on the visiting Sunday after Easter, Sean paid little attention to the solemn vespers in the main chapel. That afternoon he had had a conversation with his father that left him badly shaken.

It had never occurred to him that, with Mike Cronin's obsession about the family, it would be Sean's obligation to keep the Cronin name alive if anything ever happened to Paul. But after visiting hours, as Mike was getting into his limousine, he had turned to his son and said, "So it's understood that if Paul doesn't come back, you'll leave the seminary?"

Sean had been stunned. "Paul will come back," he said, hoping he sounded confident. "We have to believe that."

"Well, if he doesn't come back, we have to keep the family going."

That was the way it was with Michael Cronin. Decisions were made as though there had been discussion and consultation and agreement from everyone, but in fact the decisions were his and there was no appeal. Sean had always been aware that it was only luck that his desire to become a priest had corresponded with his father's wishes.

Later, at the Benediction after the vespers, the thought came to Sean that if Paul were dead he would also have to marry Nora.

She had been brought into the Cronin family after the war, not only because her father, Edward Riley, had been General Cronin's aide on Leyte Island, but because the Rileys were a family with "good blood." She had been selected to bear the children who would keep the Cronin line alive. If Paul were dead, those children would be Sean's.

As the four hundred male voices sang enthusiastically "Holy God, we praise thy name," at the end of Benediction, Sean decided that the thought of Nora Riley as his wife and the mother of his children was disconcerting perhaps but not entirely unpleasant.

CHAPTER
TWO
1938–1950

It was during the summer of 1938 that Michael Cronin decided that his elder son, Paul, was to become president of the United States and that his younger son, Sean, was to become a priest and "probably a cardinal." The decision was made spontaneously, without reflection. Nonetheless, it was permanent and irrevocable.

Their mother, whom Sean could remember only as a cloud of golden gentleness, had died four years before in an auto accident. Aunt Jane, his father's maiden elder sister who now lived with them, was watching the seven- and nine-year-old boys as they played in the sand in front of their Oakland Beach home. The sprawling house was rooted in concrete high above the lakeshore. Michael Cronin had built it for his bride at the time of their marriage, in 1928, just when he was beginning to take his money out of the stock market because "there were too many poor people owning stock." The house was called "Glendore," after the home of his ancestors in West Cork, and, although the house on Glenwood Drive in Chicago was his official residence, Michael Cronin considered Glendore his real home.

Bob Elson had finished describing another victory for the Cubs in the late-season pennant drive sparked by their new manager, Gabby Hartnett. The radio on the sundeck just above the beach was playing "You Must've Been a Beautiful Baby," while Mike and two of his business associates, Ed Connaire and Marty Hoffman, discussed the possibility of purchasing land where they were certain real-estate development would shortly begin. "If there's a war," Mike said, "the people who own the land around Chicago are going to become rich overnight."

"Is the idea of a war to defend the country or help your business?" Joan Gordon asked with a grin. She was a "friend" of Mike's from New York, a pretty woman who looked dainty in a swimsuit that had never been touched by water. The three men laughed hoarsely, and there was the sound of popping beer bottles as Mike opened another round.

It was at that moment that Paul, who had been watching the white breakers rushing up on the beach, made an impulsive dash into the lake. Sean trailed after him. Each wave was bigger than its predecessor, and one knocked Paul off his feet. The undertow, surprisingly strong for the lake, pulled him out into the churning waves.

With no awareness of what he was doing, Sean plunged into the lake after his brother. Paul lashed out at him frantically, terrified by the strength of the waves and unable to catch his breath before the next surge of water filled his mouth. One of Paul's flailing blows landed on Sean's jaw. Dazed and confused, he too slipped under the water and into the overpowering clutch of the undertow. A wall of white crashed around his head.

Sean remembered the words of his swimming instructor and permitted the water to pull him off the sand bottom. He floated free of the undertow, broke the surface of the lake, and searched desperately for his brother.

Paul was only a few feet away, screaming with fear. Back on the beach, no one, including Aunt Jane, seemed to notice the drama being enacted by the two boys. Still sputtering and choking, Sean dove back into the waves, broke water once, then plunged again toward his brother, who had sunk under the surface and was now rapidly drifting out beyond the protective sandbar.

Sean thought he had lost Paul. He was tempted to turn away to save his own life when, miraculously, it seemed, he caught sight of a frantically kicking leg. He dived once again, grabbed his brother around the chest, and pulled him toward shore just as the swimming instructor had recommended. This time Paul came peacefully enough.

They had almost made it to the beach when a gigantic breaker smashed against their backs, tumbling both of them into the waves again. Sean hit his head against the bottom, twirled over once, then struggled to his feet. Terrified and unable to move, Paul clung to him.

"Help," he whispered, almost breathless. "Help me, Sean." Sean was able to keep his balance and pull Paul back toward the shore. Choked with water, his feet slipping in the undertow, he struggled, still dragging his brother, until they were safe on the hot sand.

When Aunt Jane reached them, she pulled Paul, always her favorite, out of Sean's grasp and hugged him protectively.

"Paul, you brave, brave little thing," she wailed. "You risked your life to save that foolish child."

Sean never did know whether his father believed Aunt Jane's version of the story, although Mrs. Gordon, who enveloped him in her arms and pressed him against her soft, sweet-smelling body, whispered in his ear, "I saw what really happened."

He nestled against her, still breathing heavily. "Please don't tell," he begged. He knew instinctively that it was important to his brother to be considered heroic.

After dinner that night, before the two boys were sent to bed, Ed Connaire's wife, Margie, asked them, "What were you thinking about out there in the water?"

"I was praying to God to help me," said Sean, who had made his First Communion a few months before.

"I wasn't thinking anything. I was trying to get out of the water," said Paul.

"It sounds like you have a religious leader and a political leader here," said Marty Hoffman, rubbing the perspiration off his bald head as he sipped yet another beer.

"A president and a cardinal!" Michael Cronin exclaimed.

And that was that.

Joan Gordon, naked from her shower, peered through the drapes covering the French windows. The sun had set and there was a thin gray haze lingering over the lake.

She made certain that the latch on the window to the balcony was open. Surely Mike would come tonight, despite his sister's disapproval. It was time, past time. He had not brought her from Chicago merely to sit on the beach and listen to his strange, crude friends talk of money.

In the brief years of her widowhood she had not lacked for wealthy suitors; none, however, were so fascinating as Mike. She was both attracted to and frightened by his intense vitality and his dancing green eyes. She sighed and released the drape. Was he expecting her to come to him? He was a difficult man to understand.

She removed the featherweight rose gown from the bed and slid it over her shoulders. Then she slipped on the thin matching robe and knotted it loosely.

As she brushed her short blond hair with indifferent vigor, she noted again how much the face in the mirror looked like that of his late wife's, whose portrait hung over the fireplace. Never mentioned, Mary Eileen Morrisey Cronin was still a palpable presence in this lakeside mansion, and not merely in the face of her younger son, the gentle little boy with the soft brown eyes who had begged her to hide his heroism.

The French window opened and Mike entered, wearing a blue silk robe and carrying a bottle of champagne and two glasses. Uneasy, but preserving her outward calm, Joan Gordon continued to brush her hair. "You were joking about your sons this afternoon, weren't you?"

He was struggling with the cork on the champagne bottle. "About one being cardinal and the other president? No, I think it's a good idea. A word here, a word there, at this time in the boys' lives, will plant the seed. Get them competing with each other to see who moves up faster. Good for them." The cork popped, and a little bit of the bubbly drink flowed out of the bottle. Deftly Mike caught it in one of the champagne glasses.

"Your family is important to you, isn't it?"

"Yes, it is." He handed her the glass.

"And if Sean doesn't want to be a priest and Paul doesn't want to be a politician?"

He shrugged. "Children become what their parents want them to become. Sean and Paul will do what I want them to do. They'll have to work hard, of course, and do their part"—he poured a glass for himself—"but I'll buy their way around any obstacles."

"Money can buy anything?" She was alarmed by the cold gleam in his eye.

"Just about." Dismissing his sons abruptly, he said, "I only drink champagne with naked women." He took the glass from her hands and covered her lips with a long, searching kiss. Then, while she tried to recover her breath, he brushed aside her robe and gently pulled the gown from her shoulders. His hands were strong, yet sensitive. "Now you're really worth toasting." He drained the glass and began to kiss her again. He led her to the bed. She was paralyzed by desire as his mouth moved against her flesh. Then his teeth began to rip at her. She moaned, not with pain, since he was not hurting her.

Just as he entered her, he said in triumph, "You're mine, you know."

She knew it was true.

Mike, complacent in his male power, had watched the sun come up from Joan Gordon's balcony overlooking the lake. Then he returned to his room to dress for breakfast. Pansy, the cook, was delighted by his order for orange juice, bacon and eggs, and toast. Normally he drank only coffee in the morning.

He drained his second glass of orange juice and dug into the bacon. It had been a good night. Joan Gordon was an excellent sexual partner, infinitely more responsive than Mary Eileen had ever been. He frowned at the thought of his wife. Why did she come to his mind so often after a night of lovemaking?

Jane entered the room, her lean face grimmer than ever. She sat down at the table across from him. Her plate contained one poached egg, all she ever allowed herself for breakfast. "You were in that woman's bedroom last night," she accused him.

"Jane, how can you be so deadly dull at this hour on a lovely summer morning?"

"I will not have you carrying on in this house. We must maintain standards. If you insist on bringing your women here, I demand that you at least behave with common decency."

Mike suddenly realized how much Jane had changed in the four years since she had come to care for the boys. What little spark there had been in her had been replaced by a sour, unbending old maid. "And if I don't?"

Ignoring the threat in his voice, Jane replied, "I'll tell Joan Gordon why you can never marry her or any other woman. Your precious secret will be out in the open, and your sons will be exposed for what they are—especially Sean."

Mike felt his heart sink. The bloom had quickly worn off the day. "What do you know about that?"

"Do you think you solved everything when you pensioned off your chauffeur and sent him back to Ireland? He told me everything before he left. And you won't be able to pension me."

"You're skating on thin ice, Jane," he warned her.

She laughed, an empty, contemptuous sound. "You always were a blowhard, Mickey. I'm not afraid of you."

Mike knew that Jane was not afraid of him. But he also knew that she would never do anything to jeopardize the security of the life he offered her. Without his family, she had no one. And where else could she go to indulge her habit of secret drinking? "I think we have a standoff, Jane," he said.

He picked up his fork and piled it high with scrambled eggs. Perhaps it would be a good day after all.

On a cold Easter Sunday, in 1942, after the family had gone to Easter Mass in tiny Notre Dame Church in Oakland Beach, and after the noon meal, Aunt Jane was instructed to take the two boys to a movie at the Marquette Theater in Michigan City. She pretended to be offended by the carryings-on of the Marx Brothers, but Sean noted with satisfaction that she laughed as loudly as anyone else in the theater.

Sean had almost not been allowed to go to the movies because he had ripped his trousers in a fight the day before. Three boys from Michigan City had taunted him about his elegant clothing while he waited patiently for the Cronin Packard to turn the corner onto Lake View Drive. Sean had refused to fight them until two of them grabbed his arms and the third hit him in the stomach. Although they were bigger than he was, he broke free, chose the weakest of the attackers, and began to pummel the boy. Just then Paul arrived on the scene. When Sean and Paul were through, the three assailants went home weeping, cursing and promising vengeance.

"Not bad, kid," Paul said, ruffling his brother's hair. "For an eleven-year-old, you do pretty well."

"We ought to fight other kids more often instead of fighting each other," Sean agreed.

"Why not do both?" Paul laughed.

Although he was only eighteen months older, Paul was already half a head taller and two grades ahead of Sean in school—next year he would graduate from St. Titus and enroll, like his father before him, at Mt. Carmel. Paul did not permit Sean to forget for a moment that he was the older and the bigger and the more advanced of the two, although his manner of lording it over "little brother" was always genial.

When they returned from the movie, the reason their father wanted them out of the house became clear. While they were immersed in the Marx Brothers' antics, Michael Cronin had been readying himself for overseas duty.

The sky was a grim and brutal gray as Mike, resplendent in his colonel's uniform, told his sons that his unit had been called to active duty and bid them an emotional farewell. "In case I don't come back, I want you to remember how important your family is," Mike said. "Since your great-grandfather migrated here as a penniless farm worker, we have fought to establish the Cronin name. We were here in Chicago before Marshall Field or Potter Palmer. When my father lost his fortune in 1917, I had to leave school and forget my dream of Notre Dame and go to work. I remember hearing a man say in back of St. Bernard's Church on a Sunday morning, 'We watched 'em go up and now we watch 'em go down.'" There was rare pain in Mike's damp green eyes. "By the time I was twenty-five I had earned back the money my father lost—I showed them all that quality pays off. Do you understand that, Paul and Sean? There's nothing more important than family."

Both boys nodded.

"If I don't come back," Mike continued, "Paul, you're going into politics, and Sean, you're going into the Church."

"You bet, Dad," Paul said absently, not paying any more attention to his father's personal catechism than he usually did.

"Well, then, men," Mike said, "you have your orders and you know what has to be done."

Sean was certain that his father wanted to embrace them but didn't know how. The farewell ended with Mike saying, "Get along now and eat your dinner before it gets cold. I'll have Jeremy drive me back to Chicago."

After Sean cried himself to sleep that night, he dreamed of his mother as he often did, a soft golden radiance. When he awoke, he was not sure for a moment whether she was alive or dead. Then, fully awake, he realized sadly that she was indeed dead.

• • •

Nora Riley was an unhappy, terrified ten-year-old when Michael Cronin visited her at Angel Guardian orphanage in the autumn of 1945. Nine years of her life had been warm and peaceful: affectionate parents, a sweet young brother, a gaily decorated apartment in the Brainard district on the South Side of Chicago. Then a telegram from the War Department telling of her father's death on Leyte, followed a month later by a fire from a lighted cigarette in the apartment next door that took the lives of her mother and baby brother, and Nora Riley was a numb, grief-stricken orphan.

The doctors at the orphanage talked to her, shook their heads, and told the nuns that eventually the "poor thing" would be all right. Nora knew that too. However, "eventually" seemed a long time away, and now she was lonely and frightened.

"You look like your mother. Her eyes," said General Cronin when he met Nora. His own hard eyes watched her carefully. Her father had served with General Cronin. His last letter home, which her mother read and reread through grief-stricken tears, had praised General Cronin's bravery and goodness.

"Yes, sir," she said. But Mother had been pretty, and Nora knew that she was too tall and too thin.

"Do you like it here?"

"No, sir," she replied honestly. "I don't."

General Cronin considered for a moment. "Would you like to come and live with my family?" he asked.

Nora decided that nothing could be worse than the orphanage. "All right, sir."

"Don't call me sir," he ordered. "Call me Uncle Mike."

"Yes, sir." She found herself grinning. "Yes, sir, Uncle Mike." General Cronin laughed and kissed her.

The Cronin house on Glenwood Drive seemed like a castle on a hill, filled with friendly servants, a room of her own, and neighborhood kids who welcomed her enthusiastically. There was much less enthusiasm from Aunt Jane.

"Why did you bring her here, Michael?" Jane demanded on Nora's first day in her new home. "We have enough trouble keeping Paul and Sean out of mischief."

"I brought her home because she's Edward and Kathy's daughter, and because I wanted to," the General said calmly.

"I don't want another woman in my house," Aunt Jane said petulantly.

"She's a child, not a woman," he replied. "And she's here to stay."

Aunt Jane was silent for a moment. Then, as though admitting defeat, she said, "The child has bad teeth. We'll have to get her to an orthodontist at once."

Paul Cronin, a sixteen-year-old football star at St. Ignatius for whom Nora instantly developed a worshipful crush, hardly acknowledged her existence. His younger brother, Sean, a freshman at Quigley Seminary, who had the kindest smile Nora had ever seen, took her under his wing and explained to her who all the servants were and how to behave with them. He introduced her to the neighbors. He even walked her over to St. Titus and talked about her to the Mother Superior, a cheerful woman in black and white Dominican habit.

"Thank you, Sean," Nora said when they walked back down the drive, lined with enormous oak trees turning red and gold in the autumn sunlight. "Are you my brother now?" A little bit of warmth had slipped through the tundra in Nora Riley's young soul.

"Kind of half brother, half friend. Is that all right?"

"Great," she assented. "Perfect."

The war between Aunt Jane and Nora raged on whenever Mike was not present. It reached fever pitch by Christmas. Sean's attempts at making peace were ignored by both combatants. Aunt Jane harassed Nora about everything from the hem length on her school uniform to her table manners. Nora responded with stubborn silence. If she cried over the persecution, it was in the privacy of her room.

Christmas-tree decoration time brought the contest to a head. Normally, Sean decorated the tree with the assistance of Pansy and Erithea, the cook and the maid. It was always a huge tree, filling the front of their parlor, because his father remembered the days "before the war"—he meant the first war—when his family could afford only a tabletop tree.

After Aunt Jane discovered that Nora was going to help with the decorations, she insisted on participating for the first time that Sean could remember. Despite the Christmas music playing on their large console Philco radio, Aunt Jane had little of the Christmas spirit. Every ornament that Nora put on the tree, every string of tinsel she draped across a branch had to be changed, usually with a protest about clumsiness that must have been inherited from her parents.

Sean was fascinated by the bony little waif who had transformed their house by her slow smile and piercing blue eyes. He had learned her moods as he learned the moods of everyone he was close to, instinctively and without paying conscious attention to the process. He saw the thunderclouds building up in her eyes. Nervously, he suggested, "Maybe we ought to stop for the day. I have to go over to Titus for Midnight Mass practice. Father—"

Jane was not listening. "Can't you see that's the wrong place for the angel?" She pulled the ornament out of Nora's hand. "Put it here." The angel, a prize Michael Cronin had brought home from France, fell from Jane's hand and crashed on the floor. "You clumsy little fool!" She slapped Nora's face. "You've broken my brother's angel!"

Lightning leaped from Nora's eyes, but she said nothing.

"That's enough, Aunt Jane." Sean grabbed her wrist. He almost felt sorry for his poor lonely aunt and her silent drinking. He could smell the bourbon on her breath.

"Neither one of you have any right to be in this house," Jane hissed and fled from the parlor.

Nora, her foot on the staircase, whirled. Hands on her thin little hips, she opened her mouth as if to say something. She hesitated, then ran up the stairs.

Later, Sean knocked on the door of her room. She was huddled over the desk, weeping silently. "So you do cry."

She nodded but did not move from the desk.

He sat beside her and touched her shoulder reassuringly. "It's all right, Nora. Aunt Jane does that to everyone."

"What did she mean about neither one of us belonging here?"

"I'm not sure. She says crazy things. It's the drinking. Some sort of batty notion that I'm my mother's son and Paul is my father's son."

"That *is* odd." Nora's tearstained face turned toward him. "Whatever could she mean by that?"

"Probably that I look so much like my mother. It doesn't matter." Yet it did matter. Deep down inside, Jane's mysterious comment troubled Sean greatly.

After Michael Cronin returned from the war in 1945 with a Distinguished Service Cross, two Purple Hearts, and a matching pair of Silver Stars, he had hurled himself back into Cronin Enterprises as though he were trying to make up for the lost years. His office continued to be located in a small suite in the Field Building, with four associates and a handful of clerks and secretaries providing all the staff needed for his mysterious local, national, and international deals.

Over the next few years his sons saw him only a little more than they had when he was in the Philippines, sometimes at Oakland Beach in the company of one of the beautifully turned-out women friends who still visited him there, and sometimes at the house on Glenwood Drive, where the friends were never admitted.

One evening, when Sean had finished his third year at Quigley Seminary and Paul his freshman year at Notre Dame, the family was gathered in the parlor at Glendore. The French windows were opened and the curtains stirred in the light breeze that came off the lake. Sean was reading and Paul was shocking Aunt Jane with his description of the movie *The Lost Weekend,* which he had seen the night before with his current girl friend, a certain Caroline Flaherty, whom his father had dismissed as "not being from a good family."

Mike, hands jammed in the pockets of his white flannel trousers, paced the balcony like a captain on the bridge of his ship. He seemed tired and older than his forty-eight years. There were lines in his face that had not been there the year before, and his eyes had lost some of their vitality.

"Where's Nora?" he asked, as though only then realizing she was not at home.

"Taking a golf lesson," Sean said. "The pro at Long Beach Country Club says she may break a hundred before the summer is over."

"The kid has good blood, but she's a mess. Too tall, too thin. In a couple of years I'll have to send her to modeling school. Maybe they can teach her to stand up straight. You can't marry a girl with bad posture, can you, Paul?"

Sean was startled. This was the first he had heard of a marriage between Nora and Paul. Like all his father's other decisions, it was proclaimed as something that had already been discussed and settled.

"Certainly not," said Paul, with his customary good humor. "Make her stand up straight."

Paul didn't think his father was serious. Sean was not so sure. "She has pretty eyes," he commented.

"You're supposed to be a seminarian. You shouldn't be looking at girls' eyes." Mike, who adored his foster child, chuckled at the compliment.

"I don't think they're pretty at all." Aunt Jane entered the discussion with a predictably unflattering remark, but Mike paid no attention to it. Indeed, it often seemed he had not heard anything that Aunt Jane said in the last five years.

In the background there was the sound of a slamming door and footsteps running up the stairs.

"Hi!" Nora Riley, the subject of their conversation, entered the parlor. She was still tall and skinny, but she had deep penetrating blue eyes that demanded your attention and the beginnings of what might one day be a pretty face.

"What did you shoot, punk?" Sean asked her.

"Ninety-eight," she said. "Next summer I'll beat you." There was a faint trace of a grin.

"No more golf lessons for you, young lady. It's not dignified. I don't want to see you with those clubs again." The command was harsh but the tone was affectionate, almost caressing.

"My mother played golf, Uncle Mike," Nora said softly.

Michael Cronin grunted in disapproval. Nonetheless, the golf lessons continued.

The summer of 1948 was the best summer yet for Sean Cronin. His relationship with Paul had changed. The rivalry and competitiveness were there, but now Paul viewed him as an ally and even as a friend. They were tennis and golf partners and an enthusiastic, if as yet inexperienced, sailing crew. Paul was generous in his praise of Sean's skills, though usually the praise cast Sean in the role of the dutiful second-in-command.

Being second-in-command on the *Mary Eileen* or the tennis court didn't bother Sean. To be respected by his handsome, popular brother, and to be admitted to his circle of friends, was more than enough.

One day Sean returned in the early afternoon to the house overlooking the lake. He had been thoroughly drubbed by Nora in their eighteen-hole golf match and, after a six and five defeat, he was not ready to risk himself in another eighteen holes.

He moved to the deck chair on the balcony, nodding over a copy of *A Bell for Adano*. It was one of those humid summer days on the shores of Lake Michigan, with big thunderheads building up in the sky.

He was stirred from his sleeplike reverie by the sound of a woman pleading. "No. Please don't. Oh, no . . . don't!"

Who was the woman? he asked himself. Aunt Jane had gone to Chicago on one of her shopping expeditions. Nora was still at the club. The Packard was in the driveway, which meant that his father was in the house—alone, Sean had thought. He stirred in his chair. The French window next to him led into his father's study. The window was open and the drapes were not completely drawn. The scent of the roses that decorated the study teased his nostrils. Still in his reverie, Sean glanced lazily into the study.

His father was in the den with Mrs. Conway, a friend from Baltimore who had come to visit him frequently that summer. Mike was none too gently pulling off her clothing, despite what seemed to Sean to be her adamant resistance.

Sean watched, fascinated. He knew he shouldn't be there, but he couldn't drag himself away. Anyway, if he attempted to move, his father might hear him and that would be even worse.

"Take off your slip, woman," his father ordered, though in a pleasant tone of voice. "I can't do everything myself."

Mrs. Conway quickly obeyed. A pretty platinum blonde in her late thirties, she was breathtaking with her clothes off. Mike took off his own clothes. Then he pulled her to him and bent her over backward. He assaulted the front of her body with lingering, hungry kisses.

Mike seemed harsh, even brutal with her, but at the same time delicate and gentle. Her cries and moans turned from protest to pleasure. She pleaded with him at first to stop, then to continue, and finally to finish.

To Sean's transfixed eyes, the scene was horrifying, frightening, compelling, and beautiful. So that's what it was like. . . .

Most beautiful of all was the tenderness with which his father and Mrs. Conway caressed each other after their passions had found fulfillment.

At dinner that night, Mrs. Conway glowed with pleasure. No wonder she comes to Oakland Beach so often, thought Sean. His father seemed both self-satisfied and sad.

"There's a different set of rules for men like Dad," Paul said. He was floating on his back above the sandbar, fifty yards off the beach. "If he needs a woman after he's worked himself into exhaustion for a month to bring off a deal, why shouldn't he have one? He's discreet about it and tasteful in his choice of women. What's wrong with it?"

"How important do you have to be to get a dispensation from the moral law?"

"That stuff's fine for the seminary"—Paul sniffed contemptuously—"but it doesn't apply in the real world."

"He seems so straitlaced about everything else." Sean's toes just barely touched the sandbar six feet beneath the placid surface of the lake.

"Women are meant to be enjoyed," Paul said confidently. "Unless, of course, you're going to be a priest. Besides, you take him too seriously. He's a great man, but half of what he says is bullshit. . . . Come on, let's swim back to the beach. That mist drifting down the shore will fog everything in."

Paul rarely worried about danger and certainly not about ground fog on the beach. He obviously didn't want to discuss the subject.

They swam ashore; Sean with ease and Paul heavily, at the end, because of too much beer and too many cigarettes. As they were drying themselves, shivering in the chill mist, Sean pushed the point. "What do you mean, not take Dad seriously?"

"Oh, hell, Sean." Paul was impatient. "I don't pay attention to ninety percent of what he says. Nora doesn't take him seriously either. Even Aunt Jane doesn't, half the time. You're the only one who believes all his bullshit. Hell, I bet you really expect to be archbishop of Chicago." There was an edge of contempt in Paul's voice.

Sean felt his face grow warm. "It wouldn't be right to deliberately seek it," he said firmly. "But the Church needs good leadership, and I'll try to do the best job I can. I'm probably never going to be a cardinal, but I wouldn't turn it down."

"Come on, little brother, let's get back to the house; I need a beer." Paul patted him patronizingly on the head. "You should be the favorite, not me. You're the only one in the family who's like him. I wouldn't be surprised if you become a cardinal long before I'm even a United States senator." Now Paul's laughter was self-mocking. "Can you imagine that—Senator Paul Martin Cronin!"

CHAPTER THREE

1951

Sean Cronin slumped over the wheel of his car, too weak for the moment to drag himself out of the battered 1948 Chevy and then climb the stairs to Glendore. Working at the Maryville Orphanage for most of the summer had been a disaster. Nagging worry about Paul was never far from his mind. The pressure from his father to leave the seminary weighed heavily on him. And he did not look forward to spending two weeks on the shores of Lake Michigan. During the past week Aunt Jane had been even more frequently "under the weather," and Nora's giddy teenage crowd rasped on his nerves.

His father's business trips to the Middle East produced mixed feelings in Sean. For all his peculiarities Sean missed Mike Cronin. On the other hand, the Fourth of July weekend this year had been a disaster. Not only was there tension between his father and Mrs. Conway, a tension that his father never before permitted in his friendships, but the strain of long hours of work, compulsive business travel, and reckless living were taking their toll, though he was only fifty-one years old. When he was in full flush of energy and enthusiasm, he seemed ten years younger; yet on the few occasions when he was in temporary repose, he looked ten years older.

If Mary Eileen Cronin had lived, perhaps she could have warned her husband that the martinis and the Scotch were exacting a terrible toll. For a moment, Sean thought of his mother. He could only picture her as a young woman a few years older than he now was. He still had dreams in which she was alive, dreams which were so powerful that it took him several minutes of wakefulness to dismiss them as a childhood wish. He had read somewhere in a psychology book that such dreams about a dead parent could last all one's life. He hoped they would; they were wonderful dreams.

With a sigh, Sean pushed open the car door and walked up the steps to the main level of the house.

Nora was in the parlor with Maggie Martin, watching Milton Berle on the television set. Both were dressed in their summer uniforms, Bermuda shorts and cotton shirts. Nora's shirt was her usual unspectacular white, Maggie's an eye-stopping pink. A half foot shorter than Nora, Maggie was a pretty sixteen-year-old with long blond hair and a tendency to giggle.

"Hi, Sean," she said. "Nice to see you again." She fluttered her eyelids.

"Good evening, Maggie," he replied flatly and retreated to a corner of the room, far from the two teenagers. He turned on the reading light and buried himself in a chair with Graham Greene's *The End of the Affair*. Over the top edge of the book he saw a brief wry smile from Nora.

Berle's string of witticisms eventually ended and, even more blessedly, Maggie bounced out of the house in a crescendo of giggles.

"She's really okay," Nora said in defense of her friend. "She just doesn't know how to act when you're around."

"Hmmmmm."

"Mind if I sit down and read with you?"

"If you want," said Sean, thinking how improbable was the "affair" about which Graham Greene was writing. Nora curled up on the sofa opposite him and took a book off the coffee table. *From Here to Eternity*. Aunt Jane certainly was slipping if Nora was permitted to read such "trash."

"How's Aunt Jane?"

Nora did not look up. "Very much under the weather."

Nora's auburn hair was tied behind her head in a long ponytail, revealing the flawless bones of her face and head. Her eyes caught his watching her and he quickly turned away.

"And when will Dad be home again?" Sean asked after a pause.

"Labor Day weekend, if he finishes his business with the sheikhs."

"And Mrs. Conway?"

"That's over. They had a terrible row. She wanted marriage. Uncle Mike is only buying oil this year, not wives."

"She seemed like a nice woman. Too bad."

Nora closed her book, a finger between the pages, and regarded him coolly, almost dispassionately. "You look gray, Sean."

"The orphanage was a bad experience," he said, feeling the emotion seeping out of him. "They're not really orphans, of course, mostly kids from broken homes. Lonely, desperate for attention and love. They cling to you almost as though they're afraid you're going to let them down the way their parents did." He sighed in frustration. "I worked so hard with those kids that I was too tired to sleep at night, and none of it did a damn bit of good. In the end, I had to leave them the way everyone always has."

"Are we all that different, Sean?" she asked. "We're as hungry for love as they are, maybe more so. The only reason we don't cling is—well, how do you cling to people like Uncle Mike or Aunt Jane? When Mrs. Conway was here, I wanted to be with her all the time. That's the same thing as clinging."

Sean sighed. "You're a very remarkable sixteen-year-old, Nora," he said. "No, I don't like the way that sounds. You're a very remarkable woman."

Nora leaned forward and touched his face with amazingly tender fingers. Time stood still. For a moment it seemed that the peace would never end. Then she broke the spell of the magic moment and said, with a laugh, "*Young* woman!"

Sean was confused by his reaction to her nearness. You're a seminarian, he told himself. You're going to be a priest. You shouldn't feel this way about a girl. He retrieved *The End of the Affair*. He did not want to see the light in her eyes.

Jimmy McGuire and Sean Cronin sat on the edge of the raft watching the sun sink toward the horizon through the haze of Chicago.

"Sets earlier every day, doesn't it?" said Sean.

"They call that the changing of the seasons," replied Jimmy. "We morose Irish can make of it whatever we want, so long as we remember that after Christmas the days get longer again."

Sean's slim red-haired friend from the seminary was at Oakland Beach for a long weekend. His visit provided a welcome interlude, breaking the routine.

"Your golf game left a lot to be desired today," Sean said accusingly.

Jimmy kicked at the waters of the lake. "My God, how could anyone play a good game of golf with Nora around? I'm sorry, I know she's your sister, but a body like hers ought to be barred from the golf course."

Sean laughed. "She's not really my sister. And I'll make her wear a very loose shirt tomorrow."

"Don't you dare!" Jimmy exclaimed.

"Then don't blame me if she beats you tomorrow as badly as she beat you today."

"Losing to Nora"—Jimmy grinned mischievously—"is more fun than beating anyone else. And I know she's not your real sister, but if she isn't a sister, what is she to you?"

Such shifts from the facetious to the dead serious were characteristic of Jimmy McGuire.

"I don't really know," Sean said slowly.

"Don't you think you ought to find out?"

"I guess I'm trying to," Sean said. He was alarmed that the intensity of his feeling for Nora was so obvious.

"You're in very deep waters, Sean. If you're not careful, you and Nora are going to get hurt."

"I'll never hurt Nora," he said stubbornly. "Never."

"Excuse my skepticism," said Jimmy. "I don't see how you can possibly avoid hurting her."

Nora rested her head on the leather car upholstery as they watched *An American in Paris* on the drive-in movie screen. In the back seat of the Chevy there were smothered sighs from Maggie Martin and Tom Shields. Nora couldn't understand how Maggie could neck with so many different boys. Poor Maggie. Everyone liked her, she was the life of the parties at which Nora stood shyly on the fringes. Yet Maggie did not like herself and would turn unpredictably petulant just when she had everyone's attention and affection.

Her date, Tom Shields, was a tall thin young man with limp brown hair, destined to become a doctor like his father, Roy, the

Cronin family doctor and longtime friend. Tom was too serious for fun-loving Maggie. He had gone to Quigley Seminary with Sean and would graduate from Notre Dame next year. He was as interested in conversation as necking, but Maggie didn't think she was smart enough to talk seriously. So they necked instead.

Nora was not greatly concerned about the electricity that seemed to be leaping back and forth between her and Sean. The summer would soon be over and Sean would return to the seminary. Confident that Paul was still alive, she did not take seriously Uncle Mike's plan that Sean should leave the seminary and, in a few years, marry her. She had to admit to herself, though, that the thought of being Sean's wife was an interesting one.

Nora looked at Sean out of the corner of her eye. The movie was ending and he was removing the sound box from the car door. He was not strikingly handsome like Paul, but at six feet one, with a strong trim body, soft warm eyes, neat blond hair, and a cleanly carved face, Sean was more than merely good-looking—and when he looked sad your heart ached and you would do absolutely anything to bring back the magic smile. It occurred to Nora that she was glad she would never have to make a choice between the two brothers.

They dropped Maggie and Tom at Maggie's house and returned home. It was an unusually hot night, and Sean proposed a walk on the beach. Nora was delighted.

"I think Tom's hooked," Sean said as they arrived at the bottom of the stairs on the sundeck. "He's always been sweet on that little baggage, and she lets him do whatever he wants."

"Baggage is not a nice word," said Nora, kicking off her loafers. "And he does the things she wants him to do. They're both hooked." She felt the warm sand seep around her toes.

Then, they were in each other's arms, kissing, at first awkwardly, hesitantly, and then fiercely.

"Sweeter than wine?" Nora asked after a few minutes, quoting one of the hit songs of the summer to cover her confusion.

"Sweeter than the finest German *Eiswein*," Sean said hoarsely. He stroked the firm muscles of her back.

"Too warm for this clinging to each other," she said into his chest.

"I guess so." She felt as though they would stand there, holding each other, ankle deep in the sand of Oakland Beach, for the rest of eternity.

He tilted her chin up and brought his lips down to meet hers. His kisses became more demanding. His hands followed the contours of her body.

"Very, very nice, Sean," she murmured through the haze into which she was sinking. "Too nice, I think."

"Too nice," Sean agreed heavily, pulling back from her. "I . . . I hope you're not angry?"

"Of course I'm not angry," she said, trying to sound relaxed. "It's summer and we're young, so we must cling to each other while we still can."

Nora Riley considered the young woman opposite her in the mirror as she applied her eye makeup exactly the way she had been taught in modeling school. Not bad, she told herself.

When her instructor had told her that she had the body of a Greek goddess and the face of a Titian madonna, Nora had laughed. Then she had gone home and looked at herself in the mirror. She was astonished to find that the description was not altogether inaccurate. She had never expected to be anything more than plain.

"Getting ready for the country club dance?" Uncle Mike burst into her room, smiling cheerfully. "I don't approve of all that makeup."

"Then you wasted your money sending me to finishing school," she said, "because I'm doing exactly what they taught me."

"Sean has to leave the seminary," he said, in his direct manner. "Now that Paul's gone, he has to assume responsibility of the second-in-command."

"I keep telling you"—Nora tried to keep the hand with her makeup brush steady—"that Paul isn't dead."

"Sure he's dead," said Mike harshly. "Sean is only kidding himself by going back to the seminary this year. I can tell that he's sweet on you, and you can keep him from going back to the seminary if you want." His voice was ingratiating. Nora adored Uncle Mike, despite all his faults. She wanted him to be happy. If marrying Sean would make him happy . . . but that was ridiculous.

"Sean is never in his life going to do for someone else," she said decisively, "something that he has not already made up his own mind to do."

Father McCabe looked up at Sean, an ominous anger showing on his lank, unshaven face. "Mistah Cronin, will you ever learn that there is not a special set of rules for the Cronin family simply because your father is a rich man?"

"I do my best to keep all the rules, Father," Sean said, trying to control himself.

"Oh, you keep all the small rules." Father McCabe scratched his bristly chin. "It's the big ones you violate. You know you are not supposed to receive mail from young women, yet such letters still come to you. How do you expect us to recommend you for ordination when you have such involvements?"

Nora again, he thought helplessly. Her letters were utterly harmless, not the slightest reference to the passions of last summer. "I'm not aware of receiving anything in the mail, Father," he said uneasily, watching heavy snow flurries falling outside of the disciplinarian's window.

"What do you call this, then?" Father McCabe triumphantly displayed a blue envelope and two pages of notepaper.

"I told you many times, Father, that Nora Riley is my foster sister. She writes to me once a month."

"Sisters don't write letters like this," insisted McCabe, holding the letter between thumb and forefinger as though he were afraid it was contaminated with infectious germs.

"Nora is an innocent child," Sean said. "I'm sure, Father, that you can't find a single inappropriate phrase in her entire letter."

"Oh?" said McCabe triumphantly. "What about the way she ends the letter?"

Sean sighed with momentary relief. As he had hoped, Nora was too discreet to say anything incriminating. "Father, she's ended her letters to me for the three years I've been here at Mundelein with the words, 'All my love.' They don't mean anything more than such words would mean from anyone's sister."

Father McCabe ignored his argument, demonstrating that it was effective. "You may write to her tonight and tell her that she is never to write you again as long as you are at this seminary. Is that clear?"

"Yes, Father." Sean could hardly contain his anger. "May I have the letter so I can reply to it?"

"You certainly may not," McCabe said brusquely. With three quick twists of his thick fingers, he tore up the fragile paper into tiny pieces and threw them in the wastebasket. "Now go to your room."

Sean, his fists clenched in violent rage, pounded the desk in his room. That goddamned bastard. Why would anyone want to be a priest when a vicious fool like that had power? What right did he have to read Sean's mail, to tear it up, to forbid Nora to write him?

Abruptly he grabbed his journal, gripped his pen in rage, and began to scratch angry words on its pages. Then, slowly, he calmed down.

> *I'm as bad as McCabe. Nora's letters are innocent enough and so, for that matter, is Nora. But my feelings for her aren't innocent. Not a day, not an hour, has passed over the last five months that I have not thought about her or felt the sensation of her lips pressed against mine. I'm hungry for her like a starving man is hungry for food, and I can't persuade myself that my feelings are sinful. I suppose I ought to leave the seminary and marry her now, before Paul comes back and takes her away from me. I'll tell McCabe after dinner that I'm leaving.*

He pondered the words he had written. At the end of the seven-fifteen recreation period, he would corner McCabe and tell him what he could do with his seminary. Then he wrote a brief appendix to his decision.

> *We're not supposed to ask for signs from you, and I'm not asking for a sign. I've made up my own mind. If you want to change it, that's up to you. You'll have to do it by 7:15 tonight.*

Sean and Jimmy McGuire took a walk during the recreation period after dinner.

"I'm going to see the Moose at seven fifteen, Jimmy," Sean said. "I'm leaving."

"Don't be a fool. Of course you're not leaving."

"Dad wants me to. I have to replace Paul."

"I won't discuss it," Jimmy said. "You're the only good seminarian in this whole miserable place. You keep the rules because you believe that they really are the will of God."

"I've never told anyone, Jim, but I'm plagued by doubts all the time. Hardly a day goes by that I don't need a sign that he's out there and that he cares about me."

"Shit." Jimmy was unimpressed. "You think you're an archangel or something? Everyone has doubts. You know as well as I do that doubt and faith are compatible. Hell, I heard you say that in class last week."

"How can I go through life as a priest and not believe in God?"

"If you mean"—Jimmy was losing his patience—"how can you go through life as a priest plagued with doubts, the answer is, Why should you be different from anyone else? I'll tell you what your problem is, Cronin: you're mad at God because he took your mother away from you. Me, I wish I had a strong enough sense of God to be mad at him."

"Maybe you're right," Sean conceded. "But I'm still leaving."

"I won't bet on it, because I don't want to take your money away from you." Jimmy sounded like a professor ending a difficult lecture to which the class had paid little attention.

Sean strode into his room at seven sixteen and threw the heavy pseudo–West Point overcoat that he was required to wear onto his bed. The last time he would have to put on that goddamned thing. Just before he stormed out of the room down to McCabe's office, he noticed a tiny sheet of paper that had been slipped under his door—the carefully cut quarter size of typing paper that McCabe used for his notes. Sean picked it up impatiently.

> *Your father called this afternoon to say that the Defense Department has confirmed that your brother Paul is alive and a prisoner of war in North Korea.*

❧ BOOK II ❧

Jesus, fully aware that he had come from God and was going to God, rose from the meal and took off his cloak. He picked up a towel and tied it around himself. Then he poured water into a basin and began to wash his disciples' feet and dry them with the towel he had around him.

—John 13:3–5

CHAPTER
FOUR
1953

"You can't be brainwashed unless you have a brain." Paul Cronin grinned engagingly. "They tried but gave up when they found they had nothing to work with."

The group of young women around him, dressed in their Sunday morning summer dresses, giggled their approval.

Paul tilted his head and stuffed his hands in his trousers pockets. "They weren't exactly pleasant folks, to tell you the truth," he said soberly. "I'm glad it's all over. . . . Come on, Sean, we'd better get home for breakfast before Aunt Jane has a fit."

The gaggle of worshipers, eyes still shining, scattered. Sean got into Paul's new Corvette, wondering at how little his brother had changed. A year of combat and a year and a half in a POW camp seemed to have touched him only lightly. There was perhaps a bit more strain around the eyes and a little more restlessness. Otherwise he was the same genial, gregarious Paul.

"What's next for you, Paul?" Sean asked as the car turned down the lake drive. A thin haze hung over the lake already. It would be another humid windless day.

"I guess it will be politics, like Dad wants. I learned to make decisions and issue orders in the Marines. I'm good at it."

There was a hint of seriousness in Paul's gray eyes. Beneath the charm and the laughter there was ambition. Not, perhaps, a ruthless, compelling urge for power, but rather a relaxed low-key delight in the joys of victory.

"Law school, then?"

"Sure, why not?" Paul shrugged and turned the car into the long driveway. "But first I want to take a year off, see the country."

"Dad won't like it," Sean said.

Paul turned off the ignition. "Speaking of Dad, he seems to have changed since I left."

"Sometimes I think he's like a rubber band that is stretching and stretching and—"

"Does he really expect me to marry that overgrown tomboy?" Paul interrupted.

"You'd better ask him." Sean climbed out of the Corvette.

"Nothing against her," Paul continued, smiling cheerfully and tossing the car keys into the air. "She just isn't my kind of woman, if you know what I mean."

"Not quite," said Sean. "Anyway, Nora has a mind of her own."

"I don't think he means it," Paul pocketed his keys. "He won't insist."

"Don't bet on that, big brother."

Paul Cronin enjoyed being a war hero. It kept his father off his back, and ever since he had come home from Korea, Paul had enjoyed more girls with less effort than all the rest of the years of his life put together. Maggie Martin was only one of his conquests.

They were in her parents' house at Oakland Beach while the rest of her family was in Chicago. "Jambalaya" was playing somewhere in the background.

"Why don't you get me another beer?" he asked, giving her his most winsome boyish smile.

"Sure, Paul," she said. "Anything you want."

Outside the window, a jagged lightning flash raced madly across the sky, briefly illuminating the restless waters of the lake. Then there was a roar of thunder.

"Here's your beer, Paul," she said, pathetically eager to please him.

"I'd like more than a beer, Maggie," he said, rising from the couch and pulling her to him. He kissed her expertly, his hands caressing her back.

When it became clear that Paul would not be satisfied with only necking, Maggie at first tried to pull back. But the lure of Paul Cronin was too strong, and she finally gave in.

Later, soothing her sweat-drenched body, Paul realized that Maggie Martin, for all her wide-eyed blond innocence, was the most sensual virgin he had ever possessed. In fact, she was just about perfect—eager to learn and unbelievably hungry. There were more good times to be enjoyed with her, he thought, as he drifted to sleep, but he would have to make certain that she understood that there would never be anything more between them than just a good time. . . .

A Chinese bugle slashed the cool night air. Paul rolled over in confusion, trying desperately to clear his head of the effects of the beer he had drunk before his bout with Maggie. At first, the nightmare duplicated reality. Where was Makuch? Where the hell was that damn Polack? He twisted around in his foxhole, just as a flare exploded above him, then dropped with agonizing slowness into the smooth waters of the reservoir. Oh, my God. . . . Chinks, thousands of them, swarming up the side of the hill. Automatic weapon in one hand, hand grenades still attached to his belt, Paul squirmed out of the foxhole and began to run. The enemy was coming toward him. To hell with Makuch. To hell with the rest of the outfit. He ran in a crouch along the ridge. He had to get away. Then he tripped on a pile of loose rocks and plunged headlong down the side of the ridge. He had stumbled into a deserted .50-caliber machine-gun position. He rolled over in time to see a half dozen Chinks running toward him with bayonets in ready position. There were more coming. He grabbed at the gun, pulled the trigger, and watched as the Chinks collapsed in front of him bellowing with pain. The machine gun jammed. He fired his automatic. Then the nightmare took over. Maggie Martin, naked and screaming, was the first of the Chinks whose heads exploded in front of him. . . .

He awakened, unsure whether it was his own screams he had heard. He was soaking wet, as he always was after such dreams. They had haunted him now for two years, ever since that terrifying night by Chongun Reservoir. It was the first time he had ever killed anyone, and he must have killed scores that night. His body trembled at the memory.

He sat on the edge of the couch and automatically lit a cigarette, wondering if the nightmares would ever stop.

Makuch *knew*. He was the only one in the outfit who knew. The look of contempt in his eyes revealed that the Polack from Pittsburgh had seen his platoon commander panic and desert his command. He knew that Paul wasn't entitled to his Medal of Honor. He had seen him stumble into the machine-gun nest as he was trying to flee.

Paul stubbed out his cigarette and explained to Maggie that it had been an ordinary nightmare. Then he quickly made his excuses, kissed her good night, and left.

Sean Cronin reached for his journal impatiently. He had made no entries in it since his impetuous decision to leave the seminary, a decision that God had canceled out very quickly. Lightning was dancing across the lake. Sean watched the show with hypnotized fascination.

Your thunderstorms are much better than the human dramas for which you write the scripts, he wrote slowly. *Paul is back, as cheerful and carefree as ever, unmarked, it seems, by a year and a half in a prisoner-of-war camp. When he laughs, everybody in the room laughs. When he smiles, everybody feels happy. When he suggests that the crowd do something—like going off to a movie— we all go along.*

Paul wants to spend a year wandering around the country—getting to know America better, he said. Dad won't like it. Before the summer is over, Paul's going to have to agree to go to law school and marry Nora when she gets out of college in three years. I wonder if she'll agree, too.

I don't feel any sadness now over Paul and Nora. They're made for each other; they just don't know it yet. They're both handsome and intelligent. His laughter and her depth will balance each other perfectly.

Six months ago, I was in love with her. I've never quite said it that way to myself, but there isn't any doubt. I was head over heels in love with Nora Riley. I'm over it now, I think, but still I

*wonder if I would change places with Paul if I could. But you
don't permit things like that, do you?*

*Ah, YOU, that's the question! How can anyone want to be a
priest as much as I want to, and still doubt you? I want . . . I
want . . . what do I want?*

Mike Cronin sighed in contented satisfaction and looked down
at the woman sleeping next to him. Lorna Mahoney was proving
herself an apt pupil. It was amazing how quickly these stiff
prudish women could discover their own sexuality when he
trapped them in a mixture of adoration and fear. Mike delighted
in women, especially when he was able to transform them into the
kind of responsive instrument of pleasure to which he felt a man
such as himself was entitled.

There was no joy in buying a woman. The trick was to pursue
them, slowly, lovingly, implacably, until they were eager to give
themselves over to you.

Nor did he become disinterested after a successful conquest.
Reeducation was as important as victory—MacArthur had proven
that in Japan. It was mostly a matter of kindness and attention,
with a bit of aloofness thrown in to keep them anxious and docile.
When he was finished with his reeducation program, a woman was
as good as a Japanese geisha at giving pleasure—which was, after
all, what she was there for.

He continued to enjoy a woman until she began to hint at marriage. Then Mike ended the relationship. Some of them complained, but they usually stopped when they saw the size of his
farewell check. None of them had any trouble finding husbands,
and presumably the lucky man benefited from the skills their
wives had learned from Mike. So it all worked out.

He lit a cigarette and puffed on it complacently. You had to
control them, of course, keep them under your thumb. That was
the only way to deal with women. That was how it was with everyone. Life was a jungle. You controlled the other beasts or they
controlled you.

The only serious mistake he had ever made with a woman was
his marriage to Mary Eileen. He frowned. That had been a disaster. Thank heavens, he had been able to protect his sons from the
knowledge of the possibility of a bad inheritance from that side of

the family. Hardly a day passed when he did not worry about the weakness showing up.

He decided that he should stop thinking about his wife and pay more attention to the delectable dessert he had in bed with him. Lorna was still sound asleep, her body spread luxuriously next to him. He eased the sheet away from her so he could savor her body in the bursts of lightning that now seemed to be just outside her bedroom window. She was less spectacularly developed than some of his other companions but made up for it by her intensity. His women were older now, in their early forties instead of their middle thirties. One must maintain a sense of proportion about these things. Lorna had started to talk of marriage sooner than most of the others; one of the problems of companions who were older was that they thought of marriage a lot sooner. For a moment he permitted himself to be tempted with the thought of marriage. No, it was impossible for him.

He would have to see Paul settled down before the summer was over. He would pull strings to get him into Northwestern Law School despite his college grades. Then Paul would marry Nora when she graduated from St. Mary's. Sean would be a priest by then, and he could officiate at the ceremony.

The marriage would be a great event: Paul safely married and Sean a priest. Both would be well on their way in the careers for which they were so brilliantly fitted by family and training.

Lightning seemed to explode, bathing Lorna in an eerie blue light. Mike put his sons from his mind and pulled the sheet the rest of the way off her body.

Nora put a candle in front of her Madonna and ignited the tiny lump of incense in the blue glass dish in front of the statue. Her piety was a jealously preserved secret, unknown even to her closest friend at school, where Nora was thought of as both an athlete and an exceptional student. In the privacy of her room, Nora would kneel on bare knees, entranced by the smell of incense, the glow of the candle, and an awareness of a Presence that pervaded the atmosphere.

Ever since she had escaped from the fire that had killed her mother and her baby brother, Nora Riley knew with absolute certainty that she was supposed to do something special in life. It appeared that the something "special" was Paul Cronin, with whom she had fallen in love, even though the two of them kept a wary distance from each other. Life with Paul would be exciting. She would be the wife and mother, working in the background, guiding his life and soothing his hurts, as he walked the road to the White House.

Paul would be the first Catholic president of the United States and she would be his first lady. That was important enough, wasn't it?

The Presence, enveloping her as gently as the faint aroma of incense, did not disagree. Yet Nora realized with vague unease, as she drifted off to the hills and meadows of this special love, that it didn't agree either.

"It's time we had a serious talk." Mike Cronin stared at the neat rows of Chicago streets that extended westward from the Field Building toward the burgeoning suburbs springing up beyond the west side of the city.

"Okay, if you say so," Paul agreed. "I've only been back for a couple of months, though. I think I'm entitled—"

"You're goddamned not entitled to anything," his father barked. "Your Medal of Honor doesn't entitle you to be thrown out of every tavern of northern Indiana and to screw everything that moves in Oakland Beach. I saw more combat than you did, and I came home and settled down to business."

"You weren't in a Korean prison camp; it's different," Paul sputtered.

"If you think I'm going to support you for the rest of your life, you're wrong." The top of Mike's bald head was flaming red, a very bad sign indeed.

"Okay, okay," Paul said nervously. "I'll go up to Northwestern tomorrow and see if they'll take me."

"You'll go up there today," Mike corrected him. "And, officer in the Marine Corps or not, you'll stay away from Maggie Martin. Her parents are too powerful to offend. Find your women somewhere else besides Oakland Beach and the neighborhood. And remember—after Nora's graduation you're going to marry her, just as everyone's agreed." His father hovered over him like an angry red-faced avenging angel.

"I don't object to that," Paul said, trying to placate his father. "But I'm not sure she'll go along." He reached for his cigarettes.

"She's got no choice but to go along. You're going to be the first Catholic president of this country, and Nora's going to be the first lady—whether she wants to or not."

"I think I may be able to win her over," Paul said. He sensed that a display of confidence would soothe his father's ruffled feathers. Then, in a burst of candor, he added, "You don't have to worry about me, Dad. I found out in the Marines that if you smile at people the right way they'll do almost anything for you."

"Well, that's settled then." Mike's mind was obviously turning to something else. It was time for Paul to get out of his office. Paul was suddenly aware that life could get very difficult in the years ahead if he weren't careful. And maybe even if he were.

CHAPTER FIVE

1954

"Two more years," Roger Fitzgibbon said as he and Sean Cronin labored on the weeds in the tennis court behind the theology hall at the seminary. "Just watch. When we're ordained, they'll blacktop this court."

"I suppose so," Sean replied. He was barely listening to his friend. He knew he was in trouble with the seminary authorities. His conference with the Rector in preparation for minor orders had been postponed, a sure sign that there was a debate raging behind the scenes about whether to ordain him. At best the outcome could be a "clip": he would not be ordained to the lesser orders of acolyte and reader but rather would be kept in limbo until the following year. Not expelled exactly—although no one would be unhappy if he solved their problem for them by leaving—but not approved either. To make matters worse, Sean had no idea why he was under a cloud.

"Thinking about Motherwell?" Roger asked sympathetically as he tossed a handful of weeds into the battered bushel basket next to the net. "Are you sure you passed your STB exam?"

"Joey Jim told me that I'd passed the exam, and he wanted to see me about something else." Sean wiped the perspiration off his face. "Have you ever heard of him talking about anything besides exams?"

Roger shook his head. "Nope, not once. I thought all this business about a clip was silly talk until I heard that he wanted to see you. No matter how you look at it, it can't be good."

"That's what I think too," Sean agreed.

The seminary held one principle of priestly training absolutely sacred: no one ought to be too good at anything, much less successful at a number of things. Athletic ability was tolerated, so long as it did not include every sport or accompany "too much" intellectual curiosity. High grades were viewed with suspicion, especially when combined with a propensity to read too many books. Intellectualism was taken to be almost a sure sign of pride. Affluence, especially the rumored great wealth of the Cronin family, was also a grave danger to a priestly vocation, because it made a young man think he might be independent of Church authority.

Sean accepted the basic theory. Seminarians were in training to be curates for most of their lives, cogs in the ecclesiastical machine, neat pieces of salami, sliced off with precision by a machine that made each slice almost identical to the previous one. Pastors in the archdiocese did not need or want curates who did not fit the mold. Too much "singularity" interfered with service to the Church.

Yet, try as he might, Sean could not quite conform. He kept all the rules, he did his work, he asked few difficult questions in the classroom, he fit in smoothly with his classmates. Yet lurking in the background always was the flamboyant image of his father. The Rector and many of the faculty were terrified at the possibility that after ordination Sean might turn into a clerical Mike Cronin. Almost any excuse to "cut him down to size" would be eagerly seized as a pretext, not for expelling him, but for making his life so unpleasant that he would leave—quite possibly, as the rector once suggested to him, for another diocese. "We'll give you a strong recommendation, son," the old man had said in a conspiratorial tone.

Sean wondered what his father's reaction would be to a postponement of ordination. Probably try to buy the minor orders for him. Sean grimaced. That would only make matters worse.

Roy Shields carefully packed his stethoscope into the jacket of his white suit. "Are you ever going to slow down, Mike?" he asked. There was reproach in his voice.

"Not if I can help it." Mike Cronin buttoned his tailor-made white shirt. "Why rust out when you can burn out?"

"I'd like you to come into Little Company of Mary for a couple of days. For a full range of tests."

"There's nothing wrong?" Mike tried to sound confident.

"Nothing specific," Roy assured him. "I'd just feel better if I could run some tests."

"Your job, Major"—Mike was talking to one of his staff surgeons again—"is to make me feel better, not to make yourself feel better."

"You drink too much, you smoke too much, you're carrying ten pounds more than you should, you never relax, you drive yourself from one end of the year to the other, there's no peace or stability in your life." The normally placid Dr. Shields ticked off his litany of charges almost as though he were angry. "What's the point in it, Mike? You don't need the money. Why don't you take time off and enjoy life?"

"Goddamn it, Roy, I *do* enjoy life." Mike knotted his tie. "And I intend to continue to enjoy it until my sons are established in their careers."

The doctor sighed. "Take it just a little slower."

Mike laughed. "Okay, Roy, if it will make you happy, I'll cut down on everything." He winked. "Well, almost everything."

In his limousine, Mike admitted to himself that Roy had scared him. Maybe he ought to cut down on the drinking and smoking . . . go to Glendore for a week and enjoy the coming of spring. There was no point in burning himself out. Give up smoking and drinking altogether. He had the willpower to do it if he wanted to. Maybe even settle down with Jenny Warren. He frowned. Jane wouldn't like that, would she?

He turned that unpleasant thought off and virtuously rubbed out his cigar. Give up smoking and drinking, but not Jenny. That seemed a fair enough trade. Roy hadn't said there was anything wrong with sex. And with Jenny, sex was something special indeed. He smiled in self-satisfaction. A cool, elegant New England aristocrat, reserved to the point of iciness until she took off her clothes, Jenny Warren was the best woman he had bedded in a long time, a challenge to his ingenuity.

He thought of the things she could do with her prim and proper Bostonian mouth. "Jeremy, I want to make a call," he told his chauffeur as he reached for the phone. He dialed Jenny's number.

When she picked up the phone in her apartment, he said, "There's a flight from Midway to Frankfurt on Thursday afternoon. Let's find a castle on the Rhine and drink wine all weekend."

She agreed enthusiastically. Mike relaxed on the soft cushions of his limousine, his imagination playing with a slightly tipsy Jenny, spread-eagled beneath him on a castle bed. That was the way to stay young.

He opened the door to the bar and mixed himself a stiff Scotch as Jeremy turned the Caddy down 55th Street.

He lit a cigar and puffed on it complacently. Better to burn out than rust out. He drained the Scotch and poured himself another drink.

Paul Cronin sipped his beer thoughtfully. The Dive was a crumby, dank Rush Street bar, but it was the place where most of the law school students gathered. It was therefore also the place for Paul to be with his unlimited money and his ready laugh, doing favors, collecting friends, amassing influence. It was all pathetically easy, and a great deal more fun than studying for tests.

He had discovered that law school was like everything else in his life. He could succeed with very little effort. As an experiment, he had barely studied for the midyear exams—there was a cool delicious joy in the defiance of such a gesture, a bold toss of the dice. He had not led his class, but he had been in the middle, enough to please his father and earn him a new sports car that Nora loved to drive.

Nora . . . he paused to consider that problem. She was a knockout. Not his kind of woman, like Maggie Martin, whom he still occasionally saw for the hell of it, but the kind of girl who would make a very presentable wife. The old man was often right: Nora probably was a good idea, or at least, all things considered, not a bad one.

"You been studying hard?" Jack Coles asked him.

Paul didn't particularly like Jack, who was handsome in a dark, white-teeth-grin sort of way. But Paul was friendly toward him, as he was toward everyone.

"Not too hard," Paul said cheerfully. "Have a beer."

"Thanks. . . . Say, wouldn't it be nice to know what the questions for the finals are going to be?"

Paul suppressed a yawn. "I suppose so."

Jack sipped his beer while Paul slipped a dollar bill to the bartender.

"It can be done," Jack said softly. "It will cost a few dollars, but it can be done."

Paul's interest was aroused. "You can get the exams?"

Jack looked around nervously. "With a few dollars, maybe five hundred."

"Sounds great," Paul assented. "You want to stop by my house this evening?"

"Sure," said Jack with feigned unconcern. "I might just do that."

After Jack left, Paul wondered why he had become involved in such a crackpot scheme. It was fun to outwit the faculty, most of whom were pompous frustrated federal judges. But he wasn't going to study very hard anyway, so what difference did it make if he knew what the questions were? Besides, even senile Dean Weaver would smell something fishy if Paul Cronin did better than his gentleman's C.

Paul didn't often question his own motives. He simply wanted to be a leader of other men, to be recognized when he walked down Michigan Avenue the way he was recognized in the corridors of the law school. It seemed to him to be a perfectly legitimate ambition. And he had all the talent necessary for the task. What the hell, why not aim as high as you could? Paul felt a headache coming on, as almost always happened when he thought too much about himself. He ordered another beer. How much did he really want to "settle down" with Nora and enter politics? He knew there was a lot of work to be done, crime to be fought, racial justice to be pursued, the Russians to be watched—all the things Jack Kennedy was talking about.

The Kennedys did not bother trying to analyze themselves. Why should he?

Halfway through his beer, the headache disappeared. So, too, had all qualms about paying for the theft of the final exams.

"Sit down, young man," said Joseph James Motherwell, S.J. "You're in big trouble." His eyes widened and his lips pursed as if in wonder at the size of Sean's trouble. "I want to talk to you about it."

Joey Jim was a New Deal Democrat from downstate Illinois, a pixielike seventy-year-old who talked with a nasal twang and clipped words as though he were a cowboy. A superb teacher with impeccable academic standards, his childlike face beamed with pleasure whenever he caught a student unprepared. His thin white hair and rimless spectacles made him look like an innocent angel, one that the seminarians had learned could be very dangerous if you hadn't studied the night before.

"I guess I'm going to be clipped," Sean said.

"Clipped?" Motherwell beamed with pleasure. "Why, young man, most of the faculty want to expel you."

"What have I done?" Sean asked. He wondered why he wanted to stay.

"You've made a serious mistake, young man." Motherwell readjusted the sash of his tattered old "Jesuit" cassock. "You've been born the son of a rich father who has high ambitions for you."

"Father Motherwell, Dad is a man of taste and refinement. However, there are a few things that obsess him. One of them is his desire that I become a priest. It may be crazy, but he's my father and I won't apologize for him."

"I don't think it's a crazy idea at all," Motherwell said. "You're one of the most gifted seminarians to come through this place in the last twenty-five years. You keep the rules, you're devout, you have great influence on others, you work hard, you have vision and imagination. Perhaps you're a little too cautious and conservative, but that's a good way to begin."

Joey Jim almost never paid compliments. Sean was thunderstruck. "But—"

"But nothing, young man. Not everyone is as envious as the Rector or your classmate Mr. Fitzgibbon."

"Roger? He's one of my best friends."

"Well, now, I don't know about that." Motherwell's eyes were hard. "He was the one who told them about the tailor-made suits your father sends you. They found them in your closet."

"I'm being clipped for tailor-made suits?" Sean was astonished.

Motherwell tilted his head and became even more of a pixie.

"Don't you think that's a good reason to clip someone, young man?"

"I don't wear the suits."

"They think"—Motherwell pointed a finger at Sean—"that when your father finds out you've been clipped, he'll try to buy ordination for you. Then they'll persuade the Cardinal to dismiss you. So you'd better not tell your dad, eh?"

"Did you block the expulsion?" Sean asked.

"I wasn't the only one, young man." He pursed his lips knowingly. "A group of us said we'd go to the Cardinal and protest."

Sean stood up. "Why, Father? Why go to all that trouble for me?"

"Well, young man, let's just say that I like to keep the Rector on his toes."

The Second City playhouse was cramped, uncomfortable, and unbearably hot; the drinks were expensive and not very good; and the wit of two young comics named Alan Arkin and Severn Darden was quite beyond Paul Cronin's comprehension. Yet, when one of his Jewish classmates, Tony Swartz, proposed that they take their dates to the fashionable new comedy review, Paul had quickly assented. Swartz was a class leader and destined for one of the prestigious downtown law firms. Paul was cautious with Jews; he had not known any when he was growing up, but they seemed to fit his father's stereotype—industrious, bright, and different.

To his surprise Nora seemed to enjoy the Second City wit and to be especially amused by a skit about football returning to the University of Chicago. Nor was she put off by Tony's slightly bitchy intellectual date, a slender, dark-skinned woman named Muriel. Muriel had made a few disparaging remarks about Catholic virgins when Nora mentioned she was a student at St. Mary's College but backed off when Nora ignored her in her most aristocratic manner.

Tony had been frankly admiring Nora's cool beauty. Paul was not sure whether to be proud or offended. He was even more uncertain when Nora banned all talk about Senator Joseph McCarthy, a favorite whipping boy of the law school students: "Let's not ruin the evening with that man. The Democrats will win a majority in the Senate next autumn and he'll be finished."

"Dad wouldn't like to hear you say that," he said cautiously.

"Uncle Mike is not likely to hear me say that," she replied, ending the discussion.

"Did they call you in on the exam theft?" Tony asked Paul as they were returning from a trip to the men's room.

"Yes, but the Dean admitted that no one who had the questions beforehand could have done so poorly with the answers." Paul laughed. "I think Jack would have carried it off if he hadn't been so hungry."

"I feel badly about Jack being expelled, but he sure messed up the curve." Tony shook his head.

Paul was glad when they reached the table and the conversation ended. He did not want to remember how, in his panic, he had hinted to the Dean that Jack Coles might have been the source of the advance information.

On the whole, Nora was more of a success with his friends than he had expected. And his good-night kiss did not catch her off guard. Her lips and tongue responded eagerly and her body pressed tightly against his. Catholic virgin she might be, but she was not bashful about necking.

"You're not a bad kisser, Paul Cronin," she said appreciatively, her fingers lightly touching his neck.

"I could get to like this too," he agreed.

"We'll have to try it again." She brushed his lips quickly this time and disappeared through the door of the house on Glenwood Drive. The Old Man apparently was off in Paris or Berlin or somewhere.

A nice girl, all right, with a great build and a fierce, prickly temper. Why, he wondered, as he drove back to his apartment near Lincoln Park, was he so wary of her? Probably because she seemed in such complete control of everything, including her passions.

Outside, the birds were singing and the blue sky seemed to be smiling contentedly down on the Rhine River.

"More wine?" Jenny Warren filled Mike Cronin's glass and returned to the delicate kisses with which she had been teasing and rewarding him. Thank God he was still capable of responding to such a woman, even if she was fifteen years younger.

"I love you, Michael," she said simply. "I don't understand you, but I love you and I'd do anything for you."

"I'll probably think of something before tonight." He laughed, trying to hide his wavering emotions.

"I only wish . . ." The kisses stopped and she leaned back, her fingers tracing a light design on his chest.

"What do you only wish?"

"I only wish I knew what haunts you so I could help make it go away."

He almost told her.

"This will make a man out of you, son," said the Rector, a fat foolish man with long flowing hair. "It will teach you the danger of vanity."

Vanity was the reason being given for the delay of his ordination to minor orders. Motherwell had won a point, though. The Rector promised Sean that if he stayed out of trouble during the summer, he would catch up with his classmates in the fall. It also seemed that Jimmy McGuire had done the unheard of—defended him to the Rector in the name of his classmates.

"Vanity is a bad thing," Sean temporized, refusing to admit his guilt to a charge that had been so obscurely made. In the course of the Rector's rambling explanation, his sin seemed to be virtually nonexistent.

"We all have to be humble, son." The Rector folded his hands piously on his massive oak desk, inherited from the Cardinal Mundelein era.

"Humility is a good thing." Sean wondered why he was taking such crap from a seminary at which he did not want to stay. Why was he making such foolish sacrifices when he was not even sure that he really wanted to be a priest? Was it his vocation or his father's? If they had only thrown him out, the decision to leave would not have been his.

"Some of your teachers had very glowering things to say about you," the Rector assured him. He meant glowing.

"That was very kind of them," Sean agreed. Damn you, Motherwell. If it hadn't been for you, I might be out of here and doing what I want to do.

And what do I want to do?

I want to take Nora away from Paul. That's what I want to do.

CHAPTER SIX

1954

Sean Cronin glared at the brown spires of St. Mary's College. He could hardly wait to see Nora, yet at the same time he was resentful that he had been given the job of bringing her home at the end of the school year. It was Jeremy's day off and Paul was busy with the last details for his summer clerkship in a law office.

"This place is worse than a convent," Sean muttered to Tom Shields, who was waiting to pick up Maggie Martin.

"Academically it's excellent, Sean," the thin studious young medical student replied. "The Christian Culture program that Nora is in provides a first-class education. Much better than the one I received at Notre Dame."

"All they need is a course in cooking and diaper washing," Sean sneered.

"Come on, Sean. You don't mean that. You're proud of Nora's intelligence, just as I'm proud of Maggie's."

"I'd be even more proud of them if they'd get their asses out here so we could escape from this creepy place." Sean was still angry from the injustice and the humiliation of the clip, but he was unable to release his pent-up emotions by speaking about it, lest his father hear and make matters even worse.

Finally, the two young women appeared, both clad in the Bermuda shorts that they were strictly forbidden to wear during the school year. Nora's long auburn hair flowed loosely in the spring breeze. Maggie made a soft, cuddly counterpoint to her tall, austere friend.

Sean packed Nora's suitcases in the trunk of the Cadillac and quickly drove to the crowded streets of South Bend and then the hot concrete of Highway 20 with its gas-belching trucks and flat northern Indiana farmland. A road to hell, he often told himself, paved with bad intentions.

Finally, he broke his silence. "How can you put up with that cruddy place? Pious nuns simpering around. Rules from the late Middle Ages. Irrelevant education and phony liberal crap."

Nora had been humming "Three Coins in the Fountain," as it played on the car radio. "Maybe it is a bit old-fashioned. Yet when Sister Madeleva reads her poetry, I see something to be said for the tradition. It needs to be modernized, but I don't want it to be lost."

"Women writing poetry, the acme of irrelevance."

Nora slammed the radio dial. "What's going on? You haven't said a friendly thing since I came out of the dorm. You didn't kiss me; you didn't say it was good to see me; you've sulked, complained, and sneered. If you're trying to pick a fight with me, you've damn well succeeded. What's eating you?"

"Nothing," he snarled. "Not a goddamn thing."

"All right." She moved as far as she could from him in the copious front seat of the Cadillac. "I can sulk as long as you can . . . longer. Until judgment day if I have to. We're supposed to be friends, and I can wait till you treat me like one again and tell me what those bastards at the seminary have done to you now."

Nora's unerring instincts shocked him even more than her language, words he had never heard from her before.

"I'm sure you can outsulk me, Nora," he said sheepishly. And out poured the story.

She was sympathetic and supportive. "I won't tell Uncle Mike," she promised.

"I know you won't."

They were quiet for a time, sharing the powerful emotions of their friendship. Nora made him turn off U.S. 20 and drive toward La Porte. It was a different world: trees, shade, old, old homes, front porches, quiet side streets.

"What a lovely little town," he said.

"It means the Gate, of course," she said. "It's the northern end of what was once the Great American Forest. People traveled through here for hundreds of years because it was the gateway to the prairies. Dunes on the north and forests to the south. And what's more, Mr. Smart-ass Sophisticate Sean Cronin, it's older than Chicago and fifteen minutes from Oakland Beach. You're such a terrible conservative you've never bothered to come down here and see it."

Sean laughed. It was good to be with Nora again.

They ate hamburgers at a tiny lunch stand overlooking a small azure lake on which kids were water skiing. Nora boasted that she had learned how to ski in Fort Lauderdale at Easter and offered to teach him. He told her that he had learned the summer before at the villa—a northern Wisconsin prison of sorts to which seminarians were sent during the summer to keep them separate from the laity to whom in a few years they would be ministering—and that he would gladly beat her at a competition.

They both laughed happily.

"They *will* ordain you a priest, won't they?" Nora asked after they had ordered ice-cream sodas for dessert.

"Sure, if I want to put up with their bullshit. I half wish they'd thrown me out. Then I wouldn't have to make my own decision."

Nora was baffled. "You want to be a priest, don't you, Sean? You always have."

"I don't know." He was admitting his doubts to her for the first time, indeed the first time to anyone. "I'm not sure. Sometimes yes, sometimes no. I wonder if it's not Dad's vocation instead of mine."

"Couldn't Uncle Mike be supporting the right thing for the wrong reason?"

"Maybe so. I'm so confused I don't know. If they'd thrown me out, I would have had a sign from God."

"God doesn't work that way." She dismissed his heresy decisively. "Anyway, what would you do if you were thrown out and cheated of making your own choice?"

"Probably take you away from Paul," he said impulsively.

Nora almost choked on her soda. "Oh, Sean, I'm not Paul's. I'm not anyone's. No one is going to take me away from anybody. Besides, if you should ever marry, you don't deserve to be stuck with somebody like me. You would need someone a lot better." She grinned impishly and went back to her soda.

You declare your love for a woman and she thinks it's a joke. Serves you right, Sean thought to himself. "You *are* going to marry Paul, though?"

"He's lots of fun and he's a good kisser." She grinned again. "And he's sweet to me, and it will make Uncle Mike happy . . . and I think I love him. Don't worry, Sean, I'll make up my own mind."

Sean kept his fingers firmly on the wheel of the Caddy all the way back to Chicago. He was afraid that if he freed even one arm he would embrace Nora, kiss her, and then try to hold her in his arms for the rest of his life. It was an excellent idea. Unfortunately, he had offered to marry her and she had not even heard. It was also against what the spiritual director would have called "God's Holy Will."

The enormous front lawn of the Cronin house on Glenwood Drive was perfect for a garden party. Long green canopies were hung, tables filled with filets and lobsters and ham and corned beef were arranged around the lawn, three bars were in constant operation, serving the best wine and whiskey that money could buy. A five-piece string orchestra played Viennese and Irish music, while waiters in formal dress passed through the crowd, politely offering their trays of delicacies. God cooperated with a glorious Saturday afternoon in June.

All this was in honor of Senator Joseph R. McCarthy, the man of the hour for most Irish Catholics. Everyone in the neighborhood, as well as hordes of Mike's business associates, had been invited. They all came, no matter what they thought of "Tail Gunner Joe," because they did not want to risk offending Michael Cronin. The only exceptions were a few local Democratic politicians, who did not know whether it was safe to risk the disapproval of their new chairman, County Clerk Richard J. Daley, an unknown factor thus far in Chicago political life.

Sean was introduced to the Senator, whom he instantly sized up as a lush who needed a shave. How could his father see political greatness in the man? Paul, who was sticking like glue to the Senator, seemed unperturbed by the guest of honor's bleary eyes and slurred voice.

Jenny Warren hugged Sean vigorously and told him how well he looked. Most of his father's "friends" were fond of Sean, and

he had become sufficiently tolerant to admit they were nice
women. He wished his father would marry Jenny; she was a sweet
and lovely lady who might bring some order and calm into Mike's
life.

Sean joined Roger Fitzgibbon and Jimmy McGuire at the
fringe of the party.

"Vanity of vanities, all is vanity," cracked Jimmy.

"At least Nora isn't part of the vanity." Sean needled Jimmy
whenever he could about his longtime crush on Nora.

"She and Maggie certainly divert attention from the Tail
Gunner," Jimmy agreed. In sheath dresses with short sleeves and
matching shoes, the two young women were indeed images of con-
trasting youthful loveliness.

"I can see your brother's point," Roger said. Roger wore
French cuffs and a vest and what was surely a tailor-made suit.

"It's a long way to go before he and Nora are a definite thing."
Sean realized he didn't even like to hear a hint of eventual marriage.

"Nora?" Roger raised an elegant eyebrow. "I thought it was
Maggie. Remember the night last winter when we bumped into
them at that bar near Loyola, Jimmy? When we were on vacation?"

"I think they're just friends," Jimmy said. His red face turned
even redder.

"They looked like more than friends," Roger said.

Later, when Roger had slipped away, Sean said to Jimmy, "I
want the truth about that night, and I don't mean about why you
two were breaking rules."

"You and the rules," Jimmy said impatiently. "Well, they were
very, very affectionate before they saw us. Didn't bother her. Paul
was kind of embarrassed. They left right after they talked to us."

"How affectionate?" Sean insisted.

Jimmy gulped. "I'll give it to you straight. I wouldn't be surprised if they spent part of the night in bed."

"That's straight enough." Sean was chilled to the marrow despite the June warmth.

Jenny Warren, smelling as lovely as she looked, interrupted
them. "There's a bit of a problem with your Aunt Jane. I'm afraid
I'd make things worse."

"Okay," said Sean. It was not okay, but at least he had something else to think about. "Get Ed Connaire and tell him. I'll see what I can do."

Jane, in an out-of-date burgundy spring dress, was in back of the house, shouting drunken orders at the cook. Jane Cronin was no longer a secret drinker.

Nora arrived at the same time as Sean, in time to see Jane stumble over an evergreen bush and onto the grass in front of a case of wine bottles.

"Miserable bastards," Jane said, as they helped her to her feet. "Trash."

"Easy, Aunt Jane. We'll get you into the house for a nap."

"Don't want to nap." Jane swayed dangerously.

Sean held her firmly and breathed a sigh of relief as Ed Connaire joined them.

"Easy, Jane," said the burly red-haired construction contractor. "It's going to be all right."

"It would be better if we'd let her kill her little bastard." She waved a drunken hand at Sean. "She and her priest friend . . . bastards . . . they're all worthless."

"It's all right, Jane. It's all right." Ed circled her with his muscular arms. He whispered to Sean, "I'll take care of it from now on, son."

He led the still-muttering Jane toward the back stairs of the house. Erithea was waiting patiently at the door. Jane was tottering uncertainly.

"We're going to wait for Ed," Nora said, her jaw firmly set, "and ask him what all that means. I'm not going to have you worrying about her nasty cracks any more."

Sean felt cold. He wanted to hide in the basement.

Ed Connaire looked dubious at first when Sean and Nora cornered him; then he nodded his head thoughtfully, and the three walked silently down the hill to the sidewalk on Glenwood Drive.

"It's not as bad as it sounds, Sean. It was all so long ago. I suppose you have a right to know, although I wish it could be forgotten. It doesn't make any difference—"

"Maybe I should be the judge of that," Sean said.

Ed cracked his massive knuckles. "Sure, Sean, only please try to understand that some things happen for which no one is really to blame."

"Sean understands," Nora said. "He still needs to know."

Ed smiled appreciatively. "All right Nora, you win. Sean, your father and mother were very different kinds of people. They both tried, but the first years of marriage are always hard, and—well, your father was traveling so much. Mike pretends now that their marriage was perfect, but your mother was never really happy at the house at Oakland Beach. Even though Mike had Glendore built because he thought it was what she wanted, she was discontented. She became depressed, especially after Paul was born . . . that often happens, you know."

"I know. Please go on, Ed."

"Your mother turned to religion, and your father, with the best intentions in the world, wouldn't let her continue to see the priests she had started to bring around. He was afraid it was becoming an obsession. Then, when you came along, Mary Eileen became even more depressed. One day, when Mike was in Europe on business, your mother took the car out and had the accident. No one could ever prove that she had done it on purpose, but it was a terrible sad wake, Sean. She was so young and so lovely. And they couldn't even open the casket. Some people were mad at your father because the wake was only one night. But he was right. It was too terrible for everyone. Doc Shields said it was a blessing, because she might have been crippled for the rest of her life."

"I wonder if she thought it was a blessing," said Sean bitterly.

"Drop it, Sean," Nora said. "Ed is right. It was long ago and it was tragic and it was no one's fault."

Sean regained his self-control. "Of course. Thank you, Ed. I did have to know, and now that I do I'll forget about it."

"I sure hope I did right in telling you." Ed rubbed his hands together.

"You did, Ed," said Nora. "Now it can all be buried and left in God's hands."

"He's not telling the whole story, Nora," Sean said softly as the old giant slowly climbed the steps back to the lawn party.

"Don't torment yourself. It won't do any good."

"Our lives could have been different," Sean said.

Nora drew his face down to hers and kissed him. "That's for being Sean, the most decent person I know."

That night Nora knelt at the side of her bed, wrapped in a large bath towel. "You know what I have to say. Help him to be a good priest, help me to take care of him, help me to love him the way I should love him."

There were no answers. There never were.

As she fell asleep that night, she felt a little guilty. She had kept her love for Sean in a tightly sealed compartment of her heart, a compartment that had almost exploded open when he had awkwardly hinted at marriage in the car coming home from St. Mary's. He had been angry at the seminary and hoping that she could be a substitute for his priestly vocation. Nora had known better.

She drifted off to sleep. Tonight there would only be peace, even on the subject of Sean Cronin.

CHAPTER
SEVEN
1956

Sean could not sleep the night before ordination. He tossed and turned on the stiff mattress in his room in the Sacred Orders building at Mundelein, knowing that many of his classmates were doing exactly the same thing. Outside the window, the smell of May flowers hung in the air, sweet, gentle, young. This was the day he had worked for since entering Quigley as a freshman twelve years before. It would be the happiest day of his life, everyone assured him. Yet he did not feel happy. He was no more certain of his vocation now than he had been through the twelve long years. His faith was as thin as a communion wafer. While he was eager to work in his first parish assignment, he now found it harder to pray than ever before.

He struggled out of bed, sat at his desk, and turned on the lamp. No lights-out rule the night before ordination. He looked at the shelf at the side of his desk, at the seven brown-covered ring-binder notebooks that were his diary for the seven years at Mundelein. He slid one off the shelf. Its cover felt reassuringly smooth beneath his fingers. He slowly flipped its pages. Yes, he would be ordained tomorrow. It was too late to turn back now. He had become a subdeacon the year before and a deacon last fall. He was now committed to a life of celibacy; he might just as well be a priest.

Briefly, he thought of Nora, a nostalgic love out of a forgotten past. She and Paul would probably break the news of their engagement to him after his first Mass, with characteristic tact trying not to upstage him during the day.

He sat at his desk for a long time, hardly noticing the hours pass. The first light of day creased the eastern sky behind the red-brick auditorium. Then the sun slowly eased its way over the horizon, turning the early morning a faintly glowing rose. With a start, he noticed the clock staring at him disapprovingly from his desk. He was already late for the preliminaries in the basement of the main chapel.

Five minutes later he rushed down the steps into the noisy crowd of his classmates. Father Roache, the genial majordomo of ordination ceremonies, whose principal job was to calm the jumpy nerves of the priests-to-be, cracked into the microphone, "Okay, guys, relax; Sean's going to go through with it after all."

The laughter was inappropriately loud, but it settled a lot of nerves, Sean's not included.

"Hey, you had me worried," Jimmy McGuire whispered, already dressed in his white alb with a deacon's stole over his shoulder and the priest's chasuble over one arm. "Last-minute cold feet?"

"Do I have feet?" Sean asked innocently.

The high point of the ordination ceremony came when the newly-ordained priests, wearing the chasubles they had carried into the sanctuary, stood in ordered ranks in front of the altar in the colonial-style chapel, their hands anointed with the oil of ordination. Each priest attending the ceremony marched up and down the rows, imposing his hands on the heads of the new priests and then joining old Cardinal McNulty on the platform of the main altar. The older priests then raised their right hands in the air as though in solemn benediction. It was the moment that many said was the most inspiring and most awesome part of the three-hour-long ritual.

Sean, however, felt nothing at all, just sore knees, an aching back, and a bad headache. Was God punishing him for his lack of faith?

Then, in a tottering voice, with frequent corrections as Father Roache whispered the right words into his ear, Cardinal McNulty

chanted the form of the Sacrament of Ordination to the Priesthood over the newly ordained priests:

> *"Almighty Father, grant to these servants of yours the dignity of*
> *the priesthood. Renew within them the spirit of holiness. May*
> *they be faithful to the ministry they receive from you, Lord*
> *God, and be to others models of right conduct . . . so that the*
> *words of the Gospel be preached to the ends on the earth and*
> *the family of nations, made one in Christ, may become God's*
> *one Holy People."*

Later, at the first blessing ceremony held on the steps and lawn
surrounding the main chapel, clusters of families and friends in
bright dresses and summer suits circled around the young priests,
who were trim and self-conscious in their brand new cassocks.
Mike Cronin, uncharacteristically giving way to Irish emotion,
wept as Sean, for the first time, said, "May the blessing of al-
mighty God, Father, Son, and Holy Spirit descend upon you and
remain with you always."

Paul embraced Sean enthusiastically after his blessing and after
he had kissed the hands on which the oil of ordination had not yet
dried. "You already look like a cardinal, Sean, and you sure say
the blessing like one."

And then it was Nora's turn: Nora, glowing with fresh full
beauty in her virginal sleeveless white dress. After Nora kissed
Sean's hands, they embraced tenderly.

"I'm so proud of you, Sean," she said through her tears.

"And I'm proud to have you as a sister," he replied, wondering
as he said it whether they were the right words.

A First Mass banquet for Sean was held in the sun-filled dining
room of the Beverly Country Club. The only awkward moment
came when Mike Cronin proposed a toast to his son, "the future
cardinal," embarrassing Sean and offending most of the old and
new priests who were there.

As the banquet broke up, Nora and Paul walked up to Sean.
"We have something to tell you," Paul said, grinning.

"I can't imagine what it is." Sean grinned back.

"You tell him," Paul said.

"He's *your* brother, *you* tell him," said Nora.

"Well"—Paul's embarrassment, amazingly enough, seemed genuine—"Nora claims that sometime in August she wants to make an honest man out of me."

"Nonsense," said Nora. "When he was trying to find a toast for the newly ordained Father Cronin, he discovered a couple of wedding toasts and remembered what weddings were for."

"You'll officiate?"

"I'd have my lawyers sue if you asked anyone else."

As Paul and Nora walked away, hand in hand, a tall, glorious, handsome young couple, it occurred to Father Sean Cronin that Michael Cronin's plans for his family were well under way.

Too bad Mary Eileen could not have been there yesterday to see her son become a priest. It was working out, in spite of all the things that might have gone wrong, Mike Cronin thought, as he tightened the belt on his robe and poured himself another glass of orange juice.

Despite a bad beginning, the night had been rewarding. Jenny Warren had been reluctant to make love when they returned to the empty house on Glenwood Drive after the First Mass banquet. Mike, bristling with enthusiasm over the ordination of one son and the impending marriage of the other, had enthusiastically won her over. It would be a shame to have to give her up, but none of his women seemed to understand that marriage could never be part of the arrangement.

He dismissed Jenny from his mind and returned to thinking about Sean. The boy was a strange one; he read too much poetry, but he had the mark of greatness on him. A discreet visit to the Cardinal in a week, and a large check folded in two and placed on his desk, would doubtless guarantee Sean an excellent assignment and would be the first step in his career. After that, in a couple of years, another check would mean graduate school in Rome and a place on old McNulty's staff. It would be a lot easier, he was convinced, to buy a career for Sean in the Church than to get that damn fool Paul through his bar exam.

Jenny entered the dining room, her round pretty face soft with pleasurable memories, her thin pink negligee loose enough to hint that she would like more to remember.

"Hey, Jenny," he said softly, "do you think my boy is going to be a cardinal?"

• • •

Instead of studying for his bar exam, Paul was daydreaming over the latest issue of *Playboy,* linking in his imagination the auburn-haired centerfold with Nora. After two years of heavy necking and petting, he wanted her badly. Not because his sex life was frustrated, but because she fascinated him. Paul's taste ran usually to soft, compliant women. Nora was mysterious, aloof, and seemingly unassailable.

His near North Side "pad," just off Lake Shore Drive, was carefully furnished with pillows, cushions, low soft chairs, and throw rugs. It had all the elegance and comfort necessary to make it *the* place for his law school classmates to come with their dates.

Paul sighed happily. He had not wasted the three years in law school. He had carefully chosen as friends the young men who would be useful in the years ahead: lawyers, politicians, bankers, an occasional journalist. Flattery, fun, pleasure—these were the techniques for attracting them. It was all informal and casual, yet he could tell when he glanced around his apartment during a party that everyone in the room was calculating how they could use everyone else.

That was the way it ought to be. So much the better for him that his calculations were never revealed by his amiable, smiling eyes.

Paul knew that it was time to turn domestic and raise a family. Nora would be a stabilizing influence in his life, and he probably needed that. He would stop the screwing around, too. Political success would come easy. He was a winner, of that there was no doubt. He wanted also to be a man of substance. Nora would help give him depth.

"Are you really going to marry him?" Maggie Martin Shields shook her head in disbelief. "I mean, he's great-looking, and I know you've been dating, but you're so serious and he—well, he seems to enjoy his fun."

They were sitting on the beach, luxuriating in the feel of the mid-July sun on their smooth young skin. Nora was careful in her answer. She knew that Maggie had once had a crush on Paul, and there were signs that her three-month-old marriage to Tom Shields had not settled down yet. Maggie seemed as restless as ever.

"I'm mad about him, Maggie, and I'm impressed by how much he's grown up in the last couple of years. He's thoughtful and attentive and he's studied so hard for the bar exam. I can't think of anybody I'd rather marry than Paul Cronin."

"Not even Sean?" Maggie arched her bare shoulders suggestively.

"Sean's a priest," Nora said firmly.

"Men are men," said Maggie. "I don't care whether they're priests or not." Maggie rolled over on her stomach. "You're naive, Nora. You're going to be in for a terrible surprise. Men don't really care about women. They want a woman's body and nothing more."

"Paul's a gentleman. I'm not afraid of him," Nora insisted, knowing that she was very much afraid of being alone in a bedroom with her husband-to-be, despite all the reading she had done about sex. "In any event," Nora said, "he may be a little surprised too."

CHAPTER
EIGHT
1956

Jimmy McGuire, happy in his assignment in Oak Lawn and proud of the parish car his pastor had purchased for him—since young priests could not own cars for their first five years—stopped late one evening to talk with Sean at St. Jadwiga rectory. Sean answered the doorbell himself—housekeepers, cooks, and maids at St. Jadwiga's were irregular—and led Jimmy up the shaky staircase to his tiny room on the back of the second floor.

"Does Dudon ever come out of his room?" Jimmy jerked his thumb in the direction of the pastor's elaborate suite at the front of the house.

"Not really, save to take care of his Chihuahuas and to say the first Mass on Sunday." Sean slumped in the battered old chair that was one of the two pieces of furniture in his study.

"Chihuahuas?"

"Yes. He raises full breeds or pedigrees or whatever they call prizewinning Chihuahuas. He had a big crisis last Sunday when one of the bitches—it's not a pejorative term if you're a dog—gave birth just before the six-thirty Mass."

"How crazy is he?" Jimmy asked, now quite serious.

"Oh, I don't suppose he's any more crazy than any other unmarried man of fifty-five who has nothing except dogs to live for. Remember, Jimmy, that this was a nice little Bohemian parish where everybody loved him and he didn't have to work. It became part of the black ghetto overnight. So he just sits up in his room trying to pretend it didn't happen and hoping that the chancery office will remember him."

"While you do all the work?"

"Well, that's what we're ordained for, isn't it?"

"Do you think your father—"

"Yes, I think my father went to see the Cardinal, offered to make a contribution, and almost got away with it. Then the Cardinal dug out a file card on me from Mundelein that warned him against me. So he pocketed Dad's check and sent me here to St. Jadwiga's. But I'm glad I'm here. If we don't like working in poor parishes we don't belong in the priesthood."

"You should at least take a day off," Jimmy said.

Sean relaxed a bit. "I know I should, Jimmy," he said. "And I appreciate the concern. I'll see you guys next Thursday."

"And I'll believe that when I see you on the first tee." Jimmy paused. "Is Nora really going to marry Paul?"

Sean felt his spirits lift. "That's what they both tell me."

"You always said I had a soft spot for Nora," McGuire said awkwardly, "and you were right. I just wonder. They're such different personalities."

Sean tried to consider Jimmy's observation objectively. Jimmy was a good judge of human nature. "I know what you mean, Jimmy. I used to think the same thing myself, and I know they're going to have some tough adjustments. In a way, it will be harder on Paul. Nora has all the willpower."

Jimmy was unimpressed. "Look, do me a favor, for old times' sake and all of that. Make sure Nora knows what she's doing. Tell her about Paul and Maggie."

There was a long pause while nameless emotions struggled in Sean's heart.

"Sure," he said finally.

Nora and Sean sat in the Berghoff Restaurant on Monroe Street surrounded by frantic businessmen and lawyers, enjoying, as they always did, each other's company. His telephone call had been mysterious, and Nora, only a few days away from her wedding, was uncharacteristically falling behind schedule. Nevertheless, a call from Sean proposing lunch took precedence, and she postponed her scheduled task of arranging the seating chart for the reception.

When he saw the tall, lovely young woman wave to him and then walk gracefully across the dining room, Sean had realized again how dishonest had been his defense to the seminary that Nora was "almost a sister." There was no doubt that brothers did not react to their sisters the way he reacted to Nora. Reluctantly, he banished his fantasies to a dark corner of his imagination.

"I'm glad you were able to come," he said.

"I'll have lunch with you, Sean, any time you'd like," she said. "How's it going at St. Joshua?"

"Jadwiga." He emphasized the word and then, noting her amused smile, said sheepishly, "You know, you really are an impish little bitch."

She sank her teeth into a juicy mixture of cheese, sauerkraut, and ham. "I don't think the word 'little' is appropriate, and that doesn't answer my question. Uncle Mike is furious about your assignment."

Sean pushed his plate aside. "It's all right, Nora, it really is. I'm happy. I'm doing the work I've always wanted. Anyhow, it's you, not me, who's on the agenda for this lunch."

"Oh?" Nora wondered why her heart seemed to be sinking.

"Look." He stumbled a bit. "Well, you know how it is with me and Paul. We're competitors, we're fighters, difficult, contentious people. . . ."

"Well, you are, anyhow."

"You also know how much I love him. I know all his faults, I guess, yet I still worship him and have for as long as I can remember. Sometimes he's superficial, and sometimes he's unreliable, and sometimes he seems only interested in his own pleasures. When you know him as well as I do, you know that he has the capability of being very deep and very serious and very responsive."

Nora felt a rush of affection swelling up inside her. "Oh, Sean." She reached across the table to touch his hand. "I know Paul's failings. We all were raised in the same house, remember? I do love him and he does love me, and he's grown up so much in the past few years. Bobby Kennedy told me after the Democratic convention that Paul was the best floor leader they had, and if there were more like him it would be Stevenson and Kennedy instead of Stevenson and Kefauver this November. He'll be all right, wait and see. And I'll be all right too. Please, don't worry about us." She tightened her grip on his hand.

Sean was flustered. "I don't suppose it will be any more difficult for you and Paul than it is for other young married people." He hesitated. "It may be a little different, that's all." He could not bring himself to tell her about Paul and Maggie.

Nora released her hold on his long, tense fingers. Maybe it was a sin to touch a priest's hand that way. "Don't worry, please don't. I know what I'm doing. I'm going into this marriage with both eyes open."

CHAPTER NINE

1956

Michael Cronin was afraid. He was afraid of death.

His son Sean considered that conclusion carefully. Early in life Sean had realized that his father was not like the fathers of his friends, that he was different. Now, at the age of twenty-five, the disturbing truth hit Sean with terrible clarity. Much of his father's frantic activity was a desperate rush to escape from death. As he grew older he was losing the race. His ideas became more fixed, his gestures more nervous, his eyes more icy. The old charm and wit were still there, but they were gradually slipping away.

"Do you understand all that I've told you?" Mike's cold green eyes peered up at Sean, who was sitting across from him at the littered desk in the dark, heavily paneled study of their home on Glenwood Drive, a home which his father refused to leave, even though his vast wealth could purchase an entire neighborhood far better than Beverly.

Sean tried to concentrate. "Most of it, Dad. Counting the land and the stock portfolio and the oil interests and everything else, you're worth more than half a billion dollars. I'm afraid I don't understand all the companies and the partnerships. I'd need a diagram for that."

His father laughed. "The IRS would love to have one too."

"Well, I think I understand most of it, even without the diagram," Sean said carefully. He knew this was important to his father.

Mike sighed and relaxed in his large red leather chair. "I want you to know all these things before Paul's marriage. Paul will run the business, of course, at least until he's elected to something. But there will be a group of trustees, like my old buddies Marty Hoffman and Ed Connaire, to watch him until he's forty. You'll be too busy being a priest"—Mike was still terribly dissatisfied with Sean's calm acceptance of the St. Jadwiga's assignment—"so the trust will simply pay you a check every month for the rest of your life. They'll have the right to increase the size of the check, and if you need money for something special, for yourself, not for the Church, then you can apply to them. I'll instruct them and their successors to be generous. Do you understand?"

Sean understood very well. His father intended to keep him firmly under control for all of Michael Cronin's life and then, through the trustees, under equally firm control after he died. It didn't make any difference to Sean. "I understand."

"Mind you, any time you need anything while I'm still alive, no matter how much it is, just come and ask and I'll take care of it— no questions asked, no strings attached."

Not much, thought Sean. "And what do you do with all the money you make every year, Dad?" he asked.

The long and detailed answer left Sean flabbergasted. His father gave a great deal of money away, much of it secretly. While there were Cronin Halls being built at Fordham, Notre Dame, Boston College, and Northwestern, the typical Cronin gift was anonymous.

"You're very generous," Sean said with genuine respect.

"All you have to do is say the word and I'll build a new church and a new school and a new rectory for St. Jagoff, or whatever the hell the name is. Just say the word."

"That will be the day," Sean said softly to himself.

Sean found it difficult to deliver the sermon before the wedding ceremony. He was distracted by the glitter and brass of the military wedding—Mike had insisted that Paul be married as befitting a major in the United States Marine Corps—and by the bride's beauty in her loosely flowing old-fashioned wedding gown. Nora might have been his bride, his wife. He might have shared his life with her, enjoying her beauty and delighting in her wit and intelligence. It was God's will that he give her up, God's will that she marry his brother. Yet, as he tried to concentrate on his carefully prepared sermon, disturbing images of Nora lying next to him on their marriage bed raced through his mind.

"It is our prayer today for Paul and Nora in their married life together," Sean read, "with all its joys and sorrows, that they find not only each other but also the One whose love for His people is both a symbol and an extension. We want to tell them today that even in their most lonely and difficult moment God's love will be with them, and so will the support of the Church and of all their family and friends. And so . . ."

He stumbled through the exchange of vows and the blessings of the rings with almost as much nervousness as did the bride and groom. He was careful not to look long at Nora's ecstatic face and volcanic blue eyes. By the time he came to the nuptial blessing after the Pater Noster, he had better self-control, yet his hand trembled as he gave them Holy Communion. He was relieved when it came time for the final blessing.

> *May the Lord Jesus, who was a guest at the*
> *   wedding in Cana,*
> *bless you and your families and friends.*
> *   Amen.*
> *May Jesus, who loved his Church to the end,*
> *always fill your hearts with love.*
> *   Amen.*
> *May he grant that, as you believe in his resurrection,*
> *so you may wait for him in joy and hope.*
> *   Amen.*
> *And may almighty God bless you all,*
> *the Father, and the Son, and the Holy Spirit.*
> *   Amen.*
> *May almighty God, with his Word of blessing, unite*
> *your hearts in the never-ending bond of pure love.*
> *   Amen.*
> *May your children bring you happiness, and may your*
> *   generous love for them be returned to you, many*
> *   times over.*
> *   Amen.*

Nora was not like the other virgins Paul had deflowered. She did not try to turn off the light or scurry into the bathroom. Rather, as soon as they were inside the bridal suite of the Drake, she calmly drew the drapes on the parlor windows and with a natural poise undressed before him.

Paul's confidence evaporated. His new wife was spectacularly inviting, yet he was untouched by desire.

Their first union was a near disaster. The masculine potency of which he was so proud deserted him. His bride was utterly unaffected by their coupling, save for one soft cry of pain. His satisfaction was trivial.

Afterward, Nora cried quietly next to him on the bed. "I'm sorry, I'll try to be better next time," she murmured.

So she blamed herself? Paul sighed with relief and patted her head reassuringly. "Don't worry about it, Nora. Everything will work out fine. All we had to do today was begin." He cradled her in his arms, muttering soothing words about how beautiful she was. That seemed to calm her down. His new wife would be very easy to satisfy.

Later that night the dream about Chongun returned. Joe Makuch dressed in a Chink uniform led the charge. His face changed into Nora's as he plunged the bayonet deep into Paul Cronin's belly.

Paul woke up screaming and grabbing at his stomach. His new wife embraced him, rested his head against her chest, and crooned a soft lullaby into his ear.

Thus comforted on his wedding night, Paul Martin Cronin fell back to sleep.

Joe Makuch turned up in Paul's office a week after he returned from his honeymoon. Once a trim, tough professional master sergeant, Joe was now fat, bald, and greasy, an overweight goblin of a man who had the Midas touch in reverse—everything he did turned to rock.

"I need a favor, Major," Makuch said, nervously revolving his grimy fedora in his hands. "I wouldn't bother you if I had anyone else to turn to. But this is an emergency. They built a new highway on the other side of town, one of them freeway things, and my gas station fell flat on its face. Made ten thousand bucks last year and only a couple hundred this year. I got a chance to pick up another station near an interchange on the other side of town. It won't cost me much at all . . . and it's right off of the freeway interchange, a real gold mine."

Paul sighed. Given Joe's luck, they would close the interchange next year. The problem wasn't paying a few thousand dollars of blackmail now to shut him up about the Chongun Reservoir. The problem was that the drain could keep on forever and get bigger every year.

"Sure, I understand how it is, Joe. You saved my life a couple of times, so what the hell." He grinned reassuringly. "You name it, and if I've got it, I'll give it to you."

Joe Makuch named fifteen thousand dollars, and Paul wrote him a check. He would find an explanation for his father somehow, when he had to.

BOOK III

He came to Simon Peter, who said to him, "Lord, are you going to wash my feet?"

Jesus answered, "At the moment you do not know what I am doing, but later you will understand."

"Never!" said Peter. "You shall never wash my feet."

Jesus replied, "If I do not wash you, you could have nothing in common with me."

"Then, Lord," said Simon Peter, "not only my feet, but my hands and my head as well."

—John 13:6—9

CHAPTER TEN

1962

Nora Cronin was not pleased with the phone call she received in Washington from Maggie Shields, who still lived in Chicago. Eileen, Nora's five-year-old daughter, was in nursery school, and three-year-old Mary was taking one of her rare naps. For Nora it meant an hour and a half of peace, during which she could finish Katherine Anne Porter's *Ship of Fools*. Then the jangling telephone and Maggie's peace-shattering news.

Maggie had always needed attention, and now she was complaining about Tom's preoccupation with his growing OB practice. Indeed, Maggie seemed to be jealous of every one of Tom's patients. There was little in life that made Maggie feel important. Nora sighed. She had reluctantly given up trying to persuade Maggie that she was worthwhile. Twenty years of being told by her parents that she was cute but empty-headed could not be undone.

"And I think it's just terrible about Sean." The subject of Maggie's conversation changed abruptly.

Nora put aside the book in which her finger, until then, had kept the place. "What's the matter with Sean?"

"Well, when did you see him last?"

Nora felt guilty. Sean had been absent from her mind, it seemed, for months. There were enough other things to preoccupy her. "Only for a few days, at Oakland Beach. He didn't take much of a vacation last year."

"He never takes vacations. It's just work, work, work with

those Negroes who don't appreciate him. Tom says he thinks he's killing himself. Why doesn't he ask the new Archbishop to transfer him out of that hellhole?"

"Sean says the old Cardinal sent him to St. Jadwiga's to prove that a rich man's son couldn't last in a poor parish, and that if he asks out the Cardinal will win, even if he's dead."

"That sounds like Sean, all right," Maggie said.

"Is Tom really worried about his health?"

"Tom said he thinks Sean will end up in the hospital if he doesn't stop."

After she got rid of Maggie, Nora walked to the bay window of their old Georgetown house and looked out onto the narrow street. The leaves turned red and gold in Washington later than in Chicago. It was November, the week after the election. The falling leaves had carpeted the lawn in front of their house. She had once been in love with Sean—now from the safety of retrospect she could admit that—and she had almost forgotten about him.

Nora had been only moderately happy in her marriage. She had realized within a few months that her husband was spoiled, petulant, and self-indulgent, although charming and intelligent. He might grow up someday, but she feared it wasn't very likely.

In six years of living with Paul, she had also discovered with gratification that she could put up with a marriage that was less than satisfactory and not lose her sense of self in it the way Maggie had. Despite the fact that she was as much a mother as a wife to Paul, her life was not unhappy. Her two little girls were pure joy. She had her books, her music, and her involvement in the social and cultural life of the glittering Kennedy administration.

Anyway, there was no point in being angry at Paul. It had little effect. He was contrite, humble, apologetic, and then promptly forgot everything he said. Their sex life was low-key, mildly satisfying if not exciting. Nora suspected that she was undersexed. She also suspected that there were other women. Everyone in Washington seemed to have another woman or another man. The Kennedys set the tone there, as well as in so many other things these days. While she found their infidelities distasteful, she could not resist their charm any more than could anyone else in Washington. And especially the charm of the Attorney General.

The Kennedys were a lot like Paul: likable, at times brilliant, but they used everyone. Paul was only a high-grade errand boy, despite his title of Special Assistant to the Attorney General. If he should ever become unproductive, they would drop him in a minute. Everyone in the administration knew that was the way the Kennedys were. Still, they were all willing to take their chances, wear their PT-boat tie clasps, and hope they were among those who were admired and respected and were not being used.

Nora returned to her chair and retrieved *Ship of Fools,* but she did not open it. It would be as easy for her to have a lover as it was for Paul to have other women. Easier, perhaps. Heaven knows, there was no lack of offers. Naive, South Side Irish girl that she was, it had taken her several months to recognize the propositions for what they were. She routinely turned them down. She was simply not interested.

There were more pluses than minuses in her life, the little girls especially. Perhaps she was too objective, too dispassionate. Nora considered that possibility very carefully. Lord knew, the Kennedys liked her because they thought she was a fighter. Perhaps she was a fighter, yet now didn't seem to be the time to fight.

She had played touch ball with them the previous summer at the beach in Hyannis. Her height and speed made her a strong competitor. In sweat shirt and cutoff jeans, she intercepted pass after pass, twice taking the ball out of the outstretched hands of the Attorney General of the United States and once running the interception for a touchdown. Bobby hadn't liked that at all.

"It's not fair, Nora"—he pronounced it as though her name were "Norar"—"a woman as beautiful as you shouldn't be so fast."

"I'm not fast at all, Mr. Attorney General," she had taunted him. "I'm a virtuous housewife."

Bobby thought that was very funny, but the next time she reached over his shoulder for an interception, she found herself flying through the air and landing on the beach just as an enormous wave arrived at the same place as she.

Soaking wet and furious, she stormed out of the water and shouted, "I don't give a goddamn if you are a Kennedy, I'll get even with you!"

The touch-ball game ended then in laughter and she had become a Kennedy favorite, with the phrase, "I don't give a goddamn if you are a Kennedy," being recalled whenever she was present—much to Nora's embarrassment.

At the White House for dinner, a week before the Cuban Missile Crisis, the Attorney General had needled her. "I'm still waiting for your revenge, Nora."

"That's part of the fun," she said. "I'll get you at a time when you're least ready."

"You're a great fighter," the Attorney General had said.

Much later, or so it seemed, Eileen bounded in from school, and the nanny brought a sleepy-eyed Mary down from the nursery.

The little girls were so beautiful, much more Riley than Cronin. She sighed. Uncle Mike had not forgiven her for her failure to produce a male child. Paul's disappointment was obvious too. Her reproductive apparatus was not as healthy as the rest of her. Both births had been difficult, and Mary's dangerous. Tom Shields, who had delivered both of the little girls, had shaken his head discouragingly. "No more for a while, Nora; wait at least a couple of years."

Nora had not hesitated to use the birth control pill. Priests like Sean Cronin, who vigorously denounced it as unnatural, simply didn't understand what sex meant to a husband and wife, even the placid sex between herself and Paul. Three years was long enough, though, and she felt she ought to try again.

While she was absentmindedly mediating a quarrel at the dinner table between her blond vivacious younger daughter and her raven-haired serious older daughter, Nora thought again of Maggie's call. She decided to tell Paul about her phone conversation with Maggie and suggest that he go to Chicago to see if things were really so bad with Sean, even though Sean had discouraged such visits in the past.

The sun was shining very brightly on Paul Cronin's life. Still in his early thirties, he was an important man in Washington. He had stood at Nicholas Katzenbach's side through the integration crises at the University of Alabama and the University of Mississippi. While he had not actually been with the Attorney General in the situation room during the missile crisis, he had been waiting with a few others when Robert Kennedy returned to his office at the Justice Department.

Paul had built up a network of contacts and friends, far more powerful than the Chicago crew he still carefully tended from a distance. Paul was a Kennedy man, all right, yet there was no point in being only a Kennedy man—especially when you were in a position to do important favors for people who would still be powerful in Washington long after the Kennedys had gone.

His quiet dinner parties, presided over with classic charm by Nora, were events where some of the brightest men and women in Washington could share ideas and hopes. They were just large enough so that the Kennedys would know about them and be impressed, but not so large that they would feel threatened.

In the second Kennedy administration, he would probably begin as an undersecretary somewhere and then work his way up to being a full cabinet member before returning to Chicago to run for the Senate. He had a beautiful, gifted, and much-admired wife, two gorgeous little girls, and a life ahead of him filled with promise and possibilities. Moreover, the next time he took Christine Waverly out for an early evening cocktail, he was sure he could score. A smooth, honey-haired blonde with a trim, compact body, just a few years out of Bennington, Chris Waverly was already one of the most powerful women reporters in Washington.

Paul felt no particular guilt about calling from the office to tell his wife that he would be delayed in a conference with the Attorney General when, in fact, he would be continuing his pursuit of Chris Waverly. There was the sex that you had with your wife, which was pleasant enough, and then there was the exciting pursuit of challenging women. A man, or at least a man like him, was entitled to both. He had remained faithful to Nora through her first pregnancy, although it had driven him almost mad. Then he had fallen during the delay while she recovered. After that, he didn't try, contenting himself with being faithful most of the time. He figured that made him better than most men his age in Washington.

For Nora, he had enormous respect and even admiration. She was smart, shrewd in her evaluation of people, and extremely attractive. Paul was intrigued and fascinated by her composure and by the aura of mystery that surrounded her. Nora was always surprising, except in bed, and Paul preferred her that way.

The only real problem, he told himself as he parked his Ferrari in their driveway, was that they had no son. And Tom Shields had been blunt: "If you love your wife, no more children for a while."

Paul Cronin loved his wife, or at least he was proud of her, but he wanted a son. He could not force Nora to take another chance, but she seemed ready now.

She was reading in the parlor, wearing a beige silk robe. "You didn't have to wait up for me," he said as he entered the room and tossed a heavy briefcase on one of the easy chairs.

She closed her book and embraced him. "No problem, darling. I have a sandwich in the refrigerator for you if you're hungry."

"Wonderful," he said, patting her bottom appreciatively. After his foreplay with Chris, he would certainly need her tonight. "I don't deserve this attention. You're the only wife I know of who is sympathetic and understanding."

"Better say tolerant," she said, leaving for the kitchen.

While he munched on a roast beef sandwich, Nora perched on the side of the sofa.

"Maggie Shields called today," she said.

"What did she want?" he said, feeling some pleasure from memories of his affair with Maggie.

"Tom's worried about Sean. He thinks he's ruining his health at St. Jadwiga's. I think Sean's trying to show your father, and the priests, and the dead Cardinal, and everyone else that he can handle one of the toughest assignments in the city."

Paul paused. The sandwich did not seem quite so tasty any more. The one person in the world he really worried about, aside from himself, was his little brother. "Do you think Maggie's exaggerating?"

Nora's face tightened in a thoughtful frown. "I don't usually take Maggie all that seriously. But she's not likely to misquote Tom, and if he says that Sean is running himself into the ground, I think there's a problem."

Paul began to eat his sandwich again, slowly and thoughtfully. "There are ways we can get him out of there, I suppose, although the old man is too stubborn to eat a little bit of crow. I guess I'll have to do it."

"Why don't you go to Chicago first and see how bad Sean really is?" she said.

Paul sipped from his beer glass. "I'd like to do that, but I don't think I can get away for a few weeks."

"Sean may not have a few weeks to spare. If we wait until Christmas, he could end up in a hospital."

"No, not a hospital. Not Sean." Paul suddenly saw a way to look after Sean without inconveniencing himself. "Why don't you go? Anna can take care of the kids. You'd only be gone for a few days. Besides, Sean would have a hard time admitting to me that he's worn out."

Nora hesitated. "I will if you want me to, Paul. I don't like to leave you alone in Washington, though."

He winked at her. "Don't worry about that. Bob Kennedy works us so hard that I don't even notice women any more."

"I bet." She laughed.

Amused, he thought, but not suspicious. "Speaking of Bob, by the way, he said I should give you his best and tell you that he's still waiting for your vengeance."

Nora laughed. "And it's going to come very soon. Just tell him that!"

Later that night, Paul pretended to himself that Nora was Chris Waverly; often he could make love to his wife only if he pretended that she was someone else.

His desire for Chris pushed him into stirring depths in Nora of which he was afraid. As they lay exhausted in each other's arms, she kissed him affectionately and said, "That was very nice. Thank you."

"Do you think we ought to try for a son one of these days?" he said, sensing her vulnerability.

"I've been thinking the same thing," she said softly. "As soon as I get back from Chicago. . . ."

She was soon asleep. Paul remained awake, feeling worthless as he always did after he made love to his wife. He would never be good enough for her. He had known that from the beginning. He would be a political success, but that was not enough. Nora deserved better. Someone like Sean.

CHAPTER
ELEVEN
1962

The meeting in the Attorney General's office was inconclusive. The union leader they were after was certainly a thief, yet they had no evidence, even though they knew there were records of payoffs in the office of George Sandler, the Washington lobbyist for the union. The records were Sandler's own insurance against ending up in Chesapeake Bay if power changed hands in the union; he was not likely to tell the truth to the grand jury unless there was incriminating information against him.

When the meeting was over, Paul walked back to his office with Bud O'Hara, who was supervising the investigation.

"Can't the Bureau get into Sandler's office?" he asked softly.

O'Hara eyed him with his cold Texas eyes. "That's against the law, Paul." He spoke with equal softness.

"Come on." Paul laughed. "You were the one who was talking about functional justice the other day."

The Texan shrugged. "Truth is, we don't want to try it. You know how touchy the Director is. He only breaks the law when it's his idea. Some of us think that he's in bed—figuratively, although you never can tell about the Director—with the union president."

They stopped at the door of O'Hara's office. "Any objection if we find the evidence some other way?" Paul asked lightly.

The Texan didn't hesitate. "None whatever."

. . .

Lawrence called for Michael Cronin at the door of Little Company of Mary Hospital in the new Mercedes limousine. New chauffeur, new limousine. Mike sighed. Everyone was growing old. It didn't seem the same with Jeremy gone.

Jane was surviving, though. Seventy years old and a chronic alcoholic, she refused to die. She had just pulled through another heart attack, causing the doctors to marvel.

He no longer believed that Jane would ever reveal his secret. Even if she tried, he could shut her up. That had always been true. Why had he lost his nerve? He should have married Jenny Warren; she was a spectacular woman. Should have said to hell with Jane after the ordination and married Jenny.

Too late now. She was married to a damn fiddle player. Did she do the same things to him that had so delighted Mike? The fiddle player was seven years younger than Mike, still in his middle fifties.

Mike sighed. After Jenny he had lost interest in women, other than an occasional fling here and there.

He bid Lawrence good night and mixed himself a final drink in his lonely house. It was too big for one man, but he had to keep it as a place for the kids to come home to from Washington. And for Sean on his day off, even if he never came home on his day off.

Mike sipped his drink slowly. He worried endlessly about Sean. He seemed more like Mary Eileen with every passing day—idealistic, unreal. He wondered if Jane might be right about him. There was no way of ever knowing for sure.

The headache which had bothered him for the last couple of weeks returned. He decided to mix himself another drink. If Sean would come to his senses and get the hell out of that nigger parish . . . but it was essential not to give in to him. He had to realize his mistakes. Giving in to Mary Eileen had been a disaster. He should have been firm with her much earlier.

Then the lights went out on him. It was as though someone had clubbed him on the back of his head. The next thing he knew, the clock said three in the morning. He must have fallen asleep, he told himself. Too much to drink. He staggered upstairs to bed, wavering uncertainly as he climbed the staircase.

In the morning he told himself that nothing unusual had happened. The feeling of falling through space was merely part of a hangover.

After two drinks.

St. Jadwiga's was worse than Nora could ever have dreamed. Even the parkway in front of the battered old red and brown brick apartment buildings on Douglas Boulevard seemed decrepit and worn. The stone church, with its wooden bell tower, seemed ready to fall apart. The school next door to it badly needed tuck-pointing, and the two-story wooden rectory almost surely was a fire hazard. Worst of all was the dirt. Everything—windows, doors, gutters, sidewalks, the concrete schoolyard—was filthy. Paper, beer cans, and whiskey bottles littered the ground in front of the rectory, which once long ago may have been a lawn. No wonder Sean had forbidden them to visit his parish.

She parked her rented Chevrolet in front of the rectory. As she turned off the ignition, Nora steeled herself for her encounter with Sean. Every time she was with him her heart beat faster and her throat tightened. Realistic as always, Nora knew that a part of her wanted to go to bed with him. She smiled faintly to herself. If she had recognized those emotions the day he had blunderingly offered to leave the seminary for her, she might have taken him up on the offer.

She squared her shoulders and got out of the car. Her passion for Sean was controllable and would be controlled. After all, he was her brother-in-law, and almost her brother. She gingerly walked up the decaying wooden steps and pushed the old-fashioned bell on the door front. She heard no bell ring inside. She waited and pushed it again, and then once more. Still there was no answer. Perhaps Sean was at the school.

She walked down the steps and through the passageway between the church and the school. At the back of the rectory there was a small alleyway surrounded by high fences. On the left hand was a door that led to the church and on the right hand a stairwell descending to what seemed to be a boiler room. The church door was locked. A pounding sound seemed to be coming from downstairs. Nora turned up her coat collar against the chill November winds and picked her way through the litter down into the boiler room.

There was half a foot of water on the floor of the room, and in darkness broken only by a single dim light bulb, a man was on top of the boiler with a wrench, wrestling with the pipe fitting.

"Pardon me," she said politely. "Can you tell me where Father Cronin is?"

"He's on top of the boiler putting the finishing touches on repairs," said a weary voice. "Don't worry, Sister. Tell the principal that we'll have the heat on in another half hour. Thank God it isn't the middle of January."

"It's not *a* sister, Sean," she said, trying to hide her dismay. "It's *your* sister."

The figure on the boiler turned toward her. "Nora? Just give me another second here. . . . Ugh, this thing is hard to twist. There, that does it." He climbed down off the boiler, oblivious to the water swishing around his legs, and flipped the button at the side of the rusty old turbine. There was a cranking and groaning sound within it and then a recalcitrant and dubious hum.

"Well, it seems to be working again. Come on back to the rectory. I'll make you a cup of coffee." Sean was wearing black trousers and a black shirt with a Roman collar. He was thin and worn, at least fifteen pounds underweight.

The rectory kitchen was a mess. Dirty dishes were piled up in the sink, and the cupboards and shelves were littered with empty cans and containers. "Georgetown or Hyannisport it is not," said Sean, with a pale reflection of his once-magic smile.

"You do the cooking, the housekeeping, and the janitoring, as well as the priesting?" Nora asked incredulously. "Here, give me that. I'll make the coffee—and I'll wash the coffee cups before we use them. I'm not going to bring some infectious Douglas Boulevard disease back to my kids."

A bit more light now appeared in Sean's eyes. "Same old Nora. Move in and take charge. Yes, I do everything around here; that is, everything except teach at the school. The pastor comes for Mass on Sunday morning and then goes back to his mother's house. Otherwise, it's all mine."

"You can't afford any help?" She searched for detergent to wash the dishes.

"Every penny we have goes for heat and electricity, and food for the nuns, and salaries for the lay teachers. The chancery office"—he frowned—"is not going to provide any subsidy to a parish in which the assistant is a wealthy man. That is precisely what the late Cardinal told me. So we make do."

"Why keep the parish open then?" Nora asked, cleaning the coffee cups.

"Because we educate four hundred kids a year and give them a lot better education than the public schools. Because we salvage a couple of dozen juvenile delinquents every year. Because there are a few hundred Catholics, most of them converts, who come to Mass here every Sunday. And because somebody has to visit the people of the neighborhood when they're in the hospital or in jail."

Nora took a deep breath. "You became a priest, Sean, to do these things?"

He slumped at the chipped porcelain-top kitchen counter with a weariness that tore at her heart. "I can't imagine anything I could do that would be more priestly. Come on, after we've had the coffee, I'll take you through our school."

The school was as decrepit as the rectory and the church. The corridors and the classrooms desperately needed a coat of paint. The windows were filthy. But inside the classrooms it was no different from the St. Titus grammar school that Nora Riley had attended fifteen years before. The faces of the students might be black, but the order, the discipline, the demanding presence of "S'ter," and the vigorous pursuit of learning were all the same. The children stood respectfully when Sean entered the classroom, with the traditional "Good Morn-ing, Father" slow singsong. He introduced her as Nora, and they replied, "Good morn-ing, No-ra."

"Good morning, boys and girls," said Nora, remembering the greeting.

In the corridor after the tour of the classrooms, Sean leaned against the wall. "We have four hundred and twenty-nine kids in this school, Nora," he said proudly. "All of them will go to high school, and two thirds of them will go to college, and I don't think the Catholic Church has ever done a better thing."

"At the cost of your life?" she said hotly.

"It's a good cause to die in, Nora," Sean said, his body sagging against the wall.

• • •

Nora had decided to plead with Uncle Mike to salvage St. Jadwiga and Sean. Mike greeted her at the door of his new office with an embrace.

"You're looking as beautiful as ever, Nora," he said.

Nora thought Uncle Mike looked older, weaker. There was a tremor in his hand and already, at one thirty in the afternoon, there was the smell of whiskey on his breath.

"What brings you to Chicago?" he asked. Outside his window the Chicago skyline, a veritable museum of architectural splendor, was set sharply against the gray November sky. To the south were the railroad tracks, the drive, and a midget airfield on the island off the lake shore. No views like that in Washington.

"We had a phone call from Maggie Shields," Nora said. "Tom is worried about Sean. Paul is busy seeing that justice survives in the nation, so he sent me here to find out whether Maggie is exaggerating. She's not. Sean is sick and tired and worn out, and he must have help."

"If he wants money, he can ask me," Mike said. "I'll give him whatever he needs to take care of that slum of his."

"You know he'll never ask, Uncle Mike. He's as stubborn as you are. And while the two of you are busy being stubborn, Sean's ruining his health and probably his life."

"He's wasting his time out there, the damned fool," Mike said.

"No, he's not," Nora flared at him. "He's doing wonderful work, but he's doing it all by himself and he's done it for too long. You give money to dozens of charities. Why can't you give some to your own son?"

"I won't give him a goddamn cent. He's old enough to take care of himself and that's final, young woman. I won't hear another word about it."

Nora's temper snapped. "You're a hateful old man." She picked up her coat, yanked open the door of the apartment, slammed it in his face as he hurried after her, and ducked into a waiting elevator just as the door opened. She wept as she rode down, as much for the look of pain on Michael Cronin's face as for the plight of Father Sean Cronin.

Paul Cronin considered the "tools" he had obtained from a contact at the CIA: a tiny camera, keys, a small flashlight, gloves, tape to secure the door, a device for searching out alarm systems.

He had visited George Sandler the day before. The lobbyist was a sleek little man with ferretlike eyes and nervous hands who had glanced anxiously at a file cabinet behind his desk when Paul warned that they might subpoena his records.

"You don't have enough evidence to warrant that, Mr. Cronin," Sandler said cautiously.

Paul didn't want to frighten him into destroying the files before he had a chance to steal them. "You're right, I guess—so far. We're going to get the whole lot of you, though. There's no reason for you to go to jail. We'd provide you with a new life and protection."

"For how long?" the other man asked bitterly. "I don't trust Bob Kennedy any more than I trust Carmine da Silva."

"You should have thought of that," Paul had replied, "before you got mixed up with his union."

Paul left after that exchange, confident that he could find his way around the office at night. Sandler thought he was safe. He would be surprised to find that, in the Kennedy administration, you fought fire with fire.

Access to the building was easy. The guard at the door was sound asleep. Paul didn't have to pretend that he was a telephone repairman. He could let himself out the back door into the alley behind K Street when he was finished. He didn't need the dark glasses and the cap which were part of his repairman's disguise. He'd be careful just the same. No point in being recognized.

The keys were not much help in opening the office door, especially since in the dim corridor light he couldn't see distinctly. You would think the CIA would have better technology.

Then he saw the light above the elevator door go on. My God, someone coming up.

For the first time he thought of the consequences if he was caught. Terror gripped at his stomach. He wanted to run. The elevator light was like the flares above the Reservoir.

At the last minute he saw a door that looked as if it might be a restroom. He ran down the corridor and pushed the door open. The door swung shut after him. Paul leaned against it, breathing heavily. He was so frightened that he broke out in a heavy sweat. What would happen if they found him? He gulped for air.

After the panic came dizziness and, after the dizziness, nausea.

Paul stumbled around the men's room, found a urinal, and vomited into it. After he had emptied his dinner he felt better. He had to pull himself together and make his escape. Down the back stairs. Why the hell had he tried such a stupid trick anyway? Dumb recklessness.

When he was sure he could walk steadily, he eased open the door. No sign of anyone, no sound.

He slipped into the corridor, hesitated, and then, unexpectedly, turned not toward the exit but back down the corridor to Sandler's office.

From then on, it was astonishingly easy. The first key he tried opened the door. He had no trouble finding the file case; the second key fit that lock. Then with the thin, powerful beam of the penlight splitting the darkness, he rapidly thumbed through the contents of the cabinet until he found the incriminating financial records. O'Hara had been sure they would be there.

His heart pounding and his head light with excitement, Paul rapidly shot two rolls of film—thirty-two pictures in all. Enough to put several corrupt union leaders behind bars for a long time to come.

In the alley afterward, Paul was triumphant. He had mastered his fear. He deserved a reward. Tomorrow night he would have it. No more fooling around with Chris Waverly. Even if he had to rape her.

Nora was shopping in Marshall Field's, buying sheets, blankets, dishes, and even clothing for Sean. Paul would have to come to Chicago to see the new Archbishop. Sean should either be transferred from St. Jadwiga's or the diocese must help him out financially. Paul was persuasive enough to be able to talk to the Archbishop, who was reportedly a decent and kindly man, into forgetting the past.

She saw a familiar face on the escalator. "Jenny," she exclaimed. "Jenny Warren!"

Michael Cronin's former companion was as pretty as she had been at Nora's wedding, if perhaps a little more subdued.

Jenny hesitated, as though she did not want to recognize Nora, but then, presumably against her better judgment, she waited at the bottom of the escalator. "Jenny Marsh now, Nora. It's good to see you."

"Let's have lunch and talk about old times."

Again Jenny hesitated. "I ought not to. . . . Will you swear that you won't tell your Uncle Mike?"

"Sure," said Nora.

Over lunch they exchanged histories of the past six years. Jenny had married the first cellist with the New York Philharmonic. Her husband was in Chicago for a concert. They were very happy. Both his children and both her children were married, and they lived a pleasant, peaceful life, organized around his music.

"I really hoped back in 1956 that you'd be my stepmother," said Nora, after an awkward lull in the conversation.

Jenny's pretty face became sad. She sipped her tea. "I thought I would be. Mike . . . he didn't exactly promise, but he certainly led me to believe . . . of course. I should have known. He was so kind and so tender and so gentle to begin with, and such a marvelous lover. Well, I deceived myself about some things and pretended other things that weren't so. And then he changed. At first I didn't even notice it—maybe because I didn't want to notice it."

"What was it like?" Nora asked gently.

"He became cool and distant. Then one morning I was told by my landlord that the lease on my apartment had been canceled. I was literally out on the street."

"He dumped you without a word?"

Jenny nodded her head. "Yes. I went to stay at my sister's in New Jersey. Two weeks later a messenger delivered an envelope with fifty thousand-dollar bills." Jenny began to cry. "As though that could blot out the pain!"

For the first time in her life, Nora realized that she didn't really know Michael Cronin. She wondered if anyone did.

Clad in jeans and a black sweat shirt, Nora was standing on a rickety stepladder, painting the walls of Sean's study. Before she went back to Washington, she would fix up his room and the kitchen, stock the refrigerator and the shelves with food, and feed him a couple of solid meals.

Outside, two lanky Negro teenagers were playing basketball in the chill November sunlight. Nora wondered why they weren't in school. Were they delinquents of the sort that Sean seemed to attract to the rectory?

She took a few minutes off from her painting and went to the head of the stairway leading down into the basement. Standing there, she could hear Sean instructing potential converts in the basement classroom.

"It's hard to believe that God loves you when you're poor and hungry, when there isn't enough heat in your apartment, and when you're not sure whether you'll have a job next week. You wonder how God lets things like that happen, when other people seem to be doing okay. You wonder if there even is a God. I can't prove to you the existence of God. Nobody can prove that. All I can say is that whenever you experience love, you experience God. And God is as present on Douglas Boulevard as he is everywhere else in the world. He loves us, and some day he's going to make everything right and we're all going to be happy with him. In the meantime, you have to get ready for God by trying to love one another with all the power you have so that there may be more of God's love in the world."

Nora fled back to her brush and her bucket of paint, tears streaming down her face. Who were she and Paul to decide that Sean shouldn't be doing what he was doing, shouldn't be talking to those poor people with so much love and affection and dedication in his voice?

Still, as she painted the wall, she told herself that she and Paul loved Sean and that God could not possibly want them to stand by idly while he worked himself to death.

"Why are you doing that?" Sean said, leaning against the doorway of his study. "I mean, we could probably hire somebody to do it."

She threw the wet paintbrush at him. "Because I love you, you damn fool. Do you think you're the only one in the family that can make sacrifices for other human beings?"

He showed the first bright Sean Cronin smile she had seen since she had come to St. Jadwiga's as he picked up the brush, walked over to the ladder, and very gently put it back into the bucket. His face averted so that she couldn't see it, he said, "Some of us are just born lucky, I guess. I'm lucky that I have you for a sister."

Later that afternoon she called Paul at his office. "Just a brief progress report. It's worse than Maggie thought. I'm cleaning up the place where he lives and giving him a few good meals, but we've got to get him out of here. Mike won't help."

"Damn!" Paul said.

"I'll stay in touch, but I think you'd better practice for an interview with the new Archbishop."

"Okay . . . I've got to run now. Oh, by the way, the kids are fine, but we all miss you."

"Do you really?" Nora asked the dead telephone.

CHAPTER
TWELVE
1962

Sean Cronin looked at his face carefully in the mirror as he combed his long blond hair. He needed a haircut. He needed a new suit. He needed a rest, a long rest. No wonder Nora looked so anxious. *I scare even myself. One vacation in six years.*

Two years before, Jimmy McGuire had dragged him off to Vail, insisting that Sean had an obligation to learn how to ski. The instructor assigned to him, Sandra Walker, was a woman in her mid-twenties with long honey-blond hair and a superb body. She was spontaneous, direct, and bubbling with laughter. She even was able to make fun of Sean's initial awkwardness on skis without hurting his feelings. He did not tell her that he was a priest, and he watched with fear and pleasure the affection that grew in her lively gray eyes.

Then, one day, a substitute instructor replaced her. Sean was disappointed but asked no questions. The next day Sandra was back, subdued and snappish. Again he asked no questions and, after his lesson, trudged halfway down the slope toward his ski lodge. Then he paused and walked back to the instructor's office.

Sandra was hunched over her desk, sobbing. As naturally as though she were his daughter, he put his arms around her and drew her head to his chest. The whole story poured out. High school sweethearts who rediscovered each other in San Francisco six months before. He a Navy pilot. At first, letters every week, then every day, neither of them quite ready to say the word marriage. Then news of a crash on a carrier.

"Thanks for listening," she said as she and Sean walked back into town. "You're a nice shoulder to cry on." A little bit of bubble was back.

Sean did a lot of listening during the next week—on the ski slopes, in the dining room of the lodge, in the swimming pool. Sandra had crowded a lot of life into twenty-six years.

Then she invited him to her apartment for dinner. Sean knew he should not accept, and yet he did. Wine, fondue, cool jazz on the phonograph. A textbook seduction scene.

After dinner they sat in front of the blazing hearth. "Do you like me, Sean?"

He gathered her into his arms and caressed her back. "You know that I do, Sandra. But you deserve better than a quick grab because you're on the rebound from a tragedy." He had wanted to accept the invitation in her voice, but something held him back.

"You've been wonderful. . . . I might have killed myself."

"No, you wouldn't. And whatever help I've been would be undone if I went to bed with you. So stay in my arms for a few minutes, and then we'll say goodbye."

Jimmy McGuire was waiting for him when Sean returned to the room at the lodge. A compulsive postcard writer, Jimmy did not even look up from the stack of cards on which he was working. "Did you go to bed with her?" he asked.

"It would have been unfair to take advantage of her."

"And you're the one who thinks you don't have any faith."

Sean shook the memories from his mind. He could hear the sounds of Nora preparing dinner for him downstairs. The first woman to prepare dinner for him since Sandra Walker.

Sean studied Nora, seated across the dinner table. Even in a sweat shirt and jeans, she was beautiful. In addition to the beauty, there were now also poise and sophistication.

"Is there something wrong with me, Sean?" she asked. "You're staring."

"I was just thinking that with candlelight and wine you ought to be wearing black lace instead of a black sweat shirt."

Nora laughed. "That's a terrible thing for a priest to say!"

"Probably," he conceded. "I do appreciate what you're doing, though, Nora. And it's all right for you to give me the lecture that you've very carefully prepared."

Her forehead tightened almost imperceptibly. "I'm not going to try to persuade you that your talents are being wasted at St. Jadwiga, Sean. Your father and Paul might think so, but I don't. I've had a chance to watch you work around here for the last couple of days, and I think you're good at it. I also think you're only a couple of steps away from being Mistah Kurtz."

"Joseph Conrad's hero gone native? I suppose you're right, Nora, I have been here too long."

She pushed the roast beef platter at him, and he helped himself to another slice. "You must know that if you continue this way, your life might not be a very long one."

"Maybe. But as long as the Archbishop wants me to be here, it's God's will and I'm staying . . . and all your persuasive charms won't change my mind on that."

"It seems to me a silly way for the Church to treat a priest." She looked at him over the rim of a water glass filled with burgundy.

"There's a tremendous amount of envy in the priesthood, probably worse than in any other occupation. There aren't many rewards. Some priests resent me because they think I'm rich. Some of them because I'm getting a reputation for being good at my work. It's a heads-I-lose tails-they-win situation. If I fail here, they say, I told you so, a rich man's son can't hack it. And if I succeed, it's because of my father's money."

"Can't you do anything?"

"No. That's the way it is. The Church is not going to change."

"The Church will change, Sean," she argued. "Will because it has to."

"We disagree," he said, shrugging off her comment. He noticed that there was now a bit of fire in her eyes.

"How many of your parishioners understand Latin?" she said. "I suppose you think it sinful for married people to enjoy sex with one another? And that priests shouldn't have any friends among the laity? And that everything a pope or bishop or pastor says is God's word?"

"My parishioners like the mystery of Latin. I don't think it's sinful for married people to enjoy sex; they probably ought to enjoy it more than they do—as long as the main purpose is procreation. Priests ought to be men apart, men unlike other human beings. And yes, of course, the pope and the bishops and the pastors do represent God."

"And what happens to couples who have five or six kids? Should they stop sleeping with each other if they can't afford any more?" Her frown was now deep.

He didn't want to fight. "Look, I know it's tough. We have to be very gentle and sympathetic with them in confession. In time, someone will develop a rhythm method of birth control that will be as effective as any other. Until then, we have to resist the contraceptive mentality . . . the mentality that leads people to not want children. That's the real problem."

Nora pounded the table and almost upset the wine bottle. "Will it shock you to know, Sean Cronin, God's chosen spokesman, that I've been using the birth-control pill for a couple of years because the doctor said it would be better if I waited a while between children? Would you rather I throw Paul out of the bedroom—or do I push my luck? Do you want to see me in Holy Sepulcher Cemetery before I'm thirty? Is that God's will? Does the pope tell you that?"

Sean swallowed hard. "I can't help what I believe. Maybe I'm so rigid because I'm afraid that if I relax any of my beliefs the whole ball of wax will come apart." He buried his head in his hands. "I don't want to fight with you."

She reached across the table and took his hand. "How much do you pray, Sean?" she asked.

That question surprised him. "Not very much, I guess. Too busy. . . ."

She squeezed his hand hard. "What kind of a priest is it who doesn't pray?" It was not a judgment or an accusation but a statement of compassion.

"I don't know anything any more, Nora. Sure, I should pray. There's no time. No time to think. No time for anything. You have more faith than I do. That's why you can take chances and why I keep all the rules."

His head sagged on the linen tablecloth that she had purchased that day at Marshall Field's. She continued to hold his hand tightly.

· · ·

Paul's office phone buzzed. Bud O'Hara would see him now. He replaced the phone with a gesture of impatient annoyance: 8:30 P.M. The Kennedy administration had to show its dedication by working impossible hours. No wonder so many of the marriages were in trouble.

O'Hara had Paul's collection of photographs spread out on the desk in front of him. "Where did you find these?" he asked.

"A lucky break—from an informant." Paul gave the formal reply that was expected in such circumstances.

"Lucky for all of us. This will be the end of Carmine da Silva," the Texan said. "You'll question our friend on K Street again tomorrow? I imagine he'll turn into a cooperative witness after a few hints about what we have."

"I'll be happy to take care of it. I think he'll be ready to begin a new life at government expense."

"Fine work," O'Hara said. "We should have more breaks like this."

Paul was thoroughly pleased with himself.

Sean helped Nora on with her coat. "You're going back to Washington on Monday?"

"Yes. I guess I'll have to tell Paul that I failed at my mission. He'll worry about you, Sean." She fastened the buckle on her coat and turned up the collar. "He does care about you. Sometimes I think you're the only one in the world he really cares about."

"Don't be ridiculous," Sean said. "I'm grateful for the house cleaning and the food and the sermon and . . . and the love too."

She patted his cheek affectionately. "It was fun. Somehow it's all going to work out."

Sean wished he could believe her. "I'll walk you down to the car," he said. "These streets aren't exactly safe at night."

He opened the rectory door to discover that not even the steps of the rectory were safe. Two men with stocking caps over their faces, dressed in shabby clothes, pushed their way in. One jammed a gun in Sean's stomach. The other pointed a knife at Nora's throat. "Now, you just turn around, Father, and go back into the office," said the man with the gun. "Neither you nor your lady friend here are gonna get hurt."

Sean was frightened. Two kids, probably high on dope, both with dangerous weapons. "Be careful with those things," he pleaded. "We'll do whatever you want." His whole body was trembling.

"That's right, man, you gonna do exactly what we tell ya, and the first thing you gonna do is open that safe." The young Negro gestured the priest toward the battered iron box in the middle of the rectory office. "You gonna open that safe and give us every penny that's inside."

Sean had never bothered to lock the safe. There was very little money in it, and it had become a storehouse for parish records. With shaking fingers he pulled back the iron handle and yanked the ponderous door of the safe open.

"Now, real slow, get out the money in there and put it on the desk. Nice and easy." The thief gestured with his gun.

There was twenty-five dollars and forty-seven cents in the safe. Sean laid it on the desk.

"Hey, man, you gotta have more money than that!"

"We don't, though," said Sean. "What little we take in on Sunday goes to the bank on Monday morning."

"Man, you're rich. Everybody in the neighborhood knows that. You gotta have more money. Let me see your wallet."

Sean could not shake his terror. Nora's face was drawn, her eyes closed, the point of the knife at her neck. He removed the wallet from his black trousers and placed it on the desk. Still pointing the gun with his right hand, the thief shook four one-dollar bills out of the wallet.

"Man, you gotta do better than this, or you and your lady friend are gonna be in real trouble. Oscar, what's she got in her purse?"

Nora yielded her purse silently and without resistance. Oscar— now Sean knew who they were—opened the purse. "Shut your mouth, ya damn fool," he said. "Now this whitey priest knows who we are, and that ain't good. . . . This cunt don't have nothing except a coupla bucks, credit cards, and some traveler's checks."

The other man hefted his gun lightly in his hand. "Well now, Father. We seem to have a real problem here. There's more money in this house than we've got and you're gonna have to give us all of it, or my friend over there is gonna want to carve some fancy things on your lady friend's face."

"There isn't any more money," Sean said. He wondered if he

and Nora would have to die, now that he knew who they were. "This is a poor parish and we don't have any money."

"Well, now, that sure is a shame. Oscar, why don't you just set to work."

Oscar poked Nora's neck with the knife. A little stream of red dripped down the blade. "You're gonna be real cooperative, Father," Oscar said, "or I'm gonna have to do some mean things with this little knife of mine."

Nora's face was white. "Please, there's nothing more here." Her voice sounded small and terrified.

He jabbed at her throat again, and there was another trickle of blood.

Fury was building inside of Sean, cold, murderous hate. Something turned loose inside of him. He hurled himself on the man with the gun and knocked the gun arm aside. The gun went off, filling the room with smoke and gunpowder. Sean kicked his surprised opponent in the groin and then hit him in the face, knocking him back against the safe, where he slid to the floor, dazed. Oscar, the man with the knife, was coming toward Sean. "You asked for it, priest," Oscar said, his left arm out wide, his right arm extended. He bore down on Sean and then struck quickly with the gleaming six-inch blade.

But not quickly enough. Sean grasped the parish seal from the desktop and smashed it against Oscar's arm. The force of the blow spoiled Oscar's aim, and the knife, instead of piercing Sean's stomach, slashed against Sean's left arm. Then the knife slipped out of Oscar's fingers as he grasped his broken forearm. Sean picked up the chair behind the rectory desk and smashed it over Oscar's head. When Sean grabbed the gun lying in front of him on the floor, Oscar hobbled toward the hallway, joined by his friend, who had recovered. "Let's get out of here, man. Fuckin' priest's gonna waste us."

The invaders fled, Sean pursuing them to the door of the rectory. Only as he stood at the doorway and pointed the gun at the fugitives, disappearing into the raw November night, did he realize that he could not kill them.

He lowered the weapon and walked slowly back to the rectory. For the first time he was conscious of a sharp jabbing pain.

"Your arm!" Nora exclaimed.

He looked at the blood dripping down his arm, over his hand,

and on to the rectory floor. "Just a small cut," he said. A few more inches and it might have been an artery.

Nora huddled in her coat. "Those were the boys who were playing basketball outside this afternoon, weren't they?"

"That's right," said Sean. "They graduated from our grammar school three years ago. Sister Alicia always said they were trouble-makers."

While they waited for the police to arrive, Sean kept his good arm around Nora's shoulder. "I'm all right, Sean, I'm all right," she repeated over and over again as she strove to recover her calm before the police arrived.

"Of course you're all right, Nora. I should have listened to Sister. They were troublemakers."

It was a good thing that the police arrived quickly. Father Sean Cronin, his pulses still racing from the encounter, was filled with desire for his foster sister as he held her close and comforted her.

Chris Waverly was even better than Paul had anticipated. The drink at her apartment had turned into seduction, but she did more of the seducing than he, murmuring as she unbuttoned his shirt, "I thought you'd never give me a chance to get at you."

Paul was accustomed to passive, yielding women like Maggie Martin, and to a wife whose sexual depths he carefully avoided arousing. He had never before encountered a woman with such polished sexual skills and imperious hunger. Chris overwhelmed him. Her sleek body was a well coordinated and irresistible instrument of excitement. She aroused him, taunted him, teased him, drove him to the point of madness, and then, when he thought he could stand no more, she would begin again.

Afterward, they lay in the rumpled sheets of her bed, smoking, she coolly and he distracted and exhausted.

"You're an interesting man, Paul Cronin," she said. "A few things to learn, maybe, but worth teaching. I think you'll keep coming back for more schooling."

"It was fantastic," he said, still unable to organize his thoughts.

"No, it wasn't, not really. It was only a fair beginning. But that's all right. Come on, let's see if we can make a little more progress in today's lesson." Her hands began to explore his body.

After their second roller-coaster tumble, Paul fell asleep. The Chinese infantry attacked once again in his dream. This time a naked and deadly Chris Waverly jammed the bayonet into his belly. He woke screaming.

"Hey," she said. "I'm not that bad, am I? You're the first one who's ever awakened screaming after a tussle with me."

"It's not you," he gasped. "It's a dream I have about a night attack in Korea. It comes and goes."

"Poor Paul," she said gently. "Relax now and let mother Chris calm you down."

Chris was tender and affectionate. The terrors of the dream slowly ebbed. For a moment, Paul thought that he was in the life-preserver arms of his wife.

Joe Makuch was waiting the next day in the outer office at the Justice Department. It had been six years since Paul had seen him.

Paul mentioned a ten o'clock conference with the Attorney General, but he nonetheless had to listen to the sad tale of the decline of Joe Makuch: the bankruptcy of his gas station, his move to Los Angeles, the inevitable divorce, the children who didn't care to see their father. Now he had a marvelous opportunity to start life over with a new woman and a new auto dealership specializing in English sports cars.

"Well, I certainly hope the new dealership works out for you," Paul said nervously, glancing at his watch. "Foreign cars are going to be big in the years ahead."

"I can't purchase the place unless I come up with twenty-five thousand dollars." Joe Makuch could not meet Paul's eyes. "I thought you might lend it to me—you know, for old times' sake."

"Life here in Washington is expensive, Joe. But I'll see what I can do—for old times' sake."

"Sure. I know that things are tough all over," Makuch agreed. "But I thought you might be able to scare up the change for me. Maybe your father would be interested in investing in one of your old Marine buddies. After all, that business at the Reservoir was messy—it wouldn't look so good in the newspapers." Makuch was being much more explicit about the blackmail than he had been in the past.

"Dad has always believed that one should be loyal to the men with whom one has shared combat," Paul said. "I imagine we'll find a way to work things out. I'll be in touch with you in a few

days with the details. Now I'd better get down to the Attorney
General's office before I find myself out of a job."

As he walked down the wide corridor, honeycombed with
offices on either side, Paul's hands were covered with sweat. He
dried them off, before he entered the Attorney General's office,
and fixed his face into a casual grin, although inside he was feeling
rage—and the beginnings of a desire for revenge.

CHAPTER
—— THIRTEEN ——
1962

Eileen and Mary Cronin started to shriek with joy as soon as they saw their mother walk down the steps from the United Airlines jet at National Airport. Paul sighed with relief. It would be good to have Nora back. He missed her as he would miss a close friend. His affair with Chris had become a never-ending series of paroxysms of delight. Indeed, he had visited her apartment that morning before breakfast and returned in due time to collect his daughters for the trip to the airport. He smiled briefly at the recollection of one or two of her more ingenious tricks. Nevertheless, she could not make the Korean dreams go away, and Nora could.

Nora knelt down and hugged her two gloriously happy daughters. Then she and Paul embraced each other enthusiastically. Nora cocked a quizzical eye at him. "You must have missed me." She pressed hard against him.

Paul felt the warm security of his life preserver. "How could I help missing a wife like you?" he said, squeezing her again. "After I heard about the close call you had in Chicago . . ."

She disengaged herself. "I'm sure the newspapers here exaggerated. Nobody pushes a Cronin around."

"But it didn't melt the old man's heart?"

Nora lifted Mary into her arms and tugged at Eileen's hand. "Made him even worse. He chewed me out on the phone for ten minutes. I shouldn't have taken such chances, and Sean was responsible for risking the life of the mother of his grandchildren. I finally hung up on him."

Paul led his family toward the parking lot. In the car, riding back to Georgetown, he said, "Do you have any idea of how we can handle this Sean thing?"

"I talked with Jimmy McGuire, and he said the new Archbishop is a reasonable man, not vindictive or resentful like McNulty was. He thinks that if someone like you—well, that if you would see the Cardinal and fill him in on the background, he'd wipe the slate clean."

"I'm sure Bobby will give me a day or two off if I explain why to him. . . ." His voice trailed off.

"He goddamn well better," Nora said with uncharacteristic profanity.

"Mommy," said Eileen from the back seat, "you should *never* talk like that!"

"That's right, darling. I know I shouldn't. Mommy's just tired from the long airplane ride."

"Oh," said Eileen, granting absolution. "That's different."

Robert Kennedy frowned. "I suppose that officially we don't know how Cronin obtained these records."

"No, sir," said Bud O'Hara.

"Functional justice again?" asked the Attorney General.

"Cronin is a good man." O'Hara wanted no part of responsibility for Cronin's violation of the law.

"I know he is. But he's also a reckless gambler." He grinned. "A Kennedy can't object to that, I suppose. Yet we *could* have nailed da Silva some other way. This wasn't necessary."

"It saved us a lot of time," O'Hara replied.

"We ought to put a letter in Cronin's file commending him for progress in the investigation."

"Yes, sir," said the Texan, who never called the Attorney General by his first name.

"And perhaps we ought to reconsider his value to the administration here in Washington." He hesitated and shook his head. "We'll miss Nora."

The difference between Paul Cronin and the Attorney General was that Bob Kennedy would need a cause before he broke into the office of a citizen. Paul Cronin would break into the same office purely for the hell of it.

Cardinal Eamon McCarthy was a short, slight man of sixty-two, with salt-and-pepper hair and shrewd brown eyes peering through thick horn-rimmed glasses. "I'm very happy you came to see me, Mr. Cronin," he said. "I must say I was impressed by the newspaper account of your brother's behavior during that robbery attempt. It would seem"—he smiled briefly—"that you are not the only one in the family with heroic proclivities."

"I may have the medal, Your Excellency," said Paul smoothly, "but Sean has about four times as much courage as I do."

"Indeed?" The Archbishop's voice was mild and reedy. He seemed to be a timid, diffident sort of man. "Some of the people on my staff have tried to persuade me it was scandalous for a woman to be having supper at St. Jadwiga's rectory, even though she was a member of Father Cronin's family. It seemed to me that they were drawing a bit of a long bow."

Paul leaped at the opportunity. "Nora came to Chicago because we were advised that Sean is in failing health. I was stuck at the Justice Department, so I asked Nora to investigate. I can't imagine anyone seeing something wrong."

The Archbishop tapped his finger lightly on the manila folder that was in front of him. "As far as I've been able to gather, your brother has done remarkable work there under extraordinary conditions. I wouldn't be at all surprised if, as you say, his health is in danger." He flipped open the file. "Your brother's record at the seminary was excellent, at the top of his class most of the time. He apparently is also a man of strong commitment and dedication to the priesthood. Indeed, there is a note here in the file from one of his seminary teachers." The Archbishop held up a single-spaced letter, typed on both sides of a sheet of seminary stationery. "It recommends him for graduate study. Without making any judgments about my predecessor's decisions"—again the Archbishop smiled—"I should think that Father Cronin ought to be encouraged in such work, don't you?"

The Archbishop was making it very easy indeed. Paul would not even have to raise the question of the renewed flow of Michael Cronin's generosity to the Archdiocese of Chicago if his son was sent to graduate school. "Sean has always been a fine student. I think he would enjoy graduate school enormously."

"Yes, indeed." The Archbishop closed the file. "Very well, then," he said. "The matter is settled."

"By the way, Your Excellency, I wonder if I may make a request of you. I would just as soon Sean didn't know that I—"

The Archbishop smiled. "I understand perfectly, Mr. Cronin," he said. "I, too, have a brother."

After he left the Victorian gray pile of stone on Wabash Avenue that was the Chicago chancery office, Paul consulted his watch. He still had some time before his return trip to Washington. He could surprise Maggie Shields at her Lincoln Park West apartment. After his victory with the Archbishop, he deserved a prize. On second thought, he decided Maggie was a trivial piece of candy compared to Chris. He could wait until he reached Washington.

Maggie Shields poured herself a second gin and tonic, insisting mentally that two drinks in the afternoon were not a serious sign unless you needed them. She was not turning into one of those quietly drinking frustrated doctors' wives. She had a lot to live for. She was twenty-seven years old, her figure was in better shape than it had ever been since her marriage, her children were attractive, even if they were a nuisance when they were not out at the playground with their nurse, and her life was still ahead of her.

Only she was bored silly—with her serious husband, for whom delivering babies into the world was more important than his own sex life; with her difficult eldest daughter, Nicole; with the confines of their apartment overlooking the park; with herself. Her friends were all married and talked about nothing but teeth and toilet training. The free-floating intellectuals in the neighborhood were too highbrow. She did not like to read, and the soap operas on television held her attention for only a few hours each day. The infrequent vacations she took with Tom were no help. He tried to become amorous, and that bored her worse than anything.

She had thought about divorce, but she couldn't face being alone. Maybe she ought to open a shop somewhere, sell expensive dresses to wealthy women. She would be good at that. Her taste in clothes was excellent. The slacks and blouse she was wearing cost three hundred dollars and made her look ravishing. It might be worth trying. Tom would go along.

The telephone rang. It was Paul. He wouldn't be able to stop by after all. The Attorney General needed him back in Washington. It had been months since Paul had come to see her. She did not know how long she could stand not being with him. He was the only thing in her life that made her feel alive.

She poured herself another drink. Maybe she could invent an excuse to go to Washington.

Paul Cronin arrived late at the Kennedys' home in Virginia. The garden behind the house was illuminated by hundreds of twinkling lights. The end of the November Indian summer had lingered long enough for the Kennedys to have one of their outdoor parties.

Pleading a delay at the airport and a need to stop by his office, Paul had telephoned Nora and told her to take the Mercedes off to Virginia and he would join her in the Ferrari later.

"What about your wife?" Chris had asked when they were finished making love. She was lying casually on top of him, her flesh pressed against his.

"What do you mean, 'What about her'?" he replied. He knew that he should leave for Virginia any minute, and that he would not.

"Do you love her?"

"Does it make any difference?"

"Not especially. I just like to know where I stand." She kissed him provocatively.

"Yes, I do love her. It's not like—"

"Not very good in the sack, huh? That's her problem, I guess. I like you a lot, Paul." Her kisses were now becoming insistent. "I intend to keep you around a long time. If I make up my mind that I want you permanently, I'll do my best to take you away from your gorgeous Nora. I just thought it fair to warn you."

"I'm warned." He tried to sound casual, but under the circumstances it was impossible to make any serious response to Chris.

Now, as he searched for Nora among the crowd in the Attorney General's garden, he told himself that neither Chris nor anybody else could possibly take him away from Nora.

"There you are. I thought you would never come." This time it was Nora who initiated the passionate embrace. "You told me the news was good on the phone," she said, releasing him. "What are the details?"

"Sean is being sent to Rome to study Church history."

"Marvelous!" Nora exclaimed, embracing him again. "I knew you could charm the Archbishop."

Paul was at the bar later when the Attorney General of the United States, fully dressed, toppled into his swimming pool. When Paul heard the splash and the mixed cries of horror and delight, he pushed his way through the throng to the edge of the pool. The other Kennedys and members of the staff were there first and were helping the bedraggled but laughing Attorney General out of the pool.

"Who did it? Who did it?" The words were forming on everyone's lips.

Bob Kennedy made his way through the crowd to Nora Riley Cronin. "We're even now, Nora, I guess," he said with his most infectious grin.

"Who, me?" said Nora innocently.

The Attorney General laughed and turned to Paul. "Do you ever win any fights, Paul?"

"I have sense enough not to try," Paul said.

As the Attorney General started for the house and a dry set of clothing, he turned once more to Paul. "By the way, I'd like to see you for a few minutes tomorrow—if you have the time."

Paul could not help but notice that the Attorney General was no longer smiling.

Sean Cronin waited in the long, elaborately carpeted corridor of the chancery office that led to the Archbishop's suite. On both of the walls of the corridor were pictures from the career of George William Mundelein, the first Cardinal of Chicago. "Do you know what it's about?" Sean asked Roger Fitzgibbon, who was now acting as assistant chancellor before going to Rome to study canon law.

Fitzgibbon had been busy, rushing up and down the corridor delivering documents to the offices of the vicar general, the chancellor, and the vice-chancellor. "I don't know for sure," he said brusquely, indicating by tone and manner that he didn't have much time to talk. "I suppose, though, that there's been some complaint about Nora being in your rectory when it was robbed."

"Nora?" Sean said, incredulously.

"Not very prudent, Sean. Not very prudent at all," said Fitzgibbon, shaking his head disapprovingly.

Sean had an urge to smash Fitzgibbon's pious face, just as he had smashed the faces of the robbers at St. Jadwiga's.

When he was finally shown into the Archbishop's office, the Archbishop came immediately to the point. "Sit down, Father Cronin. First of all, let me congratulate you on the—er—well, I suppose the right word would be 'efficient' way in which you handled the attempted robbery at St. Jadwiga's."

"Thank you, Your Excellency," Sean said, trying to read the shrewd little Archbishop.

"I was wondering, Father Cronin, whether you would be willing to apply the same efficiency to a small task I have in mind?"

"Of course, Archbishop."

"You say yes before you even know what it is? Well, I certainly cannot criticize enthusiasm. My task, however, may take some time. I need a Church historian, a well-trained and competent one. I propose to send you to Rome to study history at the Gregorian University, and I would ask you to concentrate especially on the history of the Church's teaching and practice in regard to the sacrament of matrimony. I would be relieved to have someone with such competence on my personal staff both at the Vatican Council and afterward. Are you still enthusiastic about my task, Father?"

"Even more so," said Sean. He was scarcely able to believe what he had heard.

"Excellent," said the Archbishop. "We're going to see many changes in the Church in the years ahead, Father Cronin. I'm inclined to agree with the late Archbishop of Paris that the crises will be crises of growth and not of decline. I feel the American Church will suffer badly for its lack of proper scholarship. The change may be disconcerting."

"The Church won't change," Sean said. "It won't change because it can't change."

The Archbishop tapped his pencil lightly on his blotter. "I'm afraid I must disagree, Father." And then, echoing what Nora had said the week before, the Archbishop of Chicago added, "The Church will change because it has to change."

• • •

"Paul, I need help," Bobby Kennedy said, running his fingers nervously through his thick hair.

"Anything wrong?" Paul asked. There were warning gongs sounding inside his head.

Kennedy grinned his charming grin. "It's a rough assignment, but an important one. You know as well as I do, maybe better than I do, that Chicago is the center of organized crime and that our Crime Task Force in Chicago is a mess. Too damn much hanging out in bars, if you ask me. Can't tell the good guys from the bad guys any more. You've been so good here—well, I thought we might send you to Chicago. You're young for the job, although that doesn't bother me, of all people." Again the charming grin. "It's a great challenge."

Paul knew that he had no real choice. He was being dismissed from the Attorney General's staff in the nicest way possible. He was being kicked upstairs.

"We'll miss Nora, God knows," Kennedy said. Then he added, somewhat lamely, "You too, of course."

❧ BOOK IV ❧

This is my commandment. Love one another as I have loved you. A man can have no greater love than to lay down his life for his friends. You are my friends if you do what I command you. I shall not call you servants any more, because a servant does not know his master's business. I call you friends.

—John 15:11–15

CHAPTER
—— FOURTEEN ——
1963

Sean Cronin walked through the Piazza Farnese with quick steps. Although concerned that he would be late for dinner, he smiled cheerfully and said *buona sera* to a young couple walking in the opposite direction. They responded with solemn silence. Sean had learned enough history to know why the Roman people hated the clergy; the citizens of Rome had neither forgiven nor forgotten the absolutism of the papal state and the repeated crushing of their attempts to achieve democratic self-government. Yet, raised as he was on the South Side of Chicago where priests were greeted routinely and greeted in return, Sean could not adjust to the hostility of the young people.

It was one of the few things he did not like about Rome. Everything else—the catacombs, St. Peter's, the Vatican gardens, the Via Veneto, the baroque churches and palaces, the street urchins, and the noise—he enjoyed enormously.

The months had been busy: learning Italian and entering Gregorian University in the middle of the year; taking courses in the history of Christian attitudes and practices on marriage that the Archbishop wanted him to study; learning his way around Rome; meeting new friends. It had been an exciting and challenging six months that quickly blotted out the nightmare years at St. Jadwiga's. Then, a few weeks before, the death of John XXIII and the election and installation of a new pope. Sean's mind was still jammed with the sights and sounds as he stood in the Piazza of St.

Peter's and saw the white smoke go up and heard the first blessing "to the city and to the world" of Giovanni Battisti Montini, Pope Paul VI. How could anyone want to change a church that had so much grace and beauty in its ceremonies?

He continued across the Piazza Farnese toward Chicago House, trying not to notice the dirty looks his cassock and clerical hat earned him. Already some of his classmates at the Greg were abandoning clerical garb, behavior that Sean felt was dangerously close to apostasy.

The small sixteenth-century palazzo at the end of the narrow street that Sean had just left belonged to his friends the Alessandrinis—Angèlica and Francésco—members of the black, or papal, nobility who had chosen Pope Pius IX over Victor Emmanuel in 1870. The *Principio,* a thin handsome man, and the *Principessa,* who was lovely in a delicate, ethereal way, were people his own age. They now lived in only one fourth of that ancient family palace but did not seem to lack money, although it was not clear if either of them had ever worked a day in their lives. Sean had met them at a cocktail party at the American embassy, and they had promptly taken him under their wing.

Their "little party" this afternoon had included an assortment of curial bureaucrats and the great wise old Cardinal Menelli, who had dropped a few hints about what had happened at the conclave. Sean had felt vaguely uneasy. He had cheered enthusiastically for the new Pope, and it did not seem right to hear him discussed by Menelli in such a cynical manner. Moreover, while Sean was deeply opposed to changes that might impinge on the timeless serenity of the Church, and horrified by the translation of the Mass into English, his sense of fairness was affronted by the trickery and deceit that seemed to be a matter of course in Vatican politics. It had been much more pleasant to watch Angèlica's delicate fingers dance up and down the keyboard as she played "a little Vivaldi concerto" than it was to try to understand Rome.

At Chicago House, in the Via Sardegna, just off the Via Veneto, Eamon McCarthy, the Cardinal Archbishop of Chicago, shook his head unhappily. "It isn't like the first session, Father Cronin, not like it at all. The new Pope is a brilliant man. He understands what is happening in the Church intellectually, far better than did his predecessor." The Cardinal's hair was now almost entirely white and his normally serene brown eyes were troubled. "But I believe he is making a grave mistake. The forces of change have been unleashed. They should be guided, but they cannot be slowed down. I fear that he does not trust his fellow bishops. There will be deep trouble if that is the case."

Each evening at the dinner table at Chicago House, the Cardinal would discuss the events of the Aula of St. Peter's that day. The Chicago students who also lived in the elaborate palazzo that Cardinal Mundelein had purchased—to show that an American Cardinal could live as elaborately in Rome as an Italian Cardinal —listened intently to Eamon McCarthy's analysis. Sean found that he was the only one at the table who thought the Church was changing too rapidly. Jimmy McGuire, who had come to Rome in the fall to study canon law, had become more radical with each passing year. He even wore a black turtleneck at the dinner table instead of a cassock. Unaccountably, the Cardinal did not seem to mind.

"As you know, Father Cronin," the Cardinal said, directing the discussion to Sean, "I've asked you to specialize in the history of marriage and sexuality in Catholic teaching because I am convinced that that is the most corrosive issue we face. The other things we do at the Council are important, but mostly for scholars and priests. Sexuality is important to all our lay people."

Sean sensed that he was on the spot, as he frequently was in such discussions. It seemed to him that he was being tested every night. "In an age when sex has become a pleasure unto itself, Eminence, we have to remind our people that sex is basically for procreation."

Jimmy, who had remained Sean's closest friend despite their theological differences, spoke up abruptly. "Most married men and women will tell you that that's not why they sleep with one another at night."

"The pill doesn't change anything, Jimmy," Sean said. He knew from previous arguments that Jimmy thought the pill might be a legitimate Catholic form of birth control. "And I'm sure the bishops of the world have no intention of making exceptions for the pill."

"Oh, Father Cronin, are you sure of that?" The Cardinal smiled his quick little smile. "If there were a secret ballot, and if it was clear that the Pope had not prescribed beforehand the outcome of that ballot, I tell you this, Father Cronin: the bishops of the world for reasons of the pastoral good of our married people would vote for a change on birth control."

"I can't believe that, your Eminence," Sean said.

"Ah, come now, Father Cronin. You are such an idealist. A bishop, much less a cardinal archbishop, cannot afford to be that kind of an idealist. We may not understand the theology, we may not have insight into history, but if we are listening to our priests and to our people we know that *something* has to be done on the birth-control question."

"If you say so, it must be true," Sean conceded.

"Oh, it's true all right, Father," the Cardinal said quietly. "A number of us are going to try to see the Pope next week and persuade him to open up the Council for discussion of the problem. I suppose"—he sighed—"he will not listen to us."

"And what will that mean, Eminence?"

"That will mean, my dear Father Cronin," the Cardinal said in his gentle voice, "that sometime before this decade is over the Church will be confronted by disaster."

Paul Cronin realized that he was not going to eliminate organized crime in Chicago. The proper strategy was some fast and easy victories, a lot of public acclaim, and then an escape from the quicksand. He had already been successful in putting a number of small-time hoods behind bars, and he was now gearing up to uncover mob infiltration of a local labor union. Tony Swartz, who had joined him as his assistant, believed in what they were doing, with an idealism born of the Kennedy years. He seemed unaware that Paul cared little about the effects of the Chicago Strike Force, except as a stepping-stone for his own ambitions for political office and as an excuse to go to Washington frequently to see Chris Waverly.

She was now waiting for him in the Sans Souci restaurant, a block away from the White House. Paul had selected the Sans Souci because it was no longer an "in" restaurant, and there was less chance that he would run into anyone who knew Nora. A year ago, all the bright young men from the White House had gone there for lunch, usually to sit admiringly at the feet of the tall, black-haired Pat Moynihan, who was the closest thing to a house intellectual that the Kennedys had. Then the second-raters discovered that the Sans Souci was the place to be, and the White House staff found other places to eat.

Chris lit a cigarette and sampled her martini. Paul would be late. The Kennedys cared about no one's time but their own. Yet, still riding the crest of their Cuban missile crisis triumph, they were the toast of the nation. It would not last, of that Chris was sure.

Paul would be filled with his most recent triumphs in Chicago—putting some cheap hood behind bars. He might have illusions as to why he had been sent to Chicago; she had none. The Kennedys had decided he was dangerous to have around. He had been shipped out.

Chris had not made up her mind about Paul. He was fine in bed, if perhaps not the great lover he imagined himself to be. He was pleasant, attractive, and charming, and he was filthy rich. He was the kind of man Chris wanted—a nice sort with some conscience but not too much. The news business was becoming tiresome. She had never intended to stay in it after thirty, and she had been searching for a man who would be tolerable as a mate and whom she could mold into a major political power. Paul seemed to fill the bill. He had natural political skills and instincts. He was ambitious but not excessively so. Above all, he had the knack of saying exactly the right thing in exactly the right way when the red light of the television camera blinked on.

For all her cynicism, Chris felt a knot in her throat when Paul finally burst into the Sans Souci, brimming with energy and enthusiasm. Watch it, she told herself, you may be turning into a romantic.

His greeting, as he slid into the booth next to her, was a quick peck on the cheek. Chris guided his chin toward her mouth and responded with a long, lingering kiss. "When are you going to come back to Washington and make an honest woman of me?" she purred, releasing him only after she was sure that he had been thoroughly shaken.

"What do you mean?" His broad smile was briefly hesitant.

"You and I are a lot alike. Both of us want to see you go places in Washington. And both of us were behind the door when consciences were passed out. . . . Your Nora probably needs a man with a very stern conscience."

"Someone like my brother Sean?"

"A priest?"

He signaled the waiter for his drink order. "I'm only joking. Sean hardly knows that women exist."

Nora Cronin could not concentrate on the book she was reading. Her husband was in Washington at a meeting concerning the Chicago Strike Force. He would be coming home soon. Nora missed him more than she usually did when he was away. Although she had waited for Tom Shields to give her the go-ahead to become pregnant, this pregnancy was much more difficult than the other two had been.

She closed the book and rested it on what was left of her lap. Three more weeks. It was absurd to think that she would die, yet the thought kept stealing into her mind. She was only twenty-eight years old and the picture of health, save for a womb that didn't seem to want to function properly, particularly when a child was leaving it. She had learned from her mother and from the nuns at school that everything was part of God's plan. Perhaps God was punishing her. But she didn't know why.

She yearned to be at Oakland Beach, basking in the sunlight in the morning, swinging a golf club in the afternoon, and chatting with the neighbors over cocktails in the evening. Glendore seemed so far away, and she had almost forgotten what a golf club felt like.

She grabbed the edge of the table to help keep her balance as she stood. If she got much bigger, she thought, they would have to devise a pulley system to raise and lower her from a sitting position.

The first pain came. It was not like the pains of her previous labor; rather it felt as if the baby inside her was trying to tear her apart.

Luckily, Mary and Eileen, who were utterly delighted at the prospect of having a baby brother, were asleep upstairs. Somehow they had all gotten into the habit of thinking of this new baby as a boy. Undoubtedly, Mike Cronin's influence at work.

Another even more stabbing pain ripped through her. She screamed for the housekeeper. "Anna, come quickly. Something is terribly wrong!"

I'm going to die after all, she thought, as she fell to the floor, unconscious.

• • •

Sean stared in stunned disbelief at the cablegram. He was as numb as he had been when Father McCabe told him that his brother was missing in action in Korea. NORA CRITICAL. RETURN IF YOU CAN. PAUL.

Oh, God. No. Don't take her, please don't.

He went down the steps from his attic room in Chicago House to the floor below where the Cardinal lived. Eamon McCarthy was sitting at his desk in suspenders and a white collarless shirt. The new red robes of his cardinalship were hanging behind him. He was poring over a stack of papers, the flimsy sheets that came from the *typis polygattis vaticanis*.

"Your Eminence. . . ." Sean hesitated in the doorway.

The kindly man peered over his glasses. "Yes, Sean? You look troubled." It was the first time he had called Sean anything but Father Cronin.

Hardly able to speak, Sean showed him the cablegram.

"Of course you must go home at once," said the Cardinal. "Your family needs you more than I do just now."

"Thank you, Your Eminence. I'm sure Nora will be all right—"

"It's all in God's hands. In any event, catch the first plane in the morning and stay as long as necessary."

"I'll return as soon as Nora is out of danger."

"I will pray for her, Father Cronin. I shall pray very hard indeed. I'm sure that she will recover."

Sean's stomach was twisted with fear. "It's all in God's hands." Sean echoed the Cardinal's words, searching in the depths of his being for enough faith in God to believe what he was saying. He found nothing.

Nora knew that death had retreated when the hospital smells began to bother her again: the antiseptic odor at first, then overcooked food, and then human sickness. The terrible, terrible cold leaked slowly out of her veins and she found herself yearning for the warmth of the sunlight.

She had just finished giving her yet unnamed daughter her bottle. The little girl was lying next to her on the bed, tiny but alert, intrigued, it seemed, by the world into which she had been plunged so abruptly and unceremoniously. Tears of sadness flowed down Nora's cheeks.

"Why so many tears?" It was Sean. Had he been there all along? She had fallen into the habit of drifting in and out of sleep, as much a result of the depression that had taken control of her as of the medication or any actual physical exhaustion.

"She's a perfectly presentable little girl, isn't she?" she said after a long while.

"More than presentable," he said, poking his finger at his niece, who poked back with her own tiny finger. "I don't know much about babies, but this one is the most beautiful I've ever seen. The spitting image of her mother."

"No one wants her." Nora began sobbing. "Not her grandfather, or her father, or her mother. We're all angry at her because she's not a little boy."

"I've just watched you with her. I don't think you're angry at her any more," Sean said. "You just haven't had a chance to get used to the idea of another little Cronin girl. What's her name, by the way?"

"She doesn't have a name. We didn't have any girls' names ready, we were so sure it would be a boy. I've thought about Michele—"

"No," Sean said, "she's not a Michele. I know what she is. She's a Noreen. A little Nora."

Despite her weakness and her pain, Nora Riley Cronin sat up in bed and smiled. "You're right. She *is* a Noreen."

Sean baptized his new niece in the grim nondenominational chapel of the hospital on the morning of November 22.

"Noreen Marie Cronin"—Sean poured liberal amounts of water on her tiny bald head—"I baptize you in the name of the Father and of the Son and of the Holy Spirit."

Noreen Marie Cronin marked her entry among God's people not by wailing in protest at the cold water cascading over her face but rather by gurgling happily and trying to swallow some of the water.

On the way to the airport that afternoon, Sean studied his brother carefully. They had spent little time together in the last ten years. Who was Paul Cronin now? As far as appearances went, he was a tall, handsome New Frontiersman, his dark wavy hair cut in the Kennedy style, his PT-boat tie clip a discreet but impressive badge. A very successful and very important young politician.

"It doesn't make Dad happy now that we're both doing what he wanted us to do, does it, Paul?"

Paul glanced at him quickly. "Did you call him yesterday?"

"All I got was a stream of orders to pass on to the Pope, who Dad thinks is a weak-kneed sniveler."

"Probably like the orders I get to pass on to the President, who Dad calls a lightweight poseur."

They laughed together, and Sean felt a brief sensation of the old comradery that had been greatest in the past when they won a tennis match or a sailboat race together.

"He was disappointed, I suppose, that Noreen isn't a boy?" Sean said tentatively.

"Furious. Chewed Nora out, I'm afraid, while she was still having blood pumped into her. As though it were her fault. And then he invented some 'urgent business' so that he could miss the baptism."

"Sounds like Dad. Won't even give in to genetics," Sean said.

"God, I was so frightened that we were going to lose Nora. I don't know what I'd do without her, Sean. My life would fall apart."

A niggling voice in the back of Sean's brain told him that, while he ought not to doubt Paul's sincerity, the sentiment of his little speech sounded disturbingly artificial. Sean realized that he knew little about the man who was his brother, and even less about the quality of his marriage.

Paul drove the Mercedes into the parking lot at O'Hare. "I'll park here and walk with you. The Strike Force can spare me for another hour or so, I'm sure."

Something seemed to be amiss as they walked through the parking lot under the gray November sky. Little knots of people were gathered in intense conversation, and there seemed to be no one waiting for taxis or racing to the terminal building.

Paul's words echoed Sean's thoughts. "Something strange is going on here. Do you feel it too?"

At the edge of the parking lot, just across from the terminal, a stewardess in a United Airlines uniform was crying into a fragile lace handkerchief.

"Excuse me, miss." Paul turned on his considerable charm. "Can you tell me what has happened?"

The girl looked up from her handkerchief, her face red and puffy. "They've shot the President!"

CHAPTER
——— FIFTEEN ———
1963–1964

Paul Cronin waited nervously in the Mayor's outer office. The interview was important, and he needed all his cool to carry it off. At least three very important friends had interceded with the Mayor for him. He had all the right credentials: Notre Dame graduate, war hero, Kennedy aide, the Strike Force, good family. He would make an ideal "blue ribbon" candidate for state senator. He also had his father's money behind him for the campaign. If the Cook County Committee would slate him at their meeting in December, there would be no primary contest; the only other announced candidates were obvious hacks.

"I know your father well; we grew up together," the short red-faced Mayor said, pumping his hand. "And your poor mother, God rest her soul. A great Chicago family, the Cronins. And you've got a great future in politics in this city. And in the country, with your wonderful work for President Kennedy, God be good to him. . . ."

The nonstop monologue continued, with Paul being permitted only an occasional word. Finally the Mayor came to the point. "I'm glad to see you're thinking of elective office in this county. We need more fine young men like you in politics. It's a great vocation—like your brother's, though not as holy. I'm sure the slating committee will be very interested in your presentation."

It sounded like an endorsement to Paul. "Your support will be very important, Your Honor."

"The slating committee's gotta make its own decisions." The Mayor rushed on. "They have to consider *all* the candidates and choose the one they think has the best chance of being the best senator from your district. And, of course, the man who has the best chance of winning."

"I hope that I win their support, Mr. Mayor, because I'm in the race till Election Day."

"That's the kind of spunk I admire. This city of Chicago needs your kind of young man in politics," the Mayor said. He stood and held out his hand.

Paul knew when he walked out of the office that he had the nomination in the bag. It didn't have to be a very big bag, because state senator was not an important job. Springfield was dullsville, and members of the Illinois General Assembly had very little clout unless they were willing to stay in Springfield for a lot longer than he intended. But in four years the veteran Congressman from the third district would probably retire. A presentable record in Springfield would be the first step to Congress, then to the Senate, then to . . . well, any place.

Paul wondered whether Dick Daley was baffled by such a forceful application for such a small job. Probably not. The Mayor had a reputation for being able to read the cards before they were dealt.

Elizabeth Hanover, the woman who was serving as chairman of the Gallery Committee, was not Mike's kind of woman. She was tall and slender and black-haired. Moreover, she displayed none of the shy modesty that Mike usually found appealing.

Mike had been persuaded to lend his name to a civic group that would fund an impressionist gallery on the North Side. He meant to attend the first meeting and then quietly disappear. If it were not for his hope that Paul would be slated to run for the State Senate, he might not have even bothered to show up at the first meeting.

However, his kind of woman or not, Elizabeth was stunning: about ten years younger than he, smoldering black eyes, a throaty voice, and a figure that stirred welcome feelings in Mike. He wasn't over the hill yet.

Elizabeth accepted his invitation to lunch at the Mid-America Club on the top floor of the new Prudential Building. As they watched the snowflakes gently cover the brown squares of Grant Park and the ugly railroad tracks that bisected it, they talked first of Monet, then of Mike's plans for Paul's election campaign.

By the time they were finished with lunch, there was no one left in the dining room save the two of them and the always polite waiters. There was a brief silence. Elizabeth ground out her cigarette.

"Isn't your apartment on Outer Drive East?" She gestured toward the lake, now hidden by the snow.

"Great view of the lake," he said. He felt like a tongue-tied sixteen-year-old.

"Then perhaps we ought to go there and make love." She picked up her purse. "Find out whether we like each other in bed and get that out of the way."

Mike's expression never changed, although he was startled by her candor.

They held hands as they walked against the stinging lake wind and the thick blanket of snow. "Do you belong to the health club?" She pointed toward the bubble-top swimming pool at the base of the tall fog-shrouded skyscraper. "I'll bring my swimming suit the next time."

"Are you so certain there will be a next time?" he asked.

"Oh, yes," she said confidently.

She was right.

Michael Cronin was admitted to the Mayor's office promptly at the scheduled time of his appointment. There was the usual preliminary small talk. Then they got down to business. Mike was smooth and relaxed, confident that Richard Daley was no different from the Chicago politicians he had known before the war.

"I've lost touch with Chicago politics over the years," he said. "I've been out of town so much that things kind of slipped away from me until Paul came home from Washington."

"You're doing an important job in the international economic community, Mike." The Mayor spoke like a defense attorney.

"I suppose some people would think it's just selfishness that I've become interested again, now that Paul is seeking public office."

"If a man doesn't support his own son, who will he support?" The Mayor's round face was bright with admiration.

"Of course, we'll provide most of the money for Paul's campaign. . . ." He hesitated, trying to make his offer as indirect as possible. "And after that, Dick, you can be sure that my contributions to anything the party thinks important will be substantial."

The Mayor stared at Mike, his face unreadable. Mike felt his own smile fade.

"Election contributions are funny things, Mike." Daley's tone turned nostalgic. "I remember when I was running for sheriff, a man came from our friends on the West Side and offered me two hundred and fifty thousand dollars. That was a lot of money in those days. I told him I didn't want his money, and he turned around and went down the street and gave it to my opponent, Elmer Walsh, and Elmer won. So the next time when I was running for county clerk he came again and offered me fifty thousand and I took it. Then, on Election Day, I called him and gave it back. He said, 'Why did you take it if you weren't going to use it?' and I said, 'That way, you can't give it to my opponent.'"

Mike wondered if he should laugh or be angry. So he laughed and Daley laughed with him. Then the Mayor heaved himself out of his massive chair briskly, shook hands with him, and told Mike that he was sure the slating committee would listen "with deep emphasis to what Paul has to say to us."

As he walked out into the subzero gloom of Washington Boulevard, Mike decided that Richard Daley was considerably different from the politicians he had known in the 1930s.

That afternoon Elizabeth made him forget about politics. She was a firm believer in love in the afternoon, especially after a swim in the pool.

She stood above him, hands complacently on her bare hips. "You know, Michael, I can't imagine anyone more different from me in background or taste, but I'm quite besotted with you. I think I'll keep you for a while." She grinned in amusement.

Under her urging he had given up smoking, swam in the pool every day, was losing weight under a doctor's guidance, and felt twenty years younger. "I hope you do." He laughed. "You've taken all the joys out of my life. All but one."

She cocked her head. "And that one?"

"Makes everything else shine as brightly as that blue sky out there."

"Oh, Michael, you are a dear." She bent over him and teased his lips with hers, her breasts brushing against his chest. "I'm going to keep you around for a long, long time."

No woman ever had such power over him. Yet he loved it. If only Jane were not in the way.

Paul was sure to win the election. Tony Swartz had designed a superlative campaign. There was plenty of money for television advertising, Paul had routed the incumbent, Roy Flanagan, in their television debate, and the two Chicago papers had endorsed him, one dismissing Flanagan as one of the worst of the hacks. Paul had crossed and recrossed the district while Flanagan had made almost no public appearances, silenced by campaign managers who suspected that Flanagan lost votes every time he opened his mouth.

The enthusiastic cheers of the audiences were strong wine for Paul. He understood how Jack Kennedy must have felt when he set an audience on fire. Even if Paul had only the vaguest idea of how the problems of Chicago could be solved, and even if he could actually do little toward solving them, he really believed that he was the better candidate. One paper spoke enthusiastically of his "patent sincerity," a line that Nora had read aloud with some amusement in almost the same tone of voice with which Chris Waverly read it over the telephone when she had seen the endorsement on the AP wire.

The polls the day before the election showed a close race; Paul lagged a few points behind Flanagan, but there was a large undecided vote. If the weather was favorable on Election Day and the turnout in the black wards was heavy, Tony predicted they would win 58 percent of the vote.

Paul sat in their suite and watched the early returns on television, preparing his acceptance speech.

Tony came into the room, his hand clutching tally sheets. "We've cracked the black wards, Paul. We're going to beat them. Not by much, but we're going to win!"

Nora's arms were instantly around him. Paul kissed her then, and slipped away from her. He strode to the window. Outside, the El train creaked slowly down Wabash Avenue. This was it. This was the start of what he had been working toward his entire life.

Flanagan's phone call conceding the election was almost anticlimactic. It was the challenge, playing the odds, that excited Paul.

Then Richard Daley was on the television screen. "I want to congratulate young Paul Cronin for the fine race he ran. We need more men like him in Cook County politics. He'll do the Democratic Party proud in Springfield."

"I'm coming home with you," Elizabeth said as they left the ballroom of the Palmer House and walked out into the clear Chicago evening.

"I don't know that I'm up to it tonight, Elizabeth," Mike Cronin said. "This campaign's damn near drained me."

"At our age, Michael, there ought to be times when it's enough for two people just to huddle in each other's arms."

So they held each other in his king-size bed and watched the full moon turn the buildings on Michigan Avenue silver.

"I'll give it to you straight, Michael," she said, her fingers cool and soothing on his face.

"When haven't you?" He searched for a laugh and couldn't find one.

"I want to marry you. I'm not saying I'll dump you if you don't marry me. I'll come around as long as you want. Yet I think you'd better marry me. I'll keep you alive for a long time and make every day of it worth while." She snuggled closer to him. "Without me I don't think you're going to make it for long."

A deep groan welled up within him. She was right. Yet there was no way.

"And you've got to stop worrying about those sons of yours. Leave them alone. Let them live their own lives. Forget about Paul's political career. He's a sure success, even though he's not half the man you are. I don't know Sean, but I'm sure he can take care of himself. Forget them."

"I live for them," he pleaded.

"Live for me."

She was right. "You make it sound tempting, Elizabeth. I'll have to think."

"I'll be waiting." She sounded disappointed but by no means defeated.

CHAPTER
── SIXTEEN ──
1964

The first committee meeting of the Birth Control Commission, established by Pope John and expanded by Pope Paul, was in May of 1964. Among the new members added for this session were Thomas Shields, a Chicago gynecologist and a specialist in fertility, and Father Sean Cronin, who was finishing his doctoral work on the history of marriage at Pontifical Gregorian University. It was a bizarre crowd of people gathered in the plain, high-ceilinged room. Sunlight streamed through the large window, turning the slightly dull plaster that seemed to mark all Vatican buildings into a glowing yellow. Seated around the brown conference table were bishops from Africa, theologians from Western Europe, a demographer from the Philippines, an English cardinal, and some frankly bored curial staff members, including the Alessandrinis' friend, Umberto Menelli.

Everyone spoke in his own language, and there was no simultaneous translation. Sean could get along passably well in Italian and was struggling with French, but German was completely beyond him. The meeting which should have been exciting was ponderous and dull. Moreover, much to Sean's astonishment, the committee seemed to have decided that the entire birth-control doctrine was now under question. And even more to his astonishment and dismay, the weight of opinion around the table seemed to favor the possibility of change.

After the meeting, at which little was accomplished, Tom

Shields and Sean shook hands warmly. Tom had arrived a few days before, but there had been no chance to meet and talk.

"Everyone's fine." Tom's face wrinkled in a broad grin. "Nora's already hitting golf balls around the country club. Noreen's trying to walk—a little dynamo if I ever saw one. Everyone is still thrilled by Paul's victory, especially Maggie. She worked her tail off for Paul during the campaign."

Poor Maggie, Sean thought to himself, the moth flying too closely to the Cronin flame.

"My father is satisfied, I suppose?"

"You know your father. Absolutely jubilant about Paul's winning the nomination one night, and calm and serene at a board meeting the next day."

They were interrupted by a French theologian who had been hostile to Sean throughout the meeting. He was a bald-headed mean-looking man with sunken dark eyes. After a few minutes of polite conversation, the theologian said to Sean, "Monsignor wishes promotion in the Church. No?"

"Not in particular," Sean said.

"But Monsignor wears a cassock as only the curialists do, and he supports their position, does he not?" In addition to a sneer, the Frenchman had bad teeth.

"I am not a monsignor." Sean's tone was icy. "I wore a cassock today because this is my first meeting and I did not know what the proper attire would be. I support no one's position but my own." He turned his back on the Frenchman, who shrugged his shoulders and glided away.

"Pleasant cuss," Tom said.

"At the risk of sounding like my father, how the hell was I supposed to know that even the goddamned English Cardinal would wear a sport shirt?"

A continent away, Paul Cronin ambled down the street toward the Shields' Oakland Beach house. Tom Shields was in Rome, the children were at play school, and Nora was on the golf course. When he wanted to see Maggie, as he did now, he merely had to walk down Lake Shore Drive to the Shields' Dutch colonial house. It was a beautiful replica of the past, protected by a huge concrete seawall, against which the silver waves were beating on this windy Thursday of the Fourth of July weekend.

He slipped around to the side entrance of the house. No point in letting anyone see him go in. Maggie was a useful sexual resource. Nora was recovered now and they had resumed their uneventful sex life, but Paul needed other women.

Maggie was waiting for him in her frilly fourposter bed. She had been notified fifteen minutes earlier to prepare for his arrival. She held a wineglass to her mouth, although it was only ten o'clock in the morning. The Beatles were playing on the phonograph, and she wore only lace panties as a token of her residual modesty.

She kissed him, a hungry, longing kiss. "Am I better than Nora?" she asked. It was the first time she had ever mentioned Nora in these circumstances.

Paul was startled. "God, yes," he said.

"I knew I was!" She said it triumphantly and took a long sip of her wine. "Why don't you divorce her and marry me?"

Paul started to undress. "You know that kind of talk is off limits," he said cautiously. "It would be the end of my career, Nora and Tom would be destroyed, the children . . ." He sat down and drew her into his arms.

His kisses became demanding. He could sense that her sexual need had driven all other thoughts from her mind. A pleasant way to put an end to a dangerous conversation.

They were too involved in their lovemaking to hear the doorbell ring, but not so much so to miss Nora's voice at the foot of the stairs.

"Hey, Maggie. Are you up there?"

There was a rattle of golf clubs as Nora, who disdained a caddy cart, dropped her clubs somewhere in the Shields' parlor.

"Oh, my God," gasped Maggie. She slipped out from under Paul, pulled on a robe, brushed a few unruly strands of her curly blond hair away from her ashen face, and raced down the stairs.

"I went back to bed after the kids ate their breakfast. . . ." Maggie was stammering.

Oh, good God, woman, Paul pleaded mentally. Cool it. Don't let her think you've got something to hide.

"I stopped by to see if you want to come to the club with me and then have lunch—"

"Oh, no . . . no, no," Maggie said.

"Suit yourself." Nora sounded puzzled but not upset.

When Maggie returned to the bedroom, Paul was hungry for her. The danger had turned him on like a powerful aphrodisiac.

Yet he told himself, as she responded to his fervor, that something had to be done about Maggie. She was becoming too demanding.

On the morning of Noreen Marie Cronin's first birthday party, her mother opened a letter from the Collegio Santa Maria dell'Lago, Via Sardegna 44, Roma. Sean's infrequent letters were eagerly awaited, and Paul did not mind if she opened them before he came home. Her one-year-old, a vigorous, even-tempered little comedian, clung to her mother's legs as she collected the morning mail and resolutely resisted her progress back to the parlor. "Let go, Noreen," her mother pleaded absentmindedly. "I have a letter from Uncle Sean."

Noreen did not let go; mommies, after all, were for hugging. So Nora dragged her to the chair and began to read Sean's letter.

> *Dear Paul and Nora,*
> *The third session of the Vatican Council is almost over, and I'm even more confused than before about the state of the Church. I've slowly come around to the view that we need profound and systematic changes. As Nora says, the Church has lost touch with the problems and needs of contemporary human beings. Yet I don't like the change that's going on here. It's too abrupt, too European, and, if you want to know what I really think, too intellectual. There is no serious attempt to maintain continuity with the traditions of the past. Paul VI makes matters worse by his nervous hand-wringing. I find that I'm against everything. I don't like the Pope. I don't like the Roman Curia, who are a bunch of cheap political fixers. I don't like the European theologians, who are arrogant, and I don't like many of the bishops, who pretend to know everything when they don't know anything.*
> *The Cardinal is a shining light among them, a man with taste, respect for the past, and a strong sense of the problems of the present. He's right when he says that the Church has to change, and he also has the pragmatic sense to realize that if the change gets out of hand we're going to have chaos. But the change is already out of hand. The melancholy complaints of the Pope, the wild ideas on the theologians, the endless maneuvering of the Curia, and the stupidity of the bishops are all creating one monumental catastrophe. And the parish priests are going to have to be the ones to pick up the pieces.*

I'm appalled at the grimness and depression of what I have written. I've been here too long. Some days I almost think St. Jadwiga's was better. I'll be eager to get home after Christmas and begin my new work.

And that brings me to something I don't quite know how to tell you. Archbishop McCarthy has made me a vice-chancellor. Jimmy McGuire also. He is to be responsible for administration and I for personnel. It will probably be announced a few days after you get this letter. I told the Cardinal that I was far more conservative than he and therefore unqualified for the position.

He paid no attention. He said it was good to balance his liberalism with my conservatism and then smiled that quick smile of his. I'm never quite sure what it means.

Anyway, I'll be back soon to a job that may make St. Jadwiga's look easy. And Happy Birthday, of course, to Noreen.

God bless.

> *Sean.*

Nora put the letter on the coffee table in front of her, tears in her eyes. "Noreen, your Uncle Sean is a stupid sonofabitch. Unqualified, indeed."

Noreen responded with a bright one-year-old giggle.

The night before he was to return to the United States, Sean had supper with the Alessandrinis, or rather with the *Principessa,* since Francésco was unaccountably absent. No particular explanation for his absence was offered. The *Principessa* received him in a black minidress with a deep V-neck and a tightly fitting bodice. Warning bells clanged in Sean's head as soon as she opened the door. He ought to run.

He did not run, however.

The meal was a long, leisurely affair. The *Principessa* flirted outrageously with Sean as she always did. It was eleven o'clock before the espresso was served in the parlor. The lights were dim and Sean's head was reeling from the excellent wine.

"So," she said, "you go home tomorrow to America to be 'Vice-Chancellor for Personnel,' whatever that means in your foolish, capitalistic Church. You have no concern for leaving Angèlica brokenhearted in Rome."

"I doubt that you will be brokenhearted for long," he said, trying to clear his head. "Anyway, I'll be back for meetings of the

Birth Control Commission, and I suspect the Cardinal is going to use me as an envoy."

She took his hand in hers. Her fingers began to caress his arm. "It's nice to have you all alone," she said, leaving no doubt as to her meaning. She leaned against him, available, inviting.

He put one arm around her and felt the expansion and contraction of the back of her rib cage beneath his hand. "You're a beautiful woman, Angèlica. You've been a bright spot in two rather dismal years. I hope you don't mind if I say thanks, but no thanks." He kissed her forehead lightly and rose unsteadily to his feet.

Much to his surprise, she did not seem offended. "My Francésco will be so unhappy to have missed you tonight. I will absolutely insist that his fool work at the Vatican does not keep him from dinner the next time you come." Her smile glittered briefly. "It has been a marvelous evening, *caro mio*. And I will miss you." She hastily pecked his cheek.

As he walked rather uncertainly across the dark and deserted Piazza Farnese, Sean wondered what would have happened to him if he had turned down an American woman who had made herself so vulnerable. Say, an Irish-American woman from Chicago. He would be on the floor, wounded and bleeding.

It was only when he had returned to the Via Sardegna, however, that it occurred to him that he was probably neither the first nor the last priest to be caught in the *Principessa* Alessandrini's web. The thought disappointed him.

In February, Sean sat in the tiny office on the second floor of the Chicago chancery, stiff and uncertain in his new role as Vice-Chancellor for Personnel. There was a foot of snow on the streets of Chicago and the temperature was well below zero. Across from him sat his classmate, Peter Flynn. Either Peter wanted to transfer from the affluent parish in Lake Forest to which he was assigned or he was about to leave the priesthood. Sean's heart sank. Transfers he could handle easily. Defections from the priesthood shocked and horrified him.

They talked a bit about the seminary, about Rome, and about Lake Forest. Then there was an anxious pause.

Peter broke the silence. "I'm going to leave the priesthood and marry. There's a woman in the parish. She's a widow with four children. We love each other. If I could marry her and stay in the priesthood, I would. The life is too lonely. There is no one who will love me if I remain a priest, and Martha . . . well, Martha has made me want to live again."

"What about your promise to the Church?" Sean asked bluntly.

"I want to keep my promise to the Church." Peter had tears in his eyes. "The Church won't let me. If I could be a married priest, I'd stay on in the priesthood."

"I don't think you would, Peter." Sean's voice was cold. "You've had two of the best assignments in the archdiocese. Good people. Good pastors. Good fellow priests. You're unhappy in the priesthood because of something deep inside yourself. Now this woman comes along and provides you with an excuse—"

"Don't call Martha 'this woman,'" Flynn said.

"You're going to bed with her, I suppose?"

"Is that a question I have to answer to apply for a dispensation?"

"No, it's a question you have to answer if you don't want to be suspended from your parish at this moment for causing a scandal among the laity. Do you think you could carry on an illicit love affair with one of your parishioners and not shock the rest of the parish?" Sean had no evidence that there was scandal in the parish, but he was willing to wager that there was, and Flynn did not deny the charge.

"You're a vindictive bastard!"

"Because I believe that priests should keep their promise and not screw the first available woman parishioner who comes along?"

White and tense with anger, Peter Flynn rose from his chair. "Fuck your dispensation!"

Sean stared at the open doorway through which Flynn had stormed. He had handled things even worse than he feared he would.

He walked down the corridor to Jimmy McGuire's office.

"Congratulations," said that cheerful cleric as Sean slipped into the chair across from him.

"For what?"

"The boss has just made us monsignors. His secretary tells me the documents have come through from Rome. You'll look gorgeous in purple buttons, my boy. Your father will celebrate, and Nora's eyes will widen with admiration."

"Leave Nora out of it," said Sean.

"What happened?"

"Peter Flynn."

"Oh, yeah." Jimmy dropped a stack of files into a drawer of his desk. "I heard he was thinking of leaving. Chew him out?"

"I made him so angry that he didn't even apply for a dispensation."

Jimmy shrugged philosophically. "No point in chewing them out once they've made up their minds. In fact, no point in chewing them out, no matter what the circumstances."

"He seemed so damned self-righteous, so proud of himself because he'd been able to get a woman into bed with him."

"If you always doubted that you could, maybe that's something to be proud about."

"I don't know what's going wrong with the world and the Church, Jimmy. Drugs, violence, student protests, barbaric music, kids sleeping around, priests saying Mass with cocktails and hors d'oeuvres, nuns and priests shacking up during summer institutes, half-naked dancing on the altar during services . . . the world's going crazy."

Jimmy sighed. "The world has always been crazy. Go easy on people like Peter. There, but for the grace of God, and that sort of thing."

"I'd never do anything like that," Sean insisted. "Maybe I'm old-fashioned, Jimmy. When I make a commitment, I keep it."

CHAPTER
—— SEVENTEEN ——
1965

On a sticky, humid, partially overcast Thursday afternoon in late July, Paul Cronin walked impatiently back and forth in front of the broken-down South Shore railroad station in the downtown slums of Michigan City, Indiana. The escalating war in Vietnam seemed far away, as did the race riots in the nation's big cities.

Down the street, with considerable huffing and puffing, the battered old orange trolley train turned the corner and chugged to a weary stop in front of the station. Chris Waverly stepped off uneasily, her light green dress wilted and her blond hair rumpled. "So that's what it was like fifty years ago!" she said. "I'm sorry about those articles I've written in favor of mass transportation. Give me the auto and the airplane any time. Hi, lover boy." Her kiss was lingering and inviting. "See how much I'm willing to suffer just to spend a few hours with you?"

Paul looked anxiously around to make sure that none of his neighbors were at the train stop. He had pleaded with Chris to rent a car, but she assured him that she would lose her way in the wilderness of northern Indiana. "I'm sorry I couldn't come to Chicago. I didn't know that you'd be in town, and Nora left me in charge of the girls."

"Have I complained? I've always wanted to see your summer hideaway."

On the lakeshore the haze was lifting and the overcast blowing away. The winds were changing as promised, and the humidity would be gone in a few hours. Paul pushed the accelerator of his Porsche hard, and the car swept down the drive at sixty-five miles an hour.

"You're going a bit fast, aren't you?" Chris asked, clinging to his arm. "Slow down. I'll keep. Besides, these dunes and lake of yours are kind of pretty."

Paul reduced the speed slightly. He loved the thrill of reckless driving just as he loved the thrill of a reckless love affair carried on while his wife was in Chicago. The excitement of the risk he was taking was almost as good as the excitement of making love to Chris again.

At the Michianna Beach Inn, a few miles down the lake from his home, a room had been reserved for "Mr. and Mrs. Waverly." Fortunately, Paul had never been at the sleek new luxury motel. The Oakland Beach Irish preferred their own homes and the old familiar restaurants.

It was a bad day for Chris to show up with little notice. Nora had impulsively driven to Chicago to "do something" about Mary's persistent cough. It was both the housekeeper's and the baby-sitter's day off. Only at the last minute had Paul been able to draft the fifteen-year-old Hanrahan girl to watch the children. He felt rushed and anxious.

Chris was in no mood to be hurried. Their lovemaking was leisurely and fulfilling.

When Paul got up from the bed to get dressed, Chris said, "Sneaking around like this is exciting, isn't it, Paul?" He could not resist the arms stretched out to him like a hungry child's. Instantly he was back in her arms and back in bed once again.

With careful solemnity, Noreen Cronin began to negotiate the stairs from her house down to the beach, one step at a time, both feet securely on each step before she tried the next one. She kept her balance with her sand shovel, waving it in the air like a royal scepter.

Noreen knew that she was not supposed to go to the beach by herself. She was being a bad girl. Yet today everyone was being bad. Even Marcie Hanrahan's mother was bad. She had come along the beach shouting that Marcie had to go home and help with the supper, and she should "this very instant bring those little brats up to their father."

Noreen didn't like being called a little brat. She didn't like being left alone in the house with her sister Eileen, who was so busy with her friend Nicole that she wouldn't play even one game with Noreen.

If Eileen was being bad, then she could be bad too. Anyway, she had to finish her sand castle before Daddy came home. Daddy would like the castle.

She continued her careful descent.

"It's a nice area." Chris was carefully arranging her makeup as Paul rushed her back to the South Shore depot. "I think I'm going to enjoy living here."

Paul was baffled by Chris's assumption that he was going to divorce Nora and make her his wife. He had never given her any reason to think so. "Nora would never give up the house," he said, trying to make a joke of it. "And even if she did, we wouldn't dare live there."

"How terribly provincial, but then this is the provinces, isn't it? I suppose you and I don't belong in the provinces anyway." She put away her compact and squeezed his leg. "But we do belong together, don't we, Paul?"

Paul groaned inwardly. Maybe they did belong together, but he could not possibly marry her.

When Paul returned home, Eileen and Nicole Shields were in the recreation room listening to records. "Everything okay? Where's the baby-sitter?"

"Her mother came and made her go home," Eileen said, with manifest disinterest. "So we came up to the house."

"Smart girl." Paul pecked at her approvingly. "The baby in her room?"

"I suppose so."

Paul mixed himself a gin and tonic as a reward for the tensions that had accompanied the pleasures of the afternoon. Chris worried him. She had seemed a little bit too flaky today. She couldn't really believe that he would give up his family for her.

He went to his room and put on a swimsuit. A little dip in the lake would do very nicely. First he would make sure about Noreen.

Gin and tonic in hand, he pushed open the door of Noreen's

room. She wasn't there. He checked the rest of the house. No Noreen.

He rushed back to the rec room. "Where is she? Where's the baby?" he shouted at Eileen.

"I have to go home now." Nicole scurried quickly out the door and down the steps.

Eileen's face turned ashen. "Isn't she in her room?"

"You little fool. You've lost the baby!"

"You lost her," Eileen shouted back. "You went away when Mommy said you should watch us."

He slapped her and pushed her across the room. Then he raced out of the house.

He cut a furious path through the sun worshipers on the beach. Everyone had seen Noreen. The lifeguard thought she had walked up the beach. Two mothers thought she had walked down the beach. Some teenagers swore that they had seen some men take her on a boat. A younger child was certain that Noreen was somewhere building sand castles near the house.

Martin O'Riordan, an ancient Oakland Beach patriarch, announced pompously to the crowd that was gathering around Paul, "We'll organize a search party to find her."

"You goddamn fool!" Paul yelled. He was becoming irrational. "If you'd been watching her in the first place, she wouldn't be lost." He turned and ran, paying little attention to the murmurs of astonishment that trailed after him.

Halfway down the beach he lost his wind and sank into the sand, breathing heavily. Oh, God, please help me find her. Nora will never forgive me.

Then he trudged slowly back to the house. Must get hold of yourself . . . call the police . . . get professional help . . . can't crack up. . . .

Three teenagers were sitting at the foot of the stairs to the Cronin house. They stood up as he approached them.

"Hi, Mr. Cronin," one of the boys said, a tall slender lad whose name Paul remembered was Bob.

"Have you seen my baby?" he asked desperately.

"Sure. We found her sleeping on the dunes. She said she wanted to come home, so Michelle carried her here."

"Where is she?" Paul exploded.

"We brought her up to the house and Eileen put her to bed," Michelle said.

Paul dashed up the steps and into the house.

"You could at least say thank you," Michelle hollered after him, with all the Irishwoman's rage at injustice. "We saved her."

The next afternoon Paul was relaxing on the balcony with the Sunday papers, thanking all the saints in heaven that he had calmed down before Nora returned. Tom and Maggie had come for dinner the night before and not a word had been said about the disaster of the afternoon.

Nora came up from the beach from her daily swim, a towel around her shoulders.

"You made a real ass out of yourself yesterday, didn't you?" she began without any preliminaries. "You hurt Eileen, ranted at your neighbors, insulted that old fool O'Riordan, and acted like an insensitive bastard in front of the teenagers who saved your daughter. Don't look surprised. You should know you can't keep anything secret in a resort community."

"It was all a misunderstanding. . . ." He searched desperately for an excuse.

"It sure was. I want to know the name of the misunderstanding. Don't bother lying to me. I can tell by the look on your face that you were with another woman."

Paul was intimidated by her deadly composed voice.

"Well—er—now, Nora, it really isn't a very important—I mean, that is—"

"Who is she?" Nora demanded.

To his amazement, Paul found himself blurting out the name. "Chris Waverly." He reached for the empty beer can on the end table next to him and then put it down nervously. "It's not an important relationship, Nora. I mean, it isn't serious. You shouldn't—"

"Which one of us leaves?"

"Which one of us leaves where?"

"This house, this minute. Either you get out or I do."

Paul stood up awkwardly. "I guess I can move back to Glenwood Drive." He hesitated.

"Back to a hotel room in Chicago. I don't want you in this house, and I don't want you on Glenwood Drive either."

"Now, Nora, this isn't the end of everything. I'm sure we can work it out. There's no reason—"

"Get out!" She lost her composure and began to scream at him. "Get out and stay out!"

There was a stack of problems on Sean Cronin's desk that Monday morning. Two more applications for dispensations from the priesthood; three letters, two of them signed, accusing priests and nuns of fornication; a signed petition of complaint against the principal of a Catholic school in a northwestern suburb, claiming that she had ridiculed the doctrine of the Assumption to a group of children on August 15; and a complaint from a pastor that his curate was telling people in the confessional that birth control was not a sin.

Sean tore up the anonymous letter and threw it in the wastebasket. One of the priests who was accused of having a lover, he noted, was fifty-seven years old.

"No fool like an old fool," he muttered to himself. Then he felt ashamed of his snap judgment. Signed or not, a complaint was a form of character assassination that he ought not to believe until he had more evidence.

The telephone on the desk next to him jangled. He picked it up and heard the unmistakable voice of his father: "What the hell is Nora doing throwing Paul out of the house? She won't even speak to him. All she would say to me was that he can have his whores."

"I haven't heard anything. But I think we can assume that if Nora's thrown Paul out, he must have given her good reason."

"That's not the point. The point is you should fix it up. They'll both listen to you." The phone line went dead. Sean eased his phone back on its cradle and it rang almost at once.

"Cronin here," he said, knowing full well that it was a Cronin on the other end of the line too: Paul Cronin, this time.

Sean saw his brother in the office in the cathedral rectory rather than in the chancery. If Paul felt any strain, he did not show it. Indeed, he spent ten minutes discussing the National League pennant race and the St. Louis Cardinals. Finally, almost as an afterthought, he said, "I suppose Nora has talked to you?"

"No," said Sean. "She has not."

"We have a problem. She knows that I've been seeing another woman. She's thrown me out."

"Oh?"

"It's one of those things that happens. You know what I mean. Not a big deal at all. A reporter from Washington."

Sean could hardly believe his brother would be so casual about his infidelity. "I presume it's not a serious relationship?"

"Just a passing thing. Nora's a wonderful wife, but sometimes marriage and sex are just not the same thing."

"Well, what do you want me to do about it?" The dull, dark office with its heavy old furniture perfectly reflected Sean's mood at the moment.

"She won't talk to me. . . . I thought you might be able to persuade her to give me another chance."

"What makes you think Nora will listen to me?"

Paul seemed surprised at the question. "You're a priest, aren't you? Of course she'll listen to you. Aren't priests supposed to help people put their marriages back together again?"

Sean sighed. "I'll see what I can do."

It was a crisp, sunny August morning in the middle 70s, with a light breeze blowing off the lake and a faint touch of autumn in the air. Mary and Eileen were playing on the beach. Nora and Noreen were building sand castles. Sean watched them silently for some time from the bottom of the stairs. There was no doubt that Noreen was the foreman on this construction job.

"Uncle!" She gestured with her small shovel.

Nora, a sweat shirt over her bikini, glanced up. "I suppose I should have expected you."

Sean joined her by the sand castle. "Run along and play with Mary and Eileen," Nora instructed Noreen. "Uncle Sean is going to preach me a sermon."

Sean sat next to her on the beach towel. She drew her long, elegant legs up beneath her chin and said calmly, "Okay, let's have it."

"I'm not going to preach a sermon, Nora. You have every right to be furious."

"Your brother is a spoiled, self-indulgent little boy. The fool can't even understand why I'm angry." Her voice was flat and hard.

"There are times in every marriage when things are difficult—"

"Now comes the part in the sermon about the importance of commitment. You always were very good, Sean, in lecturing about commitments."

"I believe in them," said Sean. "Human life is impossible unless we keep our commitments. Paul needs you. He says he'll fall apart without you, and I'm sure that's true."

"Of course it's true," she snapped. "Right now I'd like to see him fall apart."

"Don't you love him?"

Nora dug at the sand with a tiny twig. "Love him? What's love? I've produced three children that are his. I have some feelings of affection for him. I suppose I'll take him back when I calm down. You're the expert on love, Sean. Does all that add up to love? Or does it merely add up to making the best of a bad bargain?"

Sean felt enormous tenderness for her. He wanted to put his arm around her shoulder and reassure her. Instead, he said, "That's just the way it appears now, Nora. It will get better."

"The hell it will."

"Paul says there won't be any more—"

"He probably means that promise. Maybe he'll even keep it for a few weeks."

Sean took a deep breath. "Nora, there's no way I can say this delicately, so I'm not going to try. Is the relationship sexually fulfilling to you?"

Her eyes turned hard. "None of your goddamn business."

"I know it's none of my business, but I'm making it my business."

"You want me to turn into a sex kitten and compete with his women?"

"You're a passionate woman, Nora. Your life will be desperately unfulfilling if you don't find an outlet for those passions."

"Listen to the priest turn sex expert." Her words dripped with sarcasm. "Do you want me to use Paul for sexual kicks the way he uses me? Is that what you want? Very smart of you, because then I'll be cemented to him so strongly that the Cronin family won't have to worry about a scandal. Sex as cement, that's what you have in mind, isn't it?"

"Sex as love," said Sean hesitantly.

"Love doesn't enter into it at all," she said sadly. "Go away,

Sean. You preached your sermon. You invaded my privacy, undressed me, and made me look at myself so that I don't like what I see. I hope your brother and your father are happy with the results."

Sean stood up and brushed the sand off his slacks. "I didn't do it for them, Nora."

"Go away," she said. "I'll take him back when I calm down. Maybe she'd be better for him than I am. I don't know. Anyway, I made a commitment, and I'll stand by it till he walks out on me. Now go away and leave me alone."

That night, Sean found in the bottom of the drawer in his desk in the cathedral rectory a battered brown notebook that had once been his spiritual diary. It was a long time since he had made an entry.

> *In the middle course of life, as Dante said—well, maybe not quite the middle course yet—I do not like what I see. My father is becoming a difficult old man, demanding, unpredictable. My brother, whom I worshiped most of my life, has been well described by his wife as a spoiled, self-indulgent little boy. Nora is locked into a life of unhappiness and frustration, and I'm making a mess out of my job. I'm no more confident that you're out there listening than I've ever been, probably a little less confident. Not believing in you, I tried to believe in the Church; and now the Church I believed in is collapsing all around me. Not able to make a commitment to you, I made a commitment to the priesthood; and the priesthood is crumbling. I wonder if I ought not to leave like everyone else? I wonder if commitments—any commitment and every commitment—are not tragic mistakes.*

During a lull on the Sunday of the Labor Day weekend, while Nora was on the golf course and his daughters were firmly supervised by Maggie and Tom Shields on the beach, Paul managed to sneak a phone call to Chris Waverly at her Martha's Vineyard holiday retreat.

"Hi," she said. "Where have you been hiding?"

Paul started making excuses, but Chris cut him off. "Which of us is it going to be?" she said. "You've got to choose."

"She's my wife and the mother of my children, Chris. I can't leave her."

"You will sooner or later," Chris said. "We're two of a kind, Paul. You can't do without me, and I can't do without you."

As Paul talked to Chris on the phone, there was a strong pull in her direction. He knew that when the phone conversation was over, however, the opposite tug would be irresistible again. "She'll never let me go," he said defensively.

"You mean you're too much of a coward to try to break away."

"I'm sorry you feel that way, Chris." He tried to sound reasonable and adult.

"Have it your own way, Paul, but don't think you're going to get away from me so easily."

"What do you mean?" Paul sensed the Chinese bayonet in his gut once again.

"I mean that you can't discard me like yesterday's news. Sooner or later, I'm going to make you sorry for what you've done to me."

CHAPTER
—— EIGHTEEN ——
1965

In August, Sean received a phone call from Elizabeth Hanover, who wanted to talk with him. He proposed lunch or the cathedral rectory. She responded by suggesting that they meet on neutral ground—the Lincoln Park lagoon.

She wore dark brown slacks and a beige silk shirt. She showed faint signs of nervousness, unusual in such a normally cool woman.

They sat down on an old bench at the edge of a small green meadow. A few yards from them toddlers were playing under the careful eyes of young mothers in shorts and halters. "Are you on my side, or are you against me?" she asked bluntly.

"I'm on your side, of course. And priests don't bite, Elizabeth."

She laughed and relaxed. "Sorry. I've never talked to a priest before."

"What happens when you have one for a stepson?"

A faint tinge of color appeared in her cheeks. "I'm committed to your father, Sean. Does that offend you, a mistress committed to a man?"

"I want Dad to be happy. I've never seen him as happy as he is with you."

"Does it offend you that I'm your father's mistress?" She was testing him, poking at him to make sure he was human.

"You couldn't possibly offend me, Elizabeth."

"I think I'd like to have you for a stepson. If only I could get Jane out of the way."

"You think she's an obstacle?" Sean was surprised.

Elizabeth frowned. "I don't know how or why, but she has a strange hold on Michael."

"Perhaps we Cronins are more trouble than we're worth."

"No. From the first moment Michael came into that committee meeting, he owned me. Chemistry? Love at first sight? I don't know and I don't care."

Lucky Dad, Sean thought with a touch of envy. "He's mellowing, it seems to me."

"I met him at the right time. He doesn't have to dominate women any more, and I think he's giving up trying to run his sons' careers. He's letting go of things that are good to let go of. So he can live longer."

"With you to love him," Sean agreed.

Elizabeth Hanover's tears were like everything else about her—direct and straightforward. Sean put his arm around her until the tears were over.

"I've never been hugged by a priest before." She wiped away the last traces of her weeping.

"If you have a priest stepson, you'd better get used to it."

That night Sean dreamed about Mary Eileen. He awoke and groggily wondered if he had had this same dream every night. No, this one was different. His mother was still alive, but now his mother was Elizabeth. Then his father took her away from him, just as he had taken away Mary Eileen.

That couldn't have been in the dream before.

Sean did not go back to sleep.

Jane Cronin was buried at the time the Watts riots were taking place in Los Angeles and there was concern that the same sort of thing might occur on the South Side of Chicago.

At her instructions, the Mass was said at St. Ann's Church on Garfield Boulevard, now renamed after St. Charles Luwanga, an African martyr, a fact of which Jane was probably unaware or she would have changed her will.

There was some unease as the little group of mourners filed into the old church, even though the young pastor insisted that the neighborhood would never be another Watts. Nora wondered how the dilapidated old building could possibly ever have been an elegant church for the well-to-do lace-curtain Irish of the turn of the century. According to Sean, one of the pastors was quite mad and had not opened the parish hall to parishioners for twenty years. Now the black members of the parish were enjoying it immensely. God's ways were sometimes ironic.

Paul, Marty Hoffman, Ed Connaire, and Tom Shields were pallbearers. A badly shaken Mike Cronin leaned on Nora for support as they walked down the aisle of the church, with Eileen and Mary trailing behind them.

Sean's face was an unreadable mask, as though he were trying to find some meaning in his aunt's long, unhappy life.

To the bitter end, Jane had persisted in her animosity toward Nora, despite Nora's daily visits to Little Company of Mary Hospital. Nora was certain that Aunt Jane knew a secret from the family past, something that could hurt Sean badly. There were angry and knowing hints the last days in the hospital. In fact, a few hours before she died, Jane emerged from her half coma and said, "Things are never what they seem, Nora, never what they seem. Don't forget that. You'll all die like I'm dying, lonely and afraid." It sounded like a curse.

"What do you mean, Aunt Jane?" Nora felt a hand of ice momentarily touch her heart.

"I'm the only one who knows everything. Ed Connaire thinks he knows, but he doesn't know everything. It will all come out some day, and then we'll see how proud and mighty your priest really is."

Recalling the words, Nora shuddered as the body of Jane Cronin was committed to the earth from which she came. She resolved that she would corner Ed and find out what he was holding back.

After the final prayer, she told the two girls to talk to Uncle Sean and darted back into the group of mourners to find Ed Connaire. She had hesitated at first because of the occasion, but then she steeled herself and drew him away from the open grave.

"There were a lot of mysterious remarks in the last few days at the hospital," she began without preliminaries. "I know you haven't told us everything. I want to hear it all now."

The stocky contractor's hair was white, but his eyes were lively and his face almost unlined. "I've told you almost everything, Nora," he said.

"I want to know what's not covered by the 'almost.' I've got to know."

"Let sleeping dogs lie."

She shook her head. "If she's said those terrible things to me, she's said them to Sean. You know *he* won't let sleeping dogs lie. I should be prepared."

Connaire nodded. "You're right, I suppose. It was such a long time ago. No one meant anything bad."

"Ed," she said. There was a warning note in her voice.

"All right, Nora. There never was saying 'no' to you. . . . You see, Mary Eileen was a very sick woman after Paul was born. Always misty and vague. Well, one of the priests from New Albany stopped in often to see her at Oakland Beach when your father was away. They become good friends, very close. Too close, to hear Jane tell it. Then Mary Eileen became pregnant with Sean. No one was ever sure—"

"My God," Nora said in dismay.

"Personally, I think he's Mike's son, and Mike would never tolerate any other suggestion. Anyway, Mike had the young priest transferred to the other end of the state of Michigan."

"There couldn't have been anything." Nora leaned against a large burial monument.

Connaire cracked his massive knuckles. "Poor Mary Eileen thought there was. She was even more—er—depressed after Sean's birth. She tried to smother him in his crib one night. Mike stopped her just in time. She said Sean was a child of sin and God wanted him destroyed. . . . Nora, I swear that's all there is. She died in the car crash not long after that. I hope you won't tell Sean."

"Of course not." She was numb. "I hope he never finds out. I'll be ready if he does, though. Thanks, Ed."

Her daughters bounced over to her then, fascinated by the dramas written out on the headstones. Absently Nora listened to their babble, while she studied the inscription on a discreetly expensive monument at the edge of the Cronin plot:

> Mary Eileen Morrisey Cronin
> 1908–1934
> Beloved Wife and Mother
> She Left Us Too Soon

Twenty-six years old, four years younger than I am, Nora thought. She would be only in her middle fifties today.

Elizabeth Hanover's elegant dark head disappeared into one of the limousines. Nora thought, What would Mary Eileen think of you?

And of me?

Mike Cronin poured his second drink. Elizabeth would not approve, but she was not around tonight to approve or disapprove. He had told her he wanted to be alone with his grief, and she had quietly agreed. The two years with her had been the best since Mary Eileen. No, the best since his mother died. So much peace and warmth. Now he was free to marry her. Jane was dead and no one else would stop him. Tomorrow he would ask her. Sean would do the honors. Sean and Elizabeth got along famously.

Deep down in the darkest corner of his soul was a voice that told him that, Jane or not, he could never marry Elizabeth. He groaned aloud. Goddamn it, it wasn't fair.

Still, it was the way things were. He would call her tomorrow and tell her that they had better not see each other for a few weeks. Ease out gradually.

Maybe it had all been a mistake. Maybe he should have never listened to Jane. God, how can a man know what to do? At the time it had seemed the right thing to do, the only thing to do. Now he was no longer certain of anything.

BOOK V

Do not let your hearts be troubled. Trust in God still, and trust in me. There are many rooms in my Father's house; if there were not, I would not have told you. I'm going now to prepare a place for you; after I've gone and prepared your place, I shall return to take you with me, so that where I am you may be too.

—John 14:1–3

CHAPTER NINETEEN

1966

Nora Cronin celebrated her tenth wedding anniversary with her three daughters at Oakland Beach. She played golf in the morning, and in the afternoon, keeping one eye on the three little girls frolicking on the beach, she read Masters and Johnson's *Human Sexual Response*. She decided with some dissatisfaction that her own responses were distinctly below normal.

The thought was interrupted by the ringing of the telephone which she had installed on the sundeck. It was Sean, calling to wish her a happy anniversary from O'Hare Airport.

"Well, thanks for remembering," she said.

"Has Paul called?" he asked.

"Oh, sure. He called from London. London doesn't count on your tenth anniversary. Everybody's deserted me. You're going to Rome. Tom's already over there with Maggie. And my husband is on a junket in London. I'm relegated to the backwaters of southern Michigan. Serves me right, I guess."

"You don't sound brokenhearted," Sean said.

"Of course not. Anyway, thanks for calling. I'll be looking forward to seeing you in Rome week after next."

"I wanted to ask you about that. I'm not so sure that dragging me along is a good idea. Maybe you and Paul can use the time alone—"

"Don't be silly, Sean. You'll make a good tour guide, and Paul has his heart set on the old threesome being together again."

The truth was, Nora thought as she hung up, she was as ambivalent as Sean about the trip to Europe. She wanted to see Italy. Uncle Mike had forbidden her to tour Europe when she was in college: "too dangerous for a young girl." Then she had not wanted to leave the children alone when they were young. But Paul's desire for the "old threesome" to travel through Italy together worried her. As she and Paul drifted further and further apart, the outside walls of the tightly sealed house in her brain labeled "Sean Cronin" had started crumbling. She was not so much afraid of Sean as she was afraid of herself with him. Perhaps it was the result of having passed her thirtieth birthday.

She pulled off her shirt, made sure the straps on her swimsuit were properly adjusted, told the baby-sitter to keep a close eye on the girls, and plunged into the lake for her half-mile swim.

Paul had been an instant success in the state legislature, winning high marks from both the Daley Democrats and the independents for his energy and enthusiasm. Nora was surprised and impressed by how much he loved the rough-and-tumble of legislative politics: the whispered cloakroom conversations, the long barroom sessions, the late-night phone calls in which the work of politics was really accomplished. He was good at it, all right.

She had been impressed, too, by his liberalism and compassion. It was not what she had expected from the man she married. She was sorry to see it slipping away now that the Mayor was dangling a big plum in front of him.

The week before, the *Sun-Times* had called editorially for a new aviation commissioner to "straighten out the mess at O'Hare." Then the paper went on to recommend that the Mayor appoint someone of "proven ability," such as State Senator Paul Cronin. It praised Paul's war record, his service in the Kennedy administration, his legislative ability, and his "proven compassion," none of which even to his wife seemed grounds for turning over the city's airports to his supervision.

Paul was horrified and promptly called a friend in City Hall to pass the word to the Mayor that he was not behind the article. The word came back that the Mayor knew that he wasn't, but would Paul be interested in the job?

"It would be a great challenge," Paul had replied.

Nora agreed that it would be an important step in his career, yet she hated to see his newfound concern for the poor and the oppressed disappear so quickly.

Later, after her swim and after the children were properly showered, she opened a bottle of champagne to drink a toast to her anniversary. Would the next ten years be like the last ten years? Soon Noreen would be in school and Nora would have time on her hands. She had better find something to do, or she would turn into a bored old bitch.

She felt a slight shudder of fear as she sipped the gaily bubbling liquid.

Paul Cronin celebrated his tenth wedding anniversary by making love to Maggie Shields in her room at the George V in Paris.

Flying back to London late that evening to continue his study of local government in England, he decided that he would end the relationship. The pleasure of their sex had been marred for him by Maggie's plea that he leave Nora for her.

Even worse, Maggie had insisted on taking some pills before they made love. She had purchased them from a drug dealer on the Left Bank. Marijuana was one thing. This was something else. Paul sensed that Maggie was tottering on the brink of some kind of spectacular action. He didn't want to be near her when it happened.

Why, he wondered, did he always return to Maggie despite his resolutions to stop seeing her? It wasn't the sex. It was good, but he had had better.

Now there was a look of hopelessness in her eyes. He did not want to be even partly responsible for that hopelessness. He would finish the affair for good this time. Cut it off before it got totally out of hand.

A vague thought passed through his mind. How long had that emptiness lurked in her moody brown eyes? He exorcised the thought by smiling at the pretty Air France cabin attendant and ordering a second drink.

Tom Shields waited for Sean at a sidewalk café on the Via della Conciliazione, the Tiber on his right and the great silver dome of St. Peter's on his left. He had picked up Sean, battered and worn from a delayed Alitalia trip, at Fiumicino airport the previous afternoon. He had taken the priest to Chicago House on the Via

Sardegna, told him to get a good night's sleep, and promised to meet him whenever he awakened the following morning. Tom was staying at the Columbus Hotel, next to the sidewalk café, because it was close to the committee meeting place. When Maggie came down from Paris in a few days they would move to the more luxurious Hassler. The trip through Europe with Maggie had been something less than a total success. She had complained about the inconvenience of travel and the inadequacies of even deluxe hotel accommodations, and she was unimpressed by the museums and monuments that fascinated him, although she did enjoy the night life and the expensive department stores.

Tom drained his cup of espresso and signaled the waiter for a refill as a light blue Lancia pulled up by one of the elaborate lampposts on the outer sidewalk of the Conciliazione. Sean, dressed in a light gray suit and a navy blue turtleneck, emerged from the car, turned around, and kissed—or, more precisely, was kissed by—a very pretty woman. Tom Shields was stunned.

Sean, grinning broadly, slipped between two elderly couples and joined Tom at the tiny table.

"Who was that?" Tom asked.

"Oh, just a princess I happen to know—the *Principessa* Alessandrini, as a matter of fact." Sean waved his hand as though he were kissed by a princess every day.

Actually, he knew that he should stay away from Angèlica. She was becoming an obsession with him, proof of how badly his years in Rome had affected his self-discipline. His fantasies about possessing her were vivid and explicit. She had even found her way into his dreams, often becoming confused with his mother. When he awoke he had to sort them out, to insist to himself that one woman was very much alive and one was dead.

"I'm not sure about you, Sean," Tom said. "I suspect that woman may be trying to seduce you."

Sean sat next to him at the table. "May be? She's very definitely trying to seduce me—quite obvious about it." He grinned. "Don't worry. I'm immune to that sort of thing."

Yes, if ever there was a man immune to womanly charm, Tom Shields thought, it was Sean Cronin.

"How's Maggie?" Sean asked.

Tom had never discussed his problem with anyone, but Sean was so warm and seemed so genuinely interested. "Up and down, to tell you the truth. Maggie gets depressed a lot. We had a suicide attempt a few months ago. Worries the hell out of me, and I don't know what to do about it."

"Maggie?" Sean asked incredulously.

"We've tried therapy but nothing seems to work. There's a strong strain of depression in it all, though the doctors tell me the suicide attempt was mostly an effort to gain attention. I'm afraid she might push her luck too far some day and not gain the attention quickly enough to save her."

"What's she depressed about?" Sean asked, putting his hand on Tom's arm.

"I think mostly it's the demands that life makes on her to grow up. At least that's what one of the doctors said, and it seems to me to be true. Maggie has been pouting since our wedding day. I've tried paying no attention to it, and I've tried giving it all my attention. No matter what I do, or the kids do, or what the doctors do, she's still fundamentally dissatisfied with her life. The suicide attempt, they tell me, was a protest against the injustices that have been done to her—only most of the injustices are in her mind."

"God!" exclaimed Sean, tightening the grip on Tom's arm. "How do you stand it?"

"I struggle on. I blame myself when I'm away from home, but then when I'm home it doesn't seem to make any difference. I brought her with me to Europe for this meeting, thinking a vacation together would help. Then she decided to stay in Paris, even though her big complaint about these meetings before has been that I left her alone too much. I don't know what to do. I sometimes think there's nothing I *can* do."

Sean wished that, like a magician pulling a rabbit out of a hat, he could offer an insight that would be of help to Tom. But he wasn't a magician. "There are some things we can't do anything about, Tom. We just have to let happen what's going to happen."

For no apparent reason, a picture of Nora flashed through his mind.

Roger Fitzgibbon had become more Roman than the Romans, wearing not only a cassock but a clerical hat and light overcoat even though it was the middle of a heat wave.

Roger had engineered an appointment in the Secretariat of State when Cardinal McCarthy had passed him over to make Jimmy

McGuire vice-chancellor. Sean knew that this must have galled his ambitious classmate, but there was never a sign of resentment when they crossed paths in the streets around the Vatican. Never offend a potential ally.

"Good to see you, Sean." Roger smiled his toothy grin. "Hear you're knocking them dead at the Birth Control Commission."

They were across the street from the gate to the Vatican Holy Office. The gray building looked down upon them as if with aloof disapproval.

"I hear you met my colleague, Martin Spalding Quinlan, at the Alessandrinis the other night," Roger continued. "You really are in high company, Sean. The Prince is one of the most influential of the black nobility."

"Is it true that Marty added the Spalding to his name because it sounds so Episcopal?"

Roger laughed easily. "I wouldn't know about that. But he's certainly going to be a bishop very soon. Somewhere in the West, I gather. The first step up. There are those in the Secretariat who think he may succeed our beloved Eamon some day."

"Deliver us from a faggot bishop," Sean said fervently.

Roger raised an eyebrow. "Oh, come now, Sean. That's not fair. Martin's taste is impeccable, of course, and he has a wonderful eye for line and texture, but you're sophisticated enough to know that doesn't mean anything."

Sean wondered whether or not Roger's remark meant that he agreed that Quinlan was homosexual. Regardless, Sean was certain that the man who might be his next archbishop would hear a detailed account of the conversation. Well, at least the *Principessa* Angèlica would never make a play for Martin Spalding Quinlan.

Back in his room at Chicago House on Via Sardegna, Sean recalled the final vote at the Birth Control Commission. Even the four or five bishops from Africa and Asia, about whom he was uncertain, went with the majority and voted for change. There were only seven votes for the minority, including the chairman's. A five-to-one landslide for those who thought change was possible. Paul VI had his lifeline if he wanted it.

"You do not vote, Monsignor Cronin?" the chairman had asked, his surprise evident.

"I can accept neither position." Sean weighed each word carefully. "You can show me as abstaining."

"Abstaining? What does that mean?" asked the chairman.

"It means not eating meat on Friday," joked Sir Hubert, the Aussie anthropologist.

Everyone in the room tittered.

"Just note that I was present and didn't vote," said Sean.

As the meeting was breaking up and handshakes and farewells were being exchanged, the greasy French theologian accosted him. "You try to please everyone, Monsignor Cronin, and you succeed in pleasing no one. That is the fate of ambitious men." He turned and walked away.

"Bastard," whispered Tom Shields.

"Maybe that fellow's right, Tom," Sean said, staring after the retreating Frenchman. "Maybe I *am* trying to please everyone."

"That's not what the young clergy in Chicago say about you. The young priest in our parish says that all his classmates have a tremendous amount of respect for your integrity. They say that even when you're wrong, you're wrong for the right reasons."

Sean was astonished. "The next thing you'll try to tell me is that I'm popular with the junior clergy."

"I won't try to tell you that because you're a sufficiently morose Irishman not to want to believe it. It's still true. Popular and, if the young clergy are typical, getting more popular."

If they found out about his birth control vote, Sean told himself in his room, his popularity would soon begin to wane. He looked up. Cardinal McCarthy was standing in his doorway.

"Good evening, Monsignor." The little man's voice was as mild and self-effacing as ever. The enormous responsibility of being Cardinal Archbishop of Chicago was taking its toll on him, but nothing seemed to shatter his serenity. "Need I say that everyone in the Curia is talking about your vote this morning. The cardinals I met with at the Sacred Congregation this evening were very much impressed."

"I didn't do it to impress anybody, Your Eminence," he said wearily.

"I'm sure you did not, Monsignor. Nonetheless, that was what you accomplished. Rome does not often value independence, much less integrity. Sometimes and on some issues, however, a man of independence and integrity has a uniquely powerful position."

Sean couldn't help but grin. "Your Eminence, what in the hell am I supposed to do with this unique power I've earned today?"

The Cardinal's smile lasted longer this time. "One of the things you're going to do, Monsignor Cronin, is come to Castel Gandolfo with me later on in the month, after your vacation. Macchi himself —the Pope's secretary—called me a little while ago and said the Pope very much wanted to have a personal talk with you. I trust you don't mind discussing the reasons for your vote with His Holiness?" Eamon McCarthy fingered the plain gold band on his right hand, as he always did when he was afraid he might be pushing one of his priests too hard.

"The Pope's the boss, Your Eminence. Of course I'll see him."

"I'm not sure that he's the boss any more, Monsignor Cronin. However, he still believes that he is. I will send word to Monsignor Macchi tomorrow to make the proper arrangements."

Only after the Cardinal left did Sean realize that he had refused to commit Sean to the meeting without asking him first.

Sean arranged for a dinner party when Nora arrived in Rome. He watched the interaction between Nora and the *Principessa* Angèlica as the full moon illuminated the late medieval church across from Sabatini's restaurant. The setting was perfect: pure white tablecloths, fine red wine, and the obvious admiration of the other people in the outdoor dining area. Francésco was being attentive to Paul, while Angèlica had clearly decided that there was little point in competing with Nora and chose, rather, to play the role of the gracious papal noblewoman. In turn, Nora entertained the party with stories of touch football games and swimming pool escapades with the Kennedy clan.

Both women ignored Maggie Shields, Angèlica from the very beginning and Nora after one or two unsuccessful attempts to bring her into the conversation. Maggie looked lovely. With her pretty eyes and even prettier smile, she could have been part of the entertainment. Instead, she remained distant.

By the time Nora had reached the point in her story where she had "clipped" Bob Kennedy, the other two women had faded into the background of Sean's imagination. So, too, had the other guests, and the piazza, and the moonlight, and the Tiber and the city of Rome and the world. Hard work at the Birth Control Commission meetings, weariness from his unwanted job at the Chicago chancery, disillusionment with the stupidity and venality of the Church bureaucracy, his lingering flirtation with the *Principessa*—all were taking their toll on his faith and his commitment. He knew now what he wanted. He wanted Nora. The trip through Italy with her would be a joy and a terror. With the courage that comes from despair, he didn't care what happened.

The rest of the world gradually faded back in, creating a halo around Nora's strong facial bones and radiant auburn hair. Everyone was laughing, even Angèlica, who had no idea what American football was about.

Sean felt the muddy waters of damnation swirl around him. What would happen, would happen.

CHAPTER TWENTY

1966

Despite its unquestioned elegance, the Royal Danieli Hotel on the Grand Canal in Venice served croissants that were something less than totally fresh, Nora Cronin decided. Nora hated the stingy continental breakfasts and thought that they were very little improved by the addition, as a concession to American tourists, of orange juice—at an extra charge, of course. For a woman who never had breakfast without bacon, this European custom was a profound affront.

Outside the window of her room, a fine gray mist hung over Venice, a city that was considerably less than she had expected.

She pushed aside her breakfast tray and climbed out of bed. Paul, who could not stand eating breakfast in his room, was downstairs, doubtless with Sean, who thought that breakfast in bed was too much a concession to human frailty.

Nora tugged off her badly rumpled gown and walked to the bathroom. A morning like this in Venice required a leisurely bath instead of a brisk shower.

Nora was uneasy about traveling with her two brothers—only they weren't really brothers; she had married one and was in love with the other. The trip was pleasurable but, in a deeply melancholy way, foreboding. It was absurd to think anything was going to happen . . . yet. . . .

She slipped into the soothing waters of the tub. Every woman has a built-in antenna that tells her when a man is undressing her in his imagination, Nora thought. She may be offended, frightened, or flattered, depending on who the man is. Nora was enormously flattered by the intensity in Sean's eyes when they occasionally flicked in her direction. She wanted to be undressed before him as much as he wanted her that way.

Normal human reaction, she told herself. Nothing unusual about it. Sean would never make a pass, especially not at his brother's wife. And anyway, he was a priest.

The door of the bathroom opened and Paul entered. He stood silently over the tub, regarding her with a mixture of awe and desire, a little boy in need of his mother's soothing affection. Filled with guilt at her adulterous thoughts of Sean, she reached out of the tub, unbuckled his belt, and slowly pulled down the zipper on his trousers.

They were having a late lunch in a quaint, charming fifteen-room hotel on the cliff just outside the town of Amalfi with its glittering little cathedral. On the western horizon the sun was setting fire to the deep blue waters of the Mediterranean. The remaining ten days of their vacation were going to be spent near Naples, relaxing and resting, as Sean had insisted, in small hotels and on mostly deserted beaches.

"Capri is out there in that direction." Sean pointed in the distance. "The sunsets are spectacular. You'll see why old Tiberius Caesar moved his headquarters from Rome to Capri."

"The Hyannis of his administration," Nora joked.

"Or the Johnson City," said Paul cynically. "I hope he had more comfortable beds in those days than we do in our rooms here."

"Signor Cronin?" The *proprietario* of the hotel leaned discreetly over their table. "A telephone call from America."

Paul scrambled up, as though eager to get away from the table, and quickly walked out of the dining room. He had been jumpy the past few days, barely able to hide his desire for the vacation to be over.

Sean looked at his brother's back uneasily. "I wonder who could be calling?" He would not meet Nora's eyes, afraid even to look at her while they were alone together.

Paul was back in a few moments, his eyes and his face glowing with happiness. "It was the Mayor's office. Daley's offering me the job of aviation commissioner."

Sean shook Paul's hand enthusiastically and Nora hugged him. Paul ordered a bottle of Nebbiolo, a sparkling Italian red wine. He accepted their toast with a smile.

"I don't want this to be the end of the vacation for you two," he said. "Daley only wants me home for a press conference. I'm sure I'll be able to fly right back. Do you think you can take care of Nora while I'm gone, Sean?"

"I'm sure she can take care of herself," Sean said. "I'll stay around until you get back, though."

"Wonderful!" Paul drained the Nebbiolo in his glass and filled it again. "It's a tremendously important job—three airports, one of them the busiest in the world. His Honor wants to expand operations at Midway again and thinks we may need a fourth airport. It's a terrific challenge."

Nora knew that she should protest. She ought to be at her husband's side at the press conference. The European vacation should come to an end. She should not stay at the Bay of Naples with Sean. Instead, she said, "You have to promise to hurry back." She felt like a hypocrite.

Nora had not been surprised when Paul called that morning to tell her that he would not be able to rejoin her, after all.

"I'm afraid I've got some bad news." Paul hadn't sounded as if he felt it was bad news. "The Mayor wants me to start tomorrow. He promised me a vacation afterward. He said he hoped you wouldn't be too angry."

Nora, barely able to hide the disappointment in her voice, told him that she would catch the first plane into O'Hare. To her relief, he insisted that she and Sean continue on without him.

Now she walked over to the vanity table and considered the woman in the mirror. Her thoughts were clinical. "You know what you're doing," she said to her reflection. "You know exactly what's going to happen, and you want it to happen."

She removed a container of pills from her travel case and flipped open the lid. The pills seemed to be watching her, each one in its carefully appointed daily place. This was the time each day when she took one out and swallowed it.

She shrugged her shoulders, flipped the lid closed, and tossed the container in the trash basket underneath the washbasin.

She unbuttoned her blouse and slowly removed it, then untied her hair and let it cascade over her shoulders. The day had been difficult. The electricity between her and Sean was crackling back and forth just as it had that summer when Paul had been reported missing in action. Sean had kept up the pretense of being a tour guide, lecturing on the history of the Amalfi, the reason why a small town like Amalfi had a cathedral, the religious difficulties that Catholicism had faced in Italy.

She had listened dutifully and sympathized with the problems of the Italian Church. Yet in the back of her mind she was aware of what she knew was going to happen. Even if Sean did not yet know.

She made sure the door between their two suites was unlocked on her side. She willed him to come through it. She waited on the bench in front of the vanity table.

Sean wrapped the soft robe around his wet body. The shower had not helped either his headache or his tension. The vacation had been hellish. Paul's well-meaning cheerfulness and Nora's paralyzing attractiveness were driving him out of his mind. Now he was alone with her.

He would not permit anything to happen. She was his brother's wife, his childhood sister. She was lonely and frustrated in an unsatisfying marriage.

But he wanted her. He wanted her laughter and her wit, her quick intelligence and her cool self-possession, her astonishing blue eyes and her mobile, generous smile. He wanted every inch of her superb body. This . . . this need for Nora was something very different from the desire he had felt for Sandra in Vail.

He shook his head to drive out the rationalizations. He would not succumb. He sat firmly in the chair by the window and opened a doctoral dissertation on sixth-century marriage customs. If he could only last until morning, there would be no problem. Anyway, he was an inexperienced virgin. He knew nothing about lovemaking. He would make a fool of himself. He would not be able to satisfy her.

He probably wouldn't do any worse than Paul.

He turned a page of the Latin text. Paul is her husband, you damn fool, and you're not, he said to himself.

Fifteen minutes later he threw the book aside and walked across the room. He opened the connecting door and entered Nora's room, his robe pulled tight around his long, hard body.

Nora stood up, uncertainty showing on her face as he approached her. He stopped, when their two bodies were almost touching, and stroked her cheek, his fingers light and gentle. He could feel her relax. She wanted to be his.

His hands traced the outline of her face, her shoulders, her arms, her body; slowly, as if he were unveiling a statue, he undressed her until she stood naked before him. He lifted her long auburn hair back over her shoulders so that nothing hid her from him. Again, his fingers gently outlined her body.

He untied the belt on his robe, pushed it off his shoulders, and let it fall to the floor.

Then they came together in the overwhelming love they had felt for each other since she had come into the Cronin family long ago, a lonely, frightened orphan.

As the first light creased the black waters of the Mediterranean, they were still clinging to each other, their bodies sweat-soaked. "You're a wonderful lover, Sean," she said.

"A rank amateur, I'm afraid."

"That doesn't matter. You're more concerned about me than you are about yourself."

"Who else would I be concerned about?" Sean asked. He was surprised that the tenderness of his passion would be thought remarkable. There was so much he had to learn.

They were on a beach at Capri, having walked a mile from the hotel and around several headlands to a sheltered cove. Nora spread the blanket on the beach. As she finished, she felt Sean's arms around her waist. He could not look at her, touch her, caress her enough. His fingers undid the straps of her halter.

"Sean, not in public," she said.

"Nonsense." He laughed. "This beach is reserved for nude bathing. By custom, anyhow. It's just our luck to be here this morning by ourselves."

The bottom of her suit joined the top in the sand.

They lay on the blanket holding hands. They shared a sense of

freedom enhanced by the soft sea breezes and the warm sun penetrating their bodies.

Nora felt Sean turn on his side. She opened her eyes and met
his stare. She could not remember a time in her life when she was
happier than she was at this moment.

He brought his face down to hers. "Will this be the first time a
man has ever made love to you on a beach?" he whispered against
her ear.

It was naive perhaps, Nora knew, but it meant a great deal to
Sean that their lovemaking have a purity about it. If Nora could
not be a virgin in fact, then this would have to substitute.

They made love slowly, exploring every secret of each other's
bodies. Later, they swam in the Mediterranean. Nora did most of
her half mile before she returned to the beach. Walking out of the
water naked and dripping wet, her feet crunching in the sand, she
looked at Sean, lying on the blanket, and she was filled with joy.
He was so handsome. She did not give him a chance to take the
first step in renewing their lovemaking. This time it was her turn.

On their last night together, Sean's groans of pleasure turned
into sobs. "Oh, God, what have we been doing, Nora? What terrible things have we been doing?"

"Don't go turning guilty on me now," she commanded. "I refuse to think that any of this is wrong. We're not committing sin,
and I won't have you stirring up your goddamned conscience."

"We both have commitments. Solid ones."

She covered herself with the sheet as if protecting herself from
his weakness. "Neither one of us is going to give up our commitments, Sean. I'm going back to Paul. You're going back to your
Church. This is just an interlude. Paul doesn't own my body, and
the Church doesn't own you."

"But we made promises—"

"Promises that we are going to keep. It's not our fault that we
couldn't go through life without showing our love for each other.
I'm sure God doesn't think it's wrong. You know that yourself,
Sean. It's just your clerical conscience that won't let you admit it."

"Are you saying that there are special rules for us?"

She wrapped more of the sheet around her. "No, I'm not saying
anything about rules. This has been a time when the rules don't
apply. They'll start applying again as soon as I leave for Chicago.

This has been a good thing for both of us and I won't let you say otherwise."

"I wish to God I could believe that."

He would have a hard time afterward, Nora knew, on the one hand proud of his successful conquest, and on the other, burdened with guilt because of a love that he thought was sinful.

"You know I'm right," she said soothingly. "Otherwise neither one of us would have done it."

"I don't know, I just don't know. I'm too confused to figure it out."

"Then stop trying and enjoy the time we have left," she said.

And to emphasize the command, she reasserted her control over his body with her fingers and then with her lips.

CHAPTER
——TWENTY-ONE——
1966–1967

Sean Cronin and Eamon McCarthy were shown into the summer office of Castel Gandolfo in the cool hills south of Rome. Outside the window of the tall uncomfortable old room there was a garden of flowers. The aroma, soothing and tantalizing, reminded Sean of Nora's scent. He tried to banish her from his mind. He was about to have an interview with the leader of more than 700 million Catholics. He must concentrate on other things besides a woman's body.

The Pope was even shorter than he appeared in his public audiences, a frail old man in white, with nervous hands and glowing eyes. He was relaxed and calm, a compassionate and sensitive man.

"So, Monsignor Cronin," he said, "you dissented from both sides. It seemed important to listen to your position, too." The Pope gestured tentatively and smiled disarmingly, almost diffidently.

Sean took a deep breath. "I dissented, *Santità,* because I think both sides are wrong. Any public reaffirmation of the old teaching is bound, after all these years of delay, to offend the married laity who already think we do not understand their position. On the other hand, I do not believe the Church is ready for change. We have not developed a theory of human sexuality or human nature that provides a context for such change. A decision either way will simply postpone indefinitely the development of such a theory. Either way the Church loses."

"This is very interesting, Monsignor Cronin," the Pope said thoughtfully. "However, I am the Vicar of Christ and it is my duty to defend the teachings of Christ. I do not have many years left to live, and I do not know how I would explain to my God if I failed in my responsibilities. The Catholic people all over the world live in uncertainty. Does it not seem to you that as Vicar of Christ I must end their doubt?"

"With all respect, *Santità*," Sean said, "I think most of them have very little doubt any more. You will simply create new doubt about the papacy if you decide with the minority. And if you decide with the majority, without a fully developed theory to support such a decision, you will create chaos."

"Will there not be more chaos if I postpone a decision indefinitely?" The Pope was literally wringing his hands.

"I sympathize with your problem, for you must steer a middle ground between going too fast and too slow."

"If we change, many of the simple laity will be frightened."

"I disagree, Holiness," Sean insisted. "The simple laity like the new Church; they like it, in fact, I think more than I do. Hence, my recommendation to get a few steps ahead by developing a new Catholic theory of sexuality—rooted in the past, of course. *Before* the laity are ready for it, not after."

The Pope smiled. "Ah, Monsignor Cronin, perhaps you are right. You are a perceptive young priest. And I'm an old man, perhaps pope at the wrong time. I do not know what should be done. I promise you, however, I will remember very seriously the things you have said."

Then there were medals and pictures and the usual ceremony at the end of a papal audience.

As Sean and Eamon McCarthy were walking from the entrance of the old castle to the Cardinal's Oldsmobile, Eamon shook his head. "You are a constant source of amazement to me, Sean; I think of you as a conservative, yet you have a private audience with the Vicar of Christ and read him a stern lecture about his failing as a leader of the Church, something that not even the most radical of liberals would dream of doing."

"I'm sure I didn't do that."

"Moreover, not only did you do it and get away with it, you actually earned the Pope's admiration. There are not too many men whom Giovanni Battista Montini admires."

Sean opened the door for the Cardinal and then walked around to the driver's seat. After he was inside, he said, "The Pope would make a very grave mistake if he admired me."

The bored priest who heard Sean's confession in St. Peter's muttered only a few words about stern discipline and then gave him a disgracefully light penance—two rosaries—and a hasty absolution. Such quick mechanical absolution did not even begin to reach the depths of Sean's pain. Worst of all, even though he was ashamed, he did not feel guilt. He was both confused and dismayed, but he could not escape from a sense of enormous satisfaction and complacency.

Angèlica seemed to be the only one to turn to for understanding. She listened intently as he poured out the story, occasionally nodding her head sympathetically.

She sipped her espresso at a corner table at the sidewalk café just off the Piazza del Populo where they had met. "For once in my life I will be absolutely serious. I think it is surely a good thing for you. You have loved her all your life and she has loved you. What could be more natural than that you express your love for each other? For an Italian priest, it would not be sinful at all."

"You mean that a romp in the hay is occasionally useful for a priest?" he asked skeptically.

Angèlica made a face over her espresso. "Bah, you Americans are such terrible prudes. A romp in the hay, indeed! No. I mean, it is good for Sean Cronin to learn that he does not control himself completely. You cannot escape being a man, Sean, simply because you are intelligent and have an answer for everything and a rule or a principle or a theory to apply to every situation. Welcome into the human race."

This was a very different Angèlica from the casual temptress of the Palazzo Alessandrini. Sean felt grateful to her. "Maybe you're right, Angèlica. This morning, out at Castel Gandolfo, I told off the Pope. I would not ever have thought of doing that three weeks ago."

"Did he mind?" She raised a delicate eyebrow.

"No, as a matter of fact, he seemed to like it."

• • •

Nora gave birth to Michael Paul Cronin, the long-awaited Cronin heir, in May. He was baptized by his Uncle Sean in early July of 1967 in St. Titus Church. Mayor Richard J. Daley was the godfather, and his wife, Eleanor, was godmother. Michael Cronin, the proud grandfather, glowed happily. The baby's three sisters watched the ceremony as their uncle performed it with awe and wonder, although the youngest of the three, Noreen, was concerned about whether her little brother would cry when the water was poured on him. She had been assured that she herself had not uttered a single wail of protest.

Paul Cronin seemed pleased to have a son at last. Dr. Thomas Shields, who brought Mickey into the world, smiled contentedly as the ceremony progressed. Maggie Martin Shields, as usual, seemed distracted and sad.

Mickey was the picture of health, a golden child cut from the same cloth as his sister Noreen and his Uncle Sean. He accepted all the attention as though it was his as a matter of right.

However, the one who was most serene during the baptismal ceremony was Mickey's mother. Nora was still pale and thin two months after the difficult birth of her son, and sat through the ceremony instead of standing. But the glint was still in her eyes. No one in St. Titus Church had any doubt that in a month or two her golf handicap would be back where it ought to be.

At the end of the ceremony, Sean poured the water over the infant's head, saying the time-honored words: "Michael Paul, I baptize you in the name of the Father, and of the Son, and of the Holy Spirit."

Noreen Cronin was greatly disappointed. Her little brother not only did not cry, but he licked the water with his tongue, just as legend said she had done.

At the party afterward at Glenwood Drive, Sean had a moment alone with Nora. "Whose is he?" he asked her bluntly, after months of avoiding the question.

"I don't know, Sean, I don't know. There's no way I will ever know. He's a Cronin, isn't that enough?"

"Whose do you wish he was?" He could have chopped off his tongue as soon as the words were out.

"I don't want to think about that," she said. "Do you?"

"I guess not. He's a Cronin. I suppose that's all that matters."

"Yes, look at him," she said, her face shining with a mother's love. "He certainly is a Cronin, isn't he?"

Sean knew that in his heart he would never be satisfied with that answer, even though, short of paradise, that would be the only answer he would ever have.

 BOOK VI

I leave to you my own peace, I give you a peace the world cannot give; this is my gift to you.

—John 14:27

CHAPTER
——TWENTY-TWO——
1968

"If I were a thirty-seven-year-old black man instead of a thirty-seven-year-old white man," said congressional candidate Paul Cronin, "I would be angry tonight. Martin Luther King was one of the greatest leaders ever produced in this country. Now he is dead, killed by a racist. Oh, yes, if I were a black man I would be terrified, outraged, and I would feel very destructive."

The mostly white crowd in the small park next to the Rock Island commuter station stirred uneasily. Commissioner Cronin was speaking to them from a red, white, and blue platform, decorated with CRONIN FOR CONGRESS banners. The Commissioner was popular, especially in this end of the district. With the organization's vote, he was thought to be a shoo-in for election. Yet the speech he was giving was more appropriate for the black end of the district than the white. How come Paul Cronin was taking *their* side?

"If I were a thirty-seven-year-old black storekeeper in Chicago tonight," the Commissioner continued, "I would be even more angry and more frightened, for I would not know when a Molotov cocktail would come through the window of my store. I would be furious that the violent murder of a good man, who opposed violence, would be used as an excuse for more violence and more murder and, quite possibly, for my own murder. And I would be very grateful indeed if the Mayor's influence with the President was such that one phone call could send the protection of the Hundred and First Airborne—to return order to my street, my neighborhood, my city. I would mourn Martin Luther King. I would be angry at the senseless violence, whether it be carried on by whites or blacks, and I would thank God for Richard J. Daley and Lyndon Baines Johnson."

The candidate ended his speech in a tone of ringing triumph. Paul Cronin had charmed them again. The audience cheered enthusiastically. Even the small group of well-to-do blacks who stood off on one side applauded. They had more experience with the gangs of teenage looters in the neighborhood than did the whites in the crowd.

"Just the right note," said Monsignor Sean Cronin, chancellor of the Roman Catholic Archdiocese of Chicago, to Nora Cronin, who was seated next to him. Sean suspected that she provided many of the core ideas for Paul's campaign speeches.

"No matter what happens," said Nora, "Paul is going to get elected. He's in a sweet position. He can ride on Bob Kennedy's coattails."

The candidate, boyishly handsome with his hair long, but not too long, joined them for a moment before being drawn away by a reporter. "What did you think, little brother?" He grinned. "Not bad for a district where you have to keep both whites and blacks happy."

"You're a superb politician," Sean agreed.

It was true enough, he thought, as he drove through the forest preserve toward 87th Street and the Dan Ryan Expressway. Paul was Chicago's fair-haired boy. He could do no wrong as far as the public was concerned. Even his private life was leveling out. The birth of Mickey seemed to have introduced a new element in the relationship between Paul and Nora. Sean couldn't quite put his finger on it. It was as though both Paul and Nora had come to an agreement that Nora, having produced a son, had fulfilled her family duties.

The fateful interlude in Italy had had a profound effect, even though neither of them talked about it. Nora was now more self-confident and self-possessed. Sean had become almost as reckless as his now politically cautious brother used to be. And, of course, there was Mickey, the magic, happy little boy whose father would never be known for sure and who was the result, one way or the other, of what had happened that week at the Bay of Naples.

Sean parked his car in the cathedral parking lot, but instead of going to his room he walked down the street to the new chancery building and rode up in the elevator. The light was on in Jimmy McGuire's office, next to his own.

"Hi, Sean," said the always cheerful Jimmy. "Do the paratroopers have any roadblocks on the Ryan?"

"The city's quiet," Sean said. "There's still smoke, but the fires are burning out, and the radio says there's some looting on the West Side. But the worst is over. Maybe we didn't need the troops after all."

"Me, I'm glad they're here. It will make everybody think twice. . . . You're not planning on working at this hour of the night, are you?"

"I want to go over that financial problem at St. Fintan's. No one can figure out how many different bank accounts the late pastor had and which ones reflect his money and which ones reflect the parish's money."

"You can bet on it that all of it was parish money, and by the time the lawyers are finished, we'll only get half," Jimmy said. "The boss is off confirming at St. Andrew's tonight, isn't he?"

Sean wanted to get to his own office and begin work, yet Jimmy's good humor was seductive—an endless temptation to idle away time. "I don't know how he stands it. Confirmations, graduations, parish anniversaries, meetings in Rome or in Washington, half the kooks in the city of Chicago wanting to see him, the telephone ringing from one end of the day to the other, conflicts between pastors and people and people and curates, women wanting to be ordained, priests wanting to marry . . . the old man is going to work himself into an early grave. He's the most conscientious man I've ever met."

Jimmy eyed him levelly. "The second most conscientious man I know."

Sean ignored the remark and went to his own office, where he began to pore over the complex financial machinations of Father Michael John O'Brien and the parochial funds of St. Fintan the Hermit Parish. Try as he might, however, he could not drive pictures of Nora from his mind. Sheer physical hunger for her had abated, but every time he saw her the light in her incredible blue eyes, the quick explosion of her smile, and the curves of her flawless body hit him with sledgehammer force. Nothing would ever happen between them again, he promised himself. But the guilt, the torment, and the self-contempt he now felt because of their experience, would never go away, it seemed, nor would the shattering memories of its pleasures. "Oh, God!" he sobbed, burying his head in his hands. "What have I done?"

The day after the assassination of Martin Luther King, Michael Cronin was rushed from his apartment at the new John Hancock Center to the emergency room of Passavant Hospital. The doctors diagnosed the attack as a brain "spasm," something like a small stroke, the sort of trauma Eisenhower had suffered during his first term.

"The President served four more years and is still alive at seventy-eight," the soft-spoken brown-skinned neurologist from India commented reassuringly.

Yet it seemed to Sean that the touch of death was on his father's face in the hospital bed. He seemed so frail.

While Sean stood at his bedside, Elizabeth Hanover slipped quietly into the room. She took Mike's hand, oblivious of the needles in his veins. The sick man's eyes came alive.

Good God, Sean thought, he's in love with her. Like I am with Nora. How can it be that he's never married her?

"The offer still stands, Michael." She spoke with characteristic directness.

His father seemed to begin to say yes; then the life died from his eyes, and he pulled his hand away. . . .

"I'll keep up my visits, Sean, indefinitely, if you don't mind," Elizabeth said later when she and Sean were in the corridor outside Mike's room.

That stalwart, timeless woman seemed suddenly to be showing her age. Her face was lined, her normal parade-ground back a little bent.

"Be your realistic self, Elizabeth, and find someone else. This game is over."

"You're being the sensible WASP and I'm being the sentimental Irishman." She leaned her head against his shoulder.

"We're not sentimental about death," Sean said. "Not even lingering death."

Paul Cronin walked briskly up Michigan Avenue under a brooding November sky. Despite his self-confident stride and the quick smile with which he greeted passers-by who recognized his face from television news conferences, he was worried about Sean's reaction to the suggestion he was about to make. It was the only possible solution, but Sean was so unpredictable these days that Paul could not count on his being sensible.

Paul glanced up at the towering walls of the Magnificent Mile. The top of the Hancock Tower was shrouded in fog. Planes would be stacked up at O'Hare. Before he had become Aviation Commissioner he had paid no attention to such things. Now that he knew all that could go wrong at the world's busiest airport, his hands turned sweaty when the weather was bad. He couldn't talk to the Mayor any more about a new airport. "Them protestors come out every time we mention it, Paul. Haven't we got enough of them protestors as it is? Besides, you run for Congress and let me worry about O'Hara."

The Mayor always called it "O'Hara." He liked Paul, thought he had done a good job taking the heat about airport expansion, and wanted to reward him with a return to Washington.

Paul was happy about going back to Capitol Hill; now the only complication was his father's stroke. Paul did not like having to go to the hospital. The old man was getting better, all right, but now he *looked* like an old man. Paul shuddered. He didn't want to think about his father's death.

Makuch had called him to offer sympathies and brag about his own success in the business world. Paul could tell he was still a loser. Always had been a loser. Paul had been afraid that the call was a prelude to a demand for more money, but Makuch merely wanted to pretend that he was an old friend anxious about Mike Cronin's health. He congratulated Paul on his campaign for Congress. There was an ominous note in his voice when he said, "It will be nice to have one of us in Congress."

Would he ever be rid of Makuch?

The newspapers in the lobby of Passavant Hospital had headlines about the peace demonstrators at the Pentagon. Damn fool war. How could they make the Korean mistake all over again? He was glad that his "key post" in the city government provided an excuse not to ask to have his commission activated.

His stomach jumped at the thought of huddling in a foxhole while mortars thudded all around. He had not slept for almost a week after watching the siege of Khesanh on television. Even

Nora could not exorcise the thump of the explosions and the screams of the wounded at Chongun Reservoir.

"Took you long enough," said Sean. His face looked like that of a stern novice master.

"I had a rough session with Connaire and Hoffman," Paul pleaded. "More troubles."

Sean melted, as he always did, when Paul offered an excuse. He patted his brother's shoulder affectionately. "What are those two old gombeen men up to now?"

They sat on a couch in the lobby. Snow flurries danced against the dirty windowpanes. "The IRS has been hassling the Cronin Fund for more than a year. First I've heard of it. Ed and Marty had it out with Dad. . . ." Paul was glad to find an excuse not to face his father's frail, wounded body, to postpone his visit, if only for a short time.

"How bad is it?" Sean asked. He sounded as if he were spoiling for a chance to take on the IRS.

"Bad enough. Someone has to go in and straighten out the mess, someone Dad trusts and who's smart enough to figure where all the bones are buried. And it has to be done now."

Sean raised an eyebrow. "Who? Not you. A politician can't afford to be caught in such a mess. Me?"

"No way." These brief conversations with Sean about family problems brought back the comradery of the old days. How had they lost it?

"Then who? A politician can't, a churchman shouldn't . . . who? Who does Dad trust to put his complicated generosity into the order that would satisfy the IRS?"

Paul hesitated, fearing his brother's anger. "Nora," he said tentatively.

To his surprise Sean approved enthusiastically. "Who else? Of course, she's perfect." He paused. "Wonderful idea, Paul. Who else but Nora?"

Nora tried to concentrate on *The Confessions of Nat Turner*, though her mind wandered frequently to the conversation that lay ahead of her. Something terribly important, Paul had said. What could Uncle Mike want of her that was terribly important?

"He's ready to see you now, Mrs. Cronin," said the matronly

black nurse with the smile of relief she always reserved for Nora, the only visitor who could calm down Mike Cronin.

He looked much better. In a few weeks he would be able to fly to Florida to complete his rehabilitation. "Well, tough guy"—she kissed him—"when are you going to stop this goldbricking and get back to work?"

Mike laughed. "I fooled them all, didn't I? None of them thought I'd be able to head for Florida after Christmas. Give me a few months and I'll be back in the swing of things."

"Better believe it," she said admiringly. "Now, what's this about an important conversation? Every conversation with me is important, Michael Cronin, and don't you dare think otherwise."

Mike grinned. "Stirred up your curiosity, did I? It's nothing too important. . . . I just want you to take over the Fund for a few months till I come back from Florida. I'll be busy enough running Paul's campaign for Congress from down there without having to fight off the IRS vultures too."

"Why me?" she said, after a pause to gather her thoughts.

"Why not you? One son running for Congress, another running for auxiliary bishop; who else do I have besides my daughter?"

"Uncle Mike, I'm flattered. I appreciate the vote of confidence. I don't know whether I can do it. . . ."

"Don't blubber like a damn fool, woman." He seemed remarkably happy for a man giving up a prized possession. "Of course you can do it. I wouldn't ask you if you couldn't. Anyway, it will only be for a few months."

Nora knew that she should feel hesitant over the responsibility and sad for Uncle Mike's loss. Yet her mind sang for joy. Yes, certainly she could do it.

Better than anyone else.

CHAPTER
—TWENTY-THREE—
1968

The limousine picked Nora up every morning promptly at nine thirty. By then the three girls were in school and Mickey had been fed breakfast. Nora arrived at her office at the Cronin Foundation at ten o'clock and worked straight through until three o'clock—five hours every day of the week. She was home by three thirty to supervise the girls when they stormed in from St. Titus School to play with the endlessly enjoyable Mickey. She would also preside over dinner.

Nora felt tremendous guilt over her new occupational responsibilities. She was the mother of a child still a long way from school years and she was playing in the big league of business and finance. She knew that many of the other mothers at St. Titus were muttering about her, although she spent no more time at the office than they did shopping and playing golf. Such an argument, however, assuaged neither her conscience nor the criticisms of her neighbors. To make Nora's problems worse, she reveled in the excitement of the Cronin Foundation. She enjoyed every moment in the office, as well as the forty minutes of work each day in the back of her plush Cadillac limousine.

At first, the men who worked for her, many of them older than she was, were inclined to patronize her. However, no one ever did that twice. Nor did anyone make a second pass.

Nora frowned. She did not know quite what to make of her relationship with her husband. They had made love the night be-

fore: mechanical, but still good sex. They both were now competent at satisfying each other. Yet they were drifting even further
apart. Paul had his politics and she had the business. Both were
more or less oblivious of the other's concerns, although Paul was
only too happy to take her political advice. He seemed to respect
and admire her. Was that what marriage was about after almost
twelve years? Maybe they were better off than most.

Her thoughts returned to the Cronin Foundation. One day,
when she was sitting behind the vast oak desk in what used to be
Mike Cronin's office, Nora had come across a stack of bills she
couldn't make any sense of. "Mr. Conley," she asked one of the
few remaining clerks from the early days of the business, "I can't
seem to place this bill for eighteen thousand dollars for St.
Helena's Nursing Home up in Lake County. It merely says 'Services rendered. Mary.' Do you know why we pay this bill every six
months?"

The little old man with the red nose and a few streaks of snow-
white hair became agitated. He reached for the bills. "I'm afraid
Mr. Cronin told me not to bother you with these. They shouldn't
have been sent through. I've been paying that bill every six
months, doing it for a long time, more than thirty years, as far as I
can remember."

"Back to 1938?" Nora asked incredulously.

"Is this 1968? Well, then, it's more than thirty years. I've been
paying that bill since 1934. Do you want me to stop?"

"No." She gave the bill back to the old man. "If Mr. Cronin
wants the bill paid, then of course keep on paying it."

She made a note on the pad inside of her compact notebook
with its hand-tooled leather cover: *Check St. Helena's.*

Sean Cronin's phone rang. It was the Archbishop. "Monsignor
Cronin, could you spare me a few minutes?"

"Of course, Eminence." Sean collected the information on St.
Fintan the Hermit and walked down the corridor. He smiled at the
elderly woman who was Eamon McCarthy's secretary and walked
into the office of the Cardinal Archbishop of Chicago.

The Cardinal looked pale. "Bad trip to Rome, Eminence?"
Sean asked with genuine concern.

"About the same, Monsignor." The inevitable smile. "The
Roman Curia has not changed, nor has my body clock."

"You ought to take some time off, Eminence. Get away somewhere and rest."

"I believe, Monsignor, that that is a case of the pot calling the kettle black. In any event, I see from the stack of papers you brought in that you anticipated my question. You have solved the problem of St. Fintan the Hermit?" The Archbishop folded his hands in his lap, as though waiting to hear a lecture.

"It's a complex matter, Eminence. Every one of the five bank accounts, each with approximately fifty thousand dollars in it, is almost certainly made up of money siphoned off the Sunday collections through the late pastor's long years in the parish. There is no evidence that he had appreciable income of his own, or that there was money from his family. Moreover, it appears from various checks drawn on each of these accounts that the pastor considered all these funds to be parish funds. For example, he has paid the salaries of secretaries from it, the construction of new basketball backboards in the gym, annual contracts for snow removal from the parking lots. He even reimbursed the parish for payments of the seminary tax to us here at the chancery. I'm convinced that the pastor created these accounts with no intent to embezzle money from the archdiocese, but rather with the intent of hiding from us the large reserve his parish had amassed. He must have been fearful that we would confiscate some of it or force him to buy Catholic bishop bonds with it, or perhaps lower the annual assessments of his parish. Unfortunately, he died without leaving any records to confirm that these accounts were not his own."

"As a quick estimate, Monsignor," the Cardinal asked, "how common would you say that this practice is in the archdiocese?"

Sean hesitated. Better to err on the side of being conservative. "I would suggest, Eminence"—he moved his chair closer to the Cardinal's desk—"that perhaps a third of the parishes engage in practices like this, though usually not with such extensive funds or with such sloppy records."

The Cardinal looked tired for a moment. "We would need a certified accountant in every parish to prevent this sort of thing, wouldn't we, Monsignor?"

"Yes, Eminence."

"Well, I suppose we could engage in legal combat with his heirs at the cost of considerable fees to lawyers and even more considerable scandal. Therefore, we will settle with the heirs, giving them somewhere between a fifth and a quarter of the funds that rightly belong to the Catholic bishops of Chicago and to the people of God in St. Fintan the Hermit Parish. I presume that is what you would recommend?"

"I see no other option, Eminence."

"Very well, Monsignor. See that it is done. . . . There is another matter on which I ought to remark. I learned in Rome that sometime this summer we will have a papal encyclical on the birth-control issue."

Sean's heart sank. "Oh, no," he murmured.

"Oh, yes, Monsignor. And, as you can imagine, it will be the worst kind of encyclical. The only question in Rome now is whether the Pope will choose to make it an 'infallible' encyclical. Those who know him best say that the word 'infallible' will go into the text and that he will cross it out at the last minute. I am told that the encyclical will come sometime in July. I assure you, Monsignor Cronin, I will be visiting our mission in Guatemala at that time."

"It will be an absolute disaster," Sean said hoarsely.

"A position that I myself took five years ago, if you remember, Monsignor. I'm glad you've come around to my way of thinking. For weal or woe"—the Cardinal's eyes twinkled briefly—"the Catholic laity and especially the Catholic clergy have available the majority position that some imprudent commission member released to the press."

"I can't imagine who would have done that, Eminence," Sean said softly.

"Nor can I. In any event, Monsignor, I would advise you to prepare some carefully worded thoughts on the subject. Our friends in the press will surely want your comments when the encyclical is issued . . . especially"—again the quick smile and the quicker twinkle—"since it is well known that you voted neither for the minority nor for the majority position."

"Maybe they'll put that on my gravestone," said Sean Cronin.

At fourteen months, Mickey Cronin was a skilled walker, babbler, arranger of building blocks, and charmer of women, especially his sisters.

Eileen, Mary, and Noreen bounced into Nora's study. "We want to play with Mickey."

With a show of great reluctance, Nora handed her son over to the three girls, for whom he was a fascinating live doll.

"Unfaithful punk," she murmured as Mickey eagerly extended his arms to Eileen.

Mickey would cavort with anyone. His face and his coloring were pure Cronin, and his disposition was a carbon copy of Noreen's, save for the fact that, unlike his active sister, he slept soundly through the night, every night.

As Nora watched him crawl from sister to sister, delighted by the dilemma of having to choose between three enthusiastic surrogate mothers, she murmured, "You kids will spoil the little so-and-so rotten."

That was not true. Mickey was such a happy even-tempered child that nothing ever seemed to spoil him.

Yet Nora's happiness with her son was well on the way to being spoiled. She had been slow to reflect on what had happened between her and Sean. Sickness during pregnancy, the long recovery after Mickey's birth, and her involvement at the Cronin Foundation had been excuses not to think about it. It was a subject which she had been walling away in its own separate compartment.

It would not stay within its walls, however. Nora's reactions were not the reckless guilt of Sean but rather an aloof self-disdain. She, who had so prized her own fidelity to commitments, had blithely violated the central commitment in her life and led another to do so too. That Mickey was probably the result of such a shattered commitment did not change the facts. Self-possessed and self-controlled Nora Riley Cronin was as much a victim of the fires of irrational passion as were her husband, and Uncle Mike, and Mary Eileen and Maggie Shields.

Welcome into the human race, she told herself bitterly.

Sorry? She didn't know. Given another chance, she might do the same thing again and once more drive away the loving Presence that had been with her so long and which was now gone, perhaps forever.

There would be punishments, of that Nora felt certain. She waited for them calmly, knowing that the costs would have to be met. In the meantime, the Foundation provided an outlet for those dangerous energies within her.

"He loves you more than us." Noreen broke into her mother's reverie.

Mickey had crawled to his mother's feet and was looking up expectantly, not so much demanding affection and attention as patiently and brightly waiting for what was his due.

"Poor Mickey," she said, lifting him off the floor, not altogether sure why she should say that.

CHAPTER
—TWENTY-FOUR—
1968

When Paul Cronin arrived in Los Angeles, there was a note waiting for him at the hotel that said *Maggie called*. Paul sighed. Maggie had worked like a trooper during the primary battle. Paul had avoided her carefully, both because his desire for her had cooled and because Maggie was becoming irrational. He could not afford to be mixed up with someone like that, especially when he was running for the Congress of the United States. Besides, the last-minute Kennedy campaign, shaken badly in Wisconsin, had involved a considerable number of young women, mostly graduate students, for whom sex, power, and opposition to the rules meant virtually the same thing. They were outspokenly liberated and ready for almost any sexual experimentation. Indeed, there were three of them, roommates, who were undoubtedly eagerly waiting for him in their room on the ninth floor.

He noted that there was an additional single-word message on the pink slip with Maggie's phone number. *"Urgent."* He crumpled the piece of paper and dropped it in the cigarette receptacle by the elevator door.

Maggie was waiting for Paul in front of the hotel the next morning. She was wearing a soft blue dress and looked more appealing than ever. She told Paul that Tom was tied up at a conference. She wanted only to talk to Paul for a few minutes. He was uneasy, but she brought back too many pleasant memories from the past for him to refuse.

They had barely left the hotel before she was pressing against him as though they were in a bedroom instead of a car.

"Maggie, please don't do this," he pleaded. "I thought we agreed that my father's sickness—"

"What does he have to do with it?" she said, more pathetic than sullen.

"We can't take the risks," he said. "A scandal would kill him. I . . . I can't live with that on my conscience." It was as good an excuse as any. He didn't want to hurt her. It had to stop. Yet he felt himself slipping. She was so soft and warm and ready.

"You don't care about me any more." Her voice was so low he could hardly hear her. "No one does. I might as well be dead."

The mention of death calmed his desire. "That's a foolish thing to say, Mag. You have everything going for you. You don't need me to be happy."

"Yes, I do," she insisted, but she drew back toward the other side of the car. "You're the only one who ever cared."

"That's just not so," he argued. "Everyone likes you."

She was sniffling softly. "No one has ever liked me."

Maggie needed help, but Paul knew that he wasn't the one to help her. He thought about talking to Tom. No, that would never work. The best thing he could do was to stay away from her.

Nora joined Paul in Los Angeles the night of the California primary. The energies of Camelot had slowed. Many of the familiar faces were older, and the younger faces, particularly those of the women, were much harder. Nora wondered, without too much concern, how many of them had been in bed with her husband.

There was an uncomfortable hush in the ballroom of the hotel as everyone watched the early tabulations on the huge blackboard behind the stage. Gene McCarthy was obviously doing better than anyone had expected. McCarthy was the spoiler. He had spoiled Johnson's chances for reelection, and he might well spoil Bobby's chances for the nomination, throwing the primary to his bitter rival, Hubert Humphrey. And that, Nora realized, would mean Richard Nixon in the White House. She shuddered. She had met Nixon once at a party in Washington, a strange man whose eyes and gestures were unconnected with his words.

"Glad to see you, Nora." The candidate walked over and embraced her briskly.

Nora pecked at his cheek. "I hear they have some swimming pools outside," she said.

"I like you, Nora, because you're still a fighter, but I think I'll stay away from those swimming pools." Bobby smiled. The strange mixture of diffident charm and ruthlessness had its usual effect on Nora, depriving her of her aloofness.

"How well are we going to do tonight?"

Robert Kennedy grimaced. "We're going to win and we're going to claim a big victory, but we're not going to win by much. So nothing's going to be decided. I hope you can persuade your friend Mayor Daley to support us. By the way, I hear you're doing great with the business."

"Yes—I'm getting along swimmingly."

Bobby Kennedy laughed, squeezed her hand, and walked toward the platform.

Paul joined her a few moments later. "Did you see Bobby?"

"He just walked up to the platform and then disappeared—back to the Kennedy suite, I suppose."

"We're going to win big," said Paul. "California will finish off Clean Gene."

Much later in the evening it was clear that Clean Gene had been beaten, but only by a few percentage points. Robert Kennedy's victory statement was hollow and tired, and the enthusiasm of the supporters forced. Paul and Nora were standing near the platform, and as the Senator climbed down from the stage, he signaled them to follow him.

They crowded after him into a corridor just off the main ballroom. Nora wondered how anyone could stand to be a politician with the enormous pressure of compaigning and endless media attention.

There were two quick, sharp explosions just ahead of them. People shoved forward, shouting and screaming. Someone was being wrestled to the ground. Without thinking, Nora moved ahead and then stopped in unbelieving horror.

On the floor, with part of his head blown away, was Senator Robert F. Kennedy, the second of the Kennedy brothers to fall to an assassin's bullet. The crowd swirled and pushed around Nora. Pale, worn, shattered, but very much in charge, Ethel Kennedy was giving instructions. The Senator was carried down the corridor and out of the building. Nora, still immobile, leaned against the wall, reciting over and over to herself, mechanically and automatically, the words of the Act of Contrition:

> *"Oh, my God, I am heartily sorry for having offended thee because I dread the loss of heaven and the pains of hell. But most of all because I have offended thee, my God, who art all good and deserving of all my love. . . ."*

In August of 1968, while Paul was discreetly moving into the Hubert Humphrey camp, opposing the war but also opposing the McCarthy-McGovern peace forces converging on Chicago for the Democratic Convention, Sean was interviewed by an Associated Press reporter who was doing an article on the recent birth-control encyclical.

He was on the spot. It was the spot of his own making and his own choosing, and he might just as well pay the price. He didn't much care. The birth-control encyclical was a catastrophe for the Church and would appall, insult, and infuriate American Catholics. Yet as a churchman he had to loyally honor it. To be a good churchman meant that you be a good hypocrite.

"Is it accidental that the Archbishop is in Guatemala, Monsignor?" asked the reporter.

"Quite accidental. The Cardinal's trip to Guatemala has been planned for months."

"Is your statement official?"

"I'm not making any statement. Bishop Conway's statement is the official stand of the Archdiocese. We welcome the Pope's decision and we will commend it to the Catholic faithful for their attention and their obedience."

"You were one of the few who voted with the minority in favor of the encyclical, weren't you, Monsignor?"

"No, I didn't vote with either the minority or the majority."

"Then are you in favor of or against the encyclical?"

"The encyclical is the official though not infallible teaching of the Church. I support the teaching of the Church, while I regret the fact that it was issued before the subject of sexuality in the Church was given an opportunity to achieve greater maturity."

"Does that mean, Monsignor, that you think the Pope may have made a mistake in issuing this encyclical, *Humanae Vitae?*"

"As regards to the timing, he may well have made a mistake."

Again, more furious scribbling. To hell with the reporter. To hell with the Pope. To hell with everybody.

"Do you expect American Catholics to obey the encyclical?"

"I am sure that many of them will continue their present practices," he said flatly.

"Do you think the Church will ever change on birth control, Monsignor?"

Sean stared glumly at the floor. "No one claims that this encyclical is infallible. And in the words of Harry Truman, 'Never say never, 'cause never is a helluva long time.' "

The journalist laughed. "One final question, Monsignor. If you had to do it over again, how would you have voted?"

Sean hesitated. He wasn't certain of anything any more. God, church, priesthood, doctrine—all were confusion. "I think I might very well have voted with the majority."

The Cardinal Archbishop of Chicago was exhausted upon his return from Guatemala. Even after two days resting at the house at 1555 North State Parkway, he still looked drawn and withered when his chancellor joined him in his office. "You look tired, Eminence."

"I am tired, Monsignor Cronin, very tired." He nervously fingered the press clippings on the desk in front of him. "Someday, Sean, I'm going to understand you. Six years ago you were one of the most conservative clergymen of your generation. Now you are a blunt and outspoken radical. You must know that somebody's going to send these clippings to Rome."

"Let them," Sean said.

The Cardinal sighed. "I have given your name, Sean, to the Congregation for the Making of Bishops, as my top recommendation for a new auxiliary bishop. Do you realize that your statement on the encyclical may affect the possibility of Rome's acquiescing to my recommendation?"

"To hell with them, Eminence. I don't want to be an auxiliary bishop. If you'd asked me, I would have told you no."

"That, Monsignor Cronin, is precisely why I didn't ask you."

CHAPTER
—TWENTY-FIVE—
1968

Nora Cronin, still badly shaken by the memories of the awful scene in Los Angeles, had warned her husband to stay away from the Conrad Hilton Hotel during the Chicago Democratic Convention. Even if Nixon should be elected, Paul's seat was relatively safe. He should avoid the hippies and the police and the National Guard, oppose the war, support Mayor Daley, and vote for Hubert Humphrey, who had the nomination locked up.

Nora tried to follow her own advice. She worked late at the office, since the children were at Oakland Beach with the housekeeper, but she made certain that the limousine was waiting to drive her home.

One night, however, as they made their way out of the city, she saw police, National Guard troops, and screaming kids rushing up and down Wabash Avenue. At the corner of Harrison and Michigan, a car careened by and a paper bag thrown from it exploded against the Cadillac, spilling human excrement down the side of the car door. Appalled, Nora did her best to ignore the nightmare around her: police on one side; foul-mouthed kids on the other, shouting obscenities at National Guardsmen who were, if anything, even younger than the protestors. Bullhorns bellowed, blue lights swirled, police and protestors dashed back and forth across the street. Tear-gas canisters were fired, sounding like exploding shells. Nora felt for a moment as if she were plunging into Dante's Inferno. Then the driver turned the limousine off Michigan Avenue and away from the debacle. Not until they were well away from the city did she feel the tension leave her body.

Nora had remained at her office after the others had left because she was increasingly called upon to make decisions for Cronin Enterprises. These offices were located across the corridor in the Field Building from the Cronin Foundation and were as disorderly and confused as her operation was neat and disciplined. She was becoming the *de facto* head of the enterprises. Mike always went along with her suggestions nowadays, without even consulting Marty Hoffman or Ed Connaire.

Yet it was not only the pressure of extra work that had kept her in her office. For perhaps the hundredth time, she studied carefully the file on St. Helena's. What could it mean? Ed Connaire had been vague about the priest who was perhaps Mary Eileen's lover. Could he still be alive and living at the nursing home—for some reason Mike Cronin's responsibility? Nora did not want to know. She wanted to bury the past with all its shame. Yet she had contributed her own shame to the history of the Cronins. Maybe . . .

Nora didn't know what came after maybe. There would be no real peace, however, until she rolled back the rock from the tomb that had been sealed for over thirty years and found the truth that was buried at St. Helena's.

The day after his election, Paul, realizing that his first two terms in Congress would be served under a Republican president, pondered his future. He had won handsomely in the third district: indeed, by the biggest margin a Democratic candidate had ever received. He would have to serve three or four terms in the Congress before he could think of running for the United States Senate. In 1976 he would be forty-six years old, a bit older than he had hoped to be when he got into the Senate but certainly not too old in 1980, when he could make the run for the roses. Not the Old Man's game plan, but not bad either.

Thumbing through a stack of congratulatory telegrams and messages on his desk in the City Center, he pulled out a message from Maggie Shields. Again there was the single word, *Urgent*. He crumpled the note as he had crumpled all messages from Maggie through the summer and tossed it in the wastebasket.

There would be plenty of opportunities for replacing Maggie in Washington. Nora would stay in Chicago, at least for a while, because it was awkward to change the children's schools at the present. Besides, she was now the only one who could keep Cronin Enterprises going.

Paul was not upset by his wife's success in business. It would mean that their marriage would consist of trips by her to Washington and by him to Chicago—together one or two nights a week at the most, and sometimes not that often. He could have most of the advantages of being a bachelor in Washington and none of the disadvantages. He would merely have to be careful and make sure that Nora never again caught him.

He would miss the kids. They adored him, although Eileen, the oldest, was now frequently contemptuous of him for reasons he did not at all understand.

He would phone Nora dutifully every day. Appearances must be maintained. Besides, she had sound instincts of judgment about people, and as an occasional bed partner she had certain good qualities.

The next half dozen years in his life, then, seemed to hold remarkable promise.

The Cardinal studied Sean thoughtfully. "Someday, Monsignor Cronin, you are going to have to explain your magic to me. It would be most useful to understand it during the few remaining years I have left to deal with the Vatican."

"Beg pardon, Eminence?"

"I have just had a phone message from the Apostolic Delegate," said the Cardinal. "He's informed me that the Pope, with the recommendation from the Congregation for the Creation of Bishops, has named you Titular Bishop of some city in Asia Minor, which I believe is substantially below the level of the Aegean Sea, and Auxiliary Bishop of Chicago. I would, under normal circumstances, congratulate one who has received such an important appointment. However, as I understand it, this is an appointment that you have not desired, did not want, and would be tempted not to accept. I will content myself with telling you, Bishop Cronin, that you are certainly going to accept that appointment, if I have to constrain you at the point of a gun." Eamon

McCarthy permitted himself the luxury of a broad, self-satisfied smile.

"Shit," said the new Auxiliary Bishop of Chicago.

Jimmy McGuire dreaded the dinner at the Mid-America Club, now in its new quarters atop the slender white marble pillar of the Standard Oil Building. "The fifth tallest in the world," Sean told the three visiting bishops. "We also have Number One and Number Four."

The Mid-America, Sean had assured Jimmy, would be the best place to go. Any of the more exclusive eating clubs would be a waste of money. "The Episcopal palate, James," Sean said, "is almost as undeveloped as the Episcopal conscience."

Jimmy didn't mind the guests. Martin Spalding Quinlan from Boise was indeed a pompous dullard, a neat little altar boy with precise French cuffs and carefully tinted hair. Harold Wheaton, an auxiliary from Washington, was all right; discreet, cautious, but basically a rubicund political realist. Modesto Gomez from the Southwest said very little because, if one were to believe Sean Cronin, he had very little to say.

A dinner with such men on the last day of the meeting of the national hierarchy in Chicago could be pleasant, or at worst harmless, if it were not almost certainly to be the occasion for one of Sean's reckless diatribes against his brother bishops. You had to take the good with the bad, Jimmy supposed. Something had happened to Sean around the time of the last meeting of the Birth Control Commission that had made him one of the most courageous and progressive churchmen in America. It also had made him restless, angry, and foolhardy. None of the Cronins, Jimmy mused, seemed very good at balance.

Jimmy's worst fears were realized during the main course.

Sean had ordered Château Lafite-Rothschild to follow the white Châteauneuf-du-Pape with which the meal had begun, mostly, Jimmy was certain, for the raised eyebrows such an extravagance would produce. Marty Quinlan was commending the recent document from the Holy Office on human sexuality and arguing that the bishops should have taken up his proposal to send a positive reply to Rome, thanking the Pope for such an insightful reaffirmation of the tradition. These were words, Jimmy thought, not unlike those which could have been heard from Sean during his first half-dozen years in the priesthood.

"Bullshit," Sean said. He filled his wineglass for the second time.

"It's so hard for us to know what proposals to act upon." Harold Wheaton tactfully changed the subject. "I think we ought to develop a program of in-service training for the bishops, so they can learn how to budget their time and their energies. Otherwise we spread ourselves too thin."

Sean made a grand gesture with his glass. "The most important course in such a program, Harry, would be a course in lying. You can't be a good bishop unless you're an accomplished liar. We lie to Rome about how enthusiastically we receive their bullshit; we lie to the priests and the laity about how they should enforce such rulings; we lie to the press about what we really think. We even lie to ourselves, although we know that we won't be able to sleep at night because of what that goddamn encyclical is doing in our dioceses. Some of us are ready-made psychopathic liars. The rest of us are the do-it-yourself variety."

"You don't mean that, Sean," Modesto Gomez protested mildly.

Jimmy protested much less mildly as he and Sean walked back to the cathedral rectory after leaving their guests at the Palmer House. "Cronin, you're an ass. Every word of what you said tonight will go to the delegation tomorrow morning. You know the only hope we have of continuing Eamon's policies here is for you to be the next cardinal. Do you want to give Chicago to Marty Quinlan on a silver platter?"

"Do you want a cardinal who is guilty of incest and adultery?" Sean exploded.

Jimmy was stunned. So that was it. He had better say the right thing now. "Sean, are you going to revel in guilt for the rest of your life? The truth is, you damn fool, that what bothers you is not the sin, which God forgives, but the mark on your stainless white record. Sean Cronin isn't perfect. He's a sinner like the rest of humankind. So he's excused from keeping his big mouth shut, even when it endangers the entire archdiocese?"

"You're fun when you get mad, Jimmy," Sean said through clenched teeth.

"You and Nora work it out between each other?" Jimmy softened his tone.

"Not really. How can we work it out? It happened, and that's that."

"A fine Christian you are, Bishop. You both have a long time to live, a family to share, and you love each other. You can't go around forever in a paralysis of guilt. Have you ever read the Gospel about forgiveness?" His voice rose. "No, I forgot. God forgives sinners but Sean Cronin doesn't, not when the sinner is himself."

"I don't know how to handle it," Sean said wearily. "It haunts me every day."

"It made you a brave and honest churchman and Nora a successful businesswoman, didn't it?" Jimmy was guessing, but he had no choice but to play for high stakes here on Wabash Avenue at midnight. "Isn't that the crooked lines of God, drawing good from evil?"

"A *felix culpa?*" Sean said. "I don't buy the 'happy fall' theology. Never did."

"Heretic," Jimmy mumbled. He knew that he had planted questions and doubts. He hoped his friend would ponder them, perhaps constructively.

"I'm sorry I lost my temper and told you," Sean said after they had walked another block in dead silence. "I don't want to destroy your respect for Nora."

"You really are an ass," Jimmy said. He was genuinely angry for one of the few times in his life.

CHAPTER
TWENTY-SIX
1968–1969

The nun in charge of St. Helena's, Sister Margarita, was not much older than Nora and obviously intimidated by Nora's impressive presence in her smartly tailored suit. "I hope there's nothing out of order, Mrs. Cronin," she said.

"Not at all, Sister Margarita." Nora tried to sound reassuring yet not patronizing. "There's no question but that we will continue to pay for the care of Mary, but as the person responsible now for the Cronin Foundation, I'm obliged to familiarize myself with the various expenses of the fund. Do I understand that Mary has been here since 1934?" Nora felt a terrible wrenching pain in her stomach. "And you have no idea of what her last name is?"

"None at all, Mrs. Cronin. Mr. Cronin assured the nun who was in charge in those days—there have been eight other heads of St. Helena's between her and myself—that he had all the records carefully filed in the bank, and that it was absolutely essential, as a work of Christian charity, to take care of this poor woman." She hesitated and then went on uncertainly. "Of course, I discovered the matter when I assumed responsibility the year before last. My training in hospital administration, needless to say, made me very uneasy about such a practice, but it didn't seem possible after all these years to review the case. . . . I would ask you to believe that I made this decision quite independently of the contributions Mr. Cronin regularly makes to our institution."

"Look, Sister Margarita," Nora said, "I'm newer at my job than you are at yours. I'm not going to make any trouble. I just want to know more about Mary."

The nun was visibly relieved. "She came here, as you seem to be aware, in late 1934, diagnosed as incurably psychotic. She was then, as far as we can tell, in her late twenties, which would make her now about sixty. There has been little change in her condition since then. She is mostly, though not entirely, withdrawn from the world. Yet she is patient and cooperative and almost always pleasant. You're the first visitor she's had that anyone can remember. A resident psychiatrist says that long ago all hope of progress was lost. He does think, however, that back in the late 1930s a serious effort might have been successful . . . with some remission of the problem. Of course, in the late 1930s Catholic institutions did not have available the psychiatric facilities and skills that we now have." The nun sighed. "A lot of things have changed, Mrs. Cronin."

"Indeed they have, Sister. Do you think it will do any harm if I see Mary?"

"Oh, not at all, Mrs. Cronin, but I must tell you that neither will it do any good."

On her way home from the institution, as her driver skirted the city on the tri-state toll road, Nora was too shaken even to glance at her briefcase filled with work. There was no doubt who Mary was. Her features were like those of Nora's own daughter Mary: fifty years older, perhaps, but the same. And her eyes were Sean's eyes—fragile, hurt, and yet tender. More to the point, she had suddenly become attentive when the nun introduced her as Nora Cronin. Mary's aimless chatter had ceased and she became lucid for a moment. "Nora Cronin?" she said. "Why, my name is Cronin too. I had almost forgotten."

Nora decided that she would never tell Paul, if only because she did not want to take the risk of discovering that her husband already knew about the mysterious Mary. Should she tell Sean?

Nora drew a deep breath. Sean thought his faith was weak, that he didn't believe in God, at least not strongly enough. He did, of course. He played a childish game with himself, looking for "signs" from God all the time. Nora shook her head in disapproval. As though God didn't give signs every day. Sean would think his mother some kind of sign. And he would be furious at

Uncle Mike. None of it would help anyone, not Mary Eileen, not Sean, not Uncle Mike.

She examined her reactions. Was she angry at Uncle Mike? She should be, but she was not. Poor man. He was wrong, but she was certain he had done what he thought best.

She gathered up her gloves and her purse. I guess you're elected to carry the burden of the secret, Nora, she said to herself. Who else?

Eleven-year-old Nicole Shields discovered her mother's body on her parents' bed when she returned home from school. It was a month after the 1968 Presidential election. Her mother was dressed in a pale blue dress, the one she had worn on the previous Easter Sunday. She seemed to be quietly sleeping. Nicole, who frequently fought with her mother, murmured an unenthusiastic greeting as she walked down the hall to her own room. Then, puzzled by why her mother would be sleeping with her Easter dress on, she walked back to the bedroom.

Her mother's chest did not seem to be moving.

Nicole felt a sudden chill. Reluctantly she walked toward the bed, telling herself that her mother was only asleep. She stood at the side of the bed. No, it couldn't be . . . her mother had had too much to drink. She touched her mother's face. It was cool. She picked up her hand. It was cold too. Then it seemed to close on her own, like a claw pulling her down.

Nicole jumped away, dropping the hand back on the bed. Screaming hysterically, she ran from the room. It was a long time before she calmed down enough to call her father.

Like a man in a dream, Tom Shields called one of his neighbors who was a specialist in internal medicine and summoned an ambulance from the emergency room at Little Company of Mary Hospital. Maggie had finally pushed her luck too far. She had signaled her need for attention and affection, time had run out before anyone had heard her signal. Sitting on the bed next to the lifeless body of the woman he had always loved but never understood, Tom Shields wondered, as he had so often during their marriage, what more he could have done that he had not. He was certain that the failure was his, but he could never put his finger on what the failure was. Idly, he reached for the note on the table next to the bed. Maggie's final message. She was always leaving "final messages."

He opened the envelope and began to read:

> *I can't stand it any more. I'm sick of pretending. I hate it. You're the only one I've ever loved. And after all the good times we've had, and all the things we've done together, you don't want me any more. There's no point in going on. Love, Maggie.*

Tom Shields glanced at the envelope. It was not addressed to him, as he had first assumed, but rather to Congressman Paul Cronin.

All feeling drained out of him. He put the final note from his wife in the pocket of his jacket. There was no point in letting anyone else see it.

Congressman-elect Paul Cronin was so pleased with himself that he left his office at the City Center early and took the four o'clock Rock Island train home. He whistled "Hail to the Chief" softly as he sprang up the stairs of his house and opened the door. Nora was sitting in the parlor, her hair tied severely behind her head, a handkerchief held in one hand.

"What's the matter, Nora?" He knew his wife's moods well enough to understand that something terrible had happened.

"Maggie finally did it," said Nora, her voice hoarse. "She tried to kill herself. This time she succeeded."

"Good God," Paul said. He remembered with a feeling of relief the crumpled telephone messages.

Chris Waverly eyed Paul skeptically. "You haven't changed much, Congressman," she said. Her tone was bitter. "Coming back to Washington, huh?"

Chris's figure was as crisp and trim as ever, but her face was thin and the lines on it made her look hard. She looked at least a decade older than Nora.

"I hope we can be friends, Chris," Paul said.

"Not a chance." She snubbed out her cigarette. "By the way, I heard your old flame Maggie—you know, the one you used to bed when neither Nora nor I was available—I heard she killed herself.

Any chance it was because of you? It would make an interesting story, wouldn't it? I can see the headlines, 'Mistress commits suicide after Congressman spurns her.'"

Paul's heart sank. He had been a fool to tell Chris about his longtime affair with Maggie. It seemed amusing to brag about it in those days. Damn Chris and her memory. Even worse, Maggie's daughter, Nicole, had told his daughter Eileen that Maggie had left a note addressed to Congressman Cronin but that her father had taken it. So Shields probably knew about the affair. If Chris implicated Paul in Maggie's suicide, his seat in Congress would be worthless. Daley wouldn't even slate him in 1970.

But there would be no way that Chris could know about the note. "Good hunting, Chris," he said brazenly. "You just try to involve me in this tragedy."

"Believe me, lover boy, I intend to."

Sean was surprised but delighted when his secretary told him that Congressman Cronin had come to see him, but the dull look in his brother's eyes and the lifeless tone in his voice suggested that Paul was in trouble. "What's wrong, Paul? Can I help?"

"As a matter of fact, that's what I wanted to talk about. I think you may be able to be a big help. You see—well, I don't know quite how to put it. Maggie Shields had a crush on me for a long time; you remember the way she was back when she was a teenager. Well, whatever her problems, she got the idea that she was in love with me. . . . As God is my witness, Sean, there hadn't been anything between us—it was all in her imagination—but she left a suicide note addressed to me. There's a reporter in Washington . . . if she ever gets her hands on that note, if Tom Shields should be angry and give her the note. . . . You know what Daley thinks about that sort of thing."

"You want me to go to Tom Shields and ask him to destroy the note?" Sean asked.

"You've always been close to Tom. He trusts you. You can explain that there never was anything between me and Maggie—"

"Of course, I'll try," Sean said. He couldn't refuse Paul, even though he knew that it might mean the end of his friendship with Tom Shields.

• • •

They were sitting in Tom Shields's house early on a Wednesday afternoon. The first snow of the year had dusted the barren back-yard of the house. Tom was thin, pale, haggard, still painfully mourning.

"How did he know about the letter?" he asked Sean.

"Apparently Nicole saw it on the bedstand."

"Damn, I thought she might have. I've been afraid to ask her. . . . Do you want to see it?"

"If you want to show it to me, Tom," he said gently.

Tom Shields riffled a notebook on his desk and pulled out a piece of light blue feminine stationery. He jabbed it at Sean.

Sean unfolded the note, read it quickly, and folded it up again. "Paul says that there was never anything between them, that it was all part of Maggie's problem."

"Your brother was very much part of her problem." Tom Shields was icy cold. "He's lying, Sean. He'd been carrying on with her for years, God knows how many years. Maggie was a confused, unhappy, superficial woman, God rest her. I did every-thing I could, but none of it was good enough. Still, everything I tried to do was canceled out by that lousy bastard—" Tom's voice turned into a sob.

"I don't know what to say, Tom. I'm broken up over Maggie's death too."

"But not so broken up that you won't try to take that note away from me to save your brother from scandal. . . . I suppose you know that a reporter has already called to interview me about Maggie and her relationship with Paul? And so you've come to save his hide?"

"It's up to you, Tom," Sean said. He held out the folded paper.

Tom threw a matchbook at Sean. "Burn the goddamn thing. Only don't say another word to me as long as you live."

Sean felt a momentary pang of compassion for his brother as Paul strode briskly across the lobby of the Illinois Athletic Club toward the couch where Sean was waiting for him. Paul shook hands with two men, smiled genially at another, and waved at two more men during the quick twenty-yard walk. Trim and fit in a perfectly fitting pinstriped suit, the Congressman displayed his quick wit and easy charm even though fear must have been gnaw-ing at him.

"Did you get it?" Paul's voice cracked.

"I did."

"Where is it? I can't risk anyone making a copy." Once the smile vanished, the pallor on Paul's face was evident.

"I burned it."

"Are you sure?"

"I'm sure. How long was your affair with Maggie going on? Since you came back from Korea?"

"Not really. Like I told you, it was mostly in her mind. Poor Maggie was not very well. Come on, let's have lunch." Paul tried to recapture some of his usual nonchalance.

Sean did not believe his brother. Paul was a pathetic liar. "I've got to get back to the office. There's a lot of work to do."

Paul's face registered his disappointment. "I was counting on it."

"Can't be helped."

So many things had changed since they were boys. Paul had been the bigger and older and more successful son then. Now, for all his political success, he didn't have the feel of a winner.

Sean's compassion turned to triumph. Then the triumph turned to guilt.

That night Sean sat in his room in the cathedral rectory, the old brown spiral notebook in front of him, the page empty. His pen was in his hand, but no words would come. Angrily, he put the pen aside. There was a knock at the door and Father Kane entered, one of the young priests on the cathedral staff.

"Hi, Terry," he said. Whatever the problem, he had to smile cheerfully at the other clergy lest they be afraid they were in trouble with him. "What is it?"

"Nora Cronin called when you were on the phone about twenty minutes ago." He extended a note to Sean. "I told her you were talking to the Apostolic Delegation, and she said I shouldn't interrupt you."

One of the many disadvantages of being a bishop was that you had to put up with tedious calls from supercilious Italian junior staff members of the Delegate. "Thanks, Terry, I'll call her right back."

Nora had been worried about Mickey. He didn't seem to be bouncing back from the cold he had had several weeks before. She had taken him to the hospital for tests. Sean had been so shattered by the terrible meeting with Tom Shields that he had not thought to call her to find out how the little boy was doing.

He dialed the number and a child's voice said, "Congressman Cronin's residence. This is Noreen Cronin speaking."

"Hi, Noreen, it's Uncle Sean. Is your mother home?"

"Oh, hi. Sure, Mom's home. Just a minute, I'll get her."

"Hello, Sean." Nora sounded like a stranger.

Sean knew that something was terribly, terribly wrong. "What's the matter with him, Nora?"

"He has leukemia."

Mickey Cronin died just before Christmas of 1969. He was two and a half years old. He had been a happy, golden little boy until the very end, laughing, playing, enjoying life, teasing his mother and sisters, unperturbed by his stay in the hospital and the various treatments the doctors gave him in a futile attempt to save his life. Death came quickly on the nineteenth of December. A mild cold had turned into a sudden high fever. His mother rushed him to the hospital. Then, the next morning, while Nora and the three solemn little girls stood around the bed, the life on this earth of Michael Paul Cronin came to an end. The girls, the older two imitating their mother, were solemn and self-possessed. The weeping Noreen insisted that her mother and sisters pray for Mickey. By the time Bishop Cronin arrived, Noreen had stopped crying. "Oh, Uncle Sean," she exclaimed enthusiastically, "Jesus and Mary came and took Mickey home to Heaven with them."

Congressman Cronin arrived only after the body of little Mickey had been taken to Donnellan's funeral home. He had not understood from what his wife had told him the night before that Mickey's condition was as critical as it turned out to be. And so, because of an important subcommittee meeting that he had to attend before the Christmas recess, he had taken a late plane.

Nora rejected a wake. She wanted to have a simple funeral the next morning, for only the family. The wonderful little boy's body must be quickly and discreetly put in the ground without any time for either grief or consolation. Paul agreed, and his tight-lipped brother offered no objections. But Mickey's sisters would not hear of it. Their little brother was to be sent on a long journey to Heaven, and they wanted a spectacular farewell. So the funeral was delayed a day, and the classmates of each of the girls filed into the church just before the Mass of the Resurrection began.

Most of the rest of St. Titus parish was there, and much of the Chicago political establishment. The poinsettias were already on the altar for Christmas, and young Eileen Cronin would not permit their removal. In fact, Eileen, not her mother, took charge of the funeral arrangements, even to the extent of selecting the reading for her uncle, the story of Jesus and Mary and Joseph fleeing into Egypt. The Mayor and Mrs. Daley knelt right behind the family. Michael Cronin wept through much of the Mass. Paul was stony-faced and grave through the entire service.

Sean told them that they must no longer think of Mickey as a little boy, but now as a full-fledged man, whose power of knowledge and love were only slightly less than that of an angel. Mickey now knew more things than all the people in the church put together and loved more powerfully than any of them could possibly love in this life. There were few dry eyes in the church when the Bishop's sermon was over. At the grave site, Noreen said to her uncle, "I always knew Mickey would be smarter than I am."

 BOOK VII

I am the way, the truth, and the light. No one can come to the Father except through me. If you know me, you know my father too. From this moment you know him and have seen him.

—John 14:6–7

CHAPTER
—TWENTY-SEVEN—
1970

Sean Cronin tossed aside the *Chicago Tribune* sports section. Broadway Joe Namath was telling the world how he personally would wipe out the Baltimore Colts. Sean felt a strong affinity for Broadway Joe. Tell off the world so you won't hear your own demons.

He had an appointment with Nora. It was the first time she had ever called for an appointment. At the quiet family Christmas party she had been sad but dry-eyed. When he left, she said firmly, "There's something I want to talk to you about after the first of the year."

She was waiting for him in Jimmy McGuire's office. Nora and Jimmy were joking as they had for so many years. But she was pale and shaken, the memories of her lost child haunting her.

"Come to see me or Jimmy?" Sean asked, rather more abruptly than he had intended.

"Jimmy. He smiles and laughs and you don't."

"Come on down to my office anyway." She followed him down the twisting stairway.

"Are you going to get to the lake at all?" Sean asked, fumbling with the materials to make coffee on the sideboard behind his desk. It was impossible for him to see Nora and not imagine her pain at losing her son—his son.

"Forget the coffee, for the love of Heaven, Sean," she said with unaccustomed brusqueness. "There's something I have to tell you."

Sean sat down as he was ordered. "Okay, Nora, let's have it."

Her blue eyes filled with tears. "Sean, your mother is still alive."

Sister Margarita was very deferential. Bishops did not often visit obscure nursing homes in Lake County. Moreover, her elaborate respect suggested that Bishop Cronin deserved special honor. The damn woman was probably a feminist beneath her formal mask and looked on him as a hero for his reckless, spur-of-the-moment endorsement of the ordination of women, Sean thought.

"Your Excellency must understand," she said soothingly, "that our patient is not lucid for more than a few moments at a time and that there is no continuity between lucid intervals. Sometimes she thinks Mrs. Cronin is her mother, and other times she thinks that she is her own daughter. It is all very sad, although fortunately there does not seem to be any mental pain."

"I understand," Sean said automatically as they followed the nun to his mother's room.

He had steeled himself during the ride there in Nora's Mercedes—she had refused to let him drive. Yet the first sight in over thirty-five years of the woman who had brought him into the world was like a savage blow to his chest. The soft face, the vague, kind eyes, the faded golden hair—he had seen them all many times in his dreams; age and suffering had changed her gentle beauty, not destroying it but ravaging it so that one could appreciate what she once must have been.

She did not seem to realize Sean was in the room.

"Connie Crawford," she exclaimed to Nora. "I haven't seen you in ages. Where have you been? When are you going to marry that nice Reilly boy?"

"I brought another guest," Nora said softly, gesturing with a hesitant hand toward Sean.

Mary Eileen peered at Sean as though she were seeing him through a thick fog. "Terry." She choked. "Terry . . . oh, my God, Terry . . . where have you been? They told me I'd never see you again . . . dear wonderful Terry . . . I knew you'd come back."

She embraced Sean and sobbed against his chest. "Who's Terry?" he whispered to Nora.

"I think he's the priest she knew when she was sick. Your Roman collar must bring back his memory. . . . Maybe—maybe you look like him too."

"It will be all right now, Mary Eileen, everything will be all right now." He tried to sound reassuring. "We'll take care of you." He stroked her long, carefully combed gold and silver hair until the sobbing stopped.

She pulled back. "I'm fine, Father." She was stiff and formal again. "It was good of you to come. I suppose you know Father O'Connor from New Albany. He's a very good friend of mine."

"Terry O'Connor?" said Sean cautiously.

"Of course. He's such a marvelous priest. He has a deep devotion to the Mother of Sorrows. He was a wonderful help to me when I was sick. I believe I've already introduced you to my daughter, Jane Cronin. She's named after her aunt, you know." Mary Eileen giggled. "Although she's much prettier than her aunt, don't you think?"

"As pretty as you are, Mary Eileen," said Sean.

"Don't call me that." She was briefly petulant. "Mary Eileen died a long time ago. She was so sick she tried to kill the baby. . . ." The anger passed like a brief spring shower. "Will you dance with me, Mike? It's been so long since we danced together."

Sean Cronin held his mother in his arms as tears streamed down his face. He would be many different people for Mary Eileen in future visits, he knew, but he would never be her son.

Nora slipped the Mercedes into the no-parking zone in front of Holy Name Cathedral. The police would not give a ticket to a car with Bishop Cronin in it.

"I think I'd better have the whole story, Nora," he said, breaking a somber silence that had lasted since they left St. Helena's.

Nora told him everything, from the conversation with Ed Connaire at Jane's funeral through her discovery of the check to the first visit to Mary Eileen and, finally, her decision to tell him when Mickey died. "I had no right to protect you. I'm sorry."

"Protect me from what?" His voice was thick with suppressed anger.

"God, Sean, don't talk to me that way. Protect you from anger toward your father, from guilt when that anger is over, from all the bitterness and frustration that is pent up inside you, from the self-destruction that's waiting to explode. . . ."

"Shouldn't that have been my choice?" His voice was unnaturally quiet.

"I had a choice to make too," she said simply.

"That miserable vile old man. He locked up his wife for thirty-five years because he was ashamed of a nervous breakdown he probably caused."

"That's not fair, Sean. She was unstable. She would have been in a home for thirty-five years in any case."

"And the goddamn family reputation? Can't let the rumor get around that the Cronin genes are defective."

"Sean," she pleaded.

"Who is my father, Nora?" His anger seemed momentarily spent. "I have found a mother. Have I lost a father?"

"You're Sean Cronin, and I'll always love you."

"That doesn't solve the problem, does it?"

"Don't tell Uncle Mike that you know about Mary." It was the wrong time and the wrong way to say it, but she had to.

He turned to her and examined her face as though she were a stranger. "Why the hell not?"

"It will kill him."

"He deserves to be killed."

"My God, Sean, who are you to judge that? How can anyone—"

"He deprived me of my mother for thirty-five years," he shouted. "*I* can judge that!"

"If you have any love for me, Sean, leave him alone." She had played her last card, knowing in the moment she laid it down that it was not high enough.

"You care that much about him?"

"I care about him, yes. I care more about you. After you've had the satisfaction of hurting him, you'll suffer more than he does. Don't you have enough guilt already?" She clutched at his arm, as if to physically restrain him.

Sean wrenched away from her. "You're a whore, Nora. You're as bad as he is." He jumped out of the car and ran off down Wabash Avenue in the bitter cold January twilight, his black coat flapping in the harsh winter wind.

• • •

Sean towered over his father, his fists balled into knots.

"Something wrong, Sean?" the old man asked. The perennial Christmas tree of Chicago's famous Loop glowed through one window of Mike's apartment, and the neat orderly lines of street-lights twinkled through another.

"How did you and Jane do it, Dad? How many people did you bribe? How many cops and doctors and undertakers did you have to pay off?"

Mike Cronin was shaken by every word spoken by his son. "It was easy," he said, his voice weak. "There actually was an auto accident. You were in the car. It was the third time she had tried to . . . to kill you. Our doctor, Roy Shields, was a good friend— he thought it was the best way out. We crossed state lines to confuse the police and the undertakers, had a closed casket wake. Only Jane and Roy and the chauffeur and I knew. . . ."

"Jane took me away from her."

"She had to, Sean. Mary Eileen tried to kill you. I had to bring Jane into the house to watch you. There was no one else I could trust." Mike was begging for sympathy.

"And you never visited her, not once since 1934."

"That's not true, Sean." Mike pressed knotted fingers against his forehead. "I went many times in the first years, even the day I left to go overseas in 1942. She never knew me, thought I was her father. It didn't do her any good, and it hurt me terribly. Can't you believe that I hurt too?"

"You miserable bastard!" Sean pulled his father out of the easy chair in which he had been sitting and shook him as though he were a rag doll. "I hope to hell I'm not your son!"

He threw his father back into the chair and stomped out of the apartment.

A few minutes later, when the sub-zero cold on Delaware Place stung at his face, Sean began to feel the guilt that Nora had predicted. He found a dime in his pocket and went into a phone booth to call his brother.

Sean waited for Paul in the vast Red Carpet Room above the United Airlines gates at O'Hare. Paul had told him on the telephone that this half hour before his flight back to Washington was the only time he could see him.

Sean glanced around at the executives who swarmed into the room, like sleek bees to a honeycomb of gold.

Paul arrived late, rushing breathlessly up the escalator, although not so quickly as to miss the opportunity to scan the room for possible constituents or cronies.

"Nora seems to be bouncing back pretty well," Paul said, toasting his brother with a vodka and tonic. "It's been a lot worse on her than on me. She'd been with Mickey all the time. I hardly got to know the poor little fellow."

"Our mother is still alive, Paul."

The vodka and tonic rested a moment at Paul's lips, and his darting gray eyes froze. "What? You'd better tell me all about it," he said softly and lowered the glass.

Sean told him all about it, except for the part about Nora's discovering "Mary" and then hiding her discovery for over a year. And he did not mention Father Terry O'Connor. When he finished, Paul's face was slack and pale. His fingers drummed convulsively on the arm of the plush beige sofa on which he was sitting. "My God," he said.

Sean waited, sensing that his brother was groping for an appropriate reaction. Outside, a huge 747 nosed into a jetway, its wide body gleaming silver.

"From what you say, she would have been in a home all this time anyway," Paul said. "Still, why did the old man . . . ?"

"The disgrace, damn it!" Sean snapped. "The disgrace of the mother of his sons being mad."

Paul shook his head. "Yeah, but . . . you know, he really believes that stuff about bad blood."

"Sure he does. And how could he make one son president and the other a cardinal if the world knew they had a mother who's mad? Hell, they probably would have thrown me out of the seminary if they thought there was insanity in the family."

Paul moved his empty glass around the surface of the coffee table. "Still, it's a damn fool stupid thing to do."

Sean's anger came flooding back. "Worse than stupid. He's the one that's the lunatic."

"I suppose so," Paul agreed. "He meant well. . . ."

"Do I have to tell you what the streets of Hell are paved with?" Sean retorted.

"I don't know what to say, Sean. I've got to sleep on this, figure it out, put some meaning to it. You aren't going to go public with it, are you?"

"No point in that, is there? Not now."

"No." Paul's relief was obvious. "I guess not." He reached for his hand-tooled leather attaché case and struggled out of the sofa. "I've got to catch that plane now. You don't mind?"

"You'll visit her the next time you're home? She won't know you, but—"

"Sure I will. It will take some getting used to, though." Paul seized on the promise. "Next time I'm in town."

As he watched his handsome brother walk out of the lounge, Sean knew that Paul would never set eyes on Mary Eileen Cronin.

For hours, Mike huddled in his chair, watching the lights of the city, unable to react to what had happened. Sean had discovered his secret. How didn't matter. Mike always knew that he would one day, one way or another.

He was still shaking from the terror of the confrontation. Good God, a man tried, he made mistakes, he did his best. No one ever understood, they never tried to understand. What the hell was he supposed to do? Let her kill the little kid? Even if he wasn't my son—and I suppose that he wasn't—I had to protect him. No gratitude, none at all. He doesn't realize how much I gave up.

Maybe I ought to call Elizabeth. She's the only one who came close. . . . No, I can't call her. She's married now. I gave that up too.

The lights of the Loop flickered on and off. A sharp stab of pain cut through Mike Cronin's head.

Then the lights of the Loop went out completely.

CHAPTER
—TWENTY-EIGHT—
1973

"Play it again, Sam," Bishop Sean Cronin ordered Monsignor James McGuire.

Jimmy managed an unusually wan smile. "I hadn't noticed your resemblance to Bogart until now, boss, but there *is* a similarity—around the mouth and teeth, if you get what I mean."

"Play it." Sean was in an unusually good mood, in part because he had found something that upset his normally unflappable second-in-command. Jimmy pushed the button on the tape player. The television screen came alive and Sean saw himself, calm and cool, with a touch of gray at his temples. His pale hair was too long, his suit was rumpled, and if one looked closely one could see that his shoes weren't polished. "Lovemaking between a man and woman," the person on the screen was saying, "can mean many different things. Through lovemaking, lovers forgive one another, show their gratitude to one another, declare their love, renew their vows, chase their anxieties and their anger, reestablish communication, make life livable for one another, challenge, stimulate, excite, and reassure one another. Also, of course, it is the means for continuing the human race."

The pious Jesuit who shared the panel with Sean was outraged. "Even if you are a bishop, I must be frank, Your Excellency. Those are tasteless, vulgar words."

"Really, Father? It had been my understanding that it's precisely all those complex dimensions of marriage and love that led St. Paul to call it a great sacrament."

"You're a celibate, aren't you?" the Jesuit asked with a hint of a smirk. "How would a celibate know these things?"

"I try to keep my vows, yes." A slight frown marred the Vicar General's handsome face. "I do counseling every evening in the cathedral rectory, I hear confessions on weekends, I have friends and family, and I *am* a male member of the human race with the usual male reactions . . . that's how I know."

The Jesuit exploded. "Bishop, those are scandalous things you're saying!"

"Scandalous for a bishop to be a member of the human race?"

Jimmy pushed the stop button on the video recorder.

"So that's what all the cardinals in the United States, except for Eamon, want to censure me for? Jimmy, they're full of baloney."

"My information is that they won't go after you by name. They'll simply pass a general resolution recommending that bishops not talk about intimate human relationships on radio or television programs. It's a way of getting at you and, of course, getting at Eamon too. They know he won't be at the November meeting because he's still recuperating from his heart attack. You've got to fight for his sake as well as your own."

"Don't be ridiculous, Jimmy." Sean was as relaxed as he had been on the television screen. "Eamon's quite capable of conspiring against them himself, if he wants to, and he thinks he knows better than to try to save me from my own folly. Forget it. It doesn't make a damn bit of difference."

"Sean, it will destroy you. You'll be finished in the American Church."

Sean shrugged and rose from his chair in the chancellor's office. "How many times do I have to tell you, Jimmy, I don't care about my future in the American Church?"

"What do you care about, Sean? You work here all day and then half the night at the cathedral rectory. You hear confessions Saturday afternoon and evening. You say two Masses on Sunday. You don't take a day off. You're in Washington or Rome at least once a month. You don't even see your brother or Nora and the kids. What *do* you care about?"

Sean put his hands in his pockets. "I'm not sure, Jimmy. If I ever find out I'll let you know. In the meantime, I've got to go

deal with Father Camillo of the Soldiers of Christ. I'll at least
have a little fun bouncing that so-and-so from the diocese."

"If I had a sister like Nora, I'd visit her," Jimmy said firmly.

"I'm sure you would, Jimmy, I'm sure you would."

Father Camillo had the manner and voice of a Spanish aristocrat and the looks to match, a face out of El Greco, tan skin,
liquid brown eyes. Moreover, he had the worldwide power of the
Soldiers of Christ behind him, a secret international Catholic soci-
ety made up of priests and laity, modeled to some extent after the
Communist Party with small cells and a strategy of infiltrating
elite groups in critical social positions. He had begun the conversation in Sean's office by trying to intimidate the Vicar General of
the Archdiocese of Chicago, as though the latter were something
of a peasant.

He didn't get very far. Sean cut him off and flipped open a
manila folder. "Let's see, Father Camillo, we have three reports of
your group infiltrating young people's organizations in parishes of
the archdiocese. One of the priests whose group was infiltrated
sent a young woman who could speak Spanish to a meeting where
you and your colleagues were present. She overheard some very
interesting conversations, Father, the sort of things that one would
expect from a Communist infiltrating a union, but hardly from a
priest in an organization concerned about spiritual values and
guidance."

Camillo raised his hand in protest. "But I am sure she exaggerated—"

"And then we have protests from five husbands whose wives
joined your organization. Apparently they won't sleep with their
men without permission from their spiritual guide, who, in a number of cases, seems to be you, Father Camillo."

"Slander!"

"Perhaps, Father, perhaps. Then there are a number of women
who have also protested because, once their husbands became part
of your group, they insisted that the wife kneel and ask for their
blessing before she left the house. They also claimed the right to
make all decisions of the family. That doesn't work with Irish-
women, Father. A cultural difference between them and the
Spanish, I suppose."

"The husband is the head of the home," Camillo insisted.

"Just barely, especially if he's Irish. Now let's see. Oh, yes. We have records of four young women who ended up in the hospital because they had scourged themselves rather too severely at the recommendation of their spiritual guide. Then there are parents who report their children are spying on them, pastors who find that their curates have hidden tape recorders in their offices and listened to their conversations, and faculty members at a Catholic university here who think they were denied tenure because of your group's conniving. We also have several copies of your confidential magazine, which, in effect, repudiates the Second Vatican Council. All in all, a very interesting dossier, Father Camillo."

The Spaniard's thin lips were white with rage. "You have no right to sit in judgment on what we do, Monsignor."

"Now, there you are wrong, Father Camillo. I am the Vicar General of this archdiocese, and I have the right to revoke your permission to continue to work in this archdiocese. And I am doing so. Here is a copy of a letter; the original will be put in the mail this afternoon, and you will note that I am sending a copy to the Apostolic Delegate and to the Sacred Congregation of the Clergy in Rome. I'm sure you may appeal if you want, but to tell you the truth, I doubt that it will work because if you persist in your appeal these materials may be leaked to the press with very considerable negative effect on your work around the country."

"I demand to see the Cardinal."

"No one is going to see the Cardinal for several weeks, Father Camillo. He is recovering from his heart attack, but he is not receiving visitors. I can assure you that His Eminence has given his full approval to this decision."

"You yourself are also subject to judgment," snarled the Soldier of Christ.

"Ah, yes, indeed. And I wouldn't be surprised to learn that you and your friends have something to do with the kangaroo court that's going to sit in judgment on me in November. To tell you the truth, Father Camillo, I don't care what you or they say. Whenever the Cardinal Archbishop wants my resignation, he can have it, as he well knows. Nonetheless, as long as I am his Vicar General, I will carry out his wishes. And I assure you, Father Camillo, it is his wish that you and your community leave this diocese within the month. If you have not departed then, we will be forced to take canonical action. And, incidentally, there are also ways to make things difficult for you civilly. We do have a holdover from Old Spain, you know. The civil authorities occasionally cooperate with us. I bet that place of yours in Hyde Park is violating all kinds of zoning regulations."

The Spaniard was trembling with rage as he stood up. "You will regret this, Monsignor. You will regret this as long as you live."

"Get out," Sean said. He slammed the folder shut and stood his full six feet one inch. "Get out before I lose my patience."

Father Camillo got out.

Sean checked his calendar to see what other appointments were written in. He was weary and depressed, a weariness that sleep could not cure and a depression that nothing exorcised. He was going through the motions, doing what a priest should do, trying to be what a bishop should be. His self-esteem and self-confidence were shattered, his faith still weak, and his hope, at best, paper thin.

Where was the Holy Spirit in his life?

The following Saturday, after Mass and before confessions, Sean went to visit the sick. First of all, a visit to the Cardinal at his house on North State Parkway.

Eamon McCarthy, thinner, paler, and old, was relaxing on the couch on the second floor, studying the overseas edition of *L'Osservatore Romano*. "You look much better than you did a week ago, Eminence." Sean wondered if the magnificent old man would ever look himself again.

"Very good of you to say so, Bishop Cronin. I'm feeling much better. If it were not for the doctor's instructions, I would come down Monday and relieve you of your many administrative burdens." The smile, quick and mocking, had not changed a bit.

"You'd have a hard time finding the chancery office, Eminence. We've moved it across the street. But I'm sure Monsignor McGuire would be happy to let you use his office."

"Yes, of course. I knew I could count on you to leave me at least a cubbyhole somewhere or other. Any serious problems this week . . . the kind you could tell me about without violating the doctor's orders to protect me from my own sense of responsibility?"

"Just two, Eminence." Sean hesitated, then continued. "I ordered the Soldiers of Christ out. Father Camillo was something less than cooperative. I assume he will appeal to the Apostolic Delegate, who, as you know, is no friend of yours."

"Nor a friend of yours, I might add, Bishop Cronin. But then we both know the Apostolic Delegate would not dare to overrule a Cardinal. No, I'm afraid that Father Camillo will have to take his white Freemasons somewhere else and the Archdiocese of Chicago will be spared them in the future. And I can tell from the look on your face that there is something else and you are debating whether you should tell it to me or not. You'd better tell me, Bishop."

"Jimmy has learned from one of his canon law friends that there's a movement under way to censure me at the bishops' meeting in November. The resolution will be introduced by all the cardinals—all but yourself, of course—and will not mention me explicitly but will rather lament the fact that certain bishops have said imprudent things about marital intimacy on television and urge that such things do not happen again."

Eamon McCarthy smoothed the few strands of hair still left on the top of his head. "And it is, of course," the Cardinal said thoughtfully, "a way of punishing me for tolerating you."

"As to that, Eminence, it is a punishment richly deserved."

"Doubtless. And I presume, being who you are, you intend to ignore the whole thing until after it's over, at which time you will tell the gentlemen of the press that you would say exactly the same thing on television all over again if the circumstances permitted?"

"You know me very well, don't you, Eminence?"

"Too well, Bishop Cronin, too well. Certainly so well that I will not attempt to dissuade you from your course of action. In truth, I would be somewhat disappointed if you told me you were going to do anything else, given the fact that every new foolish thing you do brings you one step closer to becoming my successor. I would imagine this particular incident will absolutely guarantee that you will be the next Cardinal Archbishop of Chicago."

"My father would be happy to hear that, Eminence."

"Yes, doubtless. Well, Bishop Cronin, you need not trouble yourself on my account. I will follow my doctor's orders and refuse to worry about your fate next month at the bishops' meeting."

But of course he would. There was not the slightest doubt in Sean's mind about that.

Michael Cronin's suite in the John Hancock Center was equipped as a sort of halfway hospital, with a nurse in attendance as well as a housekeeper. Sean visited his father every week, a ritual that left him emotionally exhausted. The doctors assured him that his father's crippling stroke had been inevitable, but Sean knew that their quarrel about Mary Eileen had been the catalyst.

When the hospital first called to tell him of the stroke he had still been so angry that he had refused to go to see his father. Then the rage faded. Who was he to sit in judgment of another human being? Nora had been right again.

The old man sat in his room and either watched television or stared at Lake Michigan. He could walk a few feet by himself and with one hand operate the television remote control. Sometimes he would scratch a few words on a pad of paper attached to the side of his wheelchair. Often, when Sean left their brief meeting, he wondered if the magical science that had saved his father's life and now kept him alive was a blessing or not.

"I think Agnew got off lucky." Sean went through the political events of the previous week. "And I can't imagine anything funnier than Gerald Ford as vice-president. You know, they say that he can't walk and chew gum at the same time."

There was a faint grimace on Mike's face.

"And Paul is calling for Nixon's impeachment for the Watergate cover-up. He's taking some heat from his constituents, but I bet by next summer Paul will get so much credit for being one of the first to call for impeachment procedures that the Mayor will be happy to slate him for the Senate in '76. What do you think?"

The cramped hand scrawled two illegible words on the note pad. Sean, who had learned with practice to understand most of his father's scrawling, peered over his shoulder and deciphered *Nixon-bum*.

"You better believe he's a bum," Sean agreed. "Too bad Paul isn't going to be able to run against him. There wouldn't be an easier man to beat for the presidency in '76."

His father's response was to turn on the television to the Notre Dame game. The Fighting Irish, everyone agreed, were destined to be national champions this year. His father's apartment in the

Hancock Center was sufficiently high for the signals from the South Bend television station to get through clearly.

Sean watched the first quarter and then excused himself. It was time to get back to the cathedral to hear confession.

His father made no sign that he heard him say goodbye or that he noticed he had left the room.

After he heard confessions, Sean went to his room and tossed his cassock on the battered old ottoman. Then he hurried down the stairs for dinner. As he went by the office at the entrance of the cathedral, the telephone operator handed him a note. *Sister Margarita from St. Helena's Home asked you to call at once. Important.*

Sean returned the call quickly, nervously jabbing at the telephone dial. "Bishop Cronin here, Sister," he said at Sister Margarita's infinitely courteous "Good evening."

"Oh, yes, Bishop. I'm glad you called. Mary seems to be slipping. I don't think she can last too much longer."

CHAPTER
——TWENTY-NINE——
1973

Most days in Washington for Congressman Paul Cronin were good days. A rising power in Congress, chairman of a subcommittee of the Judiciary Committee, admired and respected by his colleagues, and a favorite of the press, the forty-four-year-old Congressman from Illinois was marked by everyone as a man with a very promising future. He had managed to combine the Cook County organization and the support of Richard J. Daley with liberal stands on race, women's rights, and, especially, the war in Vietnam. His wit and charm and good looks made him a favorite of Washington hostesses and a popular escort for many of the unattached young women of Washington.

But this particular November day had been a disaster. First of all, a delegation from home had called upon him to express grave reservations about his resolution calling for the impeachment of President Nixon. They were not important people from the district, but blacks and whites from the East End. They had come to Washington to press for release of loan funds to stabilize their community. Paul expected their visit to him to be a gesture of gratitude for his success in prying the monies loose. It turned out, however, that they were less interested in his clout with HUD than his failure to support "Our President" against the odious John Dean.

As he sat in the bar at the Statler Hotel, waiting for Stan Carruthers, a colleague from Upstate New York, to join him for an evening on the town, Paul remembered his response.

"As a congressman of the United States, I am sworn to uphold the Constitution. As a member of the House Judiciary Committee, it is my most solemn obligation to consider whether a president—any president—is guilty of high crimes or misdemeanors in office. There is sufficient evidence, it seems to me, to warrant further investigation by my committee. I would be derelict in my constitutional obligations if I did not demand that investigation. I would like very much to have your support, but in the absence of your support, I will go ahead with my sworn obligation. I can do nothing else."

There was some applause, but Paul was well aware that there were many who were not applauding either his opposition to the war or his enthusiasm for impeaching Nixon.

Then Makuch had appeared in his office. He had decided that the twenty-thousand-dollar-a-year subsidy he was getting from Paul was not enough.

"I must say, Paul, that I'm dismayed by your opposition to the President." He flipped the envelope with the twenty thousand-dollar bills into his pocket as though it were a payment for an electric light bill.

"I have a constitutional responsibility—"

"Fuck constitutional responsibility," Makuch said. "He's our president and you'd better leave him alone, or some people are gonna find out about the Reservoir. I imagine that there are people over at the White House who would be interested in that information."

Paul felt his face flame and his fists clench. He choked back the impulse to say that Makuch had grown moderately wealthy with Cronin money, and he would be cutting off a source of regular income. Maybe Makuch didn't need the money any more. "We'll have to see what the investigations turn up," he said instead.

"Fuck the investigations," Makuch said. "You'd better think about what I'm saying. You're skating on thin ice."

After Makuch left, Paul drummed his fingers thoughtfully on his desk. Blackmail was bad enough, but now Makuch was demanding more than money. He was demanding political power, cracking the whip to see if Paul would jump. He almost certainly knew that Paul was destined for the Senate and possibly the White

House. If he enjoyed throwing his weight around politically, he would revel in the years ahead. The bind would get worse for Paul. If he waffled on the impeachment now, it would certainly be held against him when he was up for reelection next year and when he was running for the Senate. He could probably survive, but it would be awkward, very awkward. Unless he completely misread the signs, Nixon would be terribly unpopular by summer, and a liberal Democrat who voted in favor of him would look like a hypocrite. Of course Makuch might change his mind before summer. But what if he didn't?

And the bind would get worse as the years went on.

Paul nursed his drink thoughtfully. He was really not up to a night with Carruthers. It would be much better to go to Sally Grant's apartment. She was half expecting him anyway.

Carruthers finally arrived, apologizing for his tardiness. His wife and children had arrived unexpectedly from home for the weekend, and hence he was unavailable for the evening. But they might at least have a drink before he went home, he said.

"I'm taking a lot of heat," Paul said. "People from back home are leaning on me. Some fellow is even digging around in my war record trying to find something dirty."

Carruthers, a thin, sallow man with a high hairline and long black sideburns, shook his head sympathetically. "It's a rough one. The crowd over at the White House are not going to get more pleasant if the walls begin to crumble around them. Anyway, your war record is all right. You're a Medal of Honor winner, aren't you? And a POW? I mean, isn't the big line on you that a Medal of Honor winner was opposing the war in Vietnam?"

"I'm okay," responded Paul. "But it's hard to prove that charges are false once they're made. All I need with the senatorial race coming up in '76 are unsubstantiated charges like that drifting around."

Carruthers stirred his vodka martini thoughtfully. "Is this an individual or a group of people?"

"Just one guy."

"There are ways things like that can be taken care of. People can be leaned on a little bit, if you know what I mean. Nothing really messy, of course. It's usually pretty effective."

"Oh?" said Paul. "I might be interested in something like that."

Carruthers scribbled something on a napkin and passed it

across the table. "They're a very discreet bunch, Paul. You can trust them."

Paul stuffed the napkin into the pocket of his jacket without looking at it. "I hear Tip O'Neill is just about ready to send the signal to the party regulars. We're not going to be alone much longer."

"I think we already have enough on the bastard to impeach him four times over."

After Carruthers left, Paul had another drink and then walked down Massachusetts Avenue to Dupont Plaza. Under a streetlight, he took out the napkin from his pocket. On it there was the name "Eric" and a phone number. He memorized the phone number and tore the napkin into tiny pieces.

Sally Grant lived in an elegant apartment just off Dupont Plaza. A lush redhead, she was an analyst at the Securities and Exchange Commission. She had a simple, uncomplicated animal hunger. Indeed, when she opened the door of her apartment, she was dressed in thin black lace, more than ready for Paul's arrival. "God, Paul, I thought you'd never come." She hugged him ferociously and half dragged him into the bedroom.

His dreams after they made love were restless and troubled. He was back at the Reservoir, flares exploding over him in the dark. The hordes of screaming, bayonet-wielding Chinese burst out of the darkness and stabbed at his gut.

"What the hell's the matter with you?" Sally demanded, as he woke up in the middle of a scream.

"Nightmares from the war days," he said sluggishly. "They come and they go."

"The trouble with you, Paul Cronin," Sally said, "is that you're too goddamned reckless."

She scurried out of the bedroom and came back with a tumbler full of Scotch. He drained it in a single gulp.

"What do you mean, I'm too reckless?" he asked.

She sat on the edge of the bed, clutching her frilly nightgown at her throat. "I don't quite know what I mean. I guess I think you get off on taking chances, running risks, courting danger. You're a married congressman from a district where your wife is as popular as you are, if not more so, and you've got at least three different women—that I know of—in this city, and if I'm able to find out about the other two without any trouble, just about everyone in Washington must know about them too. What if you get caught? What if your wife catches you? What if the press catches you? What if the White House goes after you to stop you from pushing this impeachment?"

"I don't intend to get caught," Paul said.

"Do you know what people say on the Hill about you? They say you're smart, you work hard, you're charming, and that you're a Mississippi riverboat gambler. You lucked out on opposition to the war. You're probably going to luck out on impeachment. But one of these days you're going to draw for the high card and lose. Mississippi riverboat gamblers, they say on the Hill, never become committee chairmen, much less presidents."

Paul rubbed his eyes. "And what does all this have to do with my dreams?"

"I don't know how it figures, Paul. I have the feeling that you did something reckless a long time ago, and it comes back and haunts you in your sleep."

Paul slid out of bed and began to dress. "I am what I am, Sally," he said. "Take me or leave me." He wasn't sure which option he wanted Sally to take. She was getting too serious. She was beginning to remind him of Maggie Shields.

The next day in the kitchen of his home in Georgetown, Paul was poring over his staff's memo on impeachment. He had called "Eric" an hour before and had arranged to meet him in a bar around the corner from the Shoreham Hotel. The voice at the other end of the line had been smooth and cultivated. It asked no questions; indeed, it did not even seem particularly interested in Paul's name.

The doorbell rang and Paul, who was fending for himself since his housekeeper had Saturday off, answered it. It was his daughter Eileen and her friend, Nicole Shields. They were both high school seniors and had come to Washington for the weekend to investigate colleges for the following year. The trip was a lark for Eileen, a slightly shorter version of her mother who was certainly going to St. Mary's of Notre Dame. Nicole, an introverted but sexy-looking girl, was just as certainly not going to Notre Dame.

Tom Shields had remarried two years previously. His second wife was a black-haired nurse from Ireland with a gorgeous figure and a mind that matched Tom's. All the kids except Nicole seemed to get along well with their stepmother, but the tempestuous older daughter of Maggie Shields treated Fiona with silent contempt.

"Too bad Notre Dame isn't on national TV." Eileen hugged him dutifully. "I can't stand to listen to games on the radio. They make me so nervous."

"I think football is ridiculous," said Nicole, staring at Paul with bold appraisal.

"I'm afraid I won't even be able to listen to the game," he said. He remembered for the first time that he was supposed to take the two girls to dinner. "If I'm going to show off you beautiful young girls at the Lion d'Or tonight, I've got to finish these memos about getting rid of Mr. Nixon."

"Getting rid of Mr. Nixon?" Nicole said. "That would be a lot of fun."

Paul suspected that if Eileen were not with them her friend would almost certainly make a pass at him. It had been a long time since he had had one that young. He would bet that she was anything but inexperienced.

"We won't keep you," said Eileen with characteristic efficiency. "Just stopped by to say hello. We have to get over to Trinity College. We'll probably listen to the game there."

"I wish you were staying here tonight," he said. He was actually rather pleased with the fact that they were not. "But I know how young people like to hang around college dorms."

"It's where the action is," said Eileen brightly. She was a typical high school senior: bright, attractive, happy, her whole life stretching out ahead of her in promise. Nicole, on the other hand, with her angry, dangerous eyes, seemed doomed already. Why did Eileen hang around with her? Concern or family loyalty, he supposed. And why did Nicole hang around with Eileen? Maybe she sensed there was some chance of survival in the radiance of his eldest daughter.

"Your mother called from Panama night before last, Eileen. She was going out to San Miguelito to see about the housing project there." What did his daughters think of their parents' intermittent marriage? Indeed, what did they think of him? Lively Eileen, quiet Mary, and madcap Noreen seemed utterly unperturbed by anything their parents did. Self-possessed like their mother. Did they make the same sharp, keen judgments that Nora made?

"Is she going to stop here on the way home?" Eileen asked.

"No, she's going home for a board meeting; then she's coming here."

"Mother's just amazing," Eileen said. "I don't know how she does it, much less make it seem so easy . . . I mean, you're a marvel too, Dad, but mother's a woman."

"That she surely is, Eileen."

After the two girls left, Paul went back to his memo, although he did turn on the radio to listen to the Notre Dame–Georgia Tech game. Nora *was* an amazing woman. Eileen was right about that. His respect for her increased each year. He was now talking the feminist line in his public speeches and was thankful that his wife was a feminist role model. He could point to the proof that he practiced what he preached.

Their interludes together were cordial. Living apart some of the time, he supposed, was good for the marriage. That way he could imagine to himself that Nora was one of his mistresses. It was easier for him to deal with Nora as a part-time mistress than as a full-time wife.

Eric was a tall, handsome Nordic blond, hardly the mafioso that Paul had expected. Rather, he was a smooth businessman in impeccably tailored clothes. He had a faint Swedish accent.

"We have a full range of services, sir." He never called Paul by name. "We guarantee full satisfaction, total discretion, and we accept payment only after our task is accomplished." He hesitated for a moment. "Normally we make a minimal response to the problem. It's just as well, however, that you do not ask too many specific questions about the exact technique we will use, since it might be disruptive for you to know. I can assure you that in a case like the one you have described, it will be very likely that quite simple preventive measures will be more than adequate. Our charge, by the way, will be twenty-five thousand dollars."

"You're sure there won't be any trouble afterward?" Paul asked.

Eric gestured suavely over his glass of soda water. "None at all. There are certain kinds of pain which, when professionally administered, dissuade even the bravest men from doing anything that would risk a repetition."

Paul was horrified by the Swede's cruel businesslike attitude, yet he knew of no other way to deal with the problem of Joe Makuch. "Remarkable," he muttered softly.

"Now, if you will provide me with some more details about this Mr. Makuch, we'll be able to activate our program against him."

"You're sure it will work?"

"You may rely on us, sir. We guarantee satisfaction."

CHAPTER
THIRTY
1973

Nora considered the remaining half of her gin and tonic. She must make it last for another half hour, the time she had assigned herself to sunbathe in the comforting tropic warmth on the balcony of her hotel. In the distance, the blue of the ocean and the blue of the sky merged into a single gentle background. Nora sighed. Why couldn't the weather be like this in Chicago in November?

No more than one gin and tonic a day when she was on the road, and no drinks at all at home, save for an occasional glass of wine with dinner. Nora did not entirely accept the judgments made by her friends, that at thirty-eight she was more beautiful than ever. Nonetheless, she was not going to permit herself to go to seed, and drinking was a quick way to do just that.

The phone jangled in her hotel room. She wrapped her wrinkle-free travel robe around herself and struggled out of the lounge chair. It was the first secretary from the embassy.

"Mr. Thornton said that you had a fine time out at San Miguelito this afternoon. I'm delighted to hear it."

"It's a South Side Chicago Irish parish in the middle of the tropics," she responded enthusiastically. "Father Leo has that district organized like the most efficient ward in Chicago. The liturgy was beautiful, the little kids were wonderful, and the housing project seemed to be perfect. And Leo didn't give me a hard time, as so many of the clergy do, about my requirement that Cronin Enterprises make a small profit. He says his people don't want gifts or charity. They want the chance to do something for themselves. That's the reason the Foundation exists, you know."

"I understand, though it's an unusual approach in this part of the world. People get used to government loans they know they don't have to pay back, or to church gifts. Private businesses making loans with small interest are unusual."

Nora tightened the belt on her gown. "Leo says that both the other ways deprive people of their self-respect."

"Well, maybe they do. . . . Thornton said you seemed a little tired at the end of the day. I hope that doesn't mean you'll turn down a dinner invitation for this evening?"

"Oh, no," Nora replied cheerily. "A mile swim in the ocean and a half hour basking in the sunlight, and I'd very much appreciate dinner. Thanks for the invitation." The first secretary would make the usual pass halfway through dinner. She would reject it briskly, and the rest of the evening would be pleasant.

"I'll be by about seven thirty then."

"Fine, just fine."

Nora had had two affairs since Mickey's death, one in Paris and one in Chicago. Both brief, intense, and utterly unsatisfying. They provided neither the sweet unbearable ecstasy of her two weeks with Sean nor the routine affection of her sex life with Paul. Illicit sex had been consigned to the same ash can of rejected escapes as had gin and tonics.

Her experience with Sean convinced her that she was not undersexed and that she would be much better off with passion as a regular part of her life. Since illicit sex didn't work, she decided, she would have to make licit sex work. If affection for a charming little-boy husband wasn't much to build passion on, it was better than nothing.

Her own cold-bloodedness shocked her; as always, however, Nora was interested in discovering more about herself. Paul was a thoroughly presentable, if shallow, male, more attractive than most of the men who made passes at her. Occasional sex with a husband you don't love but don't hate either—one could do much worse.

She went back to the balcony, stretched out on the lounge, and unfastened her robe.

Part of Nora was dead. She presumed it would remain dead, killed by the poison of guilt, pain, and regret. Nora accepted the verdict. The part of her that still lived would pass out its years, doing its best, lamenting that which had been lost but refusing to quit. She would continue to be a wife, a mother, and a business-woman until the comedy was finished.

She tasted the gin and tonic carefully. Either she would have to drink it more quickly or stir out of her comfortable position and get ice cubes from the refrigerator in her room. She rolled over on her stomach. She was rich, successful, and even becoming famous. Yet part of her, the important part, the part that mattered, was numb and cold and would, it seemed, remain that way forever.

If that was the way it was to be, then so be it.

Even the businesswoman-philanthropist role was losing some of its attractiveness. She was good at it now, very good indeed, but the fun was going out of that too. Somehow, some way, she had to find greater challenges.

When Nora arrived home at eleven o'clock the following night, exhausted from the plane trip and worn out by the long wait for a cab at O'Hare, she found the parlor of the old house on Glenwood Drive decorated with streamers and a banner proclaiming *¡Bien Venidos Mama!* Her three daughters were playing samba music on their flutes, enthusiastically if not altogether precisely.

Later, when they were all laughing and exhausted, sitting closely around the coffee table in the parlor, Nora asked Eileen, "How was Dad when you saw him in Washington? I talked to him from the airport in Miami, but we only had a few minutes."

"He looked tired. And he was working hard on the impeach-ment. But otherwise he was fine. I wasn't able to spend much time with him because I was busy keeping Nicole out of trouble."

"I don't see how you put up with her," Nora said. "She drives Tom and Fiona crazy. It's good of you to take care of her."

"Taking care of people runs in the family." Eileen grinned. "Anyway, I like her . . . well, some of the time."

Mary and Noreen disappeared to their rooms, after much hug-ging and many good-night kisses. Eileen hung around. "Speaking of taking care of people. . . ." She slouched into the couch. "Did you hear the Murrays are getting a divorce? An annulment from the Church too."

"I'm not surprised," Nora said. She sensed a heart-to-heart talk, probably long overdue. A pang of guilt assailed her.

"Why haven't you ever divorced Dad?" Sixteen-year-olds can be disconcertingly direct.

"Dad, to begin with, is not an alcoholic and he doesn't beat me—"

Eileen made an annoyed face. "Oh, I know *that*. But, Mom, you're so different from each other. Doesn't it become boring?"

"All relationships are boring some of the time; there's more between me and Dad now than there ever has been." She had to choose her words very carefully. There would be no hiding from Eileen.

"I know *that* too, but Mom, he's so *shallow* and you're so deep, so much more like Uncle Sean. Why do you stay with Dad?"

"There are many kinds of love, Eileen. All loves are different and they all have their own commitments. You keep the commitments until they become absolutely impossible."

"Why? Why should you be stuck with a commitment you made a long time ago?"

Nora felt lightheaded and wished she had a cool gin and tonic. "Because if people don't keep their commitments, no one can trust anyone else."

Eileen's face was locked in a deep frown. "Will I make the same kind of mistakes?"

"You've had a much better childhood than I, Eileen. More confidence in yourself. I don't think you'll make many serious mistakes. Just so long as you don't think I'm lonely or frustrated or miserable in keeping my promises."

"Keeping promises is a good thing," Eileen agreed. "Otherwise, where would I be?" She brightened considerably, returned to being a happy teenager, and hugged her mother.

I guess I did all right, thought Nora. At least I'll be more ready for the next one.

Noreen dashed into the room. "Oh, I forgot. Uncle Sean called at dinnertime and said you were to call him at his private number no matter how late you got in. He sounded kind of worried."

Was it Uncle Mike? Nora walked across the room and looked up in her private phone book Sean's number at the cathedral. It had been a long time since she had used it. She punched the numbers on the phone. Sean answered at the first ring.

"Cronin," he said, sounding like a man who had not slept for a month.

"My name too," she said.

"Nora, thanks for calling. I hate to disturb you. Mary died this morning. I'm going to be saying the Funeral Mass at the home tomorrow at eleven thirty. Sister and I will be the only ones there. Paul says he can't get away. I thought you might—"

"I'll be there, Sean. Of course, I'll be there."

For the gospel of the Mass in the little pseudo-baroque chapel, Sean chose the story of the resurrection of Lazarus from St. John's Gospel. His homily was brief. "It may seem today that Mary's life was a foolish waste. She lived sixty-five years, and the last forty of those years she did not know who she was, did not recollect anything of her childhood, of her girlhood, of her young adult years, did not remember her family or her friends or those who loved her. She was not, as far as we could tell, lonely, but she was surely alone, a lost soul. And yet, we know that God loved Mary, and that now all the joys of life are part of a bright, glowing joy that will never go pale, never be dimmed, never end for all eternity. There is only one thing we can understand today. God loves Mary, and he loves all of us."

Sean went on with the Mass, lifting the bread and then the wine in offering. The young nun discreetly wiped her eyes. For Nora there were no tears.

Then, suddenly, the Presence, gone for so long, returned. There was no forgiveness, no blame, no lifting of burdens of guilt, no message that at last she was forgiven. Rather, the love that surrounded Nora behaved as though it had never left, chided her gently for not noticing its presence, and enveloped her in caressing and tender warmth. Embraced by such love, Nora realized how irrelevant was forgiveness, how foolish was anger, and how ridiculous was guilt. The part of her that had been numb and dead was alive again, so vital and so happy; the numbness seemed only to have been a very minor part of a faintly disturbing dream she had had long ago.

When Sean put the sacred host in her hands at communion time with the words, "Nora, the Body of Christ," tears finally came, tears of joy for Sean and for herself.

Later, Nora and Sean stopped for lunch in a quiet little restaurant just outside of Libertyville, not far from the seminary at Mundelein. As soon as they had ordered their meal, she said,

"Sean, if you can find it in your heart to forgive me, I want to be friends again. I've been a fool these last couple of years, blaming myself for Mickey's death and blaming you . . . well, blaming you for everything. It's ridiculous, and I promise it won't happen again."

"I'd much sooner have you as a friend than as an enemy, Nora. Besides, I'm the one who should be on his knees begging for forgiveness."

She felt her face grow warm. "I want to talk about Italy. . . . I—I loved you then, Sean, and I always will. The terrible physical hunger is gone. I'm sure it won't come back—"

He looked into her eyes. "I'm never going to be so sure of myself again, Nora. So I won't make any promises." His face was transformed by a smile. "But I think you're reasonably safe from me so long as we never go on vacation together again."

They both laughed, the tension eased, and they were happy and even young again.

Paul felt his fingers tremble as he read the small newspaper clipping that Eric had presented him with in the bar near the Shoreham. "I'm sorry, sir, about this regrettable incident. These things do happen occasionally, and while we assume full responsibility for them, they still cause us a great deal of concern."

The clipping said that Joseph Makuch had been found early that morning dead in his car on Interstate 98, the victim of a heart attack. Mr. Makuch had apparently felt the first pains of the attack, driven his car off to the side of the road, and then died from a massive blockage of the heart artery before he was able to get out of the car and seek help. He was forty-five years old, survived by his widow, Carolyn, and two sons, Arnold and Joseph.

Paul returned the clipping to Eric. "What happened?" he asked.

"The man had a heart condition, sir." Eric frowned. "Apparently an autopsy was done and the pathologist reported that Makuch could have died almost any time within the past year. The usual causes, I'm afraid. Overindulgences in food and drink, too many cigarettes, no exercise . . . a bad way to live."

"And your—er—uh, I mean, your operatives—"

"Merely forced his car to the side of the road and disembarked from their own car. Even in the legal sense, I'm sure they would not be held responsible. Of course there will be no charge, and I can promise you that if in the future you require our services, we will make sure that this does not happen again."

On the way back to his house in Georgetown, Paul wondered what Eric and his "associates" would have done if they had known about Joe Makuch's bad heart. He was shocked by the death of the man who had blackmailed him and exhilarated by the feeling of freedom that the death brought—the first freedom from the fear of exposure that he had experienced in all that time. Too bad Makuch had to die, of course, but Paul felt no guilt over his death. After all, the man had a bad heart. He should have taken better care of himself.

CHAPTER
——THIRTY-ONE——
1973

If Mike Cronin was surprised that Sean had come to visit him in the morning on the wrong day of the week, he did not show it. Rather, he turned away from the television set and looked at his son blankly.

"Turn it off," Sean said.

One of his father's twisted fingers pushed the button. The picture and the sound died.

"I'll be only a few moments, Mrs. Calloway," he said to the smiling, even-tempered black nurse, who took the hint and left the room.

He turned again to his father. "We buried Mary Eileen yesterday."

A strange, wild light flowed momentarily in his father's eyes. The crippled hand scrawled on the note pad. *"Where?"*

"At the home. She won't be at your side in death any more than she was in life." He turned and walked to the door, fearful that his turbulent emotions would spill out and he would say more than he wanted to say. It was not up to him to punish his father. He had done enough of that already.

As he left the room, he heard the television set click on.

Paul placed the breakfast tray next to Nora on the bed. "Orange juice, bacon, pancakes, coffee . . . you worked up a big appetite last night."

"And you've become quite the cook! The hotcakes look good."

"Out of a package." Paul kissed her forehead.

Nora drew the sheet closer to her throat. For a few moments last night, drugged by wine and loneliness, they had been lovers. It was a deception. It could never work between them. Paul was too much a child. Still, her body was satisfied and Paul was obviously pleased.

"It was wonderful last night." She felt that she owed him a compliment.

He kissed her again. "Maybe we should do it a little more often. I'd like that. . . . Did you see Sean and Dad in Chicago?"

"Only Sean. He absolutely refuses to fight this censure thing."

"Censure?" Paul frowned.

"Hasn't he told you? Some bizarre Spanish order has persuaded a group of cardinals to introduce a censure motion at the bishops' meeting—about his television interview last year."

"He doesn't deserve that!" Paul's voice took on a tone that Nora recognized from their childhood. It was the voice of the older brother ready to defend his younger sibling.

"Can you stop them?"

"I sure as hell can try," he said.

"Best restaurant in Washington." Paul gestured at the dining room of the Lion d'Or. "At this moment I can see two Senators, three other Congressmen, and one Cabinet member . . . some of them are even with their wives."

Sean, feeling pleasantly relaxed after two Irish whiskeys, smiled along with his brother. "And no other bishops, with or without wives."

"I suspect they wouldn't know about the Lion d'Or."

"Oh, some of them would, but they just wouldn't want the others to know they know about it." They laughed again. Then Paul became serious, or rather adopted the facial expression and tilt of his head that, for him, passed for seriousness.

"How's the old man? Every time I come home I mean to go see him, but there's so much of a rush with Nora and the kids and all. . . ."

Sean played with his butter knife. "About the same. I guess he slips a little bit each time I see him, but that's been going on for years now, and I think he has a long way more to slip before he hits bottom. I have no idea what he thinks, what he feels, how he manages to survive."

"It's a shame. I hope nothing like that happens to me."

"I suppose you've heard about my troubles with the cardinals?"

Paul was quickly disposing of his salad. "Yes, I read about it." He was trying to sound casual. "You can't let those bastards do it to you, Sean. Hell, what motivation am I going to have to run for Senator if you're not already Archbishop of Chicago?"

Sean's laugh was hollow. "I'm not going to be Archbishop of Chicago, Paul. I hereby proclaim the competition over. I'm not going to fight. It's not worth it. I probably deserve censure for a lot more things than that one television program. Let them do whatever they want."

"You *have* to fight them, Sean." Paul put down his salad fork. "You simply *have* to fight them."

"I'm not going to fight them. And what's more, I insist that you don't try to fight them for me. Understand?"

Paul swallowed half of his glass of wine in a single gulp, as though it were water to quench his thirst. "Sure, Sean. If you say that I shouldn't fight them, then I won't fight them."

"So good of you to come to visit me, Congressman," said Alfonse Cardinal Michaels. "You understand how very little time we have in Washington, although of course I appreciate your invitation to lunch."

"Always happy to oblige a Prince of the Church," Paul said. The Prince of the Church's suite in the Statler was not especially princely, but it was big, appropriate enough for Michaels, who was a tall, stocky man with iron-gray hair and thick glasses. He was alleged to have one of the lowest golf handicaps in the hierarchy.

"If you're ever in Chicago, Your Eminence," Paul said, "I'd like to play golf with you. Perhaps we could persuade my wife to accompany us. She was a junior champion as a young woman. Her handicap is still four, and that's without working on it."

The Cardinal laughed. "I'm afraid I wouldn't stand a chance against such skill, Congressman, but I might take you up on it sometime. Your brother the Bishop doesn't play golf, does he?"

The first mention of Sean. "He used to play, but he's been so busy being a bishop, with Cardinal McCarthy's illness, you know, that he hasn't played in a number of years."

"Yes, it's certainly a shame about poor Eamon. He's never had very strong health. He was a couple of years ahead of me at the North American, you know."

"I certainly hope"—Paul moved quickly now—"that nothing comes of this ridiculous censure motion that's aimed at Sean."

"Oh, now," said the Cardinal, "it really isn't aimed at him."

"Most people think it is, Your Eminence, and it will put me in a very awkward position."

"Oh? I don't see why you should be embarrassed."

"Sean's extremely popular in my district. If the Church censures him, the people in my district are going to demand that I take a stand. I've got enough trouble with this Watergate thing as it is, and I certainly wouldn't want to get into a fight with the hierarchy. But my district wouldn't give me any choice."

"Is that so?" The Cardinal seemed interested and sympathetic.

Paul was creating his story out of whole cloth. Sean was indeed popular, but there would be little constituent pressure to denounce the hierarchy for going after him. "I could possibly be put in a position where my people would expect me to take a vigorous stand against everything the Church wanted, from help for Catholic schools to tax exemptions for Church property—that sort of thing. You know, Your Eminence, I'd certainly hate to change my position, especially since my membership on the judiciary committee is so crucial for such issues, but our neighborhood is the kind of place where you stand up for your own or you get out."

"Are you trying to blackmail me?" The Cardinal's voice turned cold.

"Yes, Your Eminence," Paul said. "That's precisely what I'm trying to do. I'm telling you to leave my brother alone. He doesn't know I'm doing this. Indeed, he explicitly told me not to do anything. He's still my brother, however, and I'm not going to let a bunch of bullies pick on him. Leave him alone, or you'll regret it."

There was a long pause while the Cardinal's shrewd blue eyes probed into Paul Cronin's soul. Finally the great man spoke. "I've always admired family loyalty, Congressman. I've always admired it very much."

On the last day of the bishops' meeting, Paul invited Sean to the Monocle Restaurant, a sleek, plush bistro on D Street, around the corner from the Capitol.

"Order the Crab Imperial; they know how to do it here," Paul said.

Sean, however, ordered bay scallops and declined the bottle of wine Paul offered. His brother looked disappointed but quickly masked his feelings behind bluff enthusiasm.

"No censure vote after all?"

Sean shrugged indifferently. "I suspect Eamon made a few phone calls."

"I'm glad it worked out. And sorry you can't stay here until the weekend. Nora's going to be in town, and it would be nice for the three of us to be together again."

"You two certainly have a peripatetic marriage."

A tinge of sadness touched Paul's eyes. "It works out well enough. Maybe after the next election she'll be able to shift her base from Chicago to Washington. We have good times when we're together. It takes a long time to be friends, Sean. A long time." The last sentence escaped in a burst of candor.

"I'm sure it does." Sean felt guilt and anguish. How could Paul and Nora ever be close when Nora carried with her the memories of Amalfi?

"You should have married her."

"What?" Sean wished he had accepted the wine.

Paul drained his gin and tonic. "I'm not up to her. She's a woman of substance and depth. She deserves a husband more like you. You should be a politician too. The old man made a big mistake."

Sean struggled to regain his composure. "I don't know what you're talking about, Paul. You were the star athlete, the war hero, the charmer. I couldn't win a race for precinct captain."

"It takes more than those things." Paul signaled for another drink. "I don't know what to call it—character? Anyway, you'd make a good president, and I might not. You would love Nora the way she ought to be loved, and I can't." He waved a hand vaguely. "It's too late to change anything. I'm her husband and I might just end up in the White House. With any luck"—he grinned —"I won't be any worse a president than I am a husband."

The Cronins were together at Paul and Nora's home on Christmas Day, all except Mike Cronin, who refused to leave his apartment even to celebrate Christmas. For Nora, it was the best Christmas in years. She and Sean were friends again. Her daughters were safely on their way to young womanhood. And her marriage had settled into an easy and relaxed pattern.

"The daughters" arranged one of their usual performances before the Christmas meal: flute music, Christmas carols, crazy little skits, including a dialogue among the "three old Cronins," with Eileen playing her father, Mary playing a very solemn "Bishop Uncle" and Noreen, of course, playing her mother. Noreen had about half the lines in the miniature drama because she had written the skit.

After the entertainment was finished, Noreen bustled around the room, filling glasses with sparkling burgundy for the six of them. "Now, Mother, a few extra drinks on Christmas aren't going to affect your good looks at all." She giggled, as bubbling herself as the burgundy.

Eileen offered the toast. "To the old Cronins, it's good to have them here with us on Christmas Day. They're really not all that bad, not when you consider how old they are!"

The burgundy was downed with much laughter. It warmed Nora's throat and stomach. She was close to tears. She wished she could preserve the precious moment forever. From now on, she hoped and prayed, everything would go well for the "old Cronins."

Sean Cronin could not sleep. The excitement of Christmas Eve and Christmas Day at the cathedral, the brilliant liturgy, the superb choir, and the fun of Christmas afternoon with his family ought to have left him at peace. Yet for Sean there was no peace. There would never be peace. He tried to make an entry into his journal, but the words would not come.

He closed the notebook and went back to bed. Eileen's toast tormented him. Things *were* very good this day for the three "old Cronins," better than they'd been for a long time. But his mother was in a stranger's grave, and his father was alone, unloving and unloved. Was aloneness, then, the destiny of all the Cronins?

Sean shivered. The interlude of happiness this afternoon was a deception, a trick. For Paul and Nora and himself, he sensed the worst was yet to come.

BOOK VIII

Lord, God, you make use of the ministry of priests for regenerating your people. Make us persevere in serving your will that in our days by the gift of your grace the people concentrated to you may increase in merit and numbers through Jesus Christ our Lord. Amen.

—Prayer of Priestly Recommitment,
Holy Thursday Liturgy

When he had washed their feet and put on his clothes again, he went back to the table. "Do you understand," he said, "what I have done to you? You call me master and lord and rightly so I am. If I, then, the lord and master have washed your feet, you should wash each other's feet. I have given you an example so you may copy what I have done to you."

—John 13:12–15

CHAPTER
—THIRTY-TWO—
1976

March was a wonderful time in Rome. Spring had survived its tentative beginnings and the occasional rains washed away the sour smells of the decrepit, phony old city. Sean didn't even mind the hideously dull meeting of the Commission on the Revision of the Code of Canon Law. In fact, he rather enjoyed jousting with Cardinal Pèricle Felici, who was grimly determined to use every trick at his command—and they were many and clever—to undo the entire Vatican Council. From Felici's viewpoint, Sean was a dangerous combination of historical knowledge and pastoral experience. Furthermore, he spoke Latin too well, although not, of course, as well as did the Cardinal, who wrote sonnets in Latin.

In such a fine mood was Sean Cronin that he invited Roger Fitzgibbon to dinner at the Tre Scalini on the Piazza Navona. They drank a toast to their twentieth anniversary in the priesthood, which was only two months away. Roger's carefully groomed hair had vanished, he had put on weight, and the assignment as a delegate, or nuncio, for which he had been hoping had not yet appeared. He confessed, however, that the *Sostitúto,* the famous Under Secretary of State, Archbishop Benelli, had hinted broadly to him that he might well be in the running for a posting to Nairobi later in the year. Sean decided that he would put in a kind word for Roger with Cardinal McCarthy.

"You know, you're on everyone's *tèrna* for Chicago when

Eamon steps down." Roger flipped the *spaghetti alla bolognése* around his fork with practiced ease.

"Programmed number three, I hope." Sean sipped his wine.

"Not on Eamon's list. Not on a lot of people's. Benelli clearly likes you—"

"Maybe that's because I blew up at him once and told him he was an arrogant, narrow-minded son-of-a-bitch. Tell you the truth, he seemed to love it. Who are the real candidates?"

"There's some mention of O'Malley from Denver—"

"Oh, my God. He's to the right of Caesar Augustus. He'd destroy Chicago."

"And your old friend Martin Spalding Quinlan." Roger's smile was sly and complacent.

"That's enough to ruin my day." Sean shoved aside his pasta.

But it wasn't Sean's problem, it was Chicago's. If the Holy See sent a despicable little neuter, it was their fault, and God's, not Sean Cronin's.

The week after he returned from Rome, Sean called to make an appointment with the Apostolic Delegate in Washington. The next morning he was among the tens of thousands of people who swarmed into O'Hare International Airport. On the way into that vast, sprawling glass and concrete barn, he encountered Tom and Fiona Shields, the latter pregnant for the second time.

"Off to celebrate mid-Lent in Florida, I bet," said the Bishop.

"From the color of yourself," said the articulate Fiona, "you should be joining us. Or is it one of the rules of your order that bishops have to look gray and haggard all the time?"

"We've been trying to help shoulder the Archbishop's load," Sean admitted.

"Ah, 'tis now that I understand it. We worry about the Cardinal's health, but not about the health of the Bishop. Shame on ye, Sean Cronin. Shame on ye."

Her mocking grin made the Florida sunlight look doubly attractive.

"Is Nicole enjoying working on my brother's campaign?"

Tom's eyes narrowed ever so slightly. The old wounds had been healed, the old angry words forgotten. Yet, as Sean had suspected, Tom clearly did not like Nicole working for her mother's lover. "She certainly seems to enjoy it," he finally said. "And it was good of Eileen to get her the job after she dropped out of college. I'm not sure a political campaign offers quite the stability that Nicole needs—"

"What Nicole needs," Fiona commented, "is a life of her own, Tom, whether you and I like it or not."

"I guess so," Tom agreed. "At least it looks as if she's working for a winning candidate, which means she has a job until next November."

Sean was sorry he had initiated the conversation. He didn't like to discuss Paul with the late Maggie Shields's husband.

Fiona Shields didn't like to either. "And how's the lovely Nora?" she asked. "Sure, we don't see so much of her any more."

"She's spending more time in Washington now that the two older girls are in college. If Paul's elected Senator, I suppose she'll move there more or less permanently. Oh, that's my plane that's boarding over there. I'd better run." He bade the Shieldses good-bye and hurried into the boarding area for the flight to Washington. He was not happy that Nicole was working for Paul. Paul should have had more sense than to hire her.

As the plane took off, Sean jammed his *Chicago Sun-Times* into the pocket on the seat in front of him and began to struggle through *Humboldt's Gift,* more out of a sense of obligation to keep up with current literature than any enjoyment of the story. After a few pages, he closed it impatiently and reached for the latest spiral notebook in his attaché case.

He had made a momentous decision yesterday before he had phoned the Delegate. It was a decision that was inevitable. He had intended to write something in his journal the night before, but there had been a confirmation and a counseling case in the rectory, and an idiotic letter from Rome about the seminary—a letter that presumed the year was 1910—which had to be answered. When he was finished he was so tired he could barely see the pages of the notebook, so he resolved he would write something on the plane to Washington.

The words were slow in coming.

> *Holy Week is approaching again, a quarter of a century since Paul was missing in action in Korea. I have no more faith now than I did then. I plug along at my work. I have almost no faith*

*in you and now even less in the Church and the priesthood. I
have no faith in anyone or anything. What I do is mechanically
routine. If only I could believe in something.*

He hesitated and then began again.

*You refused a sign to your Judean critics who demanded to
view a miracle. So I will not ask for a sign. I will rather tell you
I need one, I desperately need some sign that you are there and
I'm not being a fool.*

The small Beechcraft twin-engine plane dropped out of the
clouds somewhere under six hundred feet, vibrated sharply in a
wind gust, and then settled into its final approach to the airport.
Senatorial candidate Paul Cronin shook himself fully awake.
"Rockford?"

"Moline," said Tim Burns, his bright and ambitious young campaign manager. "We changed that last night, remember?"

"Oh," said Paul sleepily. "I remember. Yes."

The bump of the landing awakened the third member of the
campaign party, Nicole Shields, who in some vague way was an
aide to Burns. "Explain to me again," she said, "why it's necessary to cover seven of these places the week before the primary
election even though the polls show us way ahead?"

Nicole was a disturbing presence on the plane. She was dark
and tempestuous, the most tantalizing nineteen-year-old Paul had
ever known. He wondered if she was sleeping with Burns. Probably. Paul gathered up his notes. He couldn't afford to take that
risk. Too much trouble with the Shields family as it was. Besides,
as a candidate for the United States Senate, he had to be careful—
a girl less than half his age, the daughter of a woman whose family
thought she killed herself because of him—that would be the kind
of scandal that would finish him off quickly.

As Tim Burns held the umbrella over his head and a chill
March wind assaulted his face, Paul helped Nicole out of the
Beechcraft. She managed to press her body momentarily against
his as she stumbled down the slippery stairs.

Her taunting young flesh sent a stab of sweetness through him.
God, he wished he were twenty-six instead of forty-six. He also
wished he had not seen Chris Waverly with her mocking smile
among the reporters covering his rally in Chicago the night before.

Congressman Cronin and his two aides huddled together under the umbrella as they walked toward the terminal. The local television crew was waiting for them. "The latest polls show you ahead of Mr. Mitchum by twelve points, Congressman," said an eager television journalist. "Do you have any comment?"

Paul started to quote Richard Daley on the polls and then realized that this was downstate and you didn't quote Daley downstate. "I'd rather have six points after the election," he said, smiling engagingly, "than twelve points before it."

He hoped that Nora did not see the Moline television tape. She might note how close to him Nicole Shields was standing.

"My decision is final, Monsieur l'Archevêque," Sean said to the Apostolic Delegate at his office in Washington. "I am well aware that the Cardinal has submitted his resignation effective on his birthday, September fifth. I also know that he has put my name at the top of the list for his recommended successor."

"But of course he has, Bishop Cronin," said the shrewd, charming French aristocrat who represented the Holy See in the United States. "It is no secret that you have been running the archdiocese and running it very well for the last few years while the Cardinal's health has been poor." The Delegate, as different as day was from night from the usual Italian careerists who came to Washington, had a marvelously effective diplomatic technique of being utterly candid at least half the time and totally secretive the other half.

"Be that as it may, Monsieur l'Archevêque, I do not wish to be considered as a successor. I assume that the Holy See has not taken such a possibility seriously. I am a native Chicagoan, I am too young and too outspoken. While I presume that I am not exactly the winterbook favorite to succeed His Eminence—"

The Gallic eyebrows shot up quizzically. "Winterbook favorite, Bishop Cronin?"

"An American racing term, Archbishop. You see, many months before the three-year-old thoroughbreds are tested in preliminary races, listings are made of their relative potential."

The Delegate made a note on a pad at the enormous desk behind which he was sitting. "Winterbook favorite, very interesting." There was a touch of green on the bushes in the Archbishop's garden. Spring came to Washington early. Spring, Easter

. . . Holy Thursday, a time of rebirth, a time of renewed commitments.

"The point, Monsieur l'Archevêque, is that since the Cardinal recommended me as his successor, I feel an obligation to make it clear to you, and through you to the Holy See, if necessary, that under no circumstances will I serve. In the classic words of the American General Sherman, 'I will not run if nominated, I will not serve if elected!' "

"Of this General Sherman, I have heard," said the Archbishop. "He also said 'War is hell,' did he not?"

It was said of the Delegate that he had learned more about America in three months than his predecessors had in seven years. He probably knew more about the Church in America than did many of Sean's colleagues in the hierarchy. "He did, Monsieur l'Archevêque. I hope I have made myself clear?"

The Delegate smiled. "Oh, yes, Bishop Cronin, you have made yourself very clear. I will keep in mind what you have said. I am sure, however, that if the Holy Father should insist, you would be happy to serve."

"This is not a diplomatic visit, Monsieur l'Archevêque," Sean said. "I am not engaged in complicated Irish-American politics. I gave that up a long time ago. I leave that to my brother. You would be well advised to inform the Holy See that under no circumstances will I be Archbishop of Chicago or archbishop of anyplace else."

The Delegate nodded. "But of course I will tell them if you insist, Bishop Cronin." He made another note on his pad. "I may be able to persuade them that you really mean it. However, I must tell you that . . . oh, yes"—he glanced at his notebook again and then laughed pleasantly—"oh, yes, Bishop Cronin, you are surely the winterbook favorite."

"You what?" said Harold Wheaton, one of Washington's auxiliary bishops, that evening while they were eating dinner in the high-ceilinged dining room of the rectory at the bishop's parish, a rectory that was built when Abraham Lincoln was President of the United States.

"I told the Apostolic Delegate to take my name out of the running. I meant it, Harry. I don't want you, or your boss, or any of my friends, or any of your friends, or anybody campaigning for me. If anyone asks why, tell them 'for spiritual and personal reasons.' "

"You're not going to resign from the priesthood, are you?" Harold Wheaton was incredulous.

"No, I'm not thinking of leaving the priesthood."

"What if the choice is you or Quinlan or that old fool O'Malley or some other horse's ass?"

Sean hesitated. "My answer would still be no."

"No one ever said you were an easy man to figure out, Sean. I will pass the word that this is not the usual discreet political tactic. But you know what? I think like every other crazy thing you do in your life, this is only going to enhance your chances of becoming the angel to the Church of Chicago."

Sean sighed. Damned if he did, and damned if he didn't. "They're going to be awfully embarrassed when I turn them down."

Later that evening, in the guest room of Bishop Wheaton's rectory with the street noises of Washington barely audible outside, Sean stared once again at his journal. Nothing to add. He had said no and he meant it. That was that.

The thought of calling Nora, which had been with him since he had awakened in the morning, returned again, insistent, demanding. She was spending most of the time in Washington, having opened up an office in a building just down the street from Lafayette Park. He glanced at his watch: nine thirty.

He dialed the first six numbers of the house in Georgetown, hesitated over the seventh, and then slowly replaced the phone in its cradle.

CHAPTER
—THIRTY-THREE—
1976

Nora sighed in relaxed contentment. The sun, the sound of the water, the warmth of the beach on a day in late June were the greatest tranquilizers in the world. Ever since she had been brought into the Cronin household, Glendore had been home much more than the house on Glenwood Drive. It was good to be home again. The first year in Washington had been difficult; her fortieth birthday, a husband who was a more tolerable little boy than he used to be, but still a little boy, the difficulties of opening the Washington office for Cronin Enterprises, and her trips around the country and around the world had worn her out.

"Old girl can't take it any more," she said, patting her belly and reassuring herself that it was still presentably flat.

She insisted that July was the month for the family to be at Oakland Beach. Eileen and Mary, students at Notre Dame, *not* St. Mary's—What, oh, what, is the world coming to? thought Nora—were perfectly content to put off summer employment until August. Paul, however, had managed to mess up his schedule so badly that he would only be there for part of the Fourth of July weekend.

She was angry at Paul. It was important that their far-flung family spend some time together. Paul didn't need a junket to Puerto Rico to boost his senatorial image; he was a shoo-in no matter what Jimmy Carter—the likely Democratic candidate—did or said. And subcommittee meetings in Washington in the summertime were ridiculous, especially since, even if he lost the Senate race, Paul would not return to the House of Representatives. Yet he was afraid of being accused of absenteeism, or so he said, so the most he would be in Oakland Beach was for the weekend of the Fourth and perhaps one other weekend at the end of the month.

Paul was running a remarkably intelligent and cautious campaign. Yet every once in a while he did something foolish. It had been only with grave difficulty that she had talked him out of adding South Africa to his tour. He would almost certainly say something wrong there.

Nora began to anoint her shoulders and back with suntan lotion. Noreen was on the golf course, and the older girls were sailing on the *Mary Eileen*. Another hour of peace and quiet before the three of them came storming in.

The phone next to her on the sundeck rang. "Damn!" she protested. She dropped the suntan lotion as she picked up the phone. "Nora Cronin," she said in her best businesswoman's voice.

"I want to sell the Sears Tower and buy the Merchandise Mart, Mrs. Cronin. Do you think you can act as the broker in the deal for me?"

"Good morning, Monsignor McGuire." She smiled affectionately. "I'm sorry, I've already sold the Sears Tower to someone else. He was a little short Italian who claimed that he worked for the Institute of Religious Works."

"Then you're really in the world of high finance, Mrs. Cronin. Just hang onto your purse when the people from the IOR are around."

"Nonsense, Monsignor. The Chicago Irish are much smarter than Vatican bankers."

"Funny you should mention them, but I need a favor, Nora." Jimmy was suddenly serious. "Can you come down here and take off our hands one utterly exhausted bishop? The man's literally stumbling around, bumping into things, he's so tired. When the Archbishop's resignation is effective in September, he's going to become administrator, and we don't need an administrator who hasn't had a summer vacation."

Nora hesitated, but only for a moment. "Of course, Jimmy. I'll be down there tomorrow morning and give him his marching orders. . . . Is he going to be the next archbishop?"

"Odds-on favorite, but you know Sean. He's told Rome that he absolutely, positively, will not accept the job."

Nora retrieved the fallen suntan lotion with her feet. "And I'm sure he's convinced them he means it."

"Somebody is going to have to tell him to take the job, even if he doesn't want it."

"Who?"

"Come on, Nora Riley Cronin." Jimmy was his carefree, merry self again. "There's only one person who can get away with giving orders to Sean Cronin, and it ain't the Pope."

"See you tomorrow morning, Monsignor."

She unfastened the halter on her swimsuit and rolled over on her stomach. This was the year that she and Sean were going to have to finally sort things out. It wasn't going to be easy. Mary Eileen's death had brought them together again, but there was still an awkward, halting friendship, haunted by unexorcised demons from the past.

"Sean, you look like hell," Nora said. She was standing at the door of the Auxiliary Bishop's office in the chancery skyscraper.

"Nora, I'm busy." He looked up from the desk, frowning at her.

Oh, God, he *was* tired. She had seen faces like that on the old men at the home where Mary Eileen had lived and died.

"You shouldn't come down here without an appointment."

Nora laughed. "Would you look at who's turning into a pompous churchman. Even his own sister can't come into his sacred office without getting permission."

Nora turned to the handsome black woman working in Sean's outer office. "Mrs. Jackson, will you get Monsignor McGuire for me?"

"Yes, ma'am," said Mrs. Jackson. She was no doubt overjoyed to see somebody who would give orders to the Auxiliary Bishop.

"Nora, please. I know I'm tired . . . overworked. . . . I should have called you before, but this morning is just too much. Now if you'll let me get back to work. . . ."

"No way am I going to let you get back to work, Bishop Cronin. Ah, there you are, Monsignor McGuire. I take it the Bishop has a hectic schedule of appointments for the next three weeks even though it's summertime and there are no confirmations or anniversary celebrations?"

"Yes, indeed," said Monsignor McGuire.

"Monsignor McGuire," she said, "cancel them all. The Bishop is leaving with me after lunch to spend the Fourth of July weekend with his family. He will be permitted to return here only when we are ready to certify to you that he will not be a boorish, insufferable ogre. Is that clear, Monsignor McGuire?"

"Absolutely, Your Holiness," Jimmy said. "When they call and ask for Bishop Cronin, we will just say, 'Bishop *who?*'"

She turned to Sean. "Now is *that* clear to you, Bishop Cronin?"

Sean smiled. "Yes, ma'am."

"I'll be in front of the cathedral rectory at one thirty. You be there too. With your golf clubs. Understand?" She gave up trying to hide her maternal smile.

Sean looked younger already. "Yes, Your Holiness," he said.

"Well, am I glad that's settled," Jimmy said. "Vacation for the rest of us begins when we get rid of the boss."

Nora dusted off her hands as though chewing out an overworked bishop was a piece of cake. "Where I am, Monsignor McGuire, *I'm* the boss." To herself she said, Oh, God, Nora, this is going to be a tough one.

It took until the bicentennial weekend for Sean to relax and realize how tired he really was. It seemed that he had been tired ever since he had been ordained twenty years before. St. Jadwiga's, graduate school, the council, the Birth Control Committee, parish work at the cathedral—no time to relax, no time to think, not even much time to pray. No wonder he was a wreck. No wonder even Jimmy McGuire couldn't take him any more and had to have Nora come and drag him off.

The renewal and rededication themes of the bicentennial celebration were a powerful sermon for him. Indeed, he gave a sermon on these themes at a small Mass he said for the Cronins and some of their neighbors on the morning of July Fourth. He talked about tall ships and tall spirits and freedom and hope and recommitment and persuaded himself that it was time to revive his own spirits and renew his own life—he would not work so hard, he would take more time off, he would learn how to pray again.

A tiny voice deep inside of him expressed skepticism.

In the afternoon, while Nora was presiding over the preparation of the festival dinner, Sean and his brother relaxed at the beach. Paul had been thoroughly drubbed on the golf course once again by his youngest daughter.

"It isn't even close any more," he said. "She was twelve strokes up on me yesterday. Today she was seventeen strokes—not because my game was worse but because the little brat shot a seventy-six."

It was hard to tell whether Paul was proud of his daughter or felt threatened by her.

"Will Nora let her go on the golf tour when she's older?" Sean asked.

"I'm sure she will. Not that it would make much difference. Noreen will do what she wants to do. But, as Nora says, that's one child we'll never have to worry about."

"Amazing how much she's like her mother at the same age," Sean said. He put aside the book he had been reading and tucked it under his beach chair. "A lot more confident, though, not a trace of awkwardness . . . maybe happier."

"Oh, yes, a lot happier," Paul agreed. "She doesn't have Dad around to hound her. You know, little brother, I sometimes think it's a good thing that the old man is out of our hair. He would have made life miserable for the kids."

For a moment Sean seethed. What a damn-fool, stupid, patronizing, unkind thing to say. They were having a spectacular Fourth of July weekend while their father was practically a prisoner in the Hancock Tower, with his nurse and his inevitable television set. Then he realized that Paul was probably right. Michael Cronin would have made his granddaughters' lives difficult. "Dad's slipping," he said. "I don't think it will be much longer now. I hope you get a chance to see him before you go to Puerto Rico."

"Oh, I will. No problem. It's just that my life is so crazy I don't know where I'm headed half the time." Paul shrugged, his shoulders hinting at the enormous burdens carried by a member of the House of Representatives.

"What does that labor convention in Puerto Rico have to do with the senatorial race in November?" Sean was curious. "Are there going to be that many delegates from Illinois?"

"Oh, 1976 doesn't have anything to do with it." Paul waved

aside the question and took a swallow from his beer can. "It's '80 and '84 that I have in mind. They invited me to talk, and it's a good place to start building for the future." He blew the foam off his lips.

"You're thinking that far ahead?"

"Yes, though sometimes, to tell you the truth, I'm not sure why. I'd just as soon laze around Oakland Beach all summer with Nora and the kids. However, I'm in the game and I guess I have to play it out."

And a little prudence. The words sprang into Sean's mind, but not to his lips. Although he'd become politically cautious, his brother had, if anything, grown personally more reckless through the years. He drove faster, swung his golf club more fiercely—especially when it was clear his daughter was going to beat him. And he had plunged into the lake for a swim the day before, braving a treacherous undertow and four-foot waves. What was it in Paul that made him court danger?

"What's on your mind?" Paul said. "You suddenly turned serious on me. You thinking about Dad?"

"No. I was thinking about how difficult a politician's life must be."

Paul waved both his arms expansively. "Don't feel too much pity for us. We love the attention, the public eye. Once you're addicted to it, it beats everything, even sex. Anyway, I think I'll have a swim. The little hellcat can't beat me at that. At least not yet." He strolled toward the inviting waters of the lake.

"Be careful," Sean shouted after him, instantly wishing he had swallowed his words.

"Don't worry, I can take care of myself." Paul laughed and dove under a cresting wave.

The next senator from Illinois had put on a little weight, and his muscles were not as hard and taut as they used to be. Yet, even if he was somewhat out of condition, he was a handsome and appealing figure.

The evening before Paul was to leave for San Juan, Nora and the two men in her life dined at the Apricot Restaurant in La Porte and then returned to the balcony overlooking the lake for coffee and Irish Mist. Paul lit a cigarette, Nora put the coffeepot on a small table, humming a Sousa march. The air was humid and still, the lake a black blanket under the stars. Mosquitoes and fireflies buzzed around them.

"Don't go to San Juan, Paul," Sean said suddenly. "Stay here for another week. You need the rest. We ought to spend more time together."

Nora fought to hold down her panic. For a moment it sounded like Amalfi all over again.

"Sean's right," she said. "You do look tired. You don't need that talk for your campaign. Besides, you should get a checkup."

Paul laughed. "You're beginning to sound like a worried suburban housewife. I'm fine, never better. I'll see the doc during the August recess. Besides"—he waved his cigarette—"I can't let the union leaders down."

"Don't go," Sean repeated.

"Why not?" Paul was curious.

"I don't really know why not." Sean was deadly serious. "I have a feeling about it, that's all."

Nora had never heard Sean sound so gloomy. "What kind of feeling?" she asked. He was frightening her.

Sean shrugged his shoulders. "I'm being foolish. Forgive me. Exhaustion must finally be catching up."

"Don't worry, Sean," Paul said. "If I'm not here to fight off the terrors, Nora will take care of you."

CHAPTER
——THIRTY-FOUR——
1976

Nicole Shields had persuaded Paul—nagged him, might be a better way of putting it—to leave the hotel and drive to the beach on the west side of the island. It was terribly hot, but there was a breeze coming off the Caribbean and the beach was deserted. Nicole pulled her sweat shirt over her head, undid the bra of her bikini, and ran toward the water. Paul tagged along behind.

Nicole turned to him. "Not afraid of the ocean, are you? Or are you afraid of me?"

Without high heels, she was a small woman: short like her mother but much more slender. Her body had the piquant appeal of an early teenager, but her seductiveness was not so much in her face or figure as in an enormous sexual energy. "A little bit of both," he admitted. She grabbed his hands and drew close to him, pressing his palms against her naked breasts.

"Don't be afraid of me. I won't bite. Or, if I do, you won't mind."

Two years before, Paul would have been tempted. Instead, he said, "Let's go swimming, Nicole. Senatorial candidates don't do it on the beach."

She sulked all the way back to San Juan, puffing nervously on a joint. Ever since Nora had moved to Washington, Paul had been resolutely faithful. He felt he had straightened out his life. It was time to do so. He didn't want any lurking scandals when he made his big move. Moreover, he and Nora seemed on their way at last to becoming friends. He was not going to risk ruining a good thing. He would never understand his wife, but no doubt about it, she would make a wonderful First Lady.

Nicole wasn't worth it.

Sean lay sleepless in his bed. The luminous clock face told him it was two o'clock. He could hear the waters of the lake slapping gently at the beach just below the dark window. Two weeks at Glendore had revived him physically and psychologically. He had not thought about the Church or the priesthood or the archdiocese for more than a few minutes. He had read mystery stories and science fiction—from a seemingly inexhaustible collection that Mary had gathered—swam, water skied, sailed, played golf.

He had no desire to return to the chancery office; to the telephone, the mail, the idiotic letters from Rome, the protestors, and the charismatics; and to all the myriad right-wing and left-wing organizations that demonstrated each day. He did not want to have to attend a committee meeting with a group of bishops ever again —dry, bloodless, unfeeling old men. The rest of his life, as far as he was concerned, should be spent in the peace and undemanding affection of Oakland Beach.

His desire for Nora was as strong as ever, but somehow that no longer seemed a serious problem. Nora was a hostess and a nurse and a friend. The old savage, imperious desire that had shattered his confidence and his self-esteem in Italy, that kind of desire seemed to have died out.

"Getting old, I guess," he told himself. "But if you don't want to be in that bedroom with her down the corridor, how come you're not asleep?"

Nicole Shields carefully injected the hypodermic needle into her vein. Coke was a lot quicker and more spectacular than grass and, everybody said, not nearly as dangerous as heroin. She had been able to find a source in San Juan, recommended by one of her Chicago friends, who guaranteed that San Juan coke was "pure as the driven snow."

She injected the coke slowly, carefully. She wasn't hooked on cocaine and didn't intend to be, nor did she want her arm to be marked by scars. Life was too much fun to do yourself in that quickly. But she had something to celebrate. After his speech tonight he would come to her room, and by the next morning she would own him. And then she would destroy him, just as he had destroyed her mother. She would make her affair with him public, and he would lose everything: his wife, his kids, his seat in the Senate, his future.

Ecstasy started to flow through her veins like a tropical river at flood tide, and she forgot about her mother and Paul Cronin and everything else.

There was a knock at the door. She said blissfully, "Come in."

It was Helen Colter, another junior staff aide to the Congressman. Helen was four years older than Nicole, plain and prudent. She looked disapprovingly at the sight of Nicole spread out on the bed in her underwear. "Have you made copies of the speech?" she asked.

"There . . . on the chair." Nicole's voice was languorous. "Would you like some cocaine? There's nothing in the world like it."

"No, thank you." Helen shook her head in irritation and picked up the stack of speeches.

"Well, there's nothing like it—'cept screwing a future United States senator."

"What would you know about that?"

"By tomorrow morning, honey"—she smiled sweetly—"I'll know everything there is to know about it."

Nora was trying unsuccessfully to read *Trinity*. The air-conditioning system installed after Glendore was built had broken down. The night air was sullen and humid. She had thrown open the windows in her bedroom, but her red, white, and blue bicentennial sleep shirt—a present from her daughters—was soaked with perspiration.

She shifted uneasily on her bed and put aside her reading glasses. Something had to be done about Sean. When she had sailed so blithely into the chancery at the behest of Jimmy McGuire, she was confident that a few weeks of rest would rehabilitate him and give them both a chance to exorcise all the demons of the past. It would be easy, she thought, to straighten things out with him once and for all.

Now, after having him around the house for three weeks, it did not look simple at all. Sean obviously adored her. Her own response to the quiet pain in his eyes was every bit as powerful as it had been in Italy. She had overestimated her maturity.

Yet Nora was afraid to clear the air, afraid that if she opened the door to discussion, her weakness would lead her to an even greater surrender than Amalfi. And perhaps on a deeper level she was more afraid that her strength would rule out the possibility of any such surrender in the future.

There was a soft knock on the door. "Come in," she said, her heart thudding against her chest.

It was Sean, of course. Trim and solid in a T-shirt and swimming trunks. "I thought you'd be awake. I can't sleep either. Want to try a swim?"

She almost said yes, then realized that the beach might be even more dangerous than her bedroom. "I don't think so," she said. "Too much exercise today for an old body."

The thin drapes stirred restlessly on a draft of air.

"Presentable enough body as far as I can see," he said. "Hey . . . do you want a drink?"

She wanted one desperately. It would be a mistake. Her defenses would be shattered if she had any alcohol in her. "A martini would be wonderful," she said.

While she waited for his return she tried to banish the memories of the hotel room in Amalfi. Same thing all over again. Her body, beyond her control, began its relentless preparations for sexual union. "I can't do it," she moaned under her breath. "I won't." But the stirrings she felt made her not at all sure that she wouldn't. She ought to get out of bed, put on a robe, join Sean in the parlor.

Instead, she lay on the bed, her palms pressed against the damp sheet, as though she were paralyzed.

The pitcher contained only enough for two martinis. Sean was deceiving himself as much as she was.

He sat on the far edge of the king-size bed, the blue sheets an ocean separating them. "To the next First Lady."

"You mean to Rosalyn?" She joked.

"Do you want the job?" Sean was serious.

"I like Washington. I like being a congressman's wife. I think I'll like being a senator's wife. After that, I don't know."

Sean sipped his drink and leaned toward her. "What's in it for you, Nora?"

"There are a lot of payoffs," she said uneasily.

"And you're happy?" He leaned back on his arm, one tightly knuckled hand depressing the edge of the bed.

She wet her lips. "Yes. Sometimes more than others."

"I love you, Nora," he said, his voice gentle. "I always will."

"I love you too, Sean. Of course I do. . . ." She tried to sound matter-of-fact. It came out a sigh.

Then he came around to her side of the bed and, prying the glass from her fingers, took her in his arms. He was a natural lover, knowing by instinct what to do just as he had ten years before. Gently he slid her shirt up and began to caress and kiss her body. She felt as though she were floating on a cloud of tenderness. Another few seconds and it would be too late. Neither of them would be able to stop.

As though returning from a faraway galaxy, she pushed his hands aside. "I don't think so, Sean," she murmured in a voice she hardly recognized. "If we don't stop, we'll lose each other for the rest of our lives."

He pulled back, jolted to his senses. "I'm sorry. I don't know what happened. . . ."

With as much modesty as she could summon, she rearranged her shirt, her hands trembling. "Come on, Sean, we both know what happened." She would try to get control of herself by being the efficient administrator.

"I'll leave right away," he said. "Drive back to Chicago tonight." He was almost to the door. Running away.

"You'll do no such thing," she said. "You'll sit down, and then we're going to have the talk we should have had a long time ago."

She sat up straight, her back against the headboard. "What happened in Amalfi was the natural consequence of all of our lives. It had to be. . . . You can handle it under your moral theology —the circumstances took control over us, robbed us of our freedom. . . ."

Sean laughed bitterly. "Nora Riley Cronin, moral theologian. Well, I think I'll go along with your opinion, Professor Cronin."

Nora relaxed. She was certain she would be able to handle the situation now, to establish boundaries where there were no boundaries.

"You know I'll always love you, Sean. But we both have other commitments, commitments we're not going to turn our backs on.

I'll be your mother, your sister, your friend, your inspiration, but I won't be your mistress, because that would mess you up and it would mess me up, it would mess up my family, and it would mess up your Church."

"Maybe I really came here tonight, Nora, to hear you say those things more than to make love to you."

"Can you live with this kind of love, Sean?"

"I'm going to have to learn to, aren't I?" he murmured.

Both the Cronins were really little boys, she thought, each needing her. Fair enough; she would mother them both, each according to his needs, keep her fingers crossed, and leave the rest to God.

Then, without warning, the Presence was there, enveloping the two of them, caressing, encouraging, reassuring. You never told me it was to be this way, Nora silently chided the Presence.

Rarely did the Presence say anything. Rather it absorbed, bathed, and soothed her. Tonight, however, it laughed. Not a sardonic laugh; rather it laughed at her the way she often laughed at Noreen when that teenage tomboy did something particularly wonderful.

Everyone, sighed Nora, wants to be a mother. Even you.

Esteban Muñoz was the best journeyman electrician in all of San Juan. There was not an electrical problem in the entire sky-high Barrington Hotel on the beach in San Juan that Esteban could not solve before the sun had set, and it was a very bad electrical engineer who designed that hotel's wiring.

Unfortunately for Esteban's peace of mind, the chief electrician at the hotel, under whom Esteban was forced to work, a certain José Alvarez, was jealous of Esteban's greater skills; if the management at the Barrington should ever find out that Esteban did all the work and José took all the credit, they would fire José and give Esteban the job he deserved—chief electrician at the Barrington.

Esteban took it for granted that there would be some harassment, but the harassment was especially heavy when the labor leaders were in San Juan; the hotel wished to prove that even though its workers did not belong to a union they could keep a modern hotel running efficiently.

All day Esteban ran from broken lamps to dead outlets to nonfunctioning air-conditioning units to disturbed television sets. Finally, late in the afternoon, on the very top floor, he discovered a loose wire at the end of the corridor. He was busy soldering and taping it when José came upon him and screamed many terrible curses. There were three air-conditioning units not functioning properly on the second floor. The loose electrical wire could wait; if it had not caused a fire before today, then it would not cause one today.

Esteban protested, but to no avail. He would be fired if he did not repair the air conditioners immediately. He hastily taped the dangling wire, closed the panel in the wall, and then, at the end of the corridor, flipped up the master switch for that floor.

Before he went home that night, however, Esteban stopped at the office of Señor Manuel Ramirez, the assistant general manager of the hotel, and warned him in the presence of his own good friend, Humberto García, that there were dangerous wires on the fifteenth floor that ought to be fixed.

Señor Ramirez was upset with Esteban. He told him that he knew he was only trying to obtain overtime pay for the weekend. He ordered Esteban out of the office and warned him that on Monday morning he would discuss his future at the hotel with Señor Alvarez.

Long before Monday morning, however, Esteban would thank the Madonna that he had had the presence of mind to bring Humberto García into Señor Ramirez's office when he made his complaint. It was the wisdom of the Madonna, he would tell his wife María Isabel, that protected him from perhaps going to jail and guaranteed him employment at the Barrington Hotel for as long as he wished it.

The labor leaders and their wives had been well dined and well wined. Paul Cronin realized that his role was as much entertainment as politics. He also understood that even if the labor barons and baronesses did not remember a single word he said, it was still important that he impress them as being a likable, promising, very pro-union member of the Congress of the United States.

The union leaders were not interested in practical programs. They were interested in stirring words and energetic visions, a repetition of the New Deal rallying cries tempered by the new common sense. Paul gave them exactly what they wanted. The old

Irishman who was the president of the union bellowed to the audience at the end of Paul's speech, "This is the best goddamned politician I've heard since John Kennedy talked to us in 1958."

Paul modestly disclaimed such a compliment, but he nevertheless spent forty-five minutes accepting the congratulations of the assembly. He noted how many handshakes were gnarled and rough from long years of manual labor. His father's old cliché that the labor bosses had never done an honest day's work did not seem to be true after all.

In the elevator ride to the fourteenth floor, Paul's spirits soared. He was enormously pleased with himself. The unions and the city organization would be a strong political base. Yes, indeed, it had been a very good night's work.

Esteban Muñoz had discovered the loose electrical wire on the fifteenth floor just as it became dangerous. The insulation around the wire had eroded through the years until it was little more than a live wire loose within the wall between the corridor and room 1502, a room that remained unoccupied during the convention. If Muñoz had been permitted to finish his work, there would have been no danger of fire. But he had not, and now sparks from the wire had already started to smolder in the wall.

Paul tossed his coat on the chair in the parlor of his suite, opened the small refrigerator, put some ice cubes in a tumbler, and half filled the tumbler with whiskey. He loosened his tie and took a hearty swallow of the drink. Then he noticed a piece of paper that had been slipped under the door. He picked it up and glanced at it. *I'm in room 1510 and waiting. N.*

He rolled the note into a ball and tossed it into the wastebasket. A stupid little girl, sending a note like that.

He hung his jacket in the closet and sat down on the couch. Ten thirty in San Juan, nine thirty in Chicago. Still time to call Nora.

That's what he would do, he would call Nora. He would not go up to room 1510. That would be a ridiculous thing to do. He dialed the long-distance operator and gave her the number. The line at Glendore was busy. He hung up, drummed his fingers on the telephone table, then rose, went to the closet, put on his jacket, and walked out to the corridor.

As Paul was leaving the elevator on the fifteenth floor, Helen

Colter entered it. Politely he held the door for her. "Wonderful speech tonight, Senator," she said.

"Let's not anticipate the wishes of the people of the state of Illinois, Helen," he said. "But thanks for the compliment anyway."

Helen flushed slightly and then smiled in response to his engaging boyish grin, a grin that seemed to be especially effective with unattractive girls like her.

Paul hesitated. Could Helen have guessed where he was going? But what difference would that make? She was too devoted to him to blab about it. And she certainly wouldn't tell Nora.

He knocked on 1510, and a dreamy voice said, "Come in; it's open."

Nicole Shields was stretched out invitingly on the bed, her childish body available, a languid smile on her face. It was, he told himself, a face that would not be pretty for nearly as long as her mother's had been.

She was a much more intense and inventive lover than her mother, however, and the Congressman enjoyed himself thoroughly. A flaky kid with enormous energy and kinky ways. Nothing serious, just a little bit of entertainment on a hot summer evening in San Juan, Puerto Rico.

It was only after their lovemaking was finished that Paul realized how high his partner was. "What have you been taking?" he asked her, half asleep.

"A little coke, a couple of pills, that's all," she mumbled.

Then they both were asleep.

The smell of the smoke from the fire at the other end of the corridor had teased Paul's nostrils for many precious minutes before he finally struggled awake and realized there was a fire someplace. He turned on the light. Smoke was seeping under the door. He jumped out of bed, rushed over and felt the door. It was hot; a fire in the corridor. Smoke inhalation was the danger: He must soak a towel with water, wrap it around his face, and make a dash for the exit stairway.

He pulled on his clothes and, with shoes untied, dashed into the bathroom, soaked four towels, two for him, two for Nicole. Then he hurried back to the bed where she lay peaceful and complacent, in the afterglow of lovemaking. He shook her roughly. "Come on, Nicole, wake up! This damned place is on fire!"

There was no reaction. He shook her again and yet again. Then he remembered what she had said about coke and pills.

"Oh, my God!" he exclaimed. "She's out. I'll have to carry her." He lifted her up and was surprised at how light she was, nothing but an innocent and bedraggled little child. He staggered toward the doorway and heard the crackle of flames in the corridor.

Then he was in the Reservoir again and the Chinese were attacking. He heard not the wail of the fire sirens but the screaming of the charging enemy. He saw not the wall of the room glowing red, before it burst into flames, but the flares breaking the night darkness above the cold waters of the Reservoir.

In his terrified imagination he saw himself running down the stairwell with a naked drugged-out nineteen-year-old girl in his arms. It would be the end of everything, everything he had worked for all his life.

Without any hesitation he threw the unconscious girl back on her bed, wrapped the towels around his face, yanked open the door of room 1510, and, body bent over, ran desperately for the stairs as the flames seemed to race along the corridor in pursuit of him.

On the fourteenth floor, people were emerging from their rooms, frightened, confused, uncertain what to do, and already beginning to cough from the smoke. Congressman Cronin took charge of the fourteenth floor, since many members of his staff were on it, and with cool efficiency organized its evacuation.

CHAPTER
THIRTY-FIVE
1976

At seven o'clock in the morning Nora was awakened in her bedroom at Oakland Beach by the telephone. "What's wrong?" she asked when she heard Paul's voice. She was suddenly tense.

"Everything's all right," he reassured her. "I wanted to call you before someone else did or before you heard it on the news. There was a fire here at the hotel last night. The upper six stories were burned out. They managed to evacuate everyone and there don't seem to be any fatalities—some people in the hospital with smoke inhalation, that's all."

"You're sure everyone's all right?" Nora was shaking her head to make sure she really was awake.

"Everyone's fine. They even think I'm a hero. The floor I was on was the one that was in the most danger. I helped get everybody out."

"Oh, Paul, I'm so glad you're okay."

"Well, I am too," he said. "I'll call you again later and let you know how things are."

The seven-thirty news on the *Today Show* showed pictures of the upper stories of the Barrington Hotel, blazing red against the Caribbean sky. It also carried interviews with a number of guests in the hotel, most of them union leaders and their families, praising Congressman Paul Cronin for his quick thinking and his cool nerve under pressure. Thank God I wasn't there, Nora said to herself. I'm sure I would have panicked.

She was making herself a second cup of coffee when Eileen, deathly pale, joined her in the kitchen.

"Nothing to worry about, Eileen," Nora said. "Dad's all right. He just called. Everyone escaped from the hotel alive."

"Not everyone, Mom. I just heard a special report. They found Nicole's body in a room on the fifteenth floor."

The evening news showed a grief-stricken Congressman Cronin discussing the tragedy of Nicole Shields' death. "She was so young, so energetic, she had such a wonderful future. I can't help but hold myself in some way responsible for her death."

Then the anchorman was on the television screen looking like a slightly prosperous undertaker. "Late word from San Juan indicates a probable reason why Nicole Shields did not escape from her room on the fifteenth floor. The medical examiner reports that she had taken a heavy dose of cocaine and amphetamines and was unconscious when the fire engulfed her room. The fifteenth floor of the Barrington Hotel was almost entirely unoccupied. The only other person with a room on that floor was another member of Congressman Cronin's campaign staff, who was fortunately in the coffee shop at the time of the fire."

Tears came easily to Paul at Nicole's funeral, although he did not bother to ask himself for what he was weeping. It was too bad Nicole had to die, but so far everything else had gone well. He had been the first to notice that Nicole was missing after the sun rose over the Caribbean. He had raced up to her room with one of the San Juan Police Department inspectors. Together they had discovered the body lying on what was left of the bed in the smoke-blackened room. Paul's nausea at the stench and smell were authentic enough. He had insisted on staying with the body while the police inspector went downstairs for medical personnel. This gave him time to look around the room for the one article of clothing he had forgotten the night before. He found his necktie half under the chair cushion, stuffed it into his pocket, and waited for the police to return.

The only things that unnerved him during the difficult day were the presence of Chris Waverly at the press conferences and the strange expression on Helen Colter's face. Chris had come to the convention to cover his speech. Her presence always unsettled him, and he was shaken by her whispered comment. "You're a hero again, huh, lover boy? Whenever you're a hero, other people seem to die."

Helen was harder to figure out. She seemed to be watching him uncertainly, as though wondering if he knew something more about Nicole's death. Well, she could not prove that he had ever been in Nicole's room at all, much less that he had stayed there until the fire had spread. Still, she had seen him on the fifteenth floor. If she should take a notion to talk to anyone. . . .

The grand ballroom of the Midland Hotel in Chicago was filled with a laughing, expectant crowd. It was obvious to Sean that everyone knew Congressman Paul Cronin would win an overwhelming victory. The totals on the giant blackboard on the stage showed a lead that was increasing every minute. The prediction of a 450,000-vote victory now seemed reasonable.

Sean did not want to be on the platform with the Senator-elect and his family. The suggestion of a union between Church and State in such a tableau did not seem appropriate. He was happy, nonetheless, about Paul's victory, happy especially for Nora and the kids, who had worked hard during the final six weeks of the campaign.

Nora's preoccupation with the election did not deter her from her new project of rehabilitating Sean. He grinned wryly—discreetly tailored suits ordered for him by Nora, lunch once a week, a new-style haircut about which he was given little choice.

Superficially, he felt more at ease, but his deep bafflement was not resolved. He was drifting closer to resigning from the priesthood. Yet he laughed more and slept better and found that a smile came more quickly to his lips. Not only Jimmy McGuire but the younger priests on the chancery office staff kidded him when he became moody and melancholy. "Isn't it about time you had lunch with Nora again?" one of them would say.

Sean recalled the occasion when, during his last visit to Rome for a meeting of the Ecumenical Committee to which, for some obscure reason he did not comprehend, he had been appointed, he had supped with the Alessandrinis. They were as handsome as ever with their jet-black hair, now dusted with fine white snowflakes. "Can you imagine, *càro mio*," protested the *Principessa*, "I now have two daughters in their late teens who wear jeans and T-shirts and chew gum and listen to rock and roll and talk like Americans?"

"Black nobility who talk like Americans!" said Sean. He was trying to get used once again to Campari and soda.

"You will, of course, be the next Archbishop of Chicago. Everyone in Rome says it. There is no doubt about it."

"I will not be the next Archbishop of Chicago," he said forcefully. "In fact, I'm probably going to leave the priesthood."

Francésco seemed dismayed, but Angèlica merely smiled knowingly. "You and Montini will do so on the same day, *càro mio*."

The thought had become more precise and more demanding in the months since that quiet evening off the Piazza Farnese. He had no idea what he would do after he left the priesthood, but resignation seemed to be the only way out of the agonizing dilemma that now beset him. Nora's kindness had opened to him the possibility of a life free from the burden that he had known since ordination. There were other things a man could do besides mediate conflicts between pastors and curates, attend insipid committee meetings, and screen stacks of complaining letters that seemed to get higher every day. Sean demanded a sign. If one didn't come quickly, he would leave the priesthood. Indeed, if they tried to force the archbishopric upon him, that would be enough of a negative sign and he would certainly leave.

There was a tumultuous ovation as Senator-elect Paul Cronin emerged on the platform with his family.

Chris Waverly listened to Paul's victory statement with wry amusement. Her resentment toward the new Senator had long since ebbed. Chris could carry a grudge for longer than most people, but living for vengeance was ridiculous. She occasionally hung around the Cronin campaign because of a vague, unspecified hunch that there was something just a little bit missing in Paul Cronin. There was no substance at the center of him. Someday he might provide a story. As the senatorial campaign progressed, however, Chris wondered if perhaps she was wrong. Paul Cronin had matured and run a careful, intelligent, neatly calculated campaign. His response to the tragedy in the Barrington Hotel had been, in fact, precisely the proper mixture of grace and sadness. Yet there was a tiny pinprick of doubt that would not go away.

"One final word," said the handsome, triumphant Senator-elect from the podium. "There is one person not here today whom we all miss and who should share the credit for our victory. I'm sure that in that land of happiness to which we all hope to go, Nicole Shields is celebrating with the rest of us."

The applause was again enthusiastic. As Chris turned to leave the ballroom, she noticed one of the young women on the Senator's staff. The girl's face was taut with a mixture of grief and anger. Tears were flowing down her cheeks.

"Something wrong, kid?" asked Chris sympathetically.

"The hypocritical sonofabitch," Helen Colter said. "He was in bed with Nicole when that fire started."

Tom Shields had agreed to see Chris Waverly only because she insisted she had something of personal importance to tell him. His hands trembled as he read the typed copy of her interview with Helen Colter that she had handed him without a word. "He killed them both," he said faintly. "He killed my wife and my daughter."

"Your wife too?"

"My wife too. He used Maggie as a convenience and broke her heart in the process. She attempted suicide more to gain his attention than anything else. The last time she left a note, not for me but for him."

Chris's head was whirling. "Do you have that note, Dr. Shields?" she asked gently.

"No." His response was bitter. "I gave it to his brother, Bishop Cronin, and he destroyed it."

"I see. How can you be sure then that they had an affair?"

Shields walked over to the wall, shoved aside the picture, spun the combination on a wall safe, and took out a leather-bound book. "She kept a diary. I found it among her things long after the funeral. Just like Maggie to forget about the diary. It records in very considerable detail her escapades with Paul Cronin."

"I see." Chris asked to see the diary.

"It's all yours," Tom Shields said. "Here, take the damn thing, do whatever you want with it."

"Are you sure, Dr. Shields? You and your wife and your other children might get hurt."

"I don't give a goddamn," Tom exploded. "I'm sick of Paul Cronin. It's time somebody exposed him for what he is."

●   ●   ●

The night he was sworn in as a member of the United States Senate, Paul Cronin woke up screaming. Nora put her arms around him and crooned softly and sweetly. Her power to exorcise Paul's terrible nightmares seemed to be waning. Now the Chinese attack at the Reservoir and the burning of the Barrington Hotel had blended into one nightmare, and the pain of the imagined Chinese bayonet in his stomach haunted him during the day as well as at night.

It took Paul a long time to calm down. And then, exhausted and breathing heavily, he finally relaxed in her embrace. "God, it's terrible, Nora," he whimpered.

"I don't understand it, Paul. Both in Korea and in San Juan you saved people's lives. Why do you have the nightmares? Maybe you ought to see someone."

"That wouldn't do any good." He laughed weakly. "There isn't all that much difference between a hero and a coward, you know. It would have been so easy to panic in both those situations."

"The dreams are an alternate scenario?" she asked.

"Something like that."

Nora was worried about Paul's dreams. If he wouldn't go for help, maybe she should.

"You're suggesting, Mr. Connors," Chris Waverly said, "that Senator Cronin may have ordered the execution of Joe Makuch?"

Chris had spent an exhausting few weeks tracking down Paul Cronin's old Marine Corps buddies. After reading Maggie's diary and interviewing Helen Colter, it was a short jump to the conclusion that the nightmares Paul used to have about Korea could be related to yet another skeleton hiding in his rapidly filling closet. It had not been hard for her to find Steven Connors in Atlanta and to check out his background and credentials.

Now, sitting in the cool, crisp, modern office of the Connors Construction Company, she knew she had hit the jackpot.

"I knew Makuch was blackmailing Paul," the handsome black man said. "He bragged to me about it. I didn't approve, mind you, but it was none of my business. Anyway, I figured that Cronin owed somebody something after running out on us at the Reservoir and then getting a Medal of Honor for it."

"That doesn't prove that he had Makuch killed. The autopsy showed that he died of a heart attack."

"I can't prove it, exactly. But Makuch called me the morning he died and said he was sure there were people following him. He said there had been a strange look in Paul's eyes the last time he paid the blackmail money to him."

"Are you willing to testify that Makuch told you that Senator Cronin had paid blackmail to him for twenty years?"

"Yes, I'm willing to say that," said Steven Connors. "I'm reluctant to do it. I don't want the publicity. But if Paul has his eye on the presidency . . . he's a coward, a phony, a hypocrite. I could not—I simply will not let him preside over a country in which my children and grandchildren must live."

"Thank you very much, Mr. Connors. You're a brave man."

"Or a coward for waiting so long. You *will* get him, Miss Waverly?"

"Oh, don't worry about that. I'll get him, all right."

CHAPTER
——THIRTY-SIX——
1977

On a Friday in the middle of Lent in 1977, Bishop Sean Cronin granted an off-the-record interview to Chris Waverly. He had no particular desire to see her. Her reputation was that of an able but acid-penned investigative reporter. Sean was afraid that she might have somehow found out about him and Nora and intended to use that information to embarrass Paul. Moreover, the tension of waiting for the appointment of a new archbishop—long delayed—was beginning to tell on his nerves and that of all the priests in the chancery and the diocese.

"Yes, Miss Waverly," he said. "How can I help you?"

Chris Waverly's hair had obviously been touched up to keep it blond. She was a hard-looking woman, yet still attractive. "I'll be blunt, Bishop. I have enough information about your brother to have him expelled from the United States Senate. Moreover, I have information that you have cooperated with him in at least one of his escapades, sufficient information, I should tell you, to frustrate any plans you might have of becoming the next Archbishop of Chicago."

"I believe that's a technique used by investigative reporters called 'intimidate them with the first question.' I don't intimidate, Miss Waverly."

"Intimidation or not, Bishop, I can destroy you."

"No, you can't. Nothing can destroy me. I am not interested in being Archbishop of Chicago. I intend to refuse the appointment if it's offered to me. If it is forced on me, I will resign from the priesthood. Now where does your intimidation get you?"

Chris Waverly regarded Sean intently. "Do you deny that you persuaded Dr. Thomas Shields to give you the farewell letter his wife wrote to your brother? Do you deny you destroyed that letter?"

"Of course I don't deny it. Why should I? It was an embarrassing letter for all concerned. Tom didn't have the heart to destroy it, so I did it for him."

"Do you deny that your brother had an affair with Maggie Shields?"

"I am not privy, Miss Waverly, to my brother's sex life. I don't believe a word of what you say, but I certainly have no proof that it's not true."

"Do you deny that your brother was in bed with Nicole Shields when the fire in the Barrington Hotel started? And that he paid blackmail for twenty years to a man named Makuch who knew he had been a coward and not a hero in Korea?"

"That's absurd. Let's end this interview, Miss Waverly." Sean stood up. "I can see no useful purpose in continuing it."

"You're different from Paul, Bishop," Chris said. "You may be an honorable man and be telling the truth. I'm not sure. But your precious brother is in very hot water, and unless you're careful you're going to be in hot water with him." She extended a business card. "Here's my card. Please call me if you change your mind."

"Get out," Sean said quietly. Chris Waverly shrugged and dropped the card on the floor as she left his office.

Seething with anger, Sean picked up the card, tore it in two, and threw it in the wastebasket. Then, after a few moments of brooding anger, he fished the pieces out of the basket, stared at them grimly, and put them together with Scotch tape.

"Jimmy." He buzzed the chancellor's office. "See if you can keep the world away from me for a few hours. I have to make a trip to Washington. And, by the way, it has nothing to do with who will be your next archbishop."

Paul paced nervously back and forth in his office in the Senate Office Building. Outside the window, the great dome of the Capitol stood as a reminder that this was the seat of what was surely the most powerful legislative body in the world.

"Chris Waverly has had it in for me for years. Wanted to sleep with me a long time ago. I turned her down, of course, and she's never forgiven me."

"She waved a diary at me, Paul. Said it was Maggie's, and that it had the details of your love affair."

"Tom Shields wouldn't give her a book like that, even if it were true and even if Maggie had kept such a record."

"She says that you were in bed with Nicole the night of the hotel fire." There was steel in Sean's voice.

Paul dismissed the charge with a wave of his hand, but his eyes were dancing randomly, nervously.

"She does know one true thing." Sean pushed on relentlessly. "She knows that Tom gave me Maggie's farewell letter to you and that I destroyed it."

"So much the worse for you, little brother." Paul grinned crookedly. "Chris is a bitch. She might just do a story based on that one fact and hint about a lot of other things. It will stir up a little trouble for a day or two, and then it will be forgotten. Anyway, you keep saying you don't want to be Archbishop of Chicago."

"Even if a quarter of what she says is true, you can imagine what it will do to Nora and the kids."

"Oh, the hell with Nora and the kids," Paul said. "I don't need this sort of thing just at the beginning of my career in the Senate. And I'm not going to have it. You can count on it, little brother. Not a word of this is ever going to appear in print."

"How are you going to stop it, Paul?"

"Just don't worry about it. I'll take care of everything."

Sean saw his brother clearly for the first time. Every charge Chris had made against Paul was probably true. He stood up, wanting to escape from the office as quickly as he could. There was an evil in his brother that amazed and frightened him.

As soon as Sean left the office, Paul punched a number into the telephone. "Eric? I wonder if we could get together this afternoon. It's similar to a matter we discussed last year."

"Of course, sir. We're always happy to oblige."

At National Airport, Sean stood staring at the bank of telephones, oblivious to the people streaming by him. Chris Waverly was a bitch. She had raked up a scandal that would destroy not only Paul but Nora and the children. Yet her charges were probably true. In any event. . . .

He walked to the telephones, waited until one was vacant, went inside the booth, and closed the glass door.

"Yes?" Chris Waverly said.

"Bishop Cronin, Miss Waverly. I must apologize for not believing you the other day. I hope you won't go ahead with the story. Too many innocent people are going to be hurt. I think I can promise you that Paul will step down after his first term in the Senate, and that he will never run for the presidency. Be that as it may, however, until you make a definite decision or until you've finished writing the story and have it in the hands of your editor, I suggest you disappear from sight and that you disappear with very effective security precautions."

"Is that a threat, Bishop?" Her voice was hostile.

"No, Miss Waverly," Sean said wearily. "It is not a threat. I don't especially like you or what you're doing, but I don't want any accident you may suffer on my conscience."

"I see." There was a pause on the other end of the conversation. "Very well, Bishop. I'll take your advice. You *are* different from your brother."

Sean staggered away from the telephone booth like a man who had been on an all-night drunk.

Paul poured himself a second drink with an unsteady hand. He had come to Chicago the day before. He felt more secure here. Would the damn telephone never ring? There would be little peace or relaxation for him until he received a confirmatory phone call from Eric. He could not imagine the reason for the delay.

Finally, the phone rang and Paul jumped at it.

"This is Eric. I'm sorry to disturb you at home."

"Goddammit, man, it's all right. What's happening? Why the delay?"

"We're doing the best we can, sir," Eric said. "We just have not been able to resolve the matter. Our team can't find the person in question. We'll continue to look, of course."

Paul felt his muscles and bones melt. It was over. The story would appear any day, and a quarter century of his efforts would have been wasted. "Keep on trying. It's a matter of life and death," he said.

"Of course, sir. Of course we will. I'll be back in touch with you, as soon as I have something to report."

Paul wished that the Chinese bayonet had really found his gut on the hillside by the Reservoir. Like a man in a dream, he walked out of the study and down the steps and away from the house.

A rainstorm accompanied him from Chicago to Oakland Beach. He drove recklessly, ignoring the speed limit and the slippery road. What difference would a speeding ticket make now? He drove by the white gate at Oakland Beach and on to the New Albany Marina. He would take out the *Mary Eileen* and sail away from all his problems.

The marina was deserted, only a few boats were in the water in early April. The *Mary Eileen* was rarely used before the kids arrived in June, but there were standing orders of twenty years' duration that it was to go into the harbor on the first day of spring.

He started the motor, backed out of the slip, and flipped on the weather radio. The prediction was for strong winds following the rainstorm.

The lake was smooth and there was almost no wind when he cleared the harbor mouth. He unfurled the jib, ran up the mainsail, and turned off the motor. The wind would be from the northeast. Why not make a straight run for Chicago? It was a strong boat, actually the fourth to bear the name, twenty-eight feet of solid fiberglass and carefully constructed rigging and masts. Comfortable, too. It could sleep six, although as far as he knew no one had ever spent the night on it.

He thought briefly of the nights he and Nora had spent together over the years. He was sorry he had not been kinder to Nora.

Then he admitted to himself that he had driven up to the lake so recklessly because he wanted to die. But wasn't that ridiculous? Why die when Eric could be calling that very minute to tell him of his success?

He brought the boat around. The wind and waves were picking up. Now was the time to return to the harbor. He hesitated, thinking of what would lie ahead if Eric failed. Scandal, disgrace, humiliation . . . the press, for so long his ally, riding him into the ground.

He headed back out into the lake, away from shore and into the storm.

The sun dove rapidly for the horizon as the *Mary Eileen* speeded on. She skipped from wave to wave as if she were rushing to join it. The halyards strained and the rigging screamed. Paul Cronin stood exultantly at his tiller. This was the way to go out, the wind blasting at your face, hair streaming in the fading light, the cold lake water washing over the prow of the boat and down the gunwales to form puddles at your feet.

The wind was soon more than twenty knots and the waves up to six feet. The *Mary Eileen* roared like a banshee as she rode up and down the waves. Paul screamed in harmony with her. The Reservoir, Heartbreak Ridge, Maggie, Nicole, Mickey—his life raced before him. All right, all right, I gave it a pretty good go. A few things went wrong, that's all. Get out while I'm still ahead.

One of the stays on the mast snapped. The mast tottered, swayed, and then crashed back toward the cockpit, barely missing Paul's head and enveloping him in billowing nylon. He struggled free.

Nora. Yes, Nora. He still wanted to live.

He ducked into the cabin and grabbed for the microphone on his radio. "Mayday, Mayday," he bellowed. *"Mary Eileen"* in distress two miles off Michigan City. Mayday, Mayday. This is Senator Cronin, I have lost my mast. Do you hear me? Michigan City Coast Guard, do you hear me?"

He flipped the "Receive" button, expecting the reassuring response of the Coast Guard, located only a few miles away. There was no answer.

"Mayday, Mayday," he shouted again, this time close to panic. A terrible thought occurred to him. He switched on the cabin lights. Nothing. He flicked the switch again. No battery. Only enough to start the auxiliary motor and turn on the weather radio.

"Mayday, Mayday," he sobbed into the dead microphone.

The *Mary Eileen* wallowed drunkenly in slashing waves. Paul pulled himself out of the cabin. Cut the mainsail free and use the jib as a sea anchor. He had seen it done once in a movie. The mainsail was dragging the boat broadside into the wind.

He dodged under the fallen mast and struggled back into the cabin, a freezing wave slamming into his face. He had to get the sail cut quickly. The *Mary Eileen* was "capsize proof"—but that didn't apply to storms like this when it was hull to the wind. He slammed doors open and shut in the cabinets until he came upon a knife. Not much of a knife but it would have to do.

He pushed upward against the cockpit door to get out of the cabin. It was wedged tight by the weight of the fallen mast and would not budge. The boat had imprisoned him. It would roll over and the water would sweep in in an overwhelming tide. He pounded against the door until his fists were bleeding. Then the boat spun around under the force of another huge wave that dumped water into the cockpit and through the ventilator in the cabin door. God, the water was cold.

But the door swung open. Paul heaved himself back into the slippery cockpit.

The sun was setting now, turning the throbbing waters of the lake red and purple. Paul slashed away at the sail, ripping it frantically and trying to remember how you rigged a sea anchor with a jib.

There was one last piece of sail at the top cleat of the mast. He climbed up on the cockpit seat and leaned over the stern to slash it free.

He saw the wave coming, not much larger than the others, but at a different angle. It slammed into the stern, knocking Paul from the seat and smashing him against the mast. For a moment he seemed to hang free in the air; then his fingers clutched at the mast.

It was too slippery to hold. The boat spun again and Paul Cronin plunged into Lake Michigan. He was not wearing a life jacket.

A life preserver would not help, he told himself, as he hit the lake. He would not survive more than half an hour in water that cold.

The pain in his body from the icy purple waters was like fire. He remembered the stories about Irish fishermen who refused to learn to swim lest they prolong their death agonies.

He wished he had never learned to swim.

He thought back to the time so many years before when Sean had rescued him from the lake. What had happened to him since then? Why had everything gone so wrong?

Then the parade of faces again: the old man, Maggie, Chris, Richard Daley, his girls, Nora, and then, finally, his brother.

CHAPTER
—THIRTY-SEVEN—
1977

Nora and Sean stood side by side over the closed casket in the moments before six United States Senators came to carry the sealed casket of the late Junior Senator from Illinois to the hearse in which he would make his last ride down Glenwood Drive for his final Mass at St. Titus Church.

Nora was weeping, as she had so often wept during the wake and the funeral.

"Suicide or accident, Sean?" She asked the question that they both had been afraid to ask.

"God loves us all, Nora, no matter what." He gave the only answer he could.

After the body of Senator Paul Martin Cronin had been laid to rest in Holy Sepulchre Cemetery and the mourners had eaten the traditional meal at the Rosewood Inn, Sean and Nora drove Michael Cronin back to his apartment at the Hancock Tower. It was a flawless April afternoon, a false hint of spring hovering over the city.

The girls had held up well. Mary and Eileen were dry-eyed, although their faces were pinched with pain. Noreen wept, but softly and quietly. She had appointed herself custodian of "Gramps," doggedly pushing his wheelchair down the aisle of the church.

As she grew older, Noreen seemed more like her grandmother. No wonder Uncle Mike saved his rare smiles for her. Poor Mike, the wake and funeral had been harder on him than on anyone else. He had cried through the Mass and then again at the burial ceremony. He was slipping rapidly.

"I'll hold the door, Noreen," Sean said softly as the elevator on the forty-fourth floor of the Hancock Tower opened.

"Gramps never had such a quick nurse," crowed Noreen, deftly steering through the door.

Youth bounded back so quickly. Nora would spend a long time trying to understand her own grief. She had loved Paul. A strange love, perhaps, but still a true love in its way.

The three of them stood awkwardly in the parlor of Uncle Mike's apartment, handing him over to the care of his nurse and yet not knowing how to leave.

Mike Cronin's hand scrawled an illegible word on the note pad attached to his chair. Sean bent over the pad, gently moving the twisted fingers away from the word. "Glendore," he said, puzzled.

"He wants us to take him up there," said Noreen. "Don't you, Gramps?"

Mike nodded his head.

"Tomorrow all right?" asked Nora. A trip to Oakland Beach would mean all that less time to think.

Again he nodded.

As they rode down in the elevator, Noreen broke the silence. "He wants to die up there," she said firmly.

That night Sean went to the cathedral rectory. Wabash Avenue was deserted, cold, unfriendly. In either direction, there were only the buildings and the streetlights. He hurried through the door of the white stone building, itself cold and unfriendly.

In his room he poured himself one of his rare nightcaps, swallowed it quickly, and poured another. He strove to feel grief. In a way he was responsible. If he had not warned Chris Waverly . . .

Who was Paul Cronin? Who was this brother about whose death he could feel numbness but no pain? Had there ever been a real Paul Cronin? Had pressure from their father cut the core out of his brother's personality?

Sorrow would come eventually; it was still too soon. The important thing was that the sign was as clear as it could be: Paul was dead; Nora was free to marry. The mistakes he and Nora had made a quarter of a century ago could now be canceled out. They would wait a discreet amount of time and then quietly be married.

There was no point in his applying for a dispensation, because Rome did not dispense bishops. About that he couldn't care less.

His phone rang.

"Cronin," he said.

"Chris Waverly, Bishop. I'm sorry about your brother's death." Her voice was gentle.

"Thank you, Miss Waverly. I appreciate your sympathy."

"I had been sitting up here for days trying to make up my mind whether to use the story. I finally decided not to, on the condition that Paul agree to never run for the presidency. I didn't want to hurt you . . . or his family. Then I heard."

"I appreciate that decision." Sean tried to keep his voice neutral.

"Was it suicide, Bishop?"

"We'll never know, Miss Waverly. We'll never know how much moral responsibility was involved. I suspect with Paul that there never was much of that."

"I've destroyed all the documents."

"I appreciate that."

"You are very different from your brother, Bishop Cronin. I don't believe in much myself, but I do hope you're the next Archbishop of Chicago."

"I'm not going to be the next Archbishop of Chicago, but it's nice of you to say it just the same."

"I'm sure you will be," said Chris Waverly. "Good luck."

On Palm Sunday, Noreen, Sean, and Nora rode to Oakland Beach to visit Mike. The two adults were moody and preoccupied, paying little attention to the wonderful spring day. Noreen considered talking about Easter and resurrection and decided against it. She knew that teenagers didn't preach sermons to bishops.

"You haven't heard from the Delegate yet?" Nora broke the silence.

"Not since the funeral," Sean said. "Why?"

"Jimmy told me that everyone in Rome is saying that they're going to offer you Chicago. You are going to take it, aren't you?"

"No," he said.

"You will," Nora said.

"I won't," he responded stubbornly.

"I don't want an argument on such a nice day," Noreen intervened. Poor grown-ups, she thought, all their heavy decisions made them forget what life was supposed to be about.

When they arrived at Glendore, Mathilda directed them to the study. Noreen had been told by her mother that her grandfather had built Glendore when he and her grandmother were just married. It was hard to think of him as a young man with a bride.

"Hi, Uncle Mike," Nora said in a cheery voice. Then she saw that Mike was sitting in his chair, hunched over, crying.

Outside, the waters of the lake were as smooth as a sheet of thin blue ice. Noreen wondered if Gramps was angry at the lake for taking her father.

"What is it, Dad?" Sean's voice was gentle.

"He's holding something in his hand," Nora said. "It looks like a picture."

Noreen took the picture out of his hand. "It's a picture of Daddy and Uncle Sean with Gramps and Grandma when they were little boys."

Then, not quite knowing why, Noreen threw her arms around her grandfather and wept with him.

Sean glanced at his watch. Another hour before the Holy Thursday services would begin. He was physically and emotionally drained.

On Wednesday he had received a call from the Delegate.

"I must begin, Archbishop Cronin, by telling you how very, very sorry I am for the tragedy in your family."

"I appreciate that, Archbishop." Sean repeated his now familiar response to sympathy. "My sister and her children and I also appreciate your very kind telegram and the Holy Father's cablegram."

"Yes, of course," said the Delegate mechanically. "Of course. But now, unfortunately, I must talk to you about the future instead of the past."

Sean was immediately guarded. Had they chosen someone else? Oddly enough, he felt a tinge of disappointment. He expected to turn the appointment down, not to be passed over. "Of course, Your Excellency."

"It is, Archbishop, the Holy Father's wish—" That was the second time the Delegate had called him "Archbishop." The canny Frenchman could not have made the same mistake twice.

"No."

"The Holy Father expressly commands you, in virtue of your vow of obedience—"

"Henri." He called the Delegate by his first name, something he had never done before. "Tell the Holy Father to go to hell."

"Oh, Archbishop Cronin, your response will not deter him in the least. He absolutely insists. Moreover, he told me confidentially that he is planning a Consistory before Pentecost—only seven weeks away—and then I shall have to call you Cardinal Cronin."

"No, I will not do it."

"Sean, yes, you will." So the Delegate was using first names too.

"Archbishop, we can sit here and argue about this for the next hour, and my answer will still be no."

"We will not argue about it at all. I will phone you again tomorrow before the Holy Thursday services, and you will give me your formal acceptance." The line went dead.

Ten minutes later the phone rang again. "Overseas operator," said a muffled voice. Then Sean heard the usual gibberish of transatlantic confusion followed by a bewildered Italian operator wanting "Monsignor Cronin" while a nasal Bronx voice insisted that they had a "Bishop Cronin" on the line. Finally, a soft but firm voice said, "Montini *aqui*."

Sean felt an emptiness in his stomach as he had as a little boy when Mike gave him orders. "Cronin *aqui*," he said. *"Buona sera, Santità."*

"We have called"—Paul VI spoke in hesitant but precise English, just as he had at Castel Gandolfo—"to state again what *Monsieur le délégat* has told you. It is our hope that you will agree to take up the burden of serving the Church in Chicago. It is a very important city. We need you."

A gentle voice, but Sean felt the same reaction as when Mike ordered him to leave the seminary and marry Nora. Only now he was not the same Sean.

"I cannot, *Santo Padre*," he replied. He felt his chest wrench with the trauma of refusing a parent.

"We are sorry about your brother's death, Monsignor," said the Pope, ignoring his refusal. "Life is very short for all of us. That is why—"

"My conscience does not permit it, *Santo Padre*," Sean interjected.

"We hope you will at least do us the honor of praying over it for a day." The Pope sounded even more hesitant, vulnerable as he always was to the appeal of conscience.

Eager for a compromise solution, even a transitory one, Sean agreed. "Of course, *Santità,* I will pray for it."

"*Monsieur le délégat* will call you again, my son."

After the papal voice faded, Sean rushed to the bathroom and retched violently. He had said no to a parent. It was not easy, but this time he had done it. Now he had merely to stick to his decision.

Sean looked at his watch again. Nora was going to visit and the Delegate was going to call him before he would go down to the cathedral. There, in his recommitment to priestly service, he would move his lips but he would say no words.

Then Nora was at the door, beautiful in a light blue suit; skirt, jacket, and sweater impeccably tailored. The touches of age around her eyes and her mouth somehow made her more endearing.

"Do you have a few minutes?" she asked.

"Of course. Come in and sit down. I have something I want to talk about."

"Me too," she said. "I didn't wear black because I'm not going to be able to stay for Mass at the cathedral. There are a couple of things I've got to do, and I guess I never really believed in black anyway."

"It doesn't matter," Sean said automatically. "What do you want to talk about?"

"No, you first," Nora insisted. She leaned forward, hands folded.

Sean took a deep breath, gripped the edge of his desk tightly and began. "Nora, I'm going to resign from the priesthood. I want to marry you. You need a husband. I need a wife. It's time to correct all the mistakes we made twenty-five years ago."

"I can't," she said in a small voice. "I simply can't, Sean. It's impossible. Please don't ask me."

"Why is it impossible?" He was anxious, ready to explode. "Don't you love me?"

She leaned forward. "Of course I love you, Sean. I've always loved you. If you weren't a priest, I'd marry you tomorrow. But you *are* a priest." She shook her head slowly, tears forming in her clear blue eyes.

"Holding me to my commitment?"

"That's right. I've tried to honor most of my commitments, even if a lot of them were those I made because of other people. Now I'm going to start making my own commitments freely and independently for myself. I still believe in commitments, Sean."

"You won't change your mind?" He felt as though a light had gone out inside him.

"No, I won't. Anyway, how can you possibly think of turning your back on all the priests of Chicago who love you so much, and the laity for whom you've become the Church?" She leaned forward even more intently, her face wrinkled in a frown. "How can you possibly think of letting them down?"

"Goddammit, Nora," he shouted. "I don't believe in any of it anymore. I never did. I have no commitments."

"Don't be silly, Sean, of course you do. Uncle Mike was wrong about a lot of things. He was right about you. . . . Has the Apostolic Delegate called to tell you you're the next Archbishop of Chicago?"

Sean hesitated. What was the point of keeping it a secret? "Yes, both he and the Pope called, and I turned them both down."

"Sean, call and tell them you've changed your mind. Do it before they have a chance to offer it to someone else."

"The Delegate is going to call me back sometime in the next half hour," he said lamely.

"Well, I hope you come to your senses before then," she said. And then she smiled sweetly at him. "Oh, Sean, I do love you, and I always will love you, but I won't be your wife."

He nodded, competing emotions struggling within him.

"What will happen to you? What will you do with your life?"

Nora straightened up, her back strong and firm. "That's what I wanted to talk to you about. The Governor has decided to appoint me to the Senate to fill out the remainder of Paul's term. I'm going to accept. The Governor has an odd notion that I'll step down two years from now and give him a clear shot at it. I've let him think that's what I'm going to do—but he's wrong."

"In God's name, Nora, why?"

"Because I'll be good at it. I have all the right political instincts. I've known that for years as I watched Paul's successes and failures." Nora stood up. "Well, I'd better leave now. I must buy the proper sort of dress for the announcement that I'm the new Senator from Illinois."

"I wish you happiness," Sean said, putting his arms around her.

For a moment they stood silently together. She was soft and sweet, an angel of love. He could feel her determination begin to melt into surrender. If he insisted now he could have her, he was sure, have a life with her in which the sweetness would never end. Images from their past love tumbled through his mind. Oakland Beach . . . Amalfi. . . . Yet surely the sweetness would be short-lived. Having her, he would lose her. Not having her, he could love her forever. Not for Jimmy McGuire, not for the Delegate, not for all the priests of Chicago, not even for the Pope, but for Nora . . . yes, for Nora . . . he would do what his damn fool Church and his damn fool God wanted him to do. He disengaged himself from the embrace. "I've got to get ready for Mass."

Nora walked to the door of his study. Her firm shoulders sagged. She paused and turned slowly; her face was streaked with tears.

Oh, God, Nora, he thought, his heart sinking, don't blow it now.

She bit her lip. "Buy you lunch in Washington next week?"

"In the Senate dining room," he insisted. Waves of warmth and grace surged across the room and enveloped him.

She grinned through her tears. "Where else?" She hesitated, then her head tilted up. "You *will* say yes to the Delegate." It was more an order than a question. She smiled and left the room.

Her warmth and peace lingered with Sean. He picked up a pen and a sheet of paper from his desk, since his journal was in his bedroom.

"You damn fool," he wrote. *"You missed God's sign for thirty years."*

He crossed out the words, tore the paper into little pieces, and threw them into the wastebasket. Because he had lost his mother, God sent him Nora, the best sign of God's love he would ever have. The same father who had taken away his mother brought the shy little girl into his life so long ago. Talk about the twisted lines of God.

The phone rang. "Cronin," he said.

"I trust, Archbishop Cronin, that you have changed your mind." The Delegate was being brusque and businesslike. "I assume that now you will accede to the wishes of the Holy Father imposed upon you in solemn obedience."

"Nope, Henri," said Bishop Cronin. "I don't really take that holy obedience stuff seriously." He hesitated for just the right dramatic effect and grinned to himself and said, "But I freely decide to serve."

There was a long silence at the other end of the line as the shrewd old French ex-missionary tried to sort out the meaning of those words. "Well, then, that is so much the better, no?"

"If you say so, Henri." Sean was now beginning to enjoy himself. There were many things he was going to enjoy in the years ahead.

"Congratulations, Sean," said the Delegate. "This makes me very happy personally."

"I think you'll live to regret it, but that's your problem."

The Delegate merely chuckled.

After he hung up, the new Archbishop of Chicago donned his black cassock, buttoning up carefully each of the purple buttons. He could hear the cathedral choir practicing the Holy Thursday music. They were singing a haunting medieval hymn, *"Ubi Caritas et Amor."*

Sean Cronin walked down the steps of the rectory to go into the cathedral and repeat with his priests his vows of commitment. He sang softly the words of the hymn to himself.

> *Where charity and love prevail*
> *There God is ever found;*
> *Brought here together by Christ's love*
> *By love are we thus bound.*
>
> *With grateful joy and holy fear*
> *His charity we learn;*
> *Let us with heart and mind and soul*
> *Now love him in return.*

Forgive we now each other's faults
As we our faults confess;
And let us love each other well
In Christian holiness.

Let strife among us be unknown,
Let all contention cease;
Be his the glory that we seek,
Be ours his holy peace.

Let us recall that in our midst
Dwells God's begotten Son;
As members of his Body joined
We are in him made one.

No race nor creed can love exclude
If honored by God's Name;
Our brotherhood embraces all
Whose Father is the same.

A PERSONAL AFTERWORD

Why would a priest write a novel, particularly a secular novel, about adultery, incest, and sacrilege?

Why would Jesus tell parables about secular events like wedding banquets and ne'er-do-well sons and treasure hunters and adulterous women? Why would writers in the Jewish scriptures tell tales about passionate love affairs between unmarried young people (the Song of Songs), about adulterous kings (the David Cycle) and hateful, incestuous and murderous families (the Joseph Cycle)?

The answer is that, since the beginning of humankind, religion has been most effectively communicated in stories that appeal to the whole person instead of being communicated in doctrinal treatises aimed at the intellect alone. The purpose of the religious tale is not to edify but to shatter preconceptions, to open up to the imagination new possibilities of living in the world and relating to the Ultimate.

This particular religious story will be successful if the reader is disconcerted by a tale of commitments that are imperfectly made and imperfectly kept—but that are still kept. And by the image of a God who draws straight with crooked lines, who easily and quickly forgives, and who wants to love us with the tenderness of a mother.

A.M.G.